Daughters of Deliverance

A Novel
Inspired by a true story

by
Lorry Lutz

HERITAGE BEACON
F I C T I O N

DAUGHTERS OF DELIVERANCE BY LORRY LUTZ
Published by Heritage Beacon Fiction
an imprint of Lighthouse Publishing of the Carolinas
2333 Barton Oaks Dr., Raleigh, NC, 27614

ISBN: 978-1-938499-82-1
Copyright © 2016 by Lorry Lutz
Cover design by Elaina Lee
Interior design by AtriTeX Technologies P Ltd

Available in print from your local bookstore, online, or from the publisher at:
www.lighthousepublishingofthecarolinas.com

For more information on this book and the author visit: lorrylutz.com

Brought to you by the creative team at Lighthouse Publishing of the Carolinas:
Eddie Jones, Ann Tatlock, Katie Vorreiter, Shonda Savage, Brian Cross, Paige Boggs

Library of Congress Cataloging-in-Publication Data
Lutz, Lorry.
Daughters of Deliverance / Lorry Lutz 1st ed.

Printed in the United States of America

Praise for *Daughters of Deliverance*

Daughters of Deliverance introduces us to Katharine Bushnell, a remarkable woman whose legacy is on a par with her well-known contemporaries: Catherine Booth, Mary Slessor, and Hannah Whitall Smith. Yet few people know about her. Lorry Lutz remedies that.

Daughters of Deliverance is gripping historical fiction. There were times when I literally held my breath.

~ **Edythe Draper**
Writer, editor and publishing consultant

Katharine is a fascinating character. She obviously trusts God immensely. When she was struggling with the decision to leave David and her dreams of residency to go to China, I shared in that struggle – feeling, at least in part, the anguish followed by rest in the Lord's will. It's fascinating to see someone so determined to heal and fulfill her calling that she abandons the familiar. It strikes of yearning for more, for both herself and people she serves.

~ **Joe**
23-year-old fantasy fiction writer

Daughters of Deliverance is a beautiful story of a life that demonstrates God's perfect love, compassion, and justice. Dr. Kate Bushnell was an amazing woman of courage and faith. What she saw as great injustice—whether the binding of young Chinese girls' feet, or the binding of young women's souls though sex trafficking—drove her to action in spite of the dangers.

The testimony of Kate's life is as relevant today as it was 100 year ago, as there are an estimated 30 million girls and boys enslaved in sex trafficking. This story encourages us to face the realities of evil and to courageously take action in faith.

~ **Larry D. Andrews**
President & CEO, Partners International

Acknowledgments

Every writer needs friends, advisors, and critics to birth a book. Since this one was in process for almost a decade, it would be impossible to thank everyone who played one of those roles. So, first of all, thank you to all of you who were interested enough to keep asking, "How is the book coming?"

Every book needs an editor, and I've had a crew of talented, insightful women who pushed me in the right direction. Jeanette Thomason helped to shape Kate's story and develop her character. Diane Gardner made rewriting far more pleasant than I anticipated. Katie Vorreiter fine-tuned the manuscript and made sure there were no anachronisms. Ann Tatlock, managing editor of Heritage Beacon/Lighthouse Publishing of the Carolinas, brought it to life.

All along the way I had readers who helped me make course corrections like Royalene Doyle, Jan Kyne, Lise Lutz, Rodney Lutz, Tamara Bond, Edythe Anne Draper, Larry Andrews, Nancy Hay, Emily Voorhies, and Joe Lutz. My granddaughter, Johannah Bates, physician assistant, researched numerous medical questions Kate confronted, for which I'm grateful.

Dana Hardwick's well-researched book on Katharine Bushnell, *Oh Thou Woman That Bringest Good Tidings* (Wipf and Stock Publishers), gave me a basis for my research and saved me countless hours. Kristin Kobes Du Mez, author of *A New Gospel for Women* (Oxford University Press), added fresh insights into Bushnell's life and the era in which she lived.

I praise God for His continuing strength and guidance. At one point I became very discouraged about completing the book. One morning I asked Him specifically for guidance, whether I should continue or not. I read this verse in Nehemiah 6:3 (NIV): *I am carrying on a great project and I cannot go down!*

And here it is!

Dedication

Dedicated to Dr. Mimi Haddad, PhD,

who passionately teaches women around the world

to be all that God created them to be.

"The Spirit of the Lord is upon me, because he hath anointed me to preach the gospel to the poor … to preach deliverance to the captives … and to set at liberty them that are bruised."

~ Luke 4:18

Prologue

*C*uriosity drew Kate to the massive tent set up on the Hanson's farm just outside of town. She wanted to see that strange preacher woman everyone was talking about, but none of Kate's friends would risk being seen there.

"My father doesn't think it's proper for a woman to go around speaking in public," Henrietta, her best friend, told Kate and their friends after church one Sunday. "Even if she *is* licensed by the Methodist Church. Have you heard what she says?" Henrietta parodied the mantra that was making the Reverend Maggie Van Cott famous, "I believe my tongue is my own—"

"And I will use it where I please and as I please," the other girls joined in the mimicry.

Despite their good-spirited teasing, Kate could not help but wonder about the courage and strength it must take for a woman to travel and preach to so many people. How did Mrs. Van Cott do something so bold? What kept her going? What was she really like? Kate determined to see for herself—with her friends or without.

The next Saturday afternoon, Kate hurried down the street to the edge of town where a large tent had been erected. She had come alone and didn't know what to expect. What kind of a woman would expose herself to such public scrutiny? No woman at Kate's church would dare stand up on the platform to speak. But was there something wrong with doing so?

As she reached the tent, people were standing to sing, "Jesus paid it all, all to Him I owe ..." Kate started down the middle aisle toward the front, but one of the ushers shook his head and pointed his long finger, directing her to the side where the women sat with little children. She barely held her tongue. *Even if I am a girl, I'm almost seventeen.* She wanted to get closer to see the Reverend Van Cott. The man had no right ... But she followed where he pointed.

As the congregation sat down, one of the local pastors introduced the speaker. Kate gasped. *Why, she looks a little like Mother!* Taller perhaps, though maybe it was the way she held her head: with pride, even though she must have known there were people in the audience bound to make fun of her.

Just then a man shouted, "Sit down!"

Another yelled, "Go fix your curls!" Kate heard laughter at the back of the tent. Mrs. Van Cott did curl her hair in larger spirals than most, but that was no reason to be rude.

Van Cott ignored the hecklers. She began to speak, and her words, more than her appearance, captivated Kate.

"I'm going to tell you a story from the book of Luke, about a woman so bent over she could hardly look more than a foot in front of her." Van Cott's voice rang out. She hunched down and hobbled across the platform.

"Satan bound her like this for eighteen long years." Van Cott paused with her head hung low, facing the floor. The audience had grown silent except for the whimper of a baby. Then Van Cott faced the crowd and called to the back of the tent. "Come up here!" Everyone turned—but there was no one there.

Kate sat mesmerized as Van Cott continued softly. "Imagine Jesus calling that bent-over woman up from the back of the synagogue. He simply touched her and said, 'You are free,' and she stood tall." Van Cott straightened to her full height.

Kate had heard the story many times, but not like this. There was something powerful about Van Cott's simple explanation that Jesus had come to free everyone—men, women, and children—from the sin binding them. How could anyone not love Jesus when they heard how He loves people, even the old, even the crippled?

Reverend Van Cott started to sing softly, closing her eyes and swaying to the words. "Almost persuaded, now to believe ..." People around Kate joined in. "Almost persuaded, Christ to receive." Now Van Cott's voice rose above the singing, "Come, come and receive Jesus." The singing continued. "Seems now some soul to say, go, Spirit, go Thy way." Many were weeping. Van Cott pled, "Don't let Satan convince you to wait for some more convenient day."

People poured down the aisle. Why, there was Mary Friesen, whose mother worked in the Evanston Bakery—and Miss Brookbank, one of the teachers at the Women's College.

Kate's eyes welled with unbidden tears. *Should I go?*

The voices still sang, "Almost persuaded; come, come today."

Van Cott reached her hand out, and Kate felt as though the woman was speaking directly to her. "It doesn't matter if you're young or old, Christ is calling you today."

Kate found herself walking to the front of the tent with others who filled the sawdust path. She sensed a voice, as sure as if it were audible. *Open your heart to Me. I am your savior, and I want you to let Me take your life in My hands and make you into My fruitful servant.*

Something within her wanted Christ to make a difference in her. At that moment, her desire to be a doctor—to be a healer so others could be whole—filled her heart. She determined right then and there to do something remarkable for God, to build something that mattered: not a lighthouse like her father had done, but something just as strong and shining, a legacy of her own for God.

1
The Lighthouse

Evanston, Illinois, 1874

Why had she never been allowed to climb up to the top of the lighthouse? Kate peered over the low railing of the catwalk and stared at the roiling waves. The sun glistened on the water a moment before a dark cloud turned the lake leaden. In the distance, a horn sounded from a ship as it inched south toward Chicago, well away from the reach of the dangerous shoal below. Kate watched the ship's silhouette float on the darkening waters.

The lighthouse stood on a rocky bluff that towered more than one hundred feet above Lake Michigan. From her perch, Kate could see the brilliant reds and golds of oak and maple trees in all their fall glory line the shore as far as Garrett Seminary's tower on the Northwestern University campus. A flock of seagulls floated by the lighthouse and suddenly dove in unison to perform seemingly impossible antics.

"It's beautiful," she whispered, still breathless from her climb up the dark circular stairway.

"'Tis," her father agreed as he reached the top of the stairs behind her. William Bushnell's ruddy face and short white bushy beard made him look more like a jovial grandfather than the foreman who had built this commanding outpost.

"It's worth the climb just to see those churning waters from up here, isn't it?" He gazed into the deep.

"I always wanted to come up to the catwalk when you were building." Kate slipped her arm through his. "But we weren't allowed anywhere near the construction."

"Now you understand." Her father grew quiet as he and Kate listened to the waves crash upon the bluff. "This isn't a safe place, even for adults. Look how easily someone could slip through this framework and fall to their death."

Kate stared down at the lake that thrashed against the rocks. She raised her eyes a moment to the man next to her. Her heart spoke what she could not yet voice. *Father, you still think of me as a child. I'm almost nineteen. Will you feel I'm grown-up enough to make a serious decision about my life?* Maybe this would be a good time to talk, just the two of them alone, without anyone else around to hear or interfere.

Her father interrupted her racing thoughts: "You know the story of the *Lady Elgin*?"

"How could I forget?" Kate watched her father's eyes lock onto the ship far out on the black lake waters. She knew what had haunted him for years. "You tell that story every time we have company."

Her father smiled, but it quickly faded. "I suppose I do," he said. He was quiet for a moment, then shook his head slowly, deliberately. "Three hundred lives lost when the *Lady Elgin* collided with a schooner carrying lumber. They had come too close to shore. But it won't happen again."

Kate followed his finger, which pointed above to the red conical light. "That seven-foot lantern up there warns ships nineteen miles offshore not to get hung up on these shoals."

Kate often heard him retell the story of the wreck. "Can you imagine what it must have been like for the passengers to be thrown into that freezing water? One time I met a man who had been a student at the university at the time of the accident. He told me that a group of them heard news of the wreck and rushed down to the lake to help. They worked all night to rescue several hundred people. Hearing him recount that, I could not imagine anyone surviving in the bitter cold. So many were indeed lost." Kate's father shook his head again. "How did they do it? The survivors? How did they manage to hang on to anything in those unforgiving, beating icy waves?"

Kate silently watched the churning lake. "Now that I'm old enough to understand, I can't imagine the terror: husbands looking for their wives, children thrown into the waters. To think, the excursion was to raise money for the Union Army during the war and the ship was loaded to capacity with revelers. It all ended so badly." Kate noticed her father grip the railing more tightly and placed her arm around him. "The Grosse Point Lighthouse has already saved hundreds of lives. It's an Evanston landmark."

Father's face relaxed. "If I don't ever take on another job, Kate, I'll feel I've made a difference with my life. God willing, there will never again be another shipwrecked body washing up on this shore, not as long as this lighthouse is here to warn the captains of the dangers."

They were quiet a minute, both staring into steely Lake Michigan.

"A man has to leave a legacy," her father said finally. He looked at his daughter. "This is the one God gave me."

Kate turned away and moved carefully down the narrow dark stairwell. What about a woman's legacy? Her legacy? She opened her mouth to speak, but the moment didn't seem right.

She glanced back at her father. She couldn't resist a smile at the thought of how understanding and supportive he was. But perhaps what she had to say was too much? The dream had been growing in her heart since that day two years prior when she'd promised God that she would love and serve Him with her whole life.

She knew what was expected of her: completing her training at the women's preparatory college, teaching at the Evanston grade school—*what good would my Latin and Greek do there?*—and marriage. Definitely not to the Reverend Hawkins' son Richard, regardless of what Mother thought.

God, how do I tell Father? She knew what Mother would say, but Father? Would he understand that she wanted to make her life ... more? *Lord, I want to study how to heal others. Does Father have any idea what it feels like for me to have my mind straining to learn, to be used—and be told that I can't nurture that desire?*

Kate slipped on a stair and would have fallen if her father's strong hand hadn't caught her.

"Careful there, my girl. Slow down. It's getting dark in here now that the sun is going down. I should have brought a lantern." He moved ahead to lead the way down the stairs.

Kate kept her eye on the dark figure in front of her. He was so strong and wise. She wouldn't mind marrying a man like him and having a brood of children, like he and her mother had done. They'd loved their children and made sure each of them, even the girls, received an education. Kate smiled as she thought of her parents' happiness over the choices her brothers and sisters had made. But her heart quickly sank. Would they understand hers? Would they accept that God might have something more for her?

At the bottom of the stairs, her father pushed open the heavy oak door. "I'll take the keys back to the keeper," he said over his shoulder. "I promise I won't stay and talk. I know your mother will have supper waiting."

Kate tugged her scarf around her neck to stave off the wind. She drew a deep breath and braced herself to speak boldly of her plans. She knew what her mother would say: *What are you possibly thinking? What will people say? What Christian man would want to marry a doctor?*

It had grown cold as the sun set. Kate shivered. Was she chilled by the wind or by what father might say of her dream? As the sunlight slowly disappeared, Kate felt her shoulders droop a little. Surely Father would understand. Surely he wouldn't resort to what others said of a woman intent on living her own legacy.

The unflattering things people said rang in her mind: *Women are not intelligent enough. They can't take the pressure. Only a hard, unladylike woman would have the temperament to compete with men.*

"Ready?" Father emerged from the keeper's residence attached to the lighthouse and took Kate's arm in his. "If we hustle along, we should be home in half an hour, just about time for your mother's famous chicken soup."

Kate took a deep breath. It was now or never. "Father," she blurted, "I've got something to tell you." She stopped and faced him. "I'm not going back to preparatory school in the spring. I want to transfer to the Women's Medical College connected to Northwestern University. I want to become a doctor."

There, she'd done it.

Her father stiffened. His face froze a moment, then melted into a mix of confusion and hurt. He started to say something.

Kate stopped him. "I've already talked with our neighbor Dr. Jewell—he's willing to recommend me. He'll even teach me neurology privately in his home. I can take most of my classes right here in Evanston."

William Bushnell shook his head, a look of shock on his face. Kate knew he'd always favored her, just a bit, because she was the youngest girl, sandwiched between four brothers. Her three sisters had followed the paths expected of them, but Kate suspected her father had always recognized her as a bit of a maverick. She had constantly read, consuming every book in the house and anything else she could get her hands on, something her brothers teased her about—that and her passion for Latin and Greek.

Father had never discouraged her. He was proud of her outstanding grades and her leadership in the Methodist Women's Auxiliary. Seeing his stricken face now, Kate reached out to hug him. "I'll do my best to make you proud of me."

His expression softened as he reached to tuck a strand of hair pulled loose from the long braid behind her ear. Then he began walking again. Kate hurried to keep pace.

"You know your mother will never agree to it."

No, Kate thought, *bless her, she'll worry I'll never find a husband.* "Father, she won't understand, but you will. I want to be a doctor. I won't be the only woman. Dr. Jewell says there will probably be three other women in my class. Just think about how much I can do to help—"

"But, Kate, you realize you'll have to study things that no respectable young woman should study."

Kate stopped again and grasped her father's arm. The love and concern in his eyes wrenched her heart. She spoke softly. "That's not true. You know that's not true. Florence Nightingale is respected."

"She's a nurse, Kate, not a doctor."

"But, Father, she's a *healer.* She has studied those same things in real life that I will in school. Look what a difference she's made. Consider the lives she's mended and saved. Don't you see? I want to make a difference. I want to help people heal. When Jesus healed people, they believed in Him. Being a doctor is one way I can convince people He loves them. I want to help women especially. As a woman, I will be able to understand what women are suffering in their bodies and their spirits in a way that men can't. They can speak about things with me, important things regarding a woman's body, that they might feel are, well, inappropriate to discuss with a man—even a doctor. More women are becoming doctors for these very reasons. Father, won't you help convince Mother that this is a call from God, not just a girlish idea?"

Kate felt hot tears wash down her face, but she didn't want her father to see her cry. She turned to look back at the lighthouse. She wanted her father to know she wasn't weak, just frustrated and determined. She was strong, and she knew God wanted her to do this. She just needed a chance.

In silence, they stood looking back at the lighthouse silhouetted against dark clouds forming into a threatening storm.

"The lighthouse will stand against any storm," her father said. "I know God will keep my little girl strong, even in the storms that are bound to come."

"Then you'll help Mother understand?" Kate was hopeful.

William Bushnell took his daughter's arm and turned her back toward home.

2
Difficult Choices

Evanston, 1876

Kate entered Dr. Jewell's study for her private lesson with the famous neurologist and started when she saw the young man seated in her regular seat. She looked at the clock above the doctor's desk. It was time for her lesson. So why was this man here? And who was he? She studied his face—high cheekbones, dark wavy hair worn long, steely gray eyes. He looked familiar.

The young man rose to greet her, towering over her, then bowed to offer her his hand. "Miss Bushnell, I'm David Russell. I've been looking forward to meeting you. Dr. Jewell tells me you are one of his best students."

David ... She recognized him as one of her classmates at Northwestern Medical College. Was he one of the young men who hissed and joked whenever she answered one of the professor's questions? She warmed with embarrassment—she was the only student in Dr. Jenkins' class forced to sit in a corner behind a screen. She knew the professor thought he was protecting her from the ribald remarks of the male students. But she could still hear them. She studied this Mr. David Russell cautiously.

"Thank you," she acknowledged and sat in the chair he proffered.

Dr. Jewell entered and smiled when he saw the two chatting. "I see you've met." He walked over to Kate. "I've asked Mr. Russell to join our private class since he's also interested in more intense study of the nervous system. I forgot to tell you when you were last here."

Kate smiled demurely and nodded a welcome to Mr. Russell. She wondered if the instruction would be the same with him present. She and Dr. Jewell had always been able to talk freely about any subject. She could ask—or answer—any question without feeling embarrassed. Would she now have to speak only when spoken to, like at the medical college?

She slipped off her coat, smoothed back her hair, and squared her shoulders, ready to take notes. Even while getting out her papers, her mind churned. Dr. Jewell never laughed at her, no matter how far-fetched her answers might be. He encouraged her to think independently. The men at the college, however, just expected her to parrot back rote answers from the book. She glanced at her classmate. What would this Mr. Russell expect from her?

In no time, she felt her worries melt away. Respectful debates ensued between the two students. David's brilliant solutions to the problems Dr. Jewell threw at them often impressed Kate—though not always.

One afternoon Dr. Jewell brought a skull into their study session. "Tell me why you think this lesion occurred." He pointed out a protrusion on the crown. He passed the skull to Kate, who took it in her hands and turned it to see both sides.

She'd never held a human skull in her hands before. It must have been a man—at least judging by its size. She moved her fingers gingerly over the protrusion on the top of the skull. A peek at David revealed his eyebrows raised and lips slightly curled in an amused challenge. She lifted her chin and turned back to the skull.

"He must have had some bad headaches with this." She laughed, then turned serious. "Could it have been caused by hydrocephalus? A swelling of his brain due to the accumulation of cerebrospinal fluid might be an explanation."

David reached for the skull. Kate handed it over with her own look of friendly challenge. She was sure she had him on this one.

"Let me make a guess. Miss Bushnell has made a good observation," David said with a glance at Kate and a twinkle in his eye. "But I wonder if fluid could cause such a bone protrusion? Could it perhaps be acromegaly, caused by an overgrowth from the pituitary gland?"

Dr. Jewell took the skull and pointed to the growth and another smaller protrusion at the back. "Good try, both of you. But, sadly, this gentleman died of meningioma, a cancer of the outer lining of the brain, which invades the bone and causes areas of overgrowth. Unfortunately, we have not found a treatment yet."

Kate looked over at David with a shrug. When he smiled back, she did too.

By the second year of studying with Dr. Jewell, Kate and David had become good friends. He walked Kate home regularly after class, and they continued their debates along the way. Kate treasured how the time sharpened her mind and drew her closer to a young man she so respected.

"Have you ever thought of studying abroad?" he asked after a session in which Dr. Jewell told them of his research in Egypt.

She shook her head. "No. But I sometimes wonder if I might go to India after school."

David raised an eyebrow, and Kate thought he might be one to trust with her dream.

"Lately, I've wondered if God wants me to pursue medicine not just so I can heal people's bodies, but so I can help free their souls. I suppose there's a bit of missionary in that. I can't say I've felt what people refer to as a 'call' but I'm not unwilling, even if it takes me overseas. What about you, Mr. Russell?"

David smiled down at her. Kate could get lost in those gray eyes. "I haven't given it much thought," he answered. "For now I want to complete my studies, then do some postgraduate work somewhere."

"That's my dream as well." Kate sighed. "But it may be a long way off. It's so hard for a woman to be accepted into graduate programs."

David grew quiet for a moment. "I hope that will change before long. I always feel embarrassed when those oafs in class make fun of you sitting behind that screen. What is Dr. Jenkins' point anyway?"

Kate laughed. "I believe he thinks he is protecting me from all of you, Mr. Russell."

"Come now, Miss Bushnell. Don't you think it's time you called me David? After all, we've been studying together almost two years." His eyes sparkled with hope.

Kate flushed. A lock of David's hair fell over his forehead. She was tempted to smooth it back but stopped herself. *What am I thinking?*

"You may call me Katharine—for now." She gave a wry smile. "But not in front of Dr. Jewell."

David bowed gallantly. "And when may I call you Kate?"

She thought for a moment. "That's what my family calls me. You may call me Kate when you're with my brothers." But not in front of Mother and Father—she didn't want them jumping to conclusions.

Kate hadn't noticed they had arrived at her front gate until Willie and John came running down the porch steps.

Willie tugged David's long blue scarf from his neck. "You'll have to catch me to get it back," he yelled as he and Johnnie dashed around the house.

"Excuse me, Ka-tha-rine," David yelled over his shoulder as he lunged away. "I've got to teach that young man a lesson."

Kate caught herself laughing when David captured the squealing boys and demanded his scarf. David was the only child in his family—no wonder he loved being around her bustling home.

1879

Kate hurried down the hall of the Women's and Children's Hospital, eager to get back to the nurses' residence where she'd lived since graduating from medical school. With only one woman intern, where else would they house her? Though she did cringe when she had to explain she was not a nurse.

She stopped at the housemother's apartment and lifted the knocker of the open door. "Hello," she called into the room. "Is there any mail for me?"

Mrs. Framer had overseen the household of nurses for decades and considered the girls her daughters. She hadn't quite figured out how to handle a girl doctor.

"I do believe there is a letter for you today, Dr. Katharine. Is this the one you've been looking for?"

Kate grinned self-consciously as she accepted the letter. She wondered if her anticipation had been obvious. It had been two months since David began his internship across the city at a large hospital, and he'd finally written. She rushed upstairs to her room to open the letter in private.

> Dear Kate,
>
> I can call you that since no one else will read this note. I haven't written sooner because the stories about being a resident are true, as I'm sure you've also discovered. The professors require long hours here at the hospital, but I am learning so much that the time just flies. I hope you are keeping well. I have a free day next Thursday and wonder if I may see you.
>
> Sincerely,
>
> David

"Oh no, that's tomorrow!" Kate wailed. Her mind raced as she quickly left her room. She was on call, but maybe Charlotte could change shifts with her. She stopped herself a moment. Why must she change her schedule for David at his first request? But without time to answer, she shook away the question and dashed back to the hospital to get Charlotte's consent to cover her shift for a short time.

The next afternoon, Kate hurried downstairs when she heard David arrive. "It's wonderful to see you, Kath-a-rine," he said, stretching out her name.

She giggled, remembering the first time he'd called her that. "Let's go to that little park a few blocks from the hospital," she suggested. "It's so good to be outside."

David gallantly offered his arm as they walked. "I can't believe the lilacs are already blooming. I think the last time I was out of that hospital, there was still snow on the ground."

Kate smiled. "Fortunately, I walk three blocks to the hospital every day unless I'm on night duty—then I try to sleep a bit sitting up in a chair. No lilacs along the way. Until a few weeks ago, the horses were turning the melting snow into mud."

David took her elbow to guide her around a puddle in their path. "Have you had any unusual cases lately?"

"Well, there is one that I want to talk with Dr. Jewell about. A man brought his wife into the hospital because she gets lost when she goes out for a walk and can't find her way home. She often doesn't recognize him or know him. She's frightened when he comes into the room. Have you ever heard of a condition like that?"

"One of my colleagues who works in the asylum told me of an instance like that, but no one seems to know what causes such a state."

"It's sad. What about you, David? Any more episodes with your favorite department head?"

David chortled. "He's a case, that one. He told us about a woman who gave birth in her carriage. Her husband was trying to get her to the hospital, but the baby wouldn't wait."

"Is the baby all right?"

"Dr. McBean told us the whole story as he took us to see her, and, yes, the baby is fine. So is the mother. But by the time he finished his story, he had led us down the hall"—David broke out laughing—"into the men's ward."

Kate wiped away a tear from laughing so hard. "Oh no! Maybe *he's* forgetting his way home."

Their afternoon flew by all too quickly. As they reached Kate's door, David tightened his arm against hers and promised, "I will try to write more often. But you're probably going through the same thing I am. The doctors keep us interns working day and night."

She nodded. He took her hand in farewell, then seemed reluctant to let go. For such a chilly afternoon, Kate felt surprisingly warm.

A few weeks later, Kate stared again at the strange request in her hand. Mrs. Gracey, the chair of the Women's Mission Board of the Methodist Episcopal Church, had sent a note asking to meet with her. What could she want? Kate wondered for what seemed like the hundredth time since receiving the request.

A sudden knock at the door announced that she'd soon know.

Kate ushered her guest into the small private sitting room of the nurses' dormitory. "Please, sit down." Kate gestured to the settee while she sat across from Mrs. Gracey, still curious to know why this regal older woman should seek her out. The woman's elegant, well-tailored navy suit and matching straw hat spoke of wealth. Kate noted that the chair of the Women's Mission Board was not only stylish but also commanding. Her intense eyes stared into Kate's from behind the short veil of her hat.

After a few minutes of congenial interaction, Mrs. Gracey came to the point of her visit. "Dr. Bushnell, the Women's Mission Board would like you to consider going as a medical missionary to our station in Kiukiang, China."

For a moment Kate sat speechless. Then she said slowly, "I couldn't even think of doing that for at least—"

"Hear me out, my dear." Mrs. Gracey seemed to take Kate's cautious response as a cue to plow ahead. She was used to having her own way, Kate mused.

"Our senior missionary, the Reverend Doctor Virgil Hart, has been pleading for help. He opened a clinic at the mission, the only medical facility for hundreds of miles. We've been praying for several years for a replacement for Dr. Mason, who had to leave because of illness."

Reaching forward to put her hand on Kate's knee, Mrs. Gracey looked intently into her eyes. "When we learned that you, one of our own Methodist women, are a trained doctor, the board knew God was answering our prayers."

How could Kate graciously tell her this was out of the question? "I'm honored, Mrs. Gracey, but I don't think it's possible for me to do this now. I'm just in the first year of my residency, and I would need a lot more experience."

"You don't understand," the older woman persisted. "There is no one there with any training or experience."

"But I would have to at least complete my residency." And there was the plan to pursue postgraduate work in neurology. *That's my call ... Isn't it Lord?*

Mrs. Gracey did not give up. "Dr. Mason had great plans for a hospital," she explained. "We even raised more than four thousand dollars, enough to build a whole hospital. But she became ill and had to return home."

"How sad."

"Yes, it is. Since Letitia left, an untrained missionary lady has been trying to help the hundreds of women who come for help."

"Did you say a woman was going to start the hospital?" Kate was shocked. How could there have been a woman doctor starting a hospital in China? Women had a hard time finding a position in a hospital in this country. Perhaps the missionaries figured the natives wouldn't mind the difference. Or maybe they were grateful for whatever help they could get, even a woman.

"Yes. A woman can often do more in China than here, especially where there is a scarcity of help. There's a desperate need," Mrs. Gracey said, "and we believe you are the one to meet that need."

How could they know that without even speaking to me first?

Kate promised to pray about Mrs. Gracey's request.

Over the next week, Kate struggled in prayer. Then she arranged a weekend off to go to Evanston to talk with her family. She even spent an hour with Dr. Jewell, just returned from several months of research in Egypt. Finally, once back in residence, she sent a note with a messenger to David: *Please come as soon as you can get away. I have something urgent to talk about.*

Two days later, David arrived in the lobby of the nurses' dormitory. Kate smiled when she saw him. In his long gray frock coat worn over a maroon vest and matching cravat, he looked professional, not like a poor intern. Her heart leaped at the warmth in his eyes.

"I'm glad you could get away so quickly," Kate said. She planned to delay a little, wondering how she should start talking about Mrs. Gracey's request.

But David had his own agenda. "I have something to show you." He reached into the inside pocket of his coat. "I brought this for you." He placed a small package, tied with a red silk ribbon, into Kate's hands.

She stared at the present. He had never before given her anything. She looked up and then, at his nod, undid the ribbon.

"When my grandfather died last year, my grandmother sent all his books to me. I found this among them. I think you might be able to use it."

Kate stared at the book inside the wrapping: *Novum Testamentum.* A Latin New Testament! She fingered the leather cover a long moment and looked up at David, then down at the Bible again, paging through its fine pages. "Are you sure you want to part with something of your grandfather's? He's underlined passages and even written notes in the margins." She looked up at David again. "Was your grandfather a pastor?"

"He was actually a seminary professor. He loved ancient languages, just like you do. I've heard you reminisce about your Latin and Greek classes at the women's preparatory school."

"I still love to go back to those textbooks. I don't want to forget: *amo, amas, amant.* I've never had a leather-bound Latin New Testament. Do you really think you should give this away? And to me?"

"I want you to have it," David urged. "Look at the first page."

Kate gasped. She recognized his bold handwriting.

> To Kate,
> Who challenges me with her God-given mind,
> David
> "What women these Christians have."
> ~ Libanius, fourth-century pagan scholar

"Oh, David, I will always cherish this." She tucked the testament into her bag and her hand into the crook of his arm. They walked in silence, Kate wondering how she could tell David about China now. Was this really the right thing—to go away and be so far from him? Why was God making this decision so difficult?

They strolled to the same park where they'd gone before. Even though she had told David she needed to talk about something with him, he didn't seem to notice her troubled spirit. It was time to tell him. It would not be easy. It was almost as hard as telling Father that she wanted to become a doctor.

"David?" She stopped a moment. "I've got to make a big decision in the next week. I don't know what to do. I need your advice."

David showed no emotion as Kate told about her visit with Mrs. Gracey, of how flabbergasted the request had left her, and how she had spent hours on her knees.

"I don't know what God wants me to do, David. For some time, I've felt that God called me into medicine, not only to heal bodies but also to heal souls. And I can't help but think it's all part of something greater that I can't yet get my mind around. I want to make an impact for Him, but I don't know if this is the time ... or the place. I need to know His will. I visited Dr. Jewell last week, and he agrees this request would be better timed after I complete my residency, but he also thinks going to China would be a unique experience."

David pointed to a bench along the path and motioned for her to sit down. The look on his face startled Kate. His eyes appeared clouded, and he clenched his lips as though trying to hold back his words.

"How long would you be gone?"

"Mrs. Gracey didn't say anything about how long they expected me to stay. I think I could come back for further studies once the mission has another doctor."

David reached for her hand, and a current of electricity ran up her arm straight to her heart, making her catch her breath.

"You must know how I feel about you, Kate. I planned to ask your father's permission to formally court you the next time I got back to Evanston. If you stay to finish your residency maybe ... maybe we could go to China together?"

They walked back to the dormitory in silence, each mulling over what this decision could mean for them. At the door, Kate turned to David. "I'm sorry things are turning out like this. The timing is just ... I'll let you know my decision."

David donned his hat and turned to go. Kate's heart broke at the inner struggle evident in his demeanor. She reached for his arm and offered a small smile. "Thank you for the New Testament. No matter what happens, I'll always cherish it."

Night after night, Kate dropped wearily to her knees beside her bed. "Father, show me Your will. Mrs. Gracey is so sure she's heard Your voice. My parents seem shocked, but they want Your will too." Kate put her forehead on the Bible in front of her and rocked back and forth on her haunches. "Am I the answer to the need of that clinic in China?"

She flipped the pages of the Bible back to the Old Testament. She didn't know where else to turn. David's declaration throbbed in her mind—*He wants to court me! Is that what I want? If he really loves me, won't he wait for me to come back?*

"God, I don't know who to ask but You. David said that I have to be sure of Your guidance, even if it goes against what family and friends say. I've been seeking Your guidance in scripture—nothing has spoken to me. My heart wants to finish my residency and continue my friendship with David, to see where it leads. God, I know You're always right, but the timing of all of this just doesn't seem fair. Can't it wait just a little while? Wouldn't it be better for David and me to … maybe go together?" She threw herself across the bed. "But I can't get Mrs. Gracey's words out of my mind: 'It's the only medical facility for hundreds of miles … When we learned that you, one of our own Methodist women, are a trained doctor, the board knew God was answering our prayers.' Are You, Lord?"

Kate sat up and lifted her Bible once more, paging through the Old Testament. She hardly read these books—Samuel, Kings, Chronicles—she didn't know anything in them to help her. She dropped the open Bible onto the bed and prayed again. "Lord, Mrs. Gracey is coming back tomorrow to get my answer. What should I say?"

Her eyes caught a verse in 1 Chronicles 28:20—one she'd underlined for some reason—and read, "Be strong and of good courage, and … and do it." Kate gasped. *Is this a word from You, God?* She continued reading aloud. "Fear not, nor be dismayed: for the Lord God, even my God, will be with thee; he will not fail thee, nor forsake thee, until thou hast finished all the work for the service … of the Lord."

Kate jumped off the bed and walked to the window. Tears splashed down her cheeks as the words dug themselves into her heart. "You will not forsake me nor fail me, God, until I've finished the work You've called me to do." She knew the words were meant for Solomon, but today they were meant for her. She was ready to tell Mrs. Gracey that she'd go to China. Then, as God's comfort washed over her, she let herself grieve for all she would leave behind. *Whatever happens, it's in Your hands, Lord.*

The next weeks passed by in a flurry of activity: ordering supplies, booking travel, packing, and saying farewells. Kate's mind was in a haze. It hardly seemed possible that she was actually leaving for China by the end of November. Eighteen seventy-nine would always stand out in her mind as the year she took the plunge to serve God wherever He called her.

Kate knew her mother had found it difficult to accept her youngest daughter's need to study medicine. A woman should want a home and husband and children. But China? Without a husband!

Others must have felt the same way. A few weeks before she left Evanston, Kate overheard two women talking in the church foyer.

One had pulled the other aside, as if to tell her a secret, but was far from quiet about it. "Have you heard that my Alice and Joseph are engaged? I'm so relieved that she decided to marry him. He's been courting her for a year."

"That's good news."

Kate thought, *They're probably wondering why David and I didn't get engaged. There must be something wrong with me.*

"And yours! How soon is your daughter's baby due? Your first grandchild!"

"Six more weeks. It's good to see the girls settled down in their own homes, isn't it?"

The loud woman turned around to see if anyone was listening. She must not have realized how much her voice carried. "Have you noticed how sad Mary Bushnell looks these days? Imagine her Katharine going off to China, and without a husband in sight. Do you think—" The woman stopped when she saw Kate standing in the group of young people nearby.

Yes, Mother knew what people were saying. She looked heartbroken over Kate's leaving. But in spite of her mother's sadness and the pain Kate felt whenever she thought of David, Kate's heart was flooded with peace. Many times a day, God's promise poured over her. He would not fail her nor forsake her until she'd finished the work He'd called her to do. She shook her head. *I just wonder what I'm getting into.*

3
Three Inches

China, 1881

*H*ens cackled loudly outside on the veranda, disturbing Kate's fitful sleep. She listened a moment to the coo of a mourning dove, the rhythmic sounds of Mandarin as the servants called to one another while carrying water into the house, and the happy voices of children laughing and chattering.

She had fallen in love with the Chinese people in the two years she'd been here. Yet China mystified and frustrated her. The ferocious heat debilitated her, and superstitions darkened every phase of life. In spite of warnings she'd heard from British traders on the ship coming over, the people didn't hate her. They simply couldn't figure her out. She had to admit, she hadn't figured them out yet either.

She wearily pulled herself out from under the mosquito net. If only she weren't so overworked. If she had more time, she could learn more of their ways and customs. She could improve her language skills.

She slid to the side of the bed. And if she could get that stuck-in-her-ways mission school principal, Miss Haskins, to realize that Kate was not diverting funds from the school every time she ordered medicine, things would be simpler too. She brushed the thought away with a prayer for grace.

Get going, Dr. Bushnell, she told herself. *You've got a full day ahead at the clinic.*

She peeked out her window to see the long line of sick people, some desperately ill, even a pregnant woman. At least birthing women came to the clinic for help when they ran into complications—but sometimes they waited too long. That had almost happened the night before.

33

To help treat the long lines of patients who queued up at the clinic doors every day, Kate had only Ella, who truly was a gift and a surprise. She and Ella had become friends in Illinois years before at a Sunday afternoon prayer meeting in Dean Sanford's rooms at the Women's College in Evanston. Ella had been two years behind Kate at the Medical College. And now here they were, serving God as doctors at the ends of the earth. Only Ella was not serving today. She had been sick for several weeks with a cough that wracked her feverish body and left her crumpled in bed.

Kate splashed her face at the intricately carved washstand in the corner of her room. She quickly brushed her heavy chestnut hair and pinned it into a bun at the back of her head. Concerned, she hurried down the hall to Ella's room.

She tapped on the door. "Ella, how are you feeling?"

Ella's voice was low and weak. "I'm so sorry, Kate. I won't be able to come to the clinic again this morning." She broke into a spasm of coughing, and Kate reached through the mosquito netting to help her sit up.

"I didn't expect you would." Kate had to keep herself from frowning at the gray of Ella's face, the lightness of her arm. Ella had lost weight rapidly since arriving six months prior and seemed more fragile each day. "I'll send some willow bark tea over with Tai Yau. That may help bring down your fever. I'll ask someone to sponge you off too. Won't that feel better? It's so hot under this net."

"Kate, I don't want to add to your patient burden."

Kate wiped beads of perspiration from Ella's forehead. Her friend knew how overwhelming the clinic's patient load was, but worrying about it was not going to help her get better. "Nonsense. You didn't ask for this. You'll soon be up and about."

But Ella had already dropped back to sleep. Kate gently wiped her forehead once more and then slipped out the door, concerned that her friend was not improving.

At the clinic, Kate first checked on the mother who'd survived a very difficult breech birth the day before. Once again, Kate had served not only as doctor but also as anesthesiologist and surgical nurse. She heard the baby girl suckling noisily and glanced over with a smile.

A growing murmur from outside the clinic interrupted the moment. The line of patients now reached almost to the gate of the compound. Kate's shoulders sank as she looked at today's patients, who, like every other day, had walked long miles from distant villages, some carrying crying babies, others feverish and taking care of themselves the best they could. Elderly men and women stood in the direct merciless sun with only cone-shaped straw hats for protection. Kate looked at their feet. The few men that came to bring wives or mothers had tough, calloused, dirty feet, some with visible sores. She winced when she thought of the women hobbling under all the binding. Their tiny, tiny feet must have ached. How could they walk at all? No wonder those little girls cried all the time. Kate couldn't imagine the agony.

Tai Yau, Kate's assistant, brought in the first patient, an old woman with an ulcerated sore on her leg.

Kate bowed in the traditional greeting and motioned for her to sit down.

"I'll have to ... wash ... clean this with"—she began, then interrupted her halting Mandarin—"Yau," she turned, frustrated, "just tell her I'll clean it and it may be painful."

The old woman smiled a toothless assent and sat immobile as Kate sterilized the ugly ulceration with carbolic acid and put a dressing on it. "Tell her to keep it clean and to come back if it doesn't get better."

The woman stood, favoring the bad leg but never uttering a cry. She bowed slightly, gratitude evident on her face, and shuffled out of the clinic. Kate wiped perspiration from her forehead and took stock of the fifty or so more patients lined at the door. They stood sweating in the glaring sun. May all the treatments be as simple as the old woman's.

But that was not to be, and Kate knew it the moment Yau led in the next couple. A woman hobbled behind her husband on tiny malformed feet. Even in this heat, the man was dressed in a long black gown, secured tightly at the neck. He carried a girl of five or six, her sweet face pallid and perspiring. She heaved exhaustedly, tiny moans escaping parched lips. Yau introduced Mr. Woon.

Kate saw the source of the problem immediately. Both of the girl's bound feet were bleeding through dirty bandages.

"Here, put her on this table." How she wished for the sterile table at the women's hospital in Chicago where she'd been a resident, instead of this rough wooden one used for every sort of emergency.

"What's your name?" Kate began to gently unwrap the bandages.

The child looked trustingly into her eyes. "Seen Fah," she whispered.

Seen Fah's father stepped officiously up to the table. He spoke to Yau, but Kate understood him perfectly. "My wife tried to fit Fah's feet into her shoes, but something has gone wrong." He lowered his voice as if embarrassed. "Her feet were too big."

Seen Fah's mother cowered behind her husband, nodding her head. Kate could almost see the guilt on her face, not for the damage she'd done, but that she'd failed to ensure her daughter's marriageability.

"She cut two of the toes that protruded too far, but they haven't stopped bleeding," the father explained.

Kate wanted to snap at them in horror but controlled her tongue and instead motioned to Yau, who had retreated with distaste to the corner of the room. "Ask him how long they've been bleeding."

The father shook his head. "Maybe a week. Maybe longer. We live in Wongshui. It took us a whole day to walk here. Can you fix her feet so they won't get bigger?"

Kate tried to hold back her anger as she continued to unwrap Fah's feet. The girl's moans turned to cries as a putrid odor confirmed Kate's worst fears. Gangrene. Fah shook with fever, and as her feet were unbound and the blood flowed, her pain reached new levels. Kate motioned to Yau to bring some willow bark for the fever, knowing even then there was little hope of saving those mangled feet and maybe not even the girl's life.

"Mr. Woon, I will do what I can, but Fah has a serious infection." Kate hesitated. She needed to be clear. "Yau, you must explain that I may have to amputate Fah's feet to save her life. She can stay here at the clinic for a few days until we see how things progress."

Yau rattled off Kate's advice in Mandarin.

"No!" Woon thundered. He talked so fast and loud that Kate struggled to understand Yau's translation. "I won't keep her here. I won't have you cut off her feet. Just give us some medicine, and we'll take her home."

"Medicine will not fix this," Kate said. "Tell him this, Yau." Kate looked intensely into Mr. Woon's eyes as Yau translated precisely.

Woon watched Kate's face. He seemed shocked that a woman, even a doctor, would challenge him so. "No!" he thundered again.

Kate turned back to swab Fah's feet with carbolic acid and rewrap them. When she stepped to the cabinet for some morphine to at least ease Fah's suffering, Mr. Woon scooped his daughter from the table and threw her over his shoulder. He motioned angrily at his wife, who hobbled behind him to the door.

Kate called out, "Don't go. She'll die!"

But Mr. Woon hurried past the waiting line of patients, grumbling, Kate assumed, about the useless foreign doctor.

Kate could only watch them leave, feeling helpless. She mumbled to Yau, "How can he do this to his own daughter? Is it more important to him that he marries her off well than that he tries to save her life?" She wiped the tears from her cheeks and regained her composure as another patient hobbled into the clinic.

Exhausted from the long day, the people's needs, and the insufferable heat, Kate entered the Harts' dining room just as the dinner bell rang. A welcome breeze off the Yangtze blew through the open archways and along the corridors. What a relief from the suffocating clinic.

She joined the seven women, fellow missionaries who taught here in the mission school and lived on the second floor of the Harts' home. The Methodist Episcopal Church had established the Kiukiang Mission fifteen years earlier in 1866 and opened the school and clinic soon after. The single teachers and medical staff ate with the Harts, as did guests passing through from Shanghai, so it was often a crowd that shared the day's experiences and misadventures.

Kate sat down as Mary Lyons and Sarah Fletcher were laughing about a faux pas Mary made in her Mandarin class.

"I don't know if I'll ever get those tonal sounds right," Mary said. "Today I tried to ask Mr. Chang, 'Please may I ask a question?' Instead, I dropped the tone on the first word and it came out, 'Please kiss me!'"

Everyone burst into laughter. Everyone, Kate noticed, except Eloise Haskins, the school principal. With the laughter, Kate felt the tension ease slightly in her neck and shoulders. She too had made such embarrassing mistakes speaking Mandarin, but further chatter of it felt too much tonight. She felt too weary to talk, too disturbed by the image still in her mind of Seen Fah's butchered feet and pleading face and her parents' stubborn choice to follow custom rather than acknowledge what was clear before their own eyes. Kate's heart grew heavy again.

The laughter quieted as Dr. Hart sat down to offer the blessing.

After the blessing, Mary turned to Kate. "You seem troubled. How did you manage without Ella? I noticed you had quite a line outside the clinic."

Kate didn't want Seen Fah to be light dinner conversation. "We managed to take care of them," she said. "Tai Yau is a fast learner."

"I wish we could get more of the Chinese girls into our school," Dr. Hart's wife, Adeline, interjected. "Wouldn't it be wonderful to be able to eventually train nurses?"

"But their fathers are adamant," Sarah said. "You know what Confucius says. Men are heavenly, light, and strength, and—"

"Women are earthly, dark, and weak," Mary chimed in.

Again the women laughed, but Kate could not join them. To her, the implications were no laughing matter at all. She could only see the sad faces and tiny feet of the young women of Kiukiang, the lined faces of the elderly women controlled for a lifetime by husbands who saw their wives as their property and servants, and the hard faces of the mothers-in-law, bullied themselves and harassing their daughters-in-law. Today she'd seen the cruelty at its worst. She would never forget that pleading little face and the agony it held as she'd unwrapped the child's butchered feet.

Kate sent up a silent prayer. *Lord, I just want to make a difference. To heal, yes, but so much more is needed. Show me what You have for me to do. There must be something more for me to do. But what? My heart breaks for these women and girls.*

As the laughter died, Kate could no longer keep the day's events to herself. "You should have been with me this afternoon." She told of Fah's feet. "Gangrene had already set in, but her father was absolutely furious when I mentioned we might have to amputate."

"Oh, come now, Dr. Bushnell," Eloise Haskins broke in. "Do you really have to describe such things at the table?"

Abashed, Kate looked around the table, but she could see the others wanted her to continue. "He stormed out the moment I finished wrapping the wounds again. He would not even wait for the morphine I offered, and there is no way Fah will survive this. Her suffering ..." Tears brimming, Kate turned to Dr. Hart at the head of the table. "Why do these people do this to their little girls?"

Dr. Virgil Hart had spent more than twenty years in China, heading up the work of the Methodist Episcopal Church. He understood the culture and people. A student of languages, with a far-reaching vision of planting mission stations throughout the province, he was considered a missionary statesman. But on this subject, he was not diplomatic. He set down his fork and spoke plainly, revealing a sorrow Kate recognized.

"I wish I had a reasonable answer, Dr. Bushnell. There is much after living here so many years that even I don't understand. I do know the custom goes back more than one thousand years. It must have started among the elites, the queens and dowagers, as a sign of beauty, perhaps to show that they were so rich they did not have to—in fact, they could not—work in the fields. Unfortunately, today almost every woman, at least in this part of China, has her feet bound."

Kate looked down at her plate, shaking her head. She was completely spent yet refused to accept such an answer as reasonable.

"Isn't anyone trying to stop it?" Sarah asked.

"We have talked about it in the mission," Dr. Hart said. "Some have even suggested that for a girl to be allowed to attend school she must unbind her feet."

Kate looked up in alarm. "But after so much time bound, that would be agonizing. Even Seen Fah screamed as I unwrapped her tight bandages. No wonder they resist. The feet must never be bound to begin with!"

"Yes," Dr. Hart said. "Yes. Some Chinese leaders are beginning to recognize that they have destroyed the usefulness of half their population. But many people insist women's feet must be bound—or their daughters will never find a husband."

"And it is not our place to interfere," Miss Haskins insisted. "It is up to the Chinese leaders."

Kate ignored Miss Haskins' comments. Any suggestion of change seemed to frighten her, as though her place at the mission school was fragile.

Kate plowed on, "I have a thought, Dr. Hart. Why not start requiring that the girls who start first grade must not have their feet bound in the first place? Parents want their children to attend the mission school, and that may be what it will take for them to protect their little girls from such barbarism. Over the years, the custom could be broken, at least in this region."

Miss Haskins spoke up again, her voice tense and full of anger. "It is not our place to change the Chinese culture, Dr. Bushnell. You have not been here very long. You do not understand how the people feel. You do not even speak Mandarin well enough to truly hear what they are saying. It takes time to understand this rich, historic culture. I suspect that if that were the case, they simply wouldn't send their daughters at all. They would just remain in their heathen beliefs. You do not understand and have no right to meddle in school affairs."

Why was she so angry? Didn't she realize what foot binding did to a body? Did she really think that mangling a little girl's feet was an act of beauty? Kate shook her head.

"Kate," Sarah asked, trying to diffuse the tension. "How do the mothers keep the feet as small as three inches? I've seen them hobbling around the compound. It looks impossible to me."

"Are you sure you want to hear this at the dinner table?" Kate straightened up in her chair and brushed her hair from her perspiring forehead.

The teachers nodded. Kate looked at Dr. Hart and then at Miss Haskins, who sat with her lips pinched together and her eyes on her plate.

"Every village has a foot binder," she began, "someone official, someone called in by the time a daughter is anywhere from three to six years old. There is the concern that when the mother sees her daughter's pain, she will not be able to bind the foot tightly enough. So the foot binder is called to bend the small toes underneath the ball of the foot. Often the arch is broken so the leg and arch form a straight line. The large toe is pointed up and back, and then the wrappings are wound tightly over and over around the heel and up over the toes."

Kate paused as the room fell silent. The teachers lowered their forks and spoons to the table. Sarah put a hand over her eyes as if to block the very image.

"The object," Kate continued, "is to keep the foot from growing more than three inches so that it can fit into the beautifully embroidered shoes the mother makes." Kate stopped. She didn't know whether to be angry or to cry. "Fah's foot was too big."

She looked at Dr. Hart, who nodded slightly, sadly, with full understanding. Kate looked around the room to explain. "Her mother was just trying to save her from lifelong embarrassment and rejection. Now the girl will probably die."

Several of the women gasped in shock. Miss Haskins pushed her chair back and excused herself. Kate stared at her own half-eaten rice but was no longer hungry. Even Adeline, normally cheerful and chattering, seemed overwhelmed by the suffering that surrounded them.

Dr. Hart reached out his hands for everyone to clasp their neighbors' in a circle of prayer around the table. "Father—" He stopped with emotion. "Father," he tried again. "Help us. Help us to share Thy light in this hurting place. May Jesus shine through us—"

"Doctor! Dr. Bushnell, you come! Come!" Leung, the cook, burst into the room with several Chinese servants behind him, all shouting in rapid Mandarin, pointing hysterically back across the compound.

4
A Deadly Attack

"Come quickly, Doctor. Ma Xhi stabbed. Blood everywhere."

Kate leaped from the table and grabbed the medical bag that she always left near the door. She followed Leung and the servants toward the heavy compound gates that stood open. Why weren't they bolted at this hour of the night?

"Thieves!" the crippled gardener said as if he read her thoughts. "Thieves broke in." Kate glanced at his bent figure as they hurried and saw blatant fear in his eyes. Roving gangs, impoverished and turned to crime since the recent famine, had attacked villagers. But none had dared attack the Kiukiang Mission before.

The main building loomed ahead like a ship silhouetted against a blackened sky. No candles flickered in the clinic windows to indicate a nurse checking on an ill patient. Kate's mind flashed to her friend Ella, still shaking with fever and cough. *I'm on my own again.* For the emergency tonight, she'd have to take care of everything herself.

"How did the thieves get through the gate?" she asked Leung.

"They said they had a mother about to give birth. Ma Xhi mumbled that he'd heard a woman screaming. Once he opened the gate, thieves began beating him with clubs and—"

"One drew a sword," the gardener interrupted. "See." He pointed ahead to dark splatters on the ground that glowed in the light of torches held by a growing crowd of Chinese from the outskirts of the compound. "Blood everywhere."

Kate and the band from the mission house reached the gates to find a small bundle on the ground, pools of blood all around. Lots of blood.

Ma Xhi's wife keened over her husband's body. Her son, Sz-Shan, knelt beside her, holding his mother in comfort, in support. He looked up as Kate arrived and shook his head. "Too late. Too late. He is dead. They shouldn't have called you."

Kate dropped to her knees beside the fallen man and felt his neck for a pulse. There. There! Faint, but it was there. *Work quickly now, Dr. Bushnell.*

The man's battered face was barely recognizable. Blood spilled from a deep cut across his face and another on his neck.

"Bring that torch closer," Kate called. She dug into her bag for something to staunch the blood.

"He shouted and tried to chase the robbers away, even with the blood running down over his eyes," Sz-Shan explained. "But he fell." The young man choked. "Now he is dead. Dead!"

Kate found a bandage and pressed it to the wound. "Your father is not dead," she said quietly. "His wounds are very serious. I must sew up this deep one to stop the bleeding. Do you understand? Hold this while I get what I need." With one hand, Kate grabbed Sz-Shan's hand and placed it on the bloodied bandage. "Press," she ordered. "Like this."

With her other hand, she dug in her bag for a bottle of carbolic acid and the suturing packet. "I'm going to close this wound, and then we will take your father back to the clinic." *Thank you, God, that they missed his artery.*

Sz-Shan used both hands to hold the bandage to his father's neck but was clearly confused.

"Hold this cloth tightly," Kate coached. "Tightly, see?" She reached over to show again how to apply pressure, then fished back for the coarse thread and a long needle. "I need to pull the wound together now." She moved Sz-Shan's hands and the bandage aside and grasped the gaping skin. Her hands seemed to fly as she drew the needle back and forth, pulling together the ragged edges of skin.

The crowd silenced, onlookers mesmerized by the strange woman, the foreign doctor at work. Shadows from the torchlight twisted across the horrified faces. Kate forced her focus onto her patient, yet with each stitch, she sensed the crowd grow to life.

"Can't this woman see Ma Xhi's spirit has departed?" one man murmured.

The question ignited others' questions as people leaned in, pressing closer to watch Kate at work.

Fear of the robbers and their swords had disappeared. Dr. Hart and the gardener walked to the mission entrance to pull the gate shut and drop the heavy bolt, sealing out any danger.

Kate finished closing the ghastly wound and checked Ma Xhi's pulse again. *Stronger. Maybe ...*

She passed smelling salts under his nose, and the man moaned. He started in pain, his head jerking and one hand instinctively rising to touch the wound, then dropping in weakness. The people started back, screaming. Some froze in horror; others ran away, afraid to see a dead man come to life.

Kate remained matter of fact. "I think he will pull through," she told Sz-Shan and the servants. "Let's take him back to the clinic."

No one moved to touch the body. The villagers were petrified.

"That must be an evil spirit," one man cried.

Ma Xhi stirred again, his moans louder now, and his wife put her hands over her mouth. Where grief had paralyzed her moments ago, now terror roused her. She tottered on those tiny malformed feet and tried to turn and run.

Sz-Shan caught his mother. "Honored mother, our father is not dead. The foreign doctor has brought him back to life." He motioned with his head for his wife to help his mother home.

Then Sz-Shan fell at Kate's feet. Bowing, he whispered, "Thank you, Doctor. We have heard you tell us of the man who died long ago and came back to life, but now we have seen it for ourselves."

Shocked, Kate reached down to pull Sz-Shan to his feet. She shook her head. "No, no. This has nothing to do with Jesus, who was killed. He *did* come back to life. Only God has the power to bring back life. Your father was never dead. Do you understand? Ma Xhi never died. I merely revived him."

Kate turned back to Ma Xhi, who had been eased into a sitting position by two brave villagers. He cried out in pain again. "Careful," she said to the villagers. "Put your shoulder under his arm—no, not where I've stitched the wound, the other one. That's right. Now gently ... gently lift him."

Just then Dr. Hart stepped back to help. "I will see that he gets to the clinic."

A sudden motion behind Kate caused her to turn around. Horrified, she saw the gardener and Leung on their knees before her, bowing their heads. "What are you doing?" she cried. She had lost all patience. "I didn't bring him back to life. I didn't raise the dead!"

Lord, why don't they listen to the truth?

Tears ran down Kate's cheeks as she turned to follow the men carrying Ma Xhi back to the clinic. She was exhausted. First the girl in the clinic with mangled feet and probably dying, and now Ma Xhi. The people weren't listening to her, not accepting help, not seeing what was true. *Please tell me, Lord, that the whole countryside doesn't believe I'm a miracle worker. Don't I have enough to do without raising the dead?*

5
Getting Direction

A pounding at the door wakened Kate. Night was already turning to the hot stickiness of day.

"One moment," Kate murmured, still half asleep. She pulled back the net curtains around her bed, swatted away hungry mosquitoes, and threw on a loose robe. She didn't take time to bind up her heavy hair as the pounding grew louder and more urgent.

"Yes?"

"A man has brought his dead daughter to see you," Tai Yau said excitedly. "He said he heard that you can raise the dead."

Kate's heart pounded in her throat. "I'll get my bag," she replied and turned back to her room.

"No." She heard Dr. Hart's voice as he came along the verandah outside her door. "I think it's best for you to stay there. Let me speak to him."

Kate sank into a chair. The people were saying she could raise the dead? They still believed Ma Xhi was already dead when she treated his wounds. The clamor of voices rose through the open window. Kate stood to see Dr. Hart speaking to a man cradling a girl, limp in his arms. People from the village gathered behind them.

Seen Fah! Oh ... Kate cradled her face in her hands.

Mary and some of the other missionaries rushed into her room and joined her at the window. "What is going on?"

"The people ... last night ..." Kate didn't even know how to begin. She sat back in the chair by the window.

Mary knelt beside her. "What is it?"

"The people think because I was able to revive Ma Xhi that I actually raised him from the dead!" Kate brushed back her hair with her hand. "Where do they get such ideas?"

"Reverend Hart will explain it to them. He will make them understand."

"They will believe him," Sarah piped in. "The people will listen to him."

Because he was a man? Or because he was the head of the mission? Kate was too tired to find the answer, but she knew her age and her sex worked against her.

I've been here almost three years, and what have I really accomplished? Certainly not raising a dead man, no matter what the people thought. They seemed to accept the medicine she gave them if it fit their superstitions. But she hadn't had time to teach the Bible to women in their homes or to free any of them from the bondage they lived under. She hadn't even had the nerve to ask Yau what she thought about foot binding.

"Enough," she said aloud. "I need to get ready for the clinic."

Mary, Sarah, and the others took their cue and left Kate's room. She slipped out of her robe and into a long black skirt and blouse, pulling the white bibbed apron over both. Already she felt weary and hot and rubbed the back of her neck, damp with perspiration.

She mumbled to herself as she dressed. "They won't believe me when I tell them that Jesus came back to life, but they expect me to bring people back from the dead. Maybe I should have never come to China. What made me think I could make a difference here? 'Listen to your heart,' Dr. Jewell said, and I really did. But I don't feel right about it this morning." *Oh, Lord, help me to keep listening to what You are telling me. I'm here. I'm the only doctor for miles.*

She sat down to slip on a black boot, still covered with dust from the night before, and began lacing the ties. "This may have been the worst decision of my life," she said aloud as she wound the long laces around the hooks to the top. "I'm too young for this. If I'd only finished my residency first—but, no. I shouldn't think that. God made it clear that I should be here. Even if the Chinese don't understand me, they need me." She shook her head and grumbled aloud in prayer, "Even if I don't understand *them*, Lord. The women seem to think it's perfectly normal to make their daughters suffer so they can find a good husband." She shook her head and lifted one hand toward the heavens. "That *can't* please You."

She thought of how she sometimes caught them eyeing her unbound feet with disdain. They probably figured that was why she didn't have a husband. Kate picked up the other boot, shook the dirt loose, then pushed her hair off her forehead, already wet with perspiration. *I should be thankful I can wear shoes that fit my normal feet.* She shuddered, thinking about the bound, bleeding, putrefied feet she saw yesterday.

Tai Yau returned to tap on Kate's door and crack it open to tell her she was free. The way was clear for her to come to the clinic. Tai Yau didn't seem to think Kate's feet were ugly. Kate wondered if the young woman wished she had strong feet like hers. She could ask her. Kate glanced at Tai Yau's tiny feet, wrapped in the Chinese slippers.

No, she thought. Her frustration quickly melted and changed to sympathy. "The excitement is over?"

"Reverend Hart tell people to go away with dead. Bring only sick and alive."

Kate sighed deeply. "And they are probably lined up already."

"Yes, line long."

Kate stood. "Go ahead," she told Yau. "I want to check on Dr. Ella. I'll be there in a few minutes."

Halfway to Ella's room, however, Miss Haskins blocked Kate's path. "Miss Bushnell," she began, "I need to speak with you a moment."

"Yes, Miss Haskins? I'm in a bit of a hurry. I've got quite a line at the clinic."

"I know. I am aware of what brings many of them here today. Do you realize these poor people think you can raise the dead? That is blasphemy."

"But, I never—"

"There is no excuse for this. If you do not deal with it soon, I will have no choice but to speak to the mission board. I will not have my students led astray." She turned on her heel. "This is what comes of allowing women to be doctors—nothing but a tangled mess," she mumbled under her breath as she strode away.

Kate blinked away her shock, took a deep breath, and then turned to Ella's room. She stepped in almost silently.

Ella was still asleep under her mosquito net. She was drenched with sweat. Kate dipped a cloth into the water in the bedside basin and reached under the net to wipe her sleeping friend's brow.

"Oh, Ella, why are we here?" she whispered. She wet the cloth again. Even now she was still asking—was this really the right place for her? Evidently, it was common knowledge that she didn't speak Mandarin well and that she didn't really know the Chinese people. Was that why she didn't feel like she was impacting the people's hearts? Their bodies, yes: but she had come to do more. And now this! She mustn't let Ella know about Miss Haskins' accusation.

Ella opened her eyes and seemed to read Kate's thoughts. "Don't be discouraged, Kate. The people really love you, especially the children. I see them run up to you just to touch your white hand or reach up to feel your thick brown hair."

"I know." Kate smiled. "I guess babies like me too. Yau came to the clinic yesterday with a big smile on her face. 'Dr. Bushnell, they come to invite you to Cheung Miang's birthday party.'" She mimicked Yau's high little voice. "I asked her, 'Who has invited me?'"

"'Mr. Cheung.'"

"I shook my head and told her 'But Miang is only weeks old!' How many weeks ...? You helped me deliver Miang in the middle of the night. Remember, Ella, they brought his mother in a sedan chair because she'd been in labor two days already. Then, at the clinic, the birth happened fast. That little man wanted to come out feet first."

Ella laughed. "That can only be a few weeks ago. He can't be more than three weeks old."

"But Yau told me, 'Baby thirty days tomorrow, Dr. Bushnell. And very special birthday. One year tomorrow.'"

"One year?" Ella questioned. "That doesn't make sense. I was there!"

"But Yau insists. 'Thirty days is one year birthday in China.'" Kate shook her head. "The Chinese customs baffle me. The people's expectations too. They asked me to bring my stethoscope to the party and place it next to Miang with all the other things to see which one he chooses. Do they really think whatever object the baby shows interest in will determine his future? That if Miang is fascinated with the gleam of my stethoscope he'll become a doctor?" She shook her head.

Ella just smiled.

That afternoon, as Kate got ready to go to the birthday party, Yau made sure she was fully prepared for the special event. "Miang will wear red dress. It will keep him safe."

"A red dress will keep him safe?" Kate asked.

"Yes," Yau said. "Red, the color of protection. The dress, so evil spirits think Miang a girl and not trouble him."

Yau nodded approvingly when Kate tucked a red envelope into her pocket. "You take *lysee*. Good, good. They like that best."

I am sure they will, Kate thought. *Money seems to speak all languages.*

She walked to the Cheung home in the village down the road from the mission. She carried her stethoscope around her neck and the traditional gift—the famed red envelope with a carefully calculated amount of money in crisp new bills.

Kate found the Cheung house easily. A crowd had formed along the narrow dirt path, and two of the Cheung girls, whom Kate knew from the clinic, ran up to grab her hands and lead her past the villagers into the house. She noticed that the oldest girl, Qui Qui, hobbled behind them, wiping her tear-streaked face. *Oh, look at her tiny feet. How can she even walk?*

At the house, Kate was ushered in as an honored guest. Mrs. Cheung sat proudly on a chair while her guests sat on the floor, drinking tea from their own cups. Kate marveled. For thirty days, Mrs. Cheung had by custom been quarantined, shut away, and now everyone gathered at her feet with their—oh! Kate had forgotten to bring her own teacup. Everyone else had theirs. She knew she had been missing something.

She stood awkwardly as one of Mrs. Cheung's relatives hastily brought in a chair.

Kate sat down uncomfortably, as troubled by a position apart from the other guests as by their customs. She would have been glad to sit on the floor with the others. She looked around at the happy faces and then at the cherubic Miang, wriggling in a red birthday dress.

The red dress! Kate felt sad. Here not even evil spirits had regard for a girl. After a quick, silent prayer for the family, she relaxed to enjoy the occasion and all the festivity. She needed it after Miss Haskins' accusations that morning.

Kate returned to the mission later in the afternoon to tell Ella about little Master Chiang in a red dress. "He looked so healthy and adorable."

"Oh, I would have loved to have gone with you." Ella grew silent a moment, then spoke in almost a whisper. "Do you think I'll ever get back to the village?"

"Of course you will, silly. Just get some rest first." Kate hoped she was right; Ella's symptoms frightened her. She stroked Ella's arm. *Heal quickly, my friend. I need you.* She straightened the netting around the bed and walked thoughtfully back to her room.

Kate slept restlessly the night after the party. She dreamed that she was back in the clinic. The poor girl's feet, swollen and bleeding, dominated her visions. *Hush, little one. I didn't mean to hurt you. Your feet are mangled and twisted. No one can help them.* But someone held Kate's hands, her healing hands, caressing the tiny feet, now miraculously uncurling. *Run, Seen Fah, run. You can run now.*

Seen Fah jumped up—and Kate jerked awake to reality, her body wet with perspiration. The air was heavy. Her room smelled like gangrene. She turned over and tried to put Fah from her mind, to think back to a snowy day in Evanston, or imagine a cool wind blowing off Lake Michigan. She remembered when her father took her up on the lighthouse to watch the waves billowing below. Her heart had been pounding. That was the day she told her father her dream.

How confident she'd felt about God's calling that day. She remembered her father's voice, almost resigned, at approving her request. "God has made you a compassionate young woman, Kate, and since this is God's doing, I don't see how I can stand in your way."

Kate shook her head, wanting to drown out her father's concern—and her mother's disapproval. *Lord, You've brought me here. My father's legacy was a lighthouse to save lives. What's mine?*

Sweat dripped down her forehead. There was not a breath of air. But even if there were, it would never reach her. If she could just rip down this deceitful-looking net—so sheer but trapping the air inside like a balloon. How had Fah been able to bear this heat, wrapped from her head to her bound feet? She'd had such a fever.

Kate punched her pillow into a ball and wrapped her arms around it. Anything to get some air. She poked a leg out from under the net just to catch a breeze. An ever-watchful mosquito buzzed in joy, and she quickly withdrew her foot back inside the netting.

She shouldn't think about David either. She'd never fall asleep. Why hadn't she heard from him? Was he sick? Had the mailbag been stolen from the train again?

She rolled over and stared at the clock on the wall, the hands seemingly immobile. She shouldn't think about David, but … she couldn't help herself.

Kate pushed her pillow aside and threw herself onto her stomach. She'd shocked him that day when she told him about Mrs. Gracey's request. Should she have taken more time to say yes? Did she miss God's "go slow" sign when David bared his heart to her? When he was going to ask her father's permission to court her? She saw his pleading eyes, heard his voice calling softer, and finally drifted into sleep, his words echoing: *I know God will show you what you must do, Kate. God will show you … God will …*

The next morning, the line of patients wound well beyond the clinic wall. Kate needed help, yet Yau seemed absent, running in and out of the door. Kate was beginning to lose patience just as Yau came back after leaving a fourth time in less than thirty minutes.

"Is there a problem out there?" Kate called over her shoulder.

Yau hurried to her side, head hung low. "Reverend Hart told me check if there were any patients asking you to visit them."

"I will go if I can. You know that."

"But some of the patients … their relatives dead."

Kate leaned back on the examining table. "The rumors of my

magical powers." Shaking her head, she sighed deeply. "We'll have to stop this."

Yau escorted the last patient out the door as the sun began to set. Kate left the clinic late again, discouraged. People expected her to do miracles, but she could hardly keep up with the long line of patients each day.

If only Kate's older sister were here to help her sort out things. Sarah had always been her confidante, encouraging—if not completely understanding—Kate's independence and determination.

After dinner, during which she carefully avoided eye contact with Miss Haskins, Kate went back to her room to finish a long overdue letter to Sarah. *How can these people possibly believe I am a miracle worker,* she wrote. *We have to stop these false practices. But how?*

She swatted a mosquito nibbling at her neck. Weariness began to overtake her, but she needed to finish the letter tonight. The Jorgensons were leaving for Shanghai in the morning, and they'd take it for her. *Focus, Kate. Focus.* She reread the last line and continued to finish the letter.

> But how? I haven't figured that out, Sarah. They don't seem to be able to understand about Jesus' resurrection. They've never seen Him perform miracles. They think I can because they saw Ma Xhi "come back from the dead" with their own eyes. They won't believe that he was never dead to begin with, that I'm no miracle worker! I shouldn't be so upset with them. I want to love them more. It's not their fault that they've not heard about Jesus before now. I can't solve this tonight. But you see my dilemma? Give my love to everybody, and tell them not to worry. I'm fine, just tired.
> All my love,
> Kate

In the morning, Kate stopped by Ella's room to lift her friend's spirits, and maybe her own, but left struck that Ella was not regaining her strength.

As she came out of Ella's room, she met Dr. Hart in the hall.

"Ah, Kate. Could you join me for a minute?" He beckoned her to his office. Kate sank wearily into a chair and pushed a strand of hair off her forehead.

Dr. Hart spoke kindly, "You mustn't be upset about what Miss Haskins said the other night, about the foot-binding issue. She sees you as a threat to her role as principal. She is afraid that if we enforced a rule against foot binding, the people might stop sending their children to the mission school. After thirty years, she is rather set in her ways."

"I appreciate your concern, Reverend Hart. But I've heard from some of the teachers that she was a schoolmate of Mrs. Gracey and that she's threatened to write her that I'm not fitting in here. She thinks I'm stirring up trouble and hindering her work at the school. She would like to have me removed from work with the women's mission efforts altogether because I 'don't have any understanding of the gospel.'"

"Oh, don't worry about that. They've been friends for a long time—long before Mrs. Gracey became the chairman of the women's board. I'm more worried about you, Dr. Bushnell. You look tired. You have dark circles under your eyes. It's been doubly hard to be without a nurse or a doctor to help for the past few weeks, hasn't it? How are you holding up?"

"I am getting along." She paused, avoiding Dr. Hart's searching eyes. "It's true I could use more help." She stared at her hands in her lap.

"I suspect it is more than needing help," Reverend Hart responded gently. "It is the unwarranted expectations because people in the whole province seem to believe you raised Ma Xhi from the dead, isn't it?" He tilted his head so he could look into her face.

Kate nodded. "I had another person at the clinic yesterday ask me to come to see his relative who died."

"It is getting out of hand, Kate. Mr. Cheung came running through the gate early this morning, calling your name. I intercepted him, but I could hardly calm him down. He just cried, 'Miang, Miang hurt. He fell from cart—bleeding.'

"Then he bent over sobbing. 'He not breathing. He dead.' He fell on his knees pleading, 'Where doctor? She know what to do.'"

Kate put her hands over her face. "Oh no! No! He was the picture of health two days ago at his birthday party." He even wore a red dress to chase away the spirits. And now they wanted her to undo the spirit's evil.

"I helped him up and tried to comfort him," Reverend Hart continued, "and explained again that you can't raise the dead."

He paused, allowing Kate to recover from her shock. "I think you should go away into the mountains for a few weeks. The mission has a cabin—it is very simple but peaceful—and you could restore yourself and give me time to calm things down here."

"But who would take care of all the people who come with legitimate needs? There's no one else to care for them."

"I have already heard from our hospital in Shanghai that they are sending one of their nurses for a few weeks. Several new missionaries arrived there, so they can spare someone to help us. You have trained Yau so well that she will be able to orient the new nurse. In the meantime, I am sending word to the village elders that Ma Xhi did not die but was saved by your medical care. I think the hysteria will die down."

Kate dabbed at her eyes. "Thank you, Dr. Hart."

"Oh, and another thing: I think Ella should go with you to the mountains. The cooler air away from mosquitoes may do her some good."

"I was going to ask you about her. I'm very concerned that she's not getting better. How soon do you think the nurse from Shanghai could get here?"

"You must not let that worry you. One of the teachers who took care of the dispensary before you came can help out until the new nurse gets here." Dr. Hart rose to his feet. "That is probably another reason Eloise is upset." He laughed. "Adeline can help you arrange for any food you need. We will hire some boys to take you and Ella up in sedan chairs, and I will send Leung to cook."

With a light-hearted step, Kate left the office straight for Ella's room to tell her the good news. She didn't think Ella would be surprised about being sent to the mountains to recuperate. She was a doctor too. She must know the seriousness of her symptoms.

Ella's wan face brightened at the news. She tried to sit up on the edge of the bed, fueled by a sudden energy. "I'll start packing tomorrow. Oh, won't it be wonderful, Kate? Some fresh air and a cool breeze through the window."

"We won't even need a mosquito net," Kate added. "But don't you get out of that bed, Ella. I'll send someone tomorrow morning to help you get ready. Reserve your strength for the sedan chair ride. It will be pretty bumpy going up that trail."

Kate headed over to the clinic though she couldn't help wondering whether Ella would be able to handle the thin mountain air. Some days she couldn't stop coughing, even here. But Kate refused to entertain the deeper question: what if the trip didn't help?

6
Getaway To The Mountains

Kate began to imagine long quiet days in the mountains with only the sounds of birds and waterfalls. She had heard that the water fell through a limestone fissure at the base of a nearby rock formation, making the sound of a bell that resonated from the cliffs. Wouldn't Sarah love to go with her? She had always wanted to see the mountains. There were no mountains around Evanston.

Kate stopped and stared out the window, thinking of her down-to-earth older sister and her delightfully boisterous sons. But she shook her head to clear it of longing memories. *Get back to work, Kate.* There was a lot to do. She wanted to pack the books—the English and Chinese Bibles, her Greek New Testament, the Latin New Testament from David. Kate looked at her books, standing invitingly on the shelf next to her bed—untouched. Oh to study again! She tried to read the Chinese Bible every day, but she found little time to study and dig deeper. She determined that one of the first things she'd do once in the mountains was to compare the Chinese version to the Greek. She hoped her language skills hadn't gotten too rusty.

Her thoughts drifted to the first time she translated a verse from Greek without the help of a lexicon. She carefully spoke the Greek words, *"egó eimi he hodós kai he alítheia kai he zoe*: I am the way and the truth and the life." If God hadn't made it so clear that He wanted her to be a healer, a doctor, she would have been a language professor. The thought brought a smile to her lips.

But halfway from the shelf to her bag, she stopped packing a moment and held David's Latin New Testament in her hands. Not a word from him in three months. She knew he was busy in his new job, but when she had first arrived in China, he wrote regularly. Were his feelings for her waning? She recalled the day he came to say good-bye at her home in Evanston. *Had Mother deliberately left us alone in the front room?* He'd folded her in his arms and whispered, "I'll be praying I'll see you soon. I love you, Kate," and stepped back just as her mother came in with a tray of tea and cookies.

Kate put the book down on her desk. She would write tonight. If she got a letter into the mailbag in the morning, it might catch the next ship loading at the dock in Shanghai. But even if David didn't receive her letter for another month, perhaps there would be one from him when she came back from the mountains.

> My dear David,
> Ella and I leave for the mountains in the morning.

Her pen flew across the page as she recounted the events of the past few weeks. She added a line with an update on Ella, for the two had met when Ella visited her roommate's parents. Kate shook her head at the fact they lived across the street from David's family. Small world! She didn't have time to tell him all about Seen Fah or the sad story of baby Miang.

> I miss talking over these things with you, but maybe that
> will happen sooner than we both expect. I have a feeling
> God may soon close this ministry for me so I can come
> home. Until then ...
> Affectionately,
> Kate

The men lifted the sedan chair. Kate's stomach flipped. She never felt quite safe in the box-like contraptions supported on the shoulders of two Chinese men. She tried to relax back in the seat, thankful for the shade beneath the bamboo roof.

As the men skillfully navigated the chair along a skinny trail that hugged the side of the mountain, Kate turned to look through the little back window at Ella in the sedan following behind. How good this air was for both of them; it grew cooler and fresher as they moved higher into the mountains. Suddenly Kate grew nervous. How could the men carry the heavy poles on their shoulders, hour after hour? What if even one man slipped or lost his balance and tipped them? She didn't dare look down.

Kate leaned back, eyes shut, until they reached the tiny log cabin built for the missionaries as a getaway from the heat and pressure of work. The structure was square and simple and stood in a clearing with the mountains towering behind it. Dr. Hart had described its sparseness well, for the main room boasted only a table with four chairs and a carved wooden bench along one wall, facing a huge stone fireplace. Having a fireplace was good, Kate decided. Nights could grow chilly in the mountains.

Within minutes, Leung ordered colorful cushions be taken from the chest two men had carried and tossed onto the seats of the chairs and bench. "Boys unpack bedding," Leung explained as the women breathed in the grandeur of the pines. "They go for firewood, then fix bed in each room. You rest." Leung busied himself unpacking food, and soon the savory aroma of richly seasoned chicken filled the air.

"Let's explore." Kate and Ella walked slowly around the perimeter of the cabin, taking in the views from every angle. As far as they could see, peaks of dark variegated rock thrust up through soft gray clouds that floated between the mountains and the valley below.

"Oh look." Ella pointed. "Are those flowering bushes growing right out of the rock, or am I imagining things?"

"Those red flowers are definitely growing out of the rocks, and they're higher than the trees around us. The trees—I've never seen so many shades of green." Kate stopped and nodded toward the horizon. "Look way up there. Could that be the tip of the tower of one of the ancient Buddhist temples?"

Ella shaded her eyes. "Where?" She laughed. "You're spoofing me. It's just a rock."

Kate smiled. The mountains were like medicine for both their souls and maybe their bodies too. She noted that Ella was breathing the pure air without coughing.

The next morning, Kate made sure Ella was settled outside on a cushioned bench under Leung's watchful care. Not only was he a good cook, but he was also one of the few Chinese workers who spoke passable English. Relieved that Ella was in capable hands, Kate decided to hike up farther into the mountains. She wanted to find a place where she could lay out her books—the English, Chinese, Greek, and Latin New Testaments—and get lost in them for the first time in a long while.

Each step up revealed another breathtaking view. The Lushan Mountains stretched for miles, their irregular stony peaks shaped like pillars and cones covered with colorful flowering bushes. Kate watched for a place to put her books and found a rock flat like a sunken pulpit, just the right height to sit beside and use as a table of sorts. She dropped her book bag.

Suddenly, she couldn't resist; she ran through the trees looking at every sight, feeling like colt in the spring. Silly? Yes, but she didn't care. Then she skidded to a halt. Oh, what a vista! She let out a cry of joy and listened for the echo to come back to her. How good it was to be in this silence—no crying babies, no one talking Mandarin so fast she couldn't understand a word, no litany of symptoms to decipher, no blood, no mangled feet. *Just You and me, God.*

A flood of freedom overwhelmed her, and she began to weep. She dropped beside the huge gray pulpit rock, at first crying in relief, then joy, and finally thankfulness. Her whole body felt release with the tears as though a too-heavy bucket burst. She gave in to a wholly unexpected and rare experience. The force of emotion surprised her. When she stopped to wipe her eyes, she realized she'd also been weeping in worry over Ella and in anger—yes, anger—at David.

She sat up and rested her arms on her knees. She considered how Miss Haskins was trying to turn the teachers against her. Why? Just because she tried to persuade the village women to stop binding their daughters' feet? Was the principal so afraid parents wouldn't send their daughters to *her* school?

Kate lay flat on the dewy grass, closing her eyes as the sun caressed her face. "I'm sorry. Forgive me!" She cried out aloud to God what she could not admit to another living person: "I don't like it here. I'm homesick. I want to go home. I am so dried-up from the horribly hot summers and the heavy workload. I'm exhausted every day at the mission. By the time I get back to my room each evening, I can hardly keep my eyes open. Lord, I thought I'd found Your ministry for me, but this doesn't feel right."

Kate sat up, conscious that she faced a decision. "Forgive me for my lack of faith. You clearly sent me to China so that I can help heal people's bodies. Thank You for that gift. But that's not enough, Lord. I can't help sensing Your plans are greater than this. Show me something more."

Spent, she lay in the soft grass until a breeze ruffled the pages of her Bible. She wiped her cheeks with the back of her hand and pushed her hair back from her face. *Help me, Lord, to be faithful until You make it clear You're releasing me. Help me understand what I'm studying today.* She began to read Philippians chapter four, comparing the different translations until ideas swirled in her mind.

When she looked up again, the sun had moved high in the blue sky. She wondered how the time could have passed so quickly. Had she actually read away the whole morning? But then, how could it have taken her almost six months to work through this little letter?

She gathered her books and ran down the path to the cabin. She shouldn't have left Ella alone all morning. *Lord, let her be all right.*

A sinking feeling seized her as she reached the empty verandah. Ella wasn't there.

Kate rushed inside and scanned the room. Then she breathed a sigh of relief. "Don't you look comfortable, sitting at the table," she said to Ella. "I'm sorry to be late, but it looks like I'm just in time for lunch."

They sat together, bowed in a short prayer, and began to eat. Everything tasted so much better in the crisp mountain air. Kate watched Ella enjoying her food and noticed a little color in her cheeks.

As if reading her thoughts, Ella said, "It is delicious, isn't it?"

Kate looked at her plate.

"No," Ella said, laughing, "this whole place."

She *was* better.

"What did you see up there?" Ella asked.

Kate tried to convey the beauty of the high places in the Lushan Mountains. "I wish you could see the pinnacles of gray rocks poking through the lush foliage—every color of green—and then those red flower bushes, yellow ones too, clinging to the rough rocks. It is so quiet you can hear the waterfalls plunging through the gorge. I found a giant rock like a flat pulpit where I could read and study. I couldn't help thinking how the psalmist David wrote 'the heavens declare the glory of God—'"

"'And the firmament sheweth his handywork,'" Ella completed Kate's recitation. "It's so beautiful even here, Kate. I sat outside all morning and didn't see one mosquito!"

"Now *that* is beautiful," Kate said, laughing.

"I can breathe here, too," Ella said with a reassuring look at Kate.

That evening, Leung directed one of the men to bring in an armful of logs. The roaring fire he built took off the mountain chill and cast flickering shadows across the room.

"Let's pull the chairs closer to the fire," Kate suggested as she set an oil lamp on a small fireside table so they could read in the cozy cabin.

She snuggled up in a blanket in the chair. "This has been the most wonderful day in ... oh, I don't know how long. The mountains are like the strong tower the psalmist praises. The scent of pine and grass, the white clouds making God's patterns in the sky—I can hardly take it all in. Then to be able to study to my heart's content in the midst of it all."

"I felt the same way, Kate. I hardly coughed at all."

Kate looked skeptical.

"Well," Ella admitted, "not as much as usual."

"You're looking better tonight," Kate reassured.

"I feel better."

"I'm glad, because I wanted your thoughts on something." Kate dug into her book bag and pulled out the Chinese New Testament. "It's so much easier to read Chinese than to speak those tonal words." She leaned forward with the New Testament in her hands. "I found the strangest thing. I've been studying Paul's letter to the Philippians, and this verse in the Chinese Bible doesn't follow the Greek." She ran her finger down the page, translating as she read from the Chinese: "I entreat thee, help those who labored with me in the gospel."

Ella searched Philippians in her English translation. "I entreat thee," she read. "Help those women which laboured with me in the gospel."

"Do you hear the difference?"

Ella sat quiet for a moment. "Translate the Chinese to me again." She shut her eyes to absorb every nuance.

Kate read slowly and deliberately. "I entreat thee, help those who labored with me in the gospel."

"There's no reference to women. Paul mentions two specifically, doesn't he? What are their names?"

"Euodia and Syntyche. That's what I don't understand." Kate fell silent, thinking about Yau, Seen Fah, and all the women she had treated with crippled or mangled feet, all the lives stunted.

"That would make a big difference to Chinese women, wouldn't it?" Ella sounded surprised. "Can you even imagine them working side by side with men in the church in Kiukiang?"

Kate's heart burned again with the same excitement she'd experienced on the mountainside. "Wouldn't that be a perfect passage for people to understand how men and women can serve God together?" Her voice rose. "What if people reading about these two women, Euodia and Syntyche, who were working with Clement, one of Paul's associates—"

Ella interrupted to pick up Kate's thought. "What if they realized that even if they weren't getting along, as Paul mentions, that didn't make them inconsequential or incapable or incompetent—simply human?"

Kate fell silent. After several moments, she voiced what she'd been thinking a long time. "It's been hard for me to watch how poorly women are treated here. They don't seem to have any value, purposely crippled to toddle three feet behind their fathers and husbands and sons, seen as good only for obeying whatever is demanded of them."

She hesitated a moment. "I've always felt it unbecoming for women to speak publicly ... and yet ... I became a believer listening to the Reverend Maggie Van Cott. You know, Ella, my classmates just laughed at Mrs. Van Cott's funny hats and sausage curls—they wouldn't think of really listening to what she had to say. She knew that, and I heard how people talked behind her back. Some said she behaved improperly and others thought her simply strange for doing what other women would not."

Ella looked Kate straight in the eye. "But you wouldn't be here if you hadn't heard her message that night about serving Jesus."

"Yes," Kate nodded. "Yes." She stared away, then turned to Ella again. "Maybe the Chinese women and men are laughing about my big feet when I visit them. Maybe they think me strange for doing what other women do not, but now that I'm getting a little more fluent in Mandarin, it seems the greatest thing I can do is to go into the villages to tell them about Jesus. I feel God is pleased with what I'm doing. It's really why I came. Miss Haskins may be right; my Mandarin is poor. But the people seem to understand what I'm saying."

Ella brightened. "Yes." She nodded. "I saw that from the start when I first arrived here and went with you to the village. I didn't understand a word of Mandarin. Still, I saw the people listening to you speak with ... respect."

Kate thought. Respect. Yes. Even though her Mandarin was halting, they did listen respectfully, even the men. She fell into thoughtful silence again. When would they believe that Jesus really rose from the dead? When she looked up, Ella had drifted off to sleep in her chair.

"Leung, how can I find the best trail to climb higher into the mountains?" Kate asked the next morning.

"I show you, Dr. Bushnell. I tell many missionaries best trail." He grinned broadly.

Before they returned to Kiukiang, Kate wanted a glimpse of Mount Lushan's highest peak, a reminder of God's glorious ways in nature and how they stirred her heart.

The colors and configurations of the rocks soothed her. She dropped her book bag on her pulpit rock and climbed the trail Leung had described. It grew steeper and the foliage thicker. Her long skirt caught on a thorny bush, and leaves whipped across her face as the wind grew stronger. She pulled her skirt free and forged up the rugged trail, her troubles seeming to fall behind with every step.

She reached the summit after several hours. The view of Mount Lushan's highest peak in the distance dazzled her with its majesty. She leaned against a pine, lost in the beauty until a bird called her attention to the sun beginning to lower in the west. *You're right, little bird. I daren't stay much longer.* She started down the trail, but a rustling behind her sounded bigger than a bird. She stopped to listen.

Nothing.

She plunged down again, then stopped once more, remembering the man who brought his son to the clinic just weeks ago with severe wounds from a tiger mauling. The boy had evidently wandered near her cubs. Could there be ... Kate peered into the underbrush behind her. *What a stupid thing to be thinking about now.* She was letting her imagination get the better of her.

Was that a touch of orange-gold in the brush off the trail? She stopped to listen. Nothing.

Still, she pulled up her skirt and ran as fast as she could down the path, her heart beating in her ears, lungs burning as she gasped for breath. *This is ridiculous. There's nothing up here but my imagination.*

Without warning, something tore at her long skirt. Kate screamed as she careened forward on the rocky path, clutching helplessly at some immature bushes. Her screams echoed hollowly down the mountain for a long second as everything went black.

7

A Heartbreaking Revelation

Kate slowly lifted her spinning head to see dark spots of blood on the ground. She touched her face with skinned hands and felt something wet under her nose. *Ugh!* Spitting out some gravel, Kate tried to look around but had trouble focusing her eyes. Any movement made her dizzy.

The tiger! Forgetting her pain, she pushed herself up a little so she could look back. Nothing in sight. She scanned the ground for paw prints. Just a patch of dirt she'd kicked up.

She must have simply tripped.

Kate wiggled her toes gingerly. Nothing broken. Slowly she tested her legs and arms, then tried to push up and stand. Piercing pain shot up and down her back and she collapsed back onto the ground.

The sunlight through the trees had dimmed. Kate drew one knee forward; she wanted to get up. The mountain woods would be dark within an hour. Who would know where to search for her? She struggled to rise to her feet, but her skirt was still caught on the thornbush that had thrown her forward so abruptly. She tried to free herself from it, to unhook her skirt, but stopped in agony. The muscles of her back tightened into a spasm. *At least I'm not paralyzed.* She tried to find something positive about the situation.

She thought of Ella back in the cabin. By now the room must be getting dark. Leung would be in the kitchen, starting dinner. Might he figure out where to find her? She had asked him that morning for the best place to view the highest peaks of Mount Lushan. But he had also described a more picturesque trail deep into the forest, which was the one she chose. Would he send people to look in both places? Doubts began to cloud her mind. Her head throbbed. She touched her forehead; her fingers slid over a slippery mass of blood that rose over a huge knot.

Stay awake.

She focused on a problem to solve. Ella. She was stronger in this mountain air, but her fever and cough returned at night. Surely she suspected she had consumption. Would her body heal if she could stay in the mountains all summer? Weariness blanketed Kate more with every thought. She longed to rest ...

No. I can't. I mustn't go to sleep. What were those things Confucius said about women? *Yes* ... Her eyes closed a moment. *Yes.* She recited the proverb out loud: "A good woman is an illiterate one." And then the one about the three obediences. "She is servant to the father, then servant to her husband, and then servant to her son." Did that include grandsons too?

Kate turned her head and the ground spun. She shielded her eyes against the setting sun and tried to focus on a rock alongside the path. "That one looks just like a skull. David and I looked at a lot of skulls in Dr. Jewell's office. I wonder where he got them all? He always delighted in testing our diagnostic skills." She raised a hand to her forehead again to feel the wet protrusion on her forehead. "I wouldn't have difficulty diagnosing this one."

Those were good days with Dr. Jewell ... and David. Had it really been five years since they sat around the illustrious doctor's desk, laughing at their mistakes when he tested their perceptions? She felt so alone, so far from help and her family and from what had been a deepening relationship with David.

Suddenly she thought of the Latin New Testament David had given her and the book bag she carried with her. Where were they? Where did she leave them? She tried to sit up and focus on the trail ahead, but it spun into a blur. Her head pounded and she felt a sharp pain along her spine that flattened her again. *Don't concentrate on the pain. Where did I leave my Latin New Testament?* Spasms seized her back. She cried out as she tried to raise herself, again only to crumple back down. She was helpless.

"Someone! Anyone! Help!"

Silence.

She shivered as the shadows lengthened. It would be night soon. Did tigers roam at night? The air grew cooler, but she knew the chill she felt was shock setting in from her injuries and an unbidden fear of the unknown.

Her mind suddenly stopped to focus on something faint. Murmurs? No. Voices. Men's voices. Wang calling.

"Dr. Bushnell?"

"I'm here!" Kate tried to call loudly. "Here!" Her voice was weak and wouldn't carry past the next turn in the path. Ignoring her pain, she pushed herself up from the ground with one arm and called again, "Over here!"

Wang and two of the Chinese servants popped up the ridge, broad smiles breaking across their faces. All they knew to say was "Dr. Bushnell." Forming a human gurney by locking hands, they scooped their arms under her and haltingly started down the mountain. Glad as she was to be rescued, Kate stiffened. The spasms in her back were unrelenting. As they reached the base of the trail, Leung ran to greet them.

The relieved smile across his cherubic face melted into concern as he saw the blood and strain on Kate's face. "Dr. Bushnell. You hurt! We so worried."

Kate leaned to the right to ease some of the pain and made an effort to reassure Leung. "Yes, but maybe I look worse than the injuries really are."

Taking small, sure steps, the servants carried Kate to the cabin, Leung behind them. Ella, waiting on the verandah, struggled up to help set Kate on a bench outside.

"I was so worried," Ella said. "Let me look at you. Those cuts are nasty, especially that bump on your head. Let's go inside, and I'll wash them with carbolic acid."

Suddenly Kate felt more panic than she had lying injured on the mountainside. "My Bibles! My Latin New Testament! I left them on the pulpit rock this morning. I have to get them." Pain shot up her back again. "Leung, can you help me find my books?"

Leung bustled up to her, nodding. "Doctor, no fear. I find all."

Kate gave him a fleeting smile. "Oh, thank you, Leung." She struggled to lean heavily on his shoulder as they took short, slow steps inside.

Ella followed, coughing. Kate noticed the deep concern on her face. She could imagine the wheels turning in her friend's mind as Ella helped her to bed.

"It will be all right," Kate took Ella's hand in hers. "Things could have been so much worse." She laughed. "I shouldn't have run down that narrow trail. But I thought a tiger was stalking me—and I didn't want to be his dinner."

"A tiger!" Ella looked even more alarmed. "At least in Kiukiang, we only worry about mosquitoes."

"Those mosquitoes!" The very thought reminded Kate of their mandatory return to the mission in two weeks. A return to the never-ending heat and lines of people in need—and the ever-present mosquitoes. "You know," she smiled wryly, eyebrows raised at the incredulous thought, "maybe our chances are better with imaginary tigers."

A month after her fall, Kate returned to the mission's dining room to take her first evening meal with all the other missionaries. Adeline Hart rushed to the door with open arms and greeted her with a hug. "It's so good to have you back."

Kate tried to hide a wince at Adeline's embrace, but the older woman could feel Kate's instinctual shudder of pain.

"How are you, really?" Adeline whispered. She relaxed her embrace but still held Kate close.

"I may have injured something in my spine," Kate murmured. "Mary has come over every night after dinner to massage my back, and that's been a big help."

The teachers came in a few minutes later. "She's back," Mary called out. Kate endured more hugs, but it was worth it. She realized how much she missed her second family. Even Miss Haskins gave her a stiff hug as she came into the dining room.

Mary announced to everyone at the table, "You can't keep Kate down. She's hobbled over to the clinic with a cane every day. Maybe this is proof that Kate's not a miracle healer."

Kate could not help but laugh. Their mirth made her relax. At least these women understood how exhausting the days here were.

At dinner, one of the teachers interrupted the usual rambling conversation about the day's events. "Kate, what was it like in the mountains?"

"Yes," another echoed.

"Yes, tell us what you saw."

Most of the younger teachers had not been up to the cabin and were eager to hear Kate's report.

"You won't believe the impact the beauty and the silence have on you."

"The silence?" Sarah asked.

"Yes." Kate searched for the words to explain. "Here there is constant chatter. The people speak a language that we don't always understand—morning water carriers, children playing. I love hearing the vendors hawk the chickens hanging over their shoulders—but not when I'm sleeping." Kate looked around the table with a twinkle in her eyes. "And *we* don't stop talking either."

The teachers laughed.

"There's not much silence around here!" Adeline agreed.

"So that is the first thing," Kate said. "The silence is so wonderful and also the cool mountain air and the cabin. We looked forward to sitting in front of the fire at night in silence except for an occasional crackle and pop of the burning wood."

Kate stopped, lost in the memory for a moment. "But the best part, what I've wanted to share most, is how I had hours every day to study my Chinese Bible."

Kate saw the crestfallen look on some of the women's faces. The idea of studying when in such a place for recreation seemed as distasteful to some of the teachers as the mosquitoes were to Kate. Only Dr. Hart leaned forward, clearly wanting to hear more, but Mary changed the subject, and the table talk turned to what seemed to Kate petty worries of the day.

Dr. Hart looked knowingly at Kate and shrugged slightly, almost apologetically.

She'd save her questions for him, Kate determined.

Kate waited until Dr. Hart closed their evening devotions around the table before she blurted out, "I've been meaning to ask you about a strange inconsistency between a verse in the Chinese and the English New Testaments."

Dr. Hart reached for the Chinese Bible that he always kept at hand. "Which verse is that, Kate?"

"Philippians, chapter four, verse two. The English version begins, 'I beseech Euodias and beseech Syntyche,' and verse three says, 'help those women.'"

"Oh, yes, here it is. The Chinese translates this, 'help those who labored with me in the gospel.'"

"That's my question. Why doesn't the Chinese translation say 'help those women' as the English version does?"

Kate felt the perplexed stares of the women around the table. "Paul cared about all of the workers, both the women and the men."

Some of the teachers frowned and looked down at their own Bibles. Miss Haskins shook her head. Kate could almost feel her disapproval.

"Don't you see?" She turned to Dr. Hart, who studied the passage a long moment.

"I see what you are asking," he said slowly. "Paul does refer to two women, Euodias and Syntyche, in the previous verse."

"And the Greek word for 'those' in verse three is *autais*, the feminine form of the word—he means *those* women. Right?"

Everyone around the table was silent.

Kate felt tears of frustration rising. "The Chinese translation discounts that women were involved in Paul's work. It makes no mention or reference to the women at all."

No one spoke a word.

Kate edged forward in her seat. "Perhaps this is one reason many of the Christian men here don't seem to respect their wives any more than other men do. They haven't learned this yet."

"Oh really, Dr. Bushnell," Miss Haskins said angrily. "Chinese men treat their wives in a Chinese way—something you need to understand."

Dr. Hart, ignoring Haskins' comment, rubbed his short gray beard with one hand as he traced the letter in the Chinese Bible with his finger. "I'm guessing the translator made the changes because of the pagan prejudice against women doing anything public."

Prejudice, yes, but pagan? Kate had seen prejudice within the church, but in the pages of the Bible?

Sarah broke in, stumbling for the right words. "You mean the translators changed the words of God to say that?"

"That would be shocking," Mary whispered.

Surely no translator of God's Word would tamper with Scripture like that. Kate leaned forward, wishing Dr. Hart would speak clearly on the matter, give some reasonable explanation. "Perhaps a well-meaning but little-educated missionary made the mistake?" she ventured.

Dr. Hart stood up. "I will have to look into this further." But he demonstrably closed his Bible—and the subject.

Kate sat back, stunned. She realized she'd touched a sore spot, but she couldn't ignore what she had found. She knew that Paul was talking about women serving in the church alongside men. It was clear that God loves women as much as He does men. Why wasn't anyone teaching this to women?

One of the Chinese servants cleared away the last of the teacups from the supper table as the missionaries drifted from the room. Kate watched the Chinese woman shuffle on tiny feet with tiny steps behind all the others. *There is no mistake*, she thought, resolute again. God wants little girls to run and play as much as little boys. As she started toward the door, she heard a voice down the hall—Miss Haskins angrily explaining something to Dr. Hart.

"I am afraid you do not see what she is doing, Dr. Hart. The villagers have trusted us—especially the school—for many years. Now I hear they are upset that she is trying to convince the younger mothers to stop binding their daughters' feet. I do not favor the practice. But pretty soon we will have the authorities down on us. I wonder if Mrs. Gracey knew how audacious this young woman is. And the things she said at dinner …"

Kate could barely hear Dr. Hart's response as they moved further away.

Audacious? *She really doesn't think I fit in here.* Kate sat down with her elbow on the table, her forehead resting on her hand. The last thing she expected was that one of their own missionaries would defend foot binding—because it was the culture?

Then she heard Miss Haskins speaking more loudly down the hall, "If you do not deal with it, I will. This cannot continue."

Footsteps rang down the passage, and Dr. Hart returned to the dining room. "Oh, I am glad to see you still here. Would you join me in my study for a moment?"

"Certainly." Kate pushed her chair back from the table. Now she'd done it. It was probably about Miss Haskins' complaints. Or was he going to chide her for raising that question about the Bible verse in front of the other teachers?

Dr. Hart offered her a chair, and for a moment it was like being back in Dr. Jewell's office. Kate felt safe to ask even the hard questions. She knew Dr. Hart was a good man and didn't think less of her work as a doctor in a field filled with only men. He respected her. She knew he respected other women as well. He scolded Chinese men who beat their wives. He'd even sent a letter to the provincial governor about banning foot binding.

Before she could ask what he really thought about the passage in question, Dr. Hart said, "I have some good news, Kate. The mail boat arrived from Shanghai this afternoon."

Good news? He wasn't going to talk about Miss Haskins' complaints? Kate's heart raced. Perhaps there was finally a letter from David? But the news was not about David.

"A new doctor and his wife, a nurse, have arrived in Shanghai." Dr. Hart smiled. "After some months of language study, they will be assigned here to Kiukiang."

Help? Kate felt a sudden relief. She put her face in her hands. *Thank you, God. I don't think I could have carried on like this much longer.* She lifted her face and smiled. "That's some of the best news I've heard in a long time."

"I know how difficult this has been for you, especially since you injured your back. You have been a true soldier for Christ, in spite of your pain. We are grateful. I am sure the Lord is pleased with you, Kate."

Kate felt a wave of joy at being acknowledged for her work, but it began to ebb almost as soon as it had swept over her. Like Miss Haskins so clearly stated, she should speak Mandarin better by now so she could speak to the hearts of the village women. She hadn't been able to convince mothers that binding their daughters' feet was cruel—that God had created them to be free to run. Worst of all, they didn't yet believe that Jesus was the only one who rose from the dead. That they needed Him as Savior. But how could they understand if they never had even a hint of the freedom He could bring?

There was so much more to do, so much.

"But I have sad news too."

"Ella?" Kate knew this conversation was coming. Though Ella seemed to rally during the days in the mountains, her cough and condition had worsened since they'd returned. She had consumption, and there was nothing more to be done. Not here.

Dr. Hart nodded. "The board agrees. She must go home in an effort to save her life."

"Yes, I agree," Kate responded. "But I will miss her."

"We have decided you should accompany her. She cannot travel alone in this condition."

Home? I can go home? Kate was shocked, but an unexpected sense of release poured over her.

"With your back injury and your weakened condition from frequent bouts of malaria, it seems the best for both you and Ella."

Kate smiled wanly. She didn't want him to know how pleased she was. He was trying to soothe her, but he had no idea that this was the answer to her prayers. God had made it clear that her work here was complete. But where had all this been leading? What was next?

"There is no reason you cannot come back, once you get Ella settled home in Denver," he said. "Once you have recuperated fully, of course."

"When do we leave?"

"There is a boat sailing for Shanghai that will reach here in about a week. That means you and Ella should prepare now. You should arrive at the coast in time for the next steamer to San Francisco. I will let you tell Ella."

Kate sat forward in her chair. "Yes, I will tell her—she needs to have her spirits lifted. This is just the news to do it."

Kate smoothed her hair back from her forehead and walked down the hall. Of course Ella would be thrilled to go home—but she would certainly understand the reason for sending her. *How to broach this? Will she fear that we've given up on her?* Kate stopped before Ella's door and looked out toward the fast-flowing Yangtze River. She wished answers on how to navigate this could come to her as quickly. She'd be sailing in a week, home to her family, to David, to a future. But for Ella ...

Kate breathed deep and stepped into the room.

"Hello, my friend." Ella reached her thin arm out to Kate.

"How would you like to go home?" Kate asked, rearranging the pillows and helping Ella sit up.

"Are you serious?"

"And how would you like it if I went with you?"

Ella sat up straight. Her smile melted into a slight frown.

"Reverend Hart is sending you home where you can get better medical care than here, and he's asked me to go with you. He doesn't think you should take that long journey by yourself."

"He's right. I know I'm getting worse. If I don't get out of this heat, this suffocating mosquito net ..." Her voice rose. "If I keep sweating, every drop of water in my body will seep through my pores. And I keep coughing and coughing until I see blood on my sheet—" She stopped herself. "Yes." Her voice was soft now, as though speaking to herself. "At least I'll have a chance to get better in Denver's mountain air. My parents may even send me to the sanatorium in Manitou Springs. People go there, you know, for the healing sunshine and mineral waters." She reached her hands out to Kate. "But you shouldn't have to leave your work here. I can't let you give up your work in China for me."

Kate wiped the perspiration from Ella's face. "It's not like that, Ella. You've seen my frequent bouts of malaria. And now my back. I've been feeling for some time that I need a change. That whole incident with Ma Xhi, the people wanting to turn me into a miracle healer. That's not why I came here. They don't understand when I tell them about the true healer." She pulled her chair closer to the bed. "There's so much more I want to learn. The more I see the needs of the Chinese women, the more I want to find ways to make their lives more meaningful, to help them see themselves as valued in God's eyes, not just for how beautiful their tiny feet are." She paused. "I'm convinced God wants women to enjoy being women. I know it must be somewhere in the Bible, I just need time to find it. I can't help sensing a call to do something more for women, more than just heal their bodies. But what? Where? I have no idea. It's just that the feeling has been growing. I need time to sort it out."

Ella nodded thoughtfully, choosing her words. "But once a new doctor comes, you would have more time to study and to visit the women in the villages. You know they love you, especially the grannies. I see their eyes crinkle into smiles when they bow to greet you at the clinic. Remember all the gifts they brought you last New Year? You are making a difference here, Kate. You don't have to leave for my sake."

"I'm not leaving just for your sake. I need some mending myself. The pain in my back isn't getting better. I damaged something in my spine when I fell. I need to see someone at home who can help me. Besides, I've been thinking of David. You remember David Russell? You met him once. We've been corresponding."

Ella looked down and then out the window, her attention suddenly pulled someplace far away.

Kate followed her gaze. "David's last letter said he had received an offer for a very prestigious post when he finishes his residency. I've been waiting to hear more about it, but the mail is so slow from America these days—"

"Stop." Ella turned back to Kate and put a hand on her arm. "I don't know how to tell you this, so I'll just say it outright. I received a letter from my former roommate." Tears welled up in Ella's eyes, then she folded her arms around Kate. "She told me ... she wrote that she and David are engaged."

As darkness settled across the endless horizon, Kate sat alone on the deck of the *Dauntless*, oblivious to the roiling sea or the sharp wind that blew across her face. She'd left Ella sleeping, finally, on the bottom bunk of their tiny cabin after hours of endless coughing.

In the busy rush of preparing to leave China, Kate had shut her mind to David's duplicity. Instead, she had readied the clinic to be turned over to the nurse from Shanghai and supervised packing up both Ella's and her things, filling two large steamer trunks.

Now as she sat on the deck under a sky sparkling with myriad stars and a full moon shining a path across the turbulent waters, she finally allowed herself to look squarely at her broken dream. Her anguished prayer flew out across the water. "Lord, I've got to accept that David has chosen someone else. I can no longer lean on him as the crutch that waited for me at home whenever I questioned my decision to come to China."

She had come with such anticipation of fulfilling God's design for her life. She admitted that her hidden fear had been that she would lose David ... and now that fear had been realized. She broke into overwhelming sobs, rocking back and forth in her deck chair. How could that have happened? How could David find another love so quickly? *Why didn't he tell me?* She sat up and wiped her eyes with the palms of her hands. No, of course he wouldn't tell her that he was courting another woman. He wrote—but his last letters were short and far between. She should have suspected.

She wiped a tear. Part of her recognized that she'd hoped that David would wait until she returned from China. Hadn't he given her that expectation when he told her he would ask her father's permission to court her? When he whispered that he loved her? Perhaps it wasn't right to expect that. But oh, it hurt. And though she trusted God, it ached that He required her to sacrifice this love. Didn't other women follow God's path and still fulfill their heart's desire?

"Lord, I know You're always fair, but it doesn't feel like it right now!" she cried aloud.

God would always offer the greatest love; she'd never doubt that. Yet the loss of David brought grief. And she would bring that grief back to God for comfort, for healing. So the tears fell as she lifted her broken heart to the compassionate Father who perfectly understood a woman's heart.

A short while later, Kate stood and glanced back over her shoulder to see if anyone had watched her breakdown. She walked to the stern of the ship where she looked down into the foaming wake that stretched back toward the edge of the horizon. *I'm out in the middle of nowhere. I don't even know if I'm going the right direction.*

"Lord," she cried out. "Should I have stayed in Chicago? Is that what You intended for me? No ... No! You called me to China, and now You are taking me home to fulfill Your plan for me. I have no idea what I'm facing, what You have in store, except Ella—"

"Ella!" She turned suddenly and fled down the deck to the stairs to their cabin. She'd left her alone too long.

"Oh, Dr. Bushnell!" the stewardess greeted her. "I'm so glad you've come back."

Dr. Gilmore, the ship's doctor, bent over Ella with his stethoscope in his hands. Ella lay motionless and unresponsive.

"What happened?" Kate cried, pulling her scarf from around her neck.

"I looked in on her like you asked me to," the stewardess explained. "She was burning with fever, and she wouldn't wake up when I tried to give her some water. So I ran to get Dr. Gilmore."

"Thank you. You did the right thing. I should have come back sooner." Kate turned to the doctor. "How is she?"

Dr. Gilmore stood and looked at Kate. "She'll be all right. I've given her something to help her sleep." He smiled at her. "You probably needed to get up on deck for a while. It's not easy taking care of someone day and night." He glanced down at Ella. "I'm sure you've already diagnosed your friend's consumption."

"I've suspected it for some time." Kate hesitated, fearing the worst. "I'm hoping there are better treatments in America. Do ... do you think she'll make it home?"

"I can't promise. I think it would help if we kept her out on deck as much as possible. This little cabin is stuffy, and she's not getting the oxygen she needs. The fresh air can be a medicine of its own. I'll make sure that the stewards arrange a private place shielded from the wind. The weather should be warm enough for just a light blanket." Dr. Gilmore checked Ella's pulse once more, gravely looking down at her pale face. "And I'll give her some sodium salicylate for pain. Were you able to import that to your clinic in China?"

"No." Kate shook her head.

"It seems to be more helpful than willow bark for pain and fevers. We've been using it the last two or three years."

It was strange, after she'd worked on her own for so long, to talk about new treatments with a fellow doctor. The conversation buoyed

Kate's spirits. She hoped the ocean air would do the same for Ella—that or the new medicine or the sunshine. Anything to help.

Ella improved out on the ship's deck. But once they boarded the Southern Pacific train in San Francisco for Denver, she began to deteriorate again. Kate watched her friend sleep fitfully on the padded leather seat. She whimpered, and Kate reached over. "What is it, Ella? Are you in pain?"

"Is there another blanket somewhere?" Ella whispered through a teeth-shattering shiver. "I'm so cold."

"I'll ask the porter." Kate bent and tucked her own sweater around Ella's shaking body. She held her in her arms for a moment. *She's so thin I could pick her up and hold her on my lap.* With a sinking feeling, she realized that getting Ella back to her parents was possibly a false hope.

8
A New Life in Denver

November 1882, Colorado

The train released one last belch of smoke. Denver at last! Now to find the Gilchrists in the crowd. Kate scanned the unfamiliar faces. She reached for Ella's hand to help her down from their Union Pacific coach.

"There." Ella pointed at the elderly couple hurrying toward them. "There they are!" She tried to run toward her parents but was weaker than even Kate expected and would have fallen if Kate had not quickly grabbed her. Harriet Gilchrist reached them first and threw her arms around her daughter, holding her as though she never wanted to let go. Then she stood back to look at her, tears brimming. "Oh, Ella. It's so good to have you back home, and you, Kate." She turned back to her husband, struggling through the crowd. "You remember Dr. Bushnell, don't you, George?"

But George had wrapped his bear-sized arms around his waif of a daughter, his body shaking with hidden tears. After a few moments, he turned, still holding Ella under his arm. "Of course. How was the journey?"

"Long," Kate admitted, checking herself. She couldn't tell them just yet about almost losing Ella on the *Dauntless*. But there was no hiding Ella's pale weakness now. Kate watched her friend lean on her parents as they shouldered her toward a porter to collect their trunks.

It was so obvious, Kate thought. Even Ella must know.

As if reading her thoughts, Mrs. Gilchrist sidled next to Kate. "We can't thank you enough for how you've taken care of her," she whispered. She turned to her husband, who was already picking up the hand luggage. "If you take those, George, I think Dr. Bushnell and I can help Ella to the carriage."

They walked slowly through a cavernous hall, where Kate couldn't help noticing how the women seemed to stride purposefully, as though they knew where they were going. She passed a young mother who wore a bonnet with a wide brim that shaded her face, a style Kate had only seen pictures of until now. The woman wore heavy rugged boots under a coarsely woven skirt. The boots were big, and the sight both startled and pleased Kate. Unbound feet. The woman pointed for her daughter to look at something in the eaves of the station. A bird? In delight, the girl, perhaps eight or nine years old, ran ahead of her mother. *She ran. A little girl running on unbound feet!* The beauty stopped Kate for a moment, and then it filled her soul to realize the girl was flying to her father who waited on the balcony above them.

"As it should be," Kate said to herself, then turned at a sudden weight against her. Ella was losing all energy. Kate hoped the carriage was close. She didn't think Ella would make it very far.

Mrs. Gilchrist, jaw clenched and face strained in concern, caught Kate's eye.

"I know this is the best place for her, Mrs. Gilchrist," Kate reassured. "Just to be here with you will be healing."

"It is so good already to be home with you, Mama." Ella turned to her father who walked beside them. "And you too, Papa. You look very handsome with—" Ella suddenly stopped and bent over, coughing.

Kate pulled a handkerchief from her pocket and thrust it into Ella's hand. "Here."

"Don't talk anymore, honey," Mrs. Gilchrist urged. "The carriage will be warm with quilts and hot bricks. We're almost there."

"I just wanted to tell Papa," Ella whispered with a fleeting smile, "that he looks handsome with his new beard."

At least home had her trying to rally, Kate thought later as they settled Ella in her old room. She waited for Ella to fall asleep under the plump feather quilt. Her friend was surrounded by her childhood dolls and cheery wallpaper with pale yellow roses. Could the worst be over? As she saw the peace on Ella's face, Kate prayed for it to be so. She slipped from the room to join the Gilchrists downstairs.

A roaring fire in the front room crackled comfortingly, and Kate felt the tension of the long journey and the exciting morning slip away. She sank into an overstuffed chair by the fireplace and rested her head back. China seemed so far away and long ago. The fire, flowers on the tables ... the Gilchrists must have planned a homecoming celebration. She started to rise at the sound of Mrs. Gilchrist entering the room, but Ella's mother would not accept Kate's offer to help in the kitchen.

"You sit here and relax. I can see that you haven't for a very long time."

Kate nodded, grateful, and leaned into the chair. She heard the scrape of pots and pans being readied in the kitchen and smelled a savory fragrance of something roasting in the oven. The idea of a celebration seemed foreign.

"Would you like a cup of tea?"

Kate opened her eyes to see Mrs. Gilchrist carefully extending a cup to her.

"Yes. Yes, thank you," she stammered. "I must have fallen asleep." She smiled apologetically at Mrs. Gilchrist. "I dreamed I was back in China, embarrassed that I'd forgotten my teacup."

"Your teacup?" Mrs. Gilchrist looked confused.

No use explaining, Kate decided. "Thank you." She sipped the tea and let it restore her. Almost home, wherever that was anymore. At least not China.

"It must be good to be back," George Gilchrist said, joining Kate by the fireplace. "I'm glad to have Ella home, and you too. We want you to know that we are more than happy for you to stay with us, Dr. Bushnell, even ... as long as you'd like."

Kate couldn't keep from noticing that he'd started to say what they were all thinking—even after Ella was gone.

"I want to help Ella as much as I possibly can medically," Kate said. "I can be her doctor if needed, but really I am her friend, and I am concerned ..." She couldn't bear to voice the seriousness any more than he could.

"We'll be very grateful for your help." George Gilchrist fell into a sobering silence. Then he brightened. "We live near Denver General

Hospital, just a few blocks away. You can walk there if you need supplies or anything."

"Our hospital actually has one of the best clinics for consumption." Mrs. Gilchrist paused, swallowed hard, and continued. "One of the best in the country for consumption patients. People come here from all over." She dabbed at her eyes with a handkerchief. "I never dreamed Ella would be one of them. How could she get so sick in China?" She looked pleadingly at Kate.

All Kate's medical training kicked in. "Frankly," she told Mrs. Gilchrist, "I think Ella already had consumption before she went to China. Once in the heat, with the mosquitoes and malaria—the disease simply took hold. There wasn't much more to be done but ... come home. God can heal her." Kate sat forward in her chair. "I've rested on that truth even when I've feared medicine could not. I saw some amazing healings in China, and I've heard about new treatments for consumption in the United States." She leaned back again. "She is in God's hands now."

The walk down Cherokee Road to Denver General Hospital was indeed short. Kate stepped increasingly faster, eager to meet the doctor the Gilchrists had arranged to care for Ella. In spite of the dire circumstances of her return, Kate was excited to be back in the medical world, to learn of new treatments developed while she was in China. But a sharp pain shooting down her leg threatened to stop her. Maybe there would be something to help her back, too.

She slowed to take in the sprawling red brick building ahead. What a difference such a facility would have made in Kiukiang!

That thought rattled through her mind as Dr. Chandler, who worked in the hospital's consumption clinic, toured her through the hospital's immaculate wards and well-stocked medicine cabinets.

"Have you seen these new thermometers?" He handed one to Kate. "You can get a reading in five minutes."

"Five minutes!" Kate marveled as much at the instrument as the doctor's graciousness toward her. He talked with her as though she were one of his colleagues—not condescendingly at all. It didn't seem to matter that she was young or a woman. She smiled brightly. "I heard of these before I left for China, but of course we didn't have such modern devices there."

"Not even our modern devices can help when health has deteriorated to a certain point," Dr. Chandler told Kate in a sober tone after listening to Ella's case. "It sounds like there is little more you can do, other than provide her bed rest, fresh air, and good food."

"She is getting all that," Kate assured him. And one thing more: the power of prayer to the God who can heal.

They walked down the long hall toward the hospital exit. "Before you go," Dr. Chandler said, "let me introduce you to our superintendent, Dr. Richards. This way; his office is just to the left."

Dr. Richards was warm and welcoming, with a camaraderie toward Dr. Chandler and herself that Kate hadn't experienced since the days of talking over cases with David in Dr. Jewell's study. Was it because her height allowed her to talk with them at eye level? Or simply the way of things here in the Wild West of Colorado? Could the professional environment for women in the United States have changed this much in three years? Whatever the case, it felt good to stand with colleagues and to be included in their discussion of a particular case.

"Are you looking for work, Dr. Bushnell?"

Dr. Richards' question startled Kate. She hadn't come to Denver General in search of a job, but ...

"We're always short of doctors," he said.

"Truth is, Denver is just growing too fast," Dr. Chandler said. "The gold rush is slowing down, but now silver's been discovered—and lead."

"Yes," Dr. Richards interjected, "and for us, that means more business."

"I'd like to work again." Kate thought what it might mean to practice at such a large, modern hospital. "But it could only be for a few days a week. I really came here to help care for my friend."

"We could work that out." Dr. Richards smiled. "Could you come in tomorrow to meet the rest of the staff?"

Before Kate could answer, a loud knock announced the arrival of a jovial-looking round man with Benjamin Franklin frames perched on the tip of his nose. He stood beaming from the doorway, first at the two men and then at Kate.

"Come in, come in, Hanson," Dr. Richards beckoned. "Meet our new colleague, Dr. Katharine Bushnell, just back from running a hospital in China." He turned to Kate. "Dr. Hanson works in the women's ward."

"Not quite a hospital," Kate said, smiling at the notion. "But the work did keep me running."

"I won't mind," Kate told Dr. Richards when he asked if she could work in the women's ward on Christmas Day. She hadn't been home for the holidays in four years, but Colorado may as well have been China for her inability to get back this year. Even if she'd had enough money, she wouldn't have left Ella. Her working a shift on Christmas would, however, give the Gilchrists a few hours alone as a family during the holiday. Ella was getting worse, not better. Everyone knew it.

The halls were eerily quiet as Kate settled at her desk to fill in charts. Most of the staff were gone to be with family, and even some patients had returned home.

But a low sound—music?—floated down the hall. Singing? Kate walked to the doorway to check: carolers. She smiled and watched them, still bundled from the snow falling outside, as they made their way into her ward.

> Silent night, holy night,
> All is calm, all is bright.

One of the patients, a frail old woman, sat up and joined in at the top of her voice. Kate hurried over to be sure she didn't try to get out of bed and found herself singing along, uplifted.

> Christ the Savior is born,
> Christ the Savior is born.

The carol ended, and Kate felt a lump rise in her throat. She swallowed hard. "Thank you." Her voice trembling, she mustered the power to speak to the carolers as they moved back down the hallway. "Thank you."

The silence returned and with it a sudden emptiness. She looked at the clock on her desk. Mother was probably fussing in the kitchen now. Kate could almost smell her famous yeast rolls. She thought of the tree decorated in the lounge and how her nieces and nephews would squeal when Father lit the candles on the branches later this evening. Compared to China, she was so close to home, just a few more days by train. What she wouldn't do to sing "Silent Night" with Mary or help grab Billie before he shook all the presents under the tree.

"Dr. Bushnell!" Running down the hall toward the front entrance, Nurse Jackson called for Kate over one shoulder. "We need you!"

Kate rushed from her ward to find a woman unconscious and slumped in a heap on the floor of the empty lobby. Her light jacket was ripped, one sleeve nearly torn from the shoulder. Blood covered her front, face, and hands. She was alone and had been brutally beaten, her lip cut and one side of her face already turning purple and swollen. Nurse Jackson ran out the front entrance and back in again, shaking her head. "No one," she said. "Another one who made it here on her own."

"Nurse Smith," Kate called down the hallway. "Quick. We need a wheelchair."

Nurse Smith could be rough with patients like this one—poor young women off the street. Sadly, Kate observed, tonight was no exception. Nurse Smith pushed the wheelchair to Kate's side steadily but unrushed, then reached down to pull up the injured woman.

"Careful!" Kate held back Nurse Smith's arm with force, preventing her patient from being moved. She looked hard at the nurse, who stepped back rather sullenly. "I need to finish checking her first."

Kate bent over the fallen figure and slowly moved her legs to check for paralysis. Touching one arm, she could tell there was trouble, perhaps a break. Gently, Kate unfolded the other arm so her patient lay flat on her back. She was so young. The woman's long black lashes fluttered. She moaned, and then she shifted, trying first to curl back into a ball from the pain and then attempting to get up.

"No," Kate commanded. "Let us help you." She looked around. "Nurse Jackson, help me. Nurse Smith, hold the chair steady, and then let's get her into the examining room."

The young woman shivered on the examination table, eyes closed, moaning as Nurse Jackson washed the blood from her face and hands. Kate noted her long, faded flowered skirt and thin black jacket. Her patient needed more than medical help. There was no way she would be able to pay the seventy-five cents a day that the hospital charged. How had she gotten into this trouble anyway? Who would beat her so? Kate smoothed back her blond unwashed hair to find more bruises on the woman's forehead, then held her left wrist to check her pulse. She noted the woman's hand, so red and chapped, and the cheap silver band on her ring finger. She was married. Where was her husband? Had he done this to her?

The woman stirred again, and Kate bent closer. "I'm Dr. Bushnell. I'm going to take care of you." Kate spoke in a warm, gentle tone and tucked the hospital blanket under the woman's chin.

Frightened eyes searched Kate's face and then the room. She felt the woman stiffen in fear, then shudder again in pain.

"It seems you've hurt your arm," Kate said in her softest voice. "Can you tell me your name?"

The woman shut her eyes again. "Bertha," she whispered. "Bertha Lyon."

"I'm going to help you, Mrs. Lyon, and you will have to help me do that, okay?" Kate slowly moved Bertha's slack right arm. "Where does it hurt?"

Without opening her eyes, Bertha slowly tipped her head toward her right shoulder.

Kate pressed carefully but firmly up her arm as Bertha winced. "What happened to you, Bertha? Who did this to you?"

Bertha's eyes flashed open. She shook her head vehemently. "No one, no one. I fell down the stairs." Suddenly frantic, she tried to get up from the examination table. "Oh, and my baby! My baby is there alone. I must get home."

"You can't go anywhere just yet." Kate gently but firmly held Bertha back. "I need to check that shoulder to see if it's broken, and we'll put some salve on the cuts." She looked more closely at Bertha's lip and then forehead. "This one is quite deep and still bleeding heavily. I think you need a stitch in there to keep it closed."

Bertha moaned and murmured again, "I have to go home. My baby's sick." But she could only lie still in exhaustion as Kate worked a sling around her to immobilize the shoulder.

"You'll be able to help your baby better once we get you fixed up, okay?" Kate spoke as she worked, determined the woman wouldn't leave without care.

When Kate finished stitching the wound, Nurse Jackson handed her a hot cup.

"Here." Kate took the cup in one hand and with the other raised Bertha's head to help her sip. "Tea with sodium salicylate," Kate said. "To ease the pain."

Bertha took one sip, then tried to sit up again. She swung her legs off the bed, insisting, "I have to go home."

Kate frowned. "Do you live far from here?"

"Just a few blocks."

"What street, Mrs. Lyon? I'm just about to finish up here and can walk you home. I don't think you are in any condition to walk alone."

"No," Bertha pulled her thin jacket over the sling. "It's not far, just over on Bannock Street."

Kate caught Nurse Jackson's eye, indicating for the nurse to stay with Bertha. "You're right," Kate said as she slipped out of the room. "Bannock Street isn't far. I can get you there in no time."

She rushed to her desk for her coat and hat, signed a final report, and hunted for a spare coat or wrap. Something to keep that poor soul warm. One of the janitor's hospital jackets hung over a chair in the cloakroom. It would be big on Bertha, but she could wrap it around herself almost double, and Kate would bring it back in the morning.

She brushed past Nurse Smith, announcing, "I'm leaving now. Dr. Hanson should be here any minute to take over. I'm walking Mrs. Lyon home. I need to be sure she's safe."

"You're what?" She looked shocked, almost embarrassed, but muttered a low "Merry Christmas, Dr. Bushnell."

In spite of her injuries, Bertha moved with determination through the night, crossing the snowy street.

"Slow down," Kate urged.

"But my baby. I have to get back to my baby," Bertha mumbled.

Kate felt her whole body straighten, her spirit determined. "What really happened?"

"I ... tripped." Bertha seemed to search for words. "There was a tear I didn't see in the rag rug at the top of the stairs. I ... fell." She must have seen the undisguised doubt on Kate's face. "I shouldn't have come to the hospital," Bertha muttered. "I would have been all right."

"Bertha, you needed those stitches and that salve. You must keep your arm in the sling until your collarbone heals."

Bertha lurched forward. "I really must get back. My baby has a fever."

"Wasn't your husband home, on Christmas Day, so he could take care of the baby?"

Bertha shook her head, then nodded at a signpost at the corner of Bannock and Eighth Street. "I live just down there." She handed back the jacket Kate had wrapped around her and bolted before Kate could ask another question.

"Thank you, Doctor." she called back, hugging the sling close to her chest. "Thank you."

Kate watched her mysterious patient shuffle to the door of a dark and grim three-story apartment building. Bertha fumbled with the knob, and Kate started forward to help, unready to let her go without answers. Where was her husband? Should Kate offer to look at the baby?

Bertha turned to look Kate in the eye and shook her head. Then without another word, she opened the door, slipped into the darkness beyond it, and slammed it shut behind her.

9
A Shocking Encounter

$\mathcal{A}$ timid knock on her office door at the hospital roused Kate from her reports. "Come in," she called, setting the papers aside.

A young Chinese woman peeked through the doorway. "Is doctor here?"

"I'm Dr. Bushnell. May I help you?"

"Oh. Never meet woman doctor," the woman said in halting English. Her face broke into a broad smile, and her black eyes twinkled. "I Hou Wan."

Without thinking, Kate replied in Mandarin. "How may I help you?"

Hou Wan's eyes grew big. She replied in Mandarin, "I've never met an American woman who speaks Mandarin. Where did you learn?"

"I spent three years working at the mission clinic in Kiukiang."

"Oh, we lived down river in Nanking, and my parents planned to send me to school there when I was older. But instead we came here when I turned twelve."

Kate looked over Hou Wan's shoulder. "We?"

"Yes," Hou Wan said. "My mother and I."

Kate offered Hou Wan a chair, then looked again out the doorway. "Your honorable mother is here?"

"No. But that is why I came." Hou Wan sat straight in the chair, clutching her purse, her feet barely touching the floor.

Unbound feet, Kate noticed. How did she escape binding? Most twelve-year-olds in China would have been bound for years. Kate felt Hou Wan's eyes searching her own. Another time, another day, Kate would ask.

She smiled at Hou Wan. "I'd offer you a cup of tea, like in China, but doctors' offices in America don't have such a lovely custom. I only work here at Dr. Hanson's office two afternoons a week, so I'm not in charge."

"I still miss some customs, the tea especially. Do you?"

"Yes," Kate said, stealing another glance at Hou Wan's feet. "At times." She sat and leaned forward. "Now about your honorable mother. Do you need me to come to see her?"

Relief broke across Hou Wan's face. "Would you? She fears leaving the house except to visit her Chinese friends; she can't speak English. She won't come here, but she needs to see a doctor. She can hardly walk, and her feet are swollen and painful."

Kate thought of the older women she had treated in Kiukiang and their tiny feet, malformed from the toes—broken to stunt growth, to the mangled arches, twisted bones, and cracked and bleeding skin. She imagined Hou Wan's mother's feet. Surely they had been bound. "When? Just say when, and I will be there."

"Tomorrow morning?"

"Tomorrow then."

Hou Wan beamed. "Thank you, Doctor." She scribbled an address for Kate on a piece of paper and turned to leave, but stopped as she reached the door. Head slightly tilted, shyly, she asked, "Is that a Bible on your desk?"

Kate looked to the corner of her desk. She hadn't expected this. "Why ... yes." She looked up to ask Hou Wan if she read the Bible too, but the tiny woman had already pulled the door shut and was gone.

Kate burst into Ella's room. "You will never believe who I met today!"

Ella's eyes sparkled as the story of Hou Wan gushed out.

"And to speak Mandarin again ... it came more easily than I could imagine—" Kate stopped. Ella was smiling in a way she hadn't for weeks. "What is it?"

"This is almost like old times, Kate, like in China. You used to come to my room to share your adventures from the clinic. I remember the day you dragged in, hair plastered to your forehead from the heat, to tell me about the twins."

"The twins. I haven't thought of them in months. But how could I forget? I can still see the family pushing to the front of the line outside the clinic." Images flashed through her mind of the poor young woman in labor, in a hammock, a gawking crowd around her, the people simply watching and doing nothing. "She wasn't more than a girl, really, and she had been in labor for two days. A breech birth, which is bad enough, and no sooner had I wrapped her baby girl in a cloth than I noticed the mother still in distress, and five minutes later held a tiny squirming boy in my hands too."

Ella's laughter, though weak, was a welcome sound. "I still don't know how you managed all that by yourself."

"I had Tai Yau, of course, and the mother's sister seemed to know what to do with newborns. But it was such a surprise. You can imagine how pleased the father was when I told him he also had a son to—" Kate couldn't say the words: to make up for his bad luck with the firstborn, a girl. She thought of how the father's expression changed from sheer disgust to beaming with joy upon hearing he had an unexpected boy baby following the girl, and she wondered what that sweet girl's fate was to be.

Ella fell into one of her troubled silences until she burst into a fit of coughing that would not stop.

Mrs. Gilchrist, who had rushed up the stairs, stopped at the door and tried to restrain a look of horror as blood spattered across the flowered bedspread.

Kate held Ella's head in her arms and wiped her face. "She'll be all right, Mother Gilchrist. I take the blame. I got her too excited. We were sharing old stories." She hugged Ella tighter. "She'll be all right."

But Kate could not help the uncertainty in her voice.

The horse-drawn cab stopped at The Flowering Orchid on Market Street just as Kate had directed. She'd agreed to meet Hou Wan here at her father's restaurant in Denver's Chinatown. Tattered Chinese signs fluttered in the air, and storefronts around the restaurant were boarded up. The streets felt far different from the colorful markets of Kiukiang that Kate knew.

"Welcome," Hou Wan greeted her inside the restaurant door. "Best we go together first time. Honorable mother not sure she wants foreign doctor treating her feet."

"Where else does she go for help? There are no Chinese doctors here."

Wan nodded. "Very little anything for Chinese here."

"I see," Kate said as they walked down almost deserted streets. Shopkeepers eyed Kate suspiciously and drew back against their blackened and decaying doorways. Their wariness unsettled Kate. Chinese people were usually very polite and gracious, but she felt as though they didn't like her.

"What happened here?" she asked Hou Wan. "Why is everything so ..."

"In ruin? Yes, much in ruin." Wan said with an effort. "Two years ago, two drunken Irishmen started fight with two Chinese laundrymen. By time they finish, thousand white men storm Chinatown." She slowed her pace past a building boarded up at the windows and doors, debris scuttled against its side. "Many people hurt. Several men killed. Most business burned. Some rebuild. Some never will."

Kate fell silent. White immigrants had new opportunities and didn't want cheap Chinese labor to upset their rank. No wonder Wan wanted to walk these streets to her mother's with Kate. They turned a corner and Kate noticed a tiny temple, colorfully painted with a fat golden Buddha sitting inside the door—flowers, money, and fruit heaped in front of him.

"Didn't this get destroyed?" she asked.

"Oh yes. It burned to ground, but temple first thing community rebuilt. My parents donate generously."

"Do you ... bring offerings here?" Kate searched for a way to determine if Hou Wan practiced the Buddhism of her birth country.

The tiny woman seemed to read Kate's thoughts. "Oh no. That why I asked if Bible on desk yours. I had feeling you love Jesus too. You so kind, helpful."

Kate brightened.

"But," Wan warned, "Honorable Mother does not love Jesus." She smiled mischievously. "Yet."

They stepped into Hou Wan's house, and for Kate, it was like stepping back into China. Brightly colored cushions were arranged on the floor along the walls. Outdated calendars with delicately drawn flowers covered the walls, and the solemn faces of ancestors peered from photos along the picture rail. On a shelf in the corner sat a shrine, the Buddha statue covered with beads and flowers, incense wafting from candles burning on each side.

Mrs. Hou sat cross-legged on a cushion, bowing to welcome Kate.

"Mother, this is Dr. Bushnell." Hou Wan's eyes twinkled. "She speaks Mandarin."

A smile spread across Mrs. Hou's face. She reached up to Kate's hands to pat them. "Ah, if you speak Mandarin, you are one of us. Please, sit down." She motioned to a big red cushion beside her. She clapped her hands softly. "Wan, get us some tea."

Kate could not do much for Mrs. Hou's mangled feet except to gently massage them and give her sodium salicylate for pain.

"I'm better already," Mrs. Hou said as she struggled to stand. "See?" She insisted on seeing Kate to the door. "I light a candle for you."

Wan took Kate's arm and steered her through the foreboding-looking streets again. "You see, Dr. Bushnell, mother hear story of Jesus from me many times, but she still believe candles and incense help her. Maybe you do something? She like you."

"How did you learn about Jesus?"

"In public school for Chinese children I hear prayers and stories from Bible, but I not know what they mean. It just what happen there." She slipped back into her mother tongue. "My friend Mei Lei and I walked past a church. We heard music coming from inside and wanted to sneak in to hear it. But Mei Lei was afraid. Ever since her father was killed in the riots, she was afraid of going outside of Chinatown, afraid of white people. I told her I wanted to hear the music until she finally went in with me. Then I couldn't leave. Something seemed to hold me in my seat while a man stood up and began to tell us about a God who created the world, a God who comes to live in our hearts when we believe in Jesus. This God sent His Son to live with people who hated Him even worse than those Irish men hated the Chinese."

Kate's heart jumped to her throat.

Wan stopped and looked at Kate intently. "That day my friend and I realized what Jesus did for us. We saw He made a way out of the ruin for us. It changed me. It changed my friend. Even though we still live in ruins, we are free. You understand?" She nodded, then shook her head. "But my parents do not understand. I want them to, and I want to tell other people what happened to me, but my English is so poor. So I found another way."

"Another way?"

Wan nodded. "I help women out of slavery."

"Slavery? Here?"

Wan glanced around, as though looking to see who could hear, and switched back to English. "Yes. Alcohol ruining our Chinese families. Not just buildings and businesses destroyed. People—people not free from it. The riots where my friend's father killed, where all this burned—it started in saloon. The men get paid every week, but before they get home, they stop to drink. They drink till their money gone. Their families already in ruin, so when men come home, drunk, no money, they get in fights with wives. Only way to change to stop the drinking, to get them to meet Jesus. So I work with Women's Christian Temperance Union."

They started walking again, Kate trying to keep up with all Hou Wan was confiding. "The drinking away a paycheck—that's not only true of Chinese families."

Hou Wan nodded. "True. But I work where I am."

Work how you can, where you are. That's right. Kate felt a sudden urgency. "What do you do at the meetings?"

"Sometimes there are speakers. Most meetings we pray and there is Bible study. Best is new Social Purity Department."

"Social Purity Department?"

"We help women we meet on streets, women beaten by drunken husbands." Hou Wan paused.

An image of Bertha, crumpled and beaten on the hospital floor flashed through Kate's mind.

"Women who sell their bodies to earn money for their children's food."

Kate stopped walking and turned to Hou Wan. "How do you ... find these women who sell their bodies?" This was something Kate did not expect, something more foreign than what she had already seen and experienced.

"We pray for God to lead us to them, and once a week we go to Halliday Street."

"Halliday Street ..." Kate tried to think where that was in relation to the hospital.

"That is where the brothels are, where women sell their bodies. Sometimes we give them food or pamphlets about Jesus. We try to make them know He loves them."

"Do they listen?" Kate asked.

"Not ones dressed up, waiting for business. But women beaten or chased out of homes—they take food or soap we give as gift."

Something—or perhaps Someone—urged Kate to ask, "The next time you go to Halliday Street, can I come with you?"

10
On the Streets

"We go out by twos," Hou Wan explained. "The silver miners come into the city to enjoy vice every weekend. If they had luck in the mountains, they go to Jenny Rogers' house. That's where the rich girls with their furs and fancy hats work."

Kate climbed into a carriage, followed by Hou Wan, who chattered in Mandarin. Kate found herself more and more comfortable conversing in Mandarin with Wan. "I brought my medical bag, should we meet someone who needs help."

Wan glanced at the black bag at Kate's feet and nodded approval. "Now we'll go north to a rough part of the city where women work in cheap cribs."

"Cribs?"

"Little rooms off the street. Women rent cribs for so many dollars a week."

"And the police? Don't the police watch the area?" Kate asked.

"If they do, they're blind. They don't arrest men or women in cribs. Lou Blonger makes sure of that. He's the boss there, and he has more power than the police chief. What he says, goes—and he says women work and rent cribs from him."

"Why can't they just stop?"

Wan thought for a moment. "Jobs are scarce for women, and these women—they do not read or write. They are not welcome to clean other women's homes or take care of other women's children. Do you understand?"

Kate shook her head. "No, I don't understand. Why would any woman want to do this?"

"Want?" Hou Wan heaved a sigh. She appeared to search for the right words to explain. "Last week, I met a young woman with two children back home. Her husband found another woman. She went to work in cribs to feed her children—they were hungry. I gave her the last bread I had. She couldn't stop saying thank you. It is bread they want."

Kate struggled for more. "Isn't there anything else they can do?"

"It seems they can sell their bodies. Some ladies of the night—that is what they are called—do this to get rich. They wear furs and costly bonnets. But they are not the ones who stand in the streets and work in the cribs. You'll see."

The carriage jolted to a stop outside the rail station, where members of the Women's Christian Temperance Union were gathering.

"Here." Hou Wan switched back to English as she hopped out of the carriage. "Like said. We meet to go in twos."

Kate swallowed hard and stepped out to join a pair of women who greeted Wan warmly.

A woman named Clare pulled her hand from her glove to welcome Kate. "We're so glad that you've joined us."

"Yes," her friend echoed. "I'm Ruth. We would have been one short today since Mrs. Giles couldn't come, and I don't know what we would have done then. We try not to go out on the streets alone."

Wan took Kate's arm as Clare gave instructions. "You'll go to Halliday Street. Ruth and I will go south on Market. We'll meet here at the station by five." She turned to Kate. "Just to make sure everyone is safe."

Hou Wan steered Kate ahead. "We'll turn at corner. Most cribs will be another block this way."

Kate scanned the street ahead. "I don't see any ... ladies of the night."

"See saloon at end of street? That is where Blonger rents the cribs. See other men there? They work for him. They do not like us coming here. They know we try to help women get away. They dangerous."

"Who is this man Blonger?"

"He in charge of everything here. He runs that saloon, another one on Larimer Street. Big gambler. Women say he expert swindler."

Kate studied the saloon entrance and the boarding house next to it on the corner. Other than needing fresh paint and their porches swept, both looked ordinary enough. Few people were out, except a lone carriage now and then.

Wan nodded to a police wagon pulling in front of the bar. "See! The police drink with Blonger's men. They work together so everything appears okay."

Wan stopped Kate to allow a carriage to pass before crossing the street. "Look," she cocked her head forward. "There." Kate followed the direction of Wan's gaze. A woman in a once-handsome traveling gown, now thin and faded, stood outside the door of a long low building with four doors and windows along the front.

"These are cribs. But I do not recognize her." Wan let loose of Kate's arm and stepped ahead. Kate followed slowly behind.

"Would you like a booklet?" Wan asked. "About Jesus' love."

Kate studied the woman's face. Would she be twenty-five? No. Older. She'd tried to bring the bloom of youth back in her cheeks with rouge.

The woman shook her head and pushed Wan's hand away. For a flickering second, Kate thought she saw a wistful look in her eyes, but then her face hardened with anger. "Go away. Just go away. Love ain't for people like me." She turned and ducked into her crib, slamming the door behind her.

"She wouldn't even take your book?" Kate asked, bewildered.

Wan was matter of fact. "Maybe she cannot read. I have not met her before, so I do not know. It is okay. We will talk more next time we come." Her eyes twinkled and she smiled. "Next time we offer to teach her to read. Show her God's love."

Two doors down, a red light shone through the curtains drawn on a window of one of the cribs.

"That is strange," Wan murmured. "That is where Maggie works. If she has customer, she turns off the lantern, and if not, when the lantern on, she stands on street corner so the light from the red glass globe shines on her hair—she has very long blonde hair. Gets a lot of customers that way." Wan looked sadly at Kate. "She is only sixteen."

Kate shook her head.

"We often talk about how she can leave. But she cannot read, so she does not know what to do, where to go. Mother is dead. Father drunk most of time. He kicked her out of house to keep another woman there."

Wan knocked softly on the door. No answer. "Maggie," she called, knocking again. "It is Hou Wan. Can you open, please?"

The door opened a crack, and a face appeared, partially hidden by long blonde hair. "I'm not feeling good, Miss Hou. Come back next week." She began to shut the door, but Wan stopped it with her foot.

Her big, strong, healthy foot, Kate thought.

"I have doctor here today, Maggie. She can give medicine to help you."

The golden curls shook as if saying no, but Wan persisted, gently pushing the door open wider until Maggie blinked in the daylight, face bruised and slashed.

Kate drew in a breath. Blood ran down the girl's dress. The cuts were deep—by a knife? Or broken glass? Without waiting for welcome or permission, Kate pushed into the room and set her bag on the table next to the bed.

"Come, lie down, Maggie," she ordered. "Let me look at those cuts." She turned to Wan. "Is there any clean water here?"

"A pitcher on table, but I don't think there is tap in here."

Kate inspected the pitcher. "There might be enough to wash the wounds. I have some boric acid powder to stop infection."

Maggie closed her eyes as Kate worked on the wounds.

"This will hurt," Kate warned. She began to stitch shut the longest gash across the girl's cheek. Maggie instinctively scrunched her eyes in pain as Kate struggled to be fast and precise. "I am so sorry. I don't have any morphine with me. But if I don't stitch it up, this cut won't close, and you'll have a terrible scar."

Kate worked swiftly. Fortunately, she had added silk suture and an eyelet needle to her bag that morning. She'd have to ask the hospital for more morphine. As Kate cleaned Maggie's other wounds, Wan slipped out the door, then returned with bread and a cup of hot tea from the store across the street.

Maggie sat up with Kate's help and gratefully accepted the tea and bread. "You better go now," she said. "It's not safe for you to be here. If he comes back and finds you here, he'll beat you too."

"Who is *he*?" Kate pressed.

"Jake, one of Blonger's men. He comes to collect rent every week. But he wanted to stay with me, or else I had to pay him more money today!" She hung her head. "I didn't have it, so I lied. I told him someone else was coming. No one was, not yet anyway." She looked furtively at the lantern, glowing red in the window. "But I told him to take the rent and leave. I said I'd pay him more later. Only he got mad and pulled a knife. He told me not to talk to him like that, not to try getting out of paying. 'You will pay,' he said. I tried to fight him off, and look what it got me. You better go. He is mean, and he said he would be back."

"You really think he'll come back after ..." Kate looked around the room and back to Maggie's bloodied dress. "After all this?"

"Just go," Maggie said, resigned.

Wan put her arms around Maggie's shoulders. "Dr. Bushnell pray for you."

Oh, Lord. Kate felt suddenly inadequate. *Should I ask for forgiveness for her sins? No. Not now. That will be between You and her in Your time. She's frightened and hurt and so young. Yes, Lord. We are all frightened.*

Kate took Maggie's hands as Wan put a hand on Maggie's shoulder. "Oh God, we ask Thee for mercy. We ask that Thou protect Maggie tonight. Help her. Help her through this night and into a new morning, a new life. Lord Jesus, let her know that Thou dost love her. We ask these things in Thy holy name."

Kate released Maggie's hand and slipped all the suturing materials back into her bag as Wan drew the curtains and turned down the oil lamp.

"You keep light off today," Wan told Maggie. "When we leave, lock door and put chair under handle like this." Did Wan think that would protect Maggie from Blonger's man? "If you make it hard for him to get in, he think another man here and not break in, see?"

Maggie nodded.

Wan smiled. "We be back next week, okay?"

Outside, Kate breathed deeply, grateful to be free of the crib's suffocating darkness. As she walked, she glanced back nervously. She felt a sense of urgency—not fear, but uncertainty. She felt that someone lurked around the corner.

Wan grabbed her by the elbow. "We must hurry. Almost five."

Though Kate stood a good foot taller than Wan, she pushed to keep up.

"Hurry," Wan said again. "We don't want Ruth and Clare to worry if we are not there by five."

Did she have the same feeling, that someone was watching them?

Though breathless, Kate felt a sudden impulse to burst into all the questions that had piled up inside. "How can any man do that to a girl? Does he think she's just a piece of flesh he can carve at will? Don't you think we should call the police?"

Wan put a remonstrating hand on Kate's arm. "You saw wagon there. Remember what I tell you. Police do nothing. If we call, police put Maggie in jail, not Blonger's man, and when she get out, Blonger's man waiting for her."

Kate shook her head, fueled forward by rage. Now Wan struggled to keep pace. "I know you're right, Wan. But leaving her back there alone, in such a pitiful state ... it's not right, not at all right for her to be there to begin with." Kate focused on Union Station, just in sight now, but it was Maggie's stitched, bruised face she saw. "She will be scarred, you know."

"Yes," Wan said. "Yes. They are all scarred."

Wan looked back nervously. Kate turned to see what had distracted her. The burly man at the corner slipped away, but not before Kate's heart jumped to her throat. She thought she'd seen him somewhere earlier. No. She was imagining things. She shook her head. Was her mind playing tricks on her? Unless ... that *was* one of Blonger's men?

"No!" the woman screamed. "You told me my rent was only three dollars this week. You promised me a special price. I was nice to you. Now you want more? No, I haven't got it." She pummeled the man who towered over her, but the blows fell off his chest like melting butter.

Kate felt Wan's tug on her arm to move on. Their return to Halliday Street brought even worse scenes than she had imagined, and the memories of Maggie's ruin had been plenty.

Kate watched in horror as the burly man pushed the woman against the window of her crib. Black greasy hair hung to his shoulders, concealing his face, but the woman's was plain to see—her expression changing from anger to terror.

"It's four dollars till next Friday or you can leave right now!" the man shouted. He raised a beefy fist to the woman's face.

Kate winced, expecting him to start pummeling the woman. She twitched with an instinctual urge to run across the street and somehow stop everything: the bullying, the buying and selling, the evil.

Wan pulled on her arm again. "No. Keep walking. We cannot do anything for them right now. We go where we can give hope, where we can make difference. They cannot listen now."

She turned to Maggie's crib door. The glow from the red lantern globe lit the window.

Wan knocked. "Maggie? Maggie, it is Wan and Dr. Bushnell."

But the girl who answered was not Maggie. "What do you want?" the girl asked, surly, drawing deep on the stub of a cigarette.

Wan tried to peek over her shoulder. "We come to see Maggie—"

The girl took a step forward to better block the doorway. "I don't know anything about Maggie."

Kate edged forward. "You couldn't miss her—her face was horribly bruised and stitched."

"Look, I don't know your Maggie. I just rented this crib yesterday." She took a long draw on the cigarette.

"But didn't anyone here mention her?" Kate tried again, offering her hand in greeting. "I'm Dr. Bushnell. I treated her injuries."

"We come to help," Wan added. Before she could say more, the woman took a step back and slammed the door. Wan tilted her head. "See? Some will listen. Most won't."

She pulled Kate from the door and nodded to a woman standing outside her crib up ahead. "We go on."

Just then a man exited the next crib and in his hurry almost bumped into them. Furious, he shouted, "Get out of the way. What are you doing here anyway, you Chinese—"

Wan cowered back. Kate put her arm around her friend's shaking shoulders but wanted to put her hands over her own ears. The man scowled, continuing to shout obscenities as they hurried away from him down the street.

Wan said not a word.

The sun was sinking behind Union Station after another long day trying to help women off the streets. "Safe." Wan smiled at the WCTU team waiting on the platform.

"How did things go today?" Ruth tried to sound hopeful.

Clare searched Kate's eyes. "Any news of Maggie?"

Wan shook her head. "It has been almost three months now, and no one has heard anything."

"But we have a good excuse for being late today," Kate explained. "Do you remember us telling you about Elsie, that older woman we met the first time I came down here? The one who said, 'Love ain't for people like me'?"

"The one who wouldn't listen?" Clare asked.

"Today," Wan broke in eagerly, "we find she listen. Today she talked to us."

Kate was exuberant. "She had read every pamphlet we left behind. She was listening when we didn't know it, and she was waiting for us today. She wants to know more about Jesus and to get away from here, start a new life. We said we would help her move, find a real job, start over."

A slight frown wrinkled Ruth's brow. "We're going to help her move and find a job? We've tried before …"

"It's not easy, Dr. Bushnell," Clare explained. "Mrs. Shield, the president of the WCTU's Denver union, doesn't like what we're doing. More than once I've heard her say that we should be careful around such sinful women."

Ruth added, "She's not the only one. We had a hard time getting permission from the union leaders to rent a place for the Reading Room where these women can come for help. At least they can get off the street for a while. We give them food or help them find a dress in our used clothes closet. We always read something from the Bible to them when they come. But there isn't much more we can do to help them—like finding a job."

It was Kate's turn to frown. There seemed to be a deep gulf between the desire of the women of the Purity Department to help and what some of the leaders were actually willing to do. She thought of Nurse Smith's disdain for the women from the street. But she never expected it from within the WCTU. Then it dawned on her. They thought these women had an innate blight that ruined their lives: that they were less-than because they were here, that there was something in them that could never be reformed. Kate saw the frustration in Wan's downcast eyes as she swallowed her own irritation.

"We must hurry home." Wan reached for Kate's arm. "We must go. Getting dark."

Yes, Kate thought. Definitely dark. There was darkness. As dark as it was there, they needed more than those little lights in the women's windows. A memory of her father suddenly flashed through her mind. This place would need a light as powerful as the Evanston lighthouse to reveal the damaged and broken lives that needed repair. She had a sense that this was just the beginning of her journey. *Lord, what are You getting me into?*

11
A Divine Appointment

By late afternoon, Denver General Hospital settled down as visitors left and nurses began getting their patients ready for the night. Kate finished her afternoon rounds and headed towards the main entrance to walk home.

Suddenly a voice called out, "Why, Dr. Bushnell, I didn't expect to see you here."

She knew the voice and face and those unmistakable steely gray eyes, but still it took a moment to register. David? Here?

"Dav—Dr. Russell! What brings you this far from home? I heard you were working in the neurology department in Chicago." She searched his face, ignoring the familiar lock of hair falling onto his forehead.

"I'm just out here for a week, giving lectures in neurology to the medical students."

Conversation, so natural five years ago, was now awkward.

David cleared his throat. "Is your family well? I don't get to Evanston anymore. My parents died, you know."

Kate wanted to grab his hand but stopped herself, noticing the ring there. "No." She was quiet a moment. "No, I didn't know. I'm sorry. So much has happened since—uh, I haven't been home since I came back from China last year. I've been helping care for Ella Gilchrist—you remember Ella, of course?"

"Yes," David said slowly. It was his turn to pause. "Yes, I knew you were back in the States. Ella was my—" He stopped himself again. "I got married, you know, and Ella was my wife's roommate in preparatory school. She hasn't heard from Ella in a long time. She wondered if I could find out how she is doing while I am here."

"Ella is not well, David." She paused. "She is dying." Kate looked down, the awkward moment of the talk of marriage replaced by profound sadness—for herself, for Ella. She looked up again.

"I am sorry, so very sorry." David fell quiet for a moment. "You must tell Ella that Jennie and I have two little boys." He locked eyes with Kate. "They remind me of your brothers—little rascals."

Kate laughed nervously.

"Kate ... do you think we could have dinner together one night while I'm here? I feel I owe you an explanation."

She forced a smile. "No, David. No, the time for explanations is past. But I'm glad you are happy. I really am. Look at you—you are a husband and a father and a doctor. You are doing what God called you to do."

"And you, Kate?" He seemed to look into her soul. "Are you doing what God has called you to do?"

The question lingered a moment. Kate thought of Ella and Bertha, Maggie and Elsie. "I think so. I know I am making a difference." She reached out her hand. "Good-bye, David." But as he left, his question echoed in her mind. *Are you doing what God has called you to do?*

She was glad for the walk home. Time to think, to review those last moments with a quieter mind—and heart. Time to get ready to return to Ella.

"Hello there." Kate bent over Ella's pale, perspiring face. "Sorry I am back so late. Can I get you something to help you sleep? Chamomile tea?"

Ella stirred. She tried to sit up but was too weak to raise herself even halfway. "I don't want to sleep, Kate. There will be plenty of time for that later." She smiled wanly. "Tell me what you've been doing. I must have been asleep when you came back from Halliday Street."

"Yes, I didn't want to wake you. I had the most wonderful experience yesterday. Remember Elsie, the woman I met my first day on the streets? I thought she was lost to us because she shut the door in our faces. But all this time she was reading the pamphlets Wan left, and she has thought on her life, who Jesus is, how He loves her, and how things can be better. She wants to leave the streets, the cribs. She wants to start over."

"Oh, Kate," Ella mumbled. "Someday I would like to meet her." She closed her eyes and whispered. "Someday I want to meet a woman like her. Just to share a little of God's love. Will you bring someone here? Promise?"

Kate nodded, only to see her friend fall into sleep.

She drifts in and out more frequently. Kate pulled the rocker close to the bed. "We have been through so much, you and I," she whispered to her friend. "Stay just a little longer." She tried to find a comfortable position in the rocking chair and had begun to fall asleep when she heard Mrs. Gilchrist tiptoe into the room.

"Rest," Mother Gilchrist whispered as she smoothed the blanket under her daughter's chin and threw a coverlet over Kate.

"Thank you," Kate murmured before slipping off to sleep, knowing it would be another long night.

The days grew shorter into late October. The Denver air had become brisk, and the temperatures dropped with the setting sun.

"We'll have just an hour or two before dark," Kate told Wan as they arrived at Union Station.

"We have more help tonight." Wan nodded to a slim young woman wrapped in a long black coat with a full-length mink scarf.

Clare introduced her: "I want you to meet Miss Lisa Bates. Miss Bates heard about our department at the last convention. She just moved here from Milwaukee and actually came looking for someone who knew about our weekly visits."

"I'm glad that I ran into Clare yesterday," Lisa responded enthusiastically. "Earlier I met two other women at the meeting who told me this was not an official project of the WCTU."

"It's sad," Clare chimed in. "At the business meeting last week, several women spoke up, discouraging the others from coming with us. They say it's a waste of time and that these women will never change. But just come along with us, Lisa. You'll see why we believe it's worth it."

Ruth announced, "We're going to visit Rosa May first tonight. That poor girl wants out of this life. She just doesn't know how to leave or where to go. Her father abuses her when she's home." She shook her head. "She can't go back to him. Most of the time Rosa May looks hungry."

"Here," Wan interrupted cheerfully. "Take sandwiches for her." She offered some small wrapped parcels inside her basket. "I stop at Father's restaurant and make them myself." She smiled.

Kate couldn't help but smile too. No one would go hungry on Wan's watch.

Wan's hand rested on Clare's a moment. "Maybe you try and get girl in Maggie's old crib to take food?" She searched Clare's face, then Ruth's. "Maybe she talk with you two?"

The thought of Maggie chilled Kate's heart. Where could she go with that scarred face without being noticed? She wondered what it would take to help women like her. With all the corruption, so little could be done. The law didn't even seem to be on their side.

Kate and Wan walked toward the crib next to the saloon. A woman stood outside, the red light shining on her blonde hair.

Maggie? Kate stepped forward tentatively. *I can't believe it!* But her spirit fell as the woman turned. It was not the expected scarred face. Still, she looked so familiar ...

Hou Wan offered the woman a sandwich, and she took it eagerly with reddened hands.

Kate knew her, but how, from where? She studied the face closer. The woman unconscious in the hospital waiting room last Christmas! "Bertha. Bertha Lyons. I thought I recognized you. What are you doing down here?"

Bertha stopped eating, hung her head, and turned to hide back in the crib.

"No, don't go away. I didn't mean to hurt you. I'm just surprised. Something must have happened to bring you here." Kate put her arms around the woman and felt the bony shoulders under a thin red shawl. "Look at me, Bertha. What happened? Where's your baby?"

Bertha began to weep uncontrollably.

"I know Bertha from the hospital last Christmas," Kate explained to Hou Wan. "She was badly bruised and had a broken collarbone ... from a fall, right, Bertha?"

Bertha could not speak and pushed her way back into her room, pulling Kate with her. Wan shut the door and turned off the awful red light.

The room was like all of the other cribs Kate had seen. A bed with a thin blanket, a chair in front of the window to see and be seen, a broken mirror over a shelf. Kate's gaze fixed upon a baby's knitted bootie.

"Bertha." Kate turned, glancing round. She asked again, "Where is your baby?"

Bertha looked up, her face awash in tears. She shook, trying to hold them back, but something was too much. She could not speak, only cry for several moments.

Kate took her hands, and they sat silently until Bertha heaved deeply, drew a breath, and said, "He's dead."

"Dead?" It couldn't be!

Bertha nodded. "He had whooping cough. I didn't have money for medicine." She hung her head then whispered so softly Kate could hardly hear her. "After Joey died, Frank told me to go to work, that he wasn't going to take care of me." Her voice turned monotone now, all emotion drained. "He said, 'What good are you if you can't even take care of your own son.'" The words unlocked something, and she began to cry again. "He told me I was a bad mother."

Bertha gained control of herself and looked Kate in the eyes. "I tried to find work. I went from door to door offering to wash clothes, scrub floors, anything—but nothing came of it. When I came home a few weeks ago, after another day of trying door to door, Frank told me to go buy him some whiskey." She rubbed her eyes with her chapped hand. "He was already so drunk he could hardly talk. I told him I didn't have any money, and he beat me. He told me to get out and not come back. Then he pushed me out the door and down the stairs." She looked up, locking eyes with Kate. "I didn't break any bones this time."

Kate reached for Bertha's hand.

Bertha pulled away. "Now I'm in worse trouble. Blonger's man is coming for his rent and I don't have it." She put her face in her hands.

"I don't know what to do. I don't want these drunken, foul-smelling, dirty men all over my body. It's awful. And the men can tell that I don't want them near me."

Kate looked to Wan. Neither said a word, but Kate knew Wan was thinking the same thing: they couldn't leave her here. But where could they take her?

Kate stood up. "We're going to find help, Bertha. Can you hang on just a bit more?" She reached into her bag. "I have three dollars."

Wan was already searching in her purse. "And I have two. Will that be enough for Blonger's man in the morning?"

Bertha nodded. The tears started again. "Thank you." She shook her head in shame, looking down. "How can I ever thank you?"

Wan handed Bertha the rest of the sandwiches. "These will last you a few days."

"We're coming back, Bertha," Kate said. "I promise. We will find a way to get you out of here—for good. Keep the red light off and lock the door so you can stay safe."

The women hurried down the street in the dusk, pulling their coats around them and dropping their faces against the cutting lake wind. But Kate knew it wasn't the cold that penetrated their hearts as they walked deep in thought. What could they do for Bertha?

The sky was growing dark. Shadows lengthened as they hurried along. Kate felt an odd sense of unease. Strange: she didn't usually feel that way anymore. It must just be what happened to Bertha. She shook her head and hurried her pace.

They turned down a familiar street, and Kate glanced behind her. Nothing. Although at the next corner she could almost swear …

"Wan, have you noticed anyone following us?"

"No, not that I see. No one around."

True. No one seemed to be around. How odd. It was almost like—

Suddenly two strong hands grabbed each of them by the arm and whirled them around. "You're the Jesus ladies. I've heard that you're visiting my girls."

Kate looked up into the man's face, his eyes covered by dark blue glasses. He was a giant! He wore a rakish hat tilted to the side of his head, and a thick cigar hung from his mouth. Kate tried to pull away. But his hand grasped her arm like an iron band.

"You have no right to detain us, sir." Kate hoped he didn't see through her bravado. With her free hand, she grabbed for Wan's arm to make sure he couldn't drag her away.

He laughed. "Rights? Rights? You're talking about rights? I own these streets. I keep people like you out."

Kate continued to try to squirm out of his gripping hand. "We are not interfering with what you do. We only try to help these poor women, many of them kept here unfairly by you."

"Be careful, Dr. Bushnell," Wan whispered. "This is Blonger. He could—"

"Shut up, chink!" Blonger yelled. "I'll do the talking." He released Wan and shook his finger in Kate's face. "You stay away from here, you hear? If any of my men catch either one of you on Halliday Street again, I'll have them bring you to me." He smiled wickedly so close to Kate's face that she winced at the whiskey on his breath. "And it will seem like these ladies are in paradise compared to where I'll put you." He gave Kate a push that almost toppled her and called out, "It's okay boys. I think they understand." He joined two men who'd come out of the darkness, and they walked off, laughing loudly.

Kate grabbed Wan's arm; she was shivering as though she had a fever. As they ran down the street toward the station, Kate spoke between breaths, "Don't let … his bluster … scare you, Wan. God has … protected us all … these months." She drew in a deep breath. "He will do it again." Still, she wished her hands would stop shaking.

A few days later, Kate hailed a carriage at the corner near the Gilchrists' home to take her to Halliday Street. She'd been struggling to find a way to get Bertha away from Blonger. The man frightened her, and for good reason. She swallowed the lump in her throat.

Now, as the carriage jostled along the bumpy streets, Kate's mind searched for an answer. She'd already asked Clare and Ruth for help. But they didn't know what to do with Bertha. They warned Kate not to approach union members about taking any of "the street women" into their homes. "Many of our members are shocked at what we do—what we do in the name of WCTU," Clare declared passionately.

"They would rise up in arms if we began bringing such women into our homes or meetings."

But Kate had made a promise. She wasn't going to wait any longer for the Purity Department's help to find an answer. She wasn't even going to wait on Wan to join her. Perhaps that wasn't so wise, but she did have the carriage driver.

When they reached Halliday Street, Kate asked the driver, "Could you wait over there?" pointing across the street.

He eyed the dismal street, quiet at this hour of the morning, and started to shake his head.

"Please," Kate assured. "It's all right. I shouldn't be more than five or ten minutes, but I need to be sure you will wait here for me." She handed him a few extra coins.

Kate looked around cautiously to see if any of Blonger's men was on the street. She scurried to Bertha's door and tapped lightly. "Bertha, it's me. Are you all right?"

The latch scraped open, and Bertha peeked through a crack in the door. She looked left to right. "You shouldn't be here, Dr. Bushnell. Blonger's man hasn't come for the money yet. He's usually here by now. It's not safe."

"I've come to take you away from this, Bertha." Kate pushed the door open wide enough to step into the room. "I'll help you get your things."

Bertha stood helpless and dazed in a ragged nightgown as Kate handed her a skirt and blouse from the hook on the wall.

"Hurry. Put these over your gown. Are all the things on the shelf yours?"

"Yes ... but where ..."

"We can talk once we're out of here." Kate tried to hide her own nervousness at the thought that they might be caught. Even though she didn't know where Bertha would be welcome, she was determined to get her out of danger right now. "Is the blanket yours?"

"Yes." Bertha pulled the blouse over her head as Kate held the blanket by its corners and began stuffing Bertha's things inside. They both froze at a loud bang on the door.

"Bertha, open up!"

"Jake," Bertha whispered as she stood frozen in place.

He jangled the doorknob, then burst into the room. It wasn't Blonger, but another man who looked equally dangerous.

Kate studied Jake's face, twisted in an ugly sneer. *I've seen him— the man fighting with the woman on the street months ago.* She hadn't noticed the scar running from his forehead and across his cheek. It was red and ugly—a recent wound. He was a man who fought a lot, even with women.

He recognized her too. "What have we here? You're one of those religious women interfering with Blonger's girls. He'll be happy to see you."

"I have the money." Bertha stepped forward. "It's right here, in my pocket. You don't have business with her. Here, take it." She started to fish in the skirt pocket.

As she reached for it, Jake's gaze landed on the bundled blanket. He turned and pushed Bertha back onto the bed. He slapped her face. The sound echoed in the room. "You thought you'd leave without paying, did you?" He struck her again.

Without thinking, Kate picked up the medical bag at her feet and swung it at Jake's head. He ducked and lost his balance, hit the iron bedstead, and crumpled to the floor. Kate pushed the rolled-up blanket with Bertha's possessions into her hands and grabbed her arm. "Quick, I have a carriage waiting across the road."

Without looking back, they rushed out the door and across the street.

"Hurry, we have to get away," Kate directed the driver. She gave him the Gilchrists' address and fell into shocked silence. *God, what have I done?*

Bertha cowered in the corner of the carriage as it lurched down the street. They could hear Jake running after them, yelling, "Blonger will hear about this!"

Kate scooted closer to Bertha and put an arm around her shivering shoulders. "It's going to be all right. It is." *I need time. I need counsel. But where, who? Who would understand what I've just done?* She squeezed Bertha in reassurance. "First, we must see my friend. Remember the night we walked home from the hospital? I told my friend about you, and she asked me to bring you to the house." *While she talks to Ella, I'll figure out the next step.*

Bertha looked at Kate and frowned. "Why would she want to see me?"

"She wanted to come down to Halliday Street with me to help, but she's very ill. That's why she asked me." They rode in silence the rest of the way. Kate paid the driver and started up the porch steps.

Bertha stopped on the first step. "This isn't right. Look at me. I'm dirty. I'm filthy, inside and out." She started to turn away.

Kate grabbed Bertha's hand and led her up the stairs, into the Gilchrists' entryway, and to her room.

"You can leave your things here. Ella's room is just down the hall. I haven't had a chance to tell her mother that you were coming, but don't worry. This is Ella's request ... and she won't have time to make many more." Kate swallowed hard on the words and led Bertha by the arm down the hallway.

The morning sun streamed across Ella's bed. Her body, wasted and thin, barely made a mound under the blankets. Her eyes fluttered open, wide with anticipation, as Kate approached the bed. *I haven't seen that look on her face for months.*

"Ella, I have someone I know you've wanted to meet. This is Bertha. Remember, I told you I met her at the hospital Christmas night?"

"You brought her. Come closer, Bertha. I want to meet you."

Bertha shook her head. "You don't want the likes of me here."

Ella struggled to raise herself but dropped back on the sheets. Bertha fell to her knees and adjusted Ella's pillow to prop her up a bit.

With a lump in her throat, Kate turned to step away a moment and came face to face with Mrs. Gilchrist, who held a jug of fresh water in her hands.

"What's this?"

"It's Bertha, Mother Gilchrist," Kate whispered, edging out of the room and forcing Ella's mother to step back into the hallway too. "Remember Bertha? I helped her that night at the hospital and met her again with Wan—"

Mrs. Gilchrist's eyes flared with fury. "How could you bring one of those women here, Kate?"

"I had to—where else could I bring her? Besides, Ella made me promise." She looked pleadingly at Ella's mother. "It was her wish, and I *promised*."

Mrs. Gilchrist was silent, but shook her head, her eyes locked on Bertha by Ella's bedside. "Look how dirty she is. She shouldn't be that close to Ella."

Kate put her hand on Mrs. Gilchrist's arm. She looked her in the eyes and spoke gently. "Ella wants this. Don't you see? It's something she can do—to encourage Bertha, to share about Jesus, how He loves her. It's her way of doing some mission work, what she wanted to do in China but didn't have a chance to before we had to leave." Kate glanced back into the room. "She needs to matter for God. Even now. Especially now."

Mrs. Gilchrist choked on a sob and hugged the pitcher to her chest.

"I don't understand any of this," Mrs. Gilchrist half-whispered, half-sobbed into Kate's shoulder.

"Nor do I." She held the hurting mother tight for a few moments, feeling them both strengthen, then they stepped back toward the room.

They stood in the doorway and watched Ella and Bertha talk softly in their own world, bathed in the light that shone across the bed and their faces. Kate strained to hear the exchange, as she knew Mother Gilchrist was doing too. But Bertha's voice was so faint and Ella's fading. Her shallow breaths seemed even slower.

Life was so strange, Kate thought. One body could fail even with a spirit that shone so brightly, and another could be strong with a spirit so frail. She watched Ella struggle to put a weak hand on Bertha's tear-stained face. The hardness and fear melted from Bertha's face, and Kate knew Ella must be praying.

Mrs. Gilchrist noticed too and stopped crying. "Even as a girl," she said almost to herself, "she had the heart of a missionary."

"Yes," Kate whispered. "Then maybe this was Bertha's gift." Maybe this was a divine appointment.

12
Good-bye

November 1885

"She's gone." Kate couldn't believe the sound of her own words.

The Gilchrists sobbed as Kate stroked Ella's forehead, smoothing back her hair. She looked up at Mrs. Gilchrist. "She was my best friend. Sometimes in China, I thought we were sisters, with but one heartbeat." She kissed Ella's forehead and slipped from the bedside. Mrs. Gilchrist collapsed over her daughter who was still and at peace.

"I'll leave you with her," Kate whispered to Mr. Gilchrist, who stood awkward and lost. Kate added, "I'll send for Reverend Bristol too—as soon as it is light." He nodded.

Kate turned to find Bertha kneeling in the doorway. She reached out a hand to pull her up. "How long have you been here?" she whispered.

"I couldn't sleep," Bertha said through tears. "I think God woke me so I could come up and pray for Miss Ella."

"Let's go down to make a pot of tea."

"I can make the tea, Dr. Bushnell. You go and rest. You've been up for three nights now."

Weariness swept over Kate. She nodded and turned to her room as Bertha slipped downstairs. Bertha had become invaluable these last few weeks. Even Mrs. Gilchrist acknowledged how diligently and efficiently she worked in the kitchen, saving them many trips up and down the stairs and giving them more time to sit with Ella.

Kate dragged herself up the stairs to her room, a black emptiness rolling through her body and soul. She'd known this day was coming, but knowing did not make the letting go any easier, she thought, throwing herself onto the bed without changing her clothes. *I am so tired, Lord. Tired.*

For a long while, she lay still, spent, wishing the sadness to fall away with sleep. But sleep wouldn't come.

"This is ridiculous," she announced to herself. She got up, lit the oil lamp on the table, and grabbed a pen to write her parents. They would want to know about Ella. Kate felt guilty, but writing had been difficult for weeks.

> Dear Mother and Father,
> Ella has just died. We thought this moment would come a dozen times over the last three nights. Her wrenching cough was merciless, and she wasted away. But she would rally and fight a little more each night. I stayed in her room until this morning. It is over before the sun has risen on the day. I am exhausted, and yet I cannot sleep. I need to notify the minister. There will be all sorts of details to attend to for the funeral preparations. The Gilchrists have come to rely upon me. It is still dark outside. And it feels dark inside too. I long to see you. I'm sure you have wondered what has been happening here. There is so much to tell, but now maybe you understand?

Kate stopped and smoothed her hair back from her forehead. How could she make them understand? She continued writing, shoulders hunched over the table.

> Once a week, I visit women whose husbands drink up their weekly pay and beat their wives. I take my medical bag to help where needed. Don't worry, I don't go alone.

She stopped herself again. She didn't think Bertha's story would make sense to Mother and Father in a letter. "Some things are difficult to translate even in our own language," she said to herself.

> Had you heard that David Russell is married? I was shocked to meet him in the hall of our hospital the other day.

Kate leaned back in her chair and straightened her shoulders. *Yes, David, you shocked us all, and maybe I shocked you too.* Maybe it was a blessing to have had so many other things pressing these last weeks, that she had not replayed over and over the moment David stood before her in the halls of Denver General.

She rubbed a thumb along the pen in her hand and became strongly aware of the bare ring finger of her left hand. She remembered that good-bye handshake once again. If she had come home from China earlier, would she have been a wife and a mother of two little boys now? She bent over the desk and continued writing.

> I hope you are feeling better, Father. I didn't learn of your illness until I received Sarah's letter, full of family news. I miss you all so much and hope to be home for a visit soon.

> Until then, pray for me. I thought China was where I was called, and now that I am here and Ella is gone, I know there must be a next step. I believe "all things work together for good" and one day even this will make sense. All I know is that God has put something in my heart— to help these troubled women—but whether it's here in Denver or somewhere else, He's not shown me yet.

> Give my love to all the family. I can't wait to see Sarah's new baby and to meet Ellen, William's new wife.

> All my love,

> Katharine

The long night and sense of loss finally pushed Kate to rest her head on her folded arms on the desk, the last conversation with David replaying again. *So much has happened.*

Sunlight streamed into the foyer below as Kate came down the stairs. The reality and ache of Ella's death set in once again as it had a dozen times since the morning she passed away a week prior. As she stepped into the foyer, a knock pulled her attention to the door.

She turned the knob and peeked through to see a familiar smiling face. "Wan!" Kate opened the door wider and practically pulled her friend inside. "Come in, come in. It's been too long."

"I wasn't sure if proper to call so soon," Wan said.

"Of course it's okay." Kate led her to the sitting room. "I've stayed close to the Gilchrists. They needed me." She looked at Wan knowingly. "It's been hard, but I know the work on Halliday Street is hard and I'm needed there too."

Wan was silent but nodded gently. "Blonger not come back again." She smiled.

"Oh!" Kate saw Bertha in the foyer and called her over. "Look who's here. You remember Hou Wan? She came with me when we first visited you on Halliday Street."

Bertha's tight embrace seemed to surprise Wan, who beamed and then held Bertha at arm's length. "Bertha! You look wonderful."

She did, Kate thought. Her shining blonde hair was piled into a luxurious bun. Her hands were no longer red and chapped from the wind and the streets, but soft and smooth. Wearing one of Ella's pretty dresses, she was clean and neat, even amid the housework she insisted upon doing.

Kate could tell Bertha was pleased by the compliment, but she simply asked, "Shall I fix some tea, Dr. Bushnell?"

"Yes, please." Kate nodded. "Wan, tell me everything. What's been happening downtown?"

Wan turned from marveling at Bertha's transformation. "Much has happened. The biggest news is that we found work for Rosa May as a servant in one of the women's homes. They provide her room and board."

"Oh!" Good news—she needed some good news. Kate smiled. "And your mother? How is your mother? I am sorry I haven't been back to treat her feet."

Wan's smile faded. "She is the same. She burns incense every day for healing, but her feet do not get better."

"I'm afraid her feet have been too damaged for me to give her any relief either. Her arch and big toe were too badly broken and malformed. She's developed serious rheumatism in the joints."

"Rheuma ..." Wan's voice trailed off in the difficult pronunciation.

"Rheumatism. It causes deep aching pain and the joints to stiffen. I have seen its horrors in too many women whose feet were bound."

Wan nodded knowingly.

Kate hesitated, then asked what she had wanted to since the day they met. "Wan, how is it your feet were never bound?"

"A miracle." She slipped into Mandarin. "Mother and I were in China while Father worked on the railroad here in Colorado. He sent money to us every few months. Mother asked him for extra money for the foot binder." She paused. "You have heard about the foot binder? She is the one who is called in because she is cruel enough to break a little girl's foot. The screams do not bother her. She is tougher than the mother who hires her."

Kate grimaced.

"Father refused to send the money for the foot binder. He ordered Mother not to bind my feet. But it was another reason that made Mother listen. He said he was saving money so we could join him here in America." Wan nodded to Kate's feet. "And girls in America did not have bound feet."

"But how did you go unnoticed up to twelve years old, not having your feet bound? Didn't the other girls poke fun at you and the women shun your mother?"

"They did. I felt embarrassed by my big feet. I wore long baggy trousers, hoping no one would notice. Honorable Mother took much abuse from the other women. But we were poor, and she said she did not have the money for the foot binder. Sometimes people took pity on us."

Bertha entered and slid a tray with the tea and cups onto the table by Kate, who motioned for her to join them. "No," Bertha said shyly. "I have things to finish in the kitchen." She turned to Wan. "I am so grateful."

As she took the cup of tea Kate poured for her, Wan watched Bertha slip from the room.

"We are the grateful ones," Kate said. "She has been such a help."

"She just needed a chance."

"Yes," Kate said. "Everyone needs a chance."

"That is one of the reasons I did not wait any more to come," Wan said, returning to English. "We have chance to hear someone who helps many women."

Kate looked curiously over her teacup.

"You have heard of Miss Frances Willard, the president of the WCTU?"

Kate set down her cup. "Miss Willard!"

"Yes, Miss Frances Willard is coming to speak in Denver—and women of the WCTU have been invited to attend. Much of Denver will be there!"

"Miss Willard, here? Why, Miss Willard was my favorite teacher at the Evanston Preparatory School for Women. Ella will—" Kate stopped midsentence. The ache inside awakened once again. She thought of school days that seemed so long ago, of Ella and the many lectures they heard from Miss Willard with all her idiosyncrasies. She had actually told the girls not to travel in mixed company because "men won't hold intellectual conversations with women."

Kate smiled. "Miss Willard has come a long way. Now the men are listening to her."

"You knew her well?"

Kate looked into her cup and nodded. "She had such high goals for her students. She wanted us to have a life objective, a daily objective, an hourly objective."

Wan looked perplexed.

"She expected a lot of us," Kate explained. "She wanted us to make our lives matter, every moment. She could be demanding in our schoolwork, but when she visited our rooms in the evening, she was like a kindly aunt." Kate laughed at herself. She looked up at Wan. "Forgive me. I'm reminiscing like an old lady. When is she coming?"

"She is coming next week. She will speak in the hall above Empire Bakery. You come?"

13
Stirrings

*I*cy winds bounced off the mountains and across Blake Street. As Kate neared the Empire Bakery, she pulled her long cloak tightly around her. She'd taken off her white medical coat before leaving the hospital but had no time to change from the black dress she wore for work.

Women's voices, singing with great gusto, drew her up the stairs to the hall above the bakery: "Rescue the perishing, care for the dying ... Jesus is merciful, Jesus will save."

Excitement hovered over the several hundred women who filled the dimly lit hall. Colorful banners dangled from the ceiling: *Down with the Saloon and Up with the Home*, and the WCTU slogan, *For God and Home and Native Land*. Baskets of flowers adorned the platform.

Where did they find those in this weather? Kate wondered, astonished by it all. Here and there a few gentlemen squirmed uncomfortably, out of place in this bastion of femininity. Kate sent them curious glances. They'd probably escorted their wives. She spotted an empty seat several rows from the back and inched her way along, just as the women around her settled into their places. Suddenly she spotted Jessie, one of the nurses from the hospital, seated in front of her. She tapped her on the shoulder and mouthed, *Glad you could make it.*

The chairman struck her gavel on the podium to begin the meeting. Mrs. Mary Shields, president of the Denver union, began honoring the illustrious guests present: "I'm so glad to introduce President Mrs. Laura Beecher, coming all the way from the Colorado Springs chapter; Miss Sarah Bolton, corresponding secretary ..."

Kate strained her neck to look between two broad-brimmed hats that nearly blocked her view of the platform. *I can't see her. Is she really here? Oh—yes.*

She sat back for the rest of the introductions that seemed interminable. She was exhausted from a long day at the hospital. At last, the announcement she'd been waiting to hear. "And now I have the great privilege of introducing our honored guest. She has crisscrossed our nation by rail and carriage to bring the message of prohibition to every city and town of this great land."

The introduction roused the women around Kate to their feet. They clapped loudly and waved white handkerchiefs and ribbons.

"For more than five years, our dear Miss Willard has led the National Women's Christian Temperance Union to greater and greater heights. In 1883, just two years ago, she became the world president of our great organization."

Kate found herself applauding with those around her. It seemed almost unbelievable that her former English teacher held such a place of honor. Her mind flashed back to a time when Miss Willard had stood up to the male faculty at Northwestern, insisting the female students have the same rights as male students. She'd eventually lost her job for that. Could it have been that she was meant to do something bigger?

"Ladies," the chairman called, motioning for attention. "Ladies, without further ado, I introduce to you Miss Frances Willard, World President of the Women's Christian Temperance Union."

The applause and cheers felt electric now. Kate's height gave her the advantage of seeing over the ornate hats in front of her. She was conscious of how big Miss Willard's presence loomed, though her former teacher was really quite short in stature and almost somber in attire. Only a tiny bit of lace peeking above her tight collar softened the dark blue suit Miss Willard wore. As usual, her only jewelry was the cameo brooch given to her by her mother years ago.

Erect and confident, Miss Willard stepped up to the lectern and pinched her pince-nez onto her nose. Kate was amused. She still did that! She hadn't changed much since Kate had seen her almost ten years prior. As in years past, Kate thought her teacher just looked ... imperial.

Miss Willard held only a Bible in her hands. For a moment, her face looked severe, thin lips pinched together, brown hair parted down the middle and caught behind her ears. Kate remembered how she and the other students had sat a little straighter whenever Miss Willard pulled back her shoulders to gain every inch of height as she began to teach. The memory of her oft-repeated refrain came back to Kate: "Be quiet, diligent, occupied, and punctual." *If only we knew then that those boundaries would actually help us gain the freedom Miss Willard spoke about.*

Now Miss Willard opened her Bible and began reading, "Whatsoever ye do in word or deed, do all in the name of the Lord Jesus, giving thanks to God and the Father by him. Amen." She closed her Bible and removed her pince-nez. Her expression changed, and her brown eyes sparkled.

"Dear sisters, as your president, I have sought to fulfill Paul's command to the Colossians as I have represented our cause across the nation. I have visited every state and territory and all but two capitals—those of Arizona and Idaho—in a single year, speaking for our cause in more than a thousand towns."

Kate marveled that Miss Willard had the energy to take her to all corners of the country. Then it struck her—*Miss Willard is at least fifteen years older than I!*

"My purpose," Miss Willard continued, "is to gather a million signatures on our petition revoking liquor licenses and the sale of any and all intoxicating drinks in any town, in any locality." Her voice grew louder. "This must be determined by ballot."

Now the women cheered even more loudly, waved prohibition flags, and stomped their feet, chanting, "The ballot for women! The ballot for women!"

Miss Willard waved her hands to still the crowd. "Please," she said, motioning for everyone to sit down. "It is our intention for women of lawful age to be privileged to take part in this vote in the same manner as men."

Pausing for a moment, as the room became quiet, Miss Willard continued with the teacher's commanding attitude that Kate remembered so well. "You've heard it before. The life-insurance statistics prove that while the average life span of the moderate drinker is but thirty-five and a half, that of the total abstainer is sixty-four."

After some time, Kate found it hard to concentrate. A glance down at her pendant watch confirmed that her former teacher had continued for more than an hour. With a deep breath, she determined not to miss a moment. She was weary to the bone from hours on her feet, but then outbreaks of more clapping made her sit straighter in her chair.

"In 1883," Miss Willard said, "we wished to give the Republicans one more chance. Their temperance plan was suspiciously succinct and stated that a constitutional amendment *relative* to the liquor traffic ought to be submitted; but how near a relative—whether a third cousin or a mother-in-law—was not indicated."

Laughter erupted from the audience, jarring Kate to even greater wakefulness. She looked around to see if anyone had noticed that she hadn't caught the joke.

Kate struggled to keep her eyes open as Miss Willard described the irrevocably divided national parties, whose funding came from the liquor industry. *I don't share her passion for political concerns,* Kate mused as she discreetly covered a yawn and blinked a few times.

"Before I close, I would like to talk about our new department for suppression of social evils, the Social Purity Department."

Kate suddenly felt wide awake. *Finally!* This was why she had come. She drew herself up to her full height in her chair so that she could see Miss Willard clearly.

"This department is as yet not fully operative. It is greatly to be regretted that we have not yet succeeded in winning the services of a superintendent. I wonder if you, my dear sisters, realize that, in many states, the age of consent has been as low as seven years— *seven years!* Little girls, not just women, across the country are being forced into debauchery because of the brutalizing influence of liquor upon sexual desire."

A unified gasp punctuated Miss Willard's words. The women around Kate raised their hands to their mouths in shock as if to silence the very idea. Kate felt a sense of kinship with her old teacher. A longing surged for these other women to meet someone like Bertha so they would know how important this work was. They would be more concerned with the wasted lives down on Halliday Street than with these flowers and politics.

Miss Willard paused in momentary silence as if to give time for her every word to stick. Then wild applause burst from the crowd once again, this time also with shouts and cheers: "For God, for home, for native land! For God, for home, for native land!"

Kate also stood, but with a sober determinedness. She thought of the women she knew, forced into lives of shame by drunken men— Maggie with her scarred face, Elsie's rouged cheeks and hardened eyes, Bertha, and Rosa May. After listening to Miss Willard, how could anyone doubt that prohibition was part of the answer?

The applause died and the crowd broke up as the women emptied the hall and headed to their cabs waiting along the street.

Something compelled Kate to head against the tide, toward the front of the hall. She waited for the many women pressed around Miss Willard to finish their praises so she could greet her old teacher. "Thank you for coming, Miss Willard." "What a powerful message." "You can count on us here in Denver."

"I know you'll stand with us," Miss Willard said warmly as she moved the women along gently in a practiced manner.

Remembering Miss Willard's previous energy, Kate was surprised, however, to now see the hints of gray in the fine brown hair and the tiny wrinkles around weary eyes. It was a weariness she felt in herself. Of course Miss Willard would be tired. Such a woman of influence and power. Kate started to turn away, hesitant to add one more person to whom her teacher must extend a smile and handshake. But more women from the audience crowded behind her, pushing her forward. Unable to turn back, Kate felt an inner urgency she couldn't explain.

She felt her hands clasped tightly in Miss Willard's. "Why, Katharine Bushnell! Indeed, *Doctor* Bushnell! I hoped to see you tonight. I have heard so many good things about your work with the Social Purity Department here in Denver."

Kate felt herself blushing. "It's the best part of my week."

"You must come to see me while I am here, my dear." Miss Willard turned and called over her shoulder, "Anna, would you arrange for Dr. Bushnell to meet with me tomorrow before I leave?" Just as quickly, Miss Willard released Kate's hand to greet the woman behind her.

No, Miss Willard had not changed one bit. She always got her objective. *I wonder what plan she has for me?* Kate thought with slight amusement.

A shy young woman with a gentle smile slipped through the crowd and touched Kate's arm. "Would you be able to meet Miss Willard tomorrow afternoon at Mrs. Shields' home?" She opened a small ledger with a stiff black cover. "Let me see. It looks as though she has time between ... 3:10 and 3:30. Her train leaves at ten after six for Kansas City, so we must allow time to get to the station."

Anna looked up with the largest brown eyes Kate had ever seen. "Oh, forgive me! I didn't introduce myself. I'm Anna Gordon, Miss Willard's travel companion. I take care of her schedule and appointments. She's been talking about your work here in Denver and hoped she would have time to meet with you."

Bewildered, Kate looked at the paper Anna gave her with Mrs. Shields' address. "I suppose I could reschedule my patients ..." But before she could finish, Anna and Miss Willard were pulled away.

Kate slowly turned to leave the nearly empty hall. She felt inexplicably exhilarated. Yet she couldn't shake a sense of deep concern. Its source suddenly dawned on her. *What exactly does she expect of me?* Her mind flashed back to the last time a strong woman leader had asked for her help, and memories of China washed over her.

She silenced the turmoil in her mind and hurried down the street, thinking about how to rearrange her appointments. At three, she was to meet with Rachel Potts, a mother of four who was pregnant again with her fifth. At three-thirty, she was to see Wilbur, an eight-year-old with a broken arm. *Oh, and I suppose I'll have to hire a carriage to take me to Mrs. Shields'.* She stopped her quick pace. Honestly. All this fuss for a twenty-minute meeting? *I should just send a note of regret. I can't simply cancel on my patients.*

She shook her head and started forward again. Miss Willard's words came back to her, as did her own: *I've heard so much about your good work here in Denver ... It's the best part of my week.* No! She couldn't miss the chance to talk more with Miss Willard. Kate looked up at the stars. "God, You must have some reason for bringing Frances Willard back into my life after ten years ... just don't make it another slow boat to China."

14
Miss Willard's Invitation

All seemed dark on the other side of Mrs. Shields' massive front door. Kate couldn't see much through the opaque oval glass, but no light glimmered from inside. She hesitated, impatience beginning to flare inside her. Was no one there? Had she come for nothing?

She pulled the cord and heard the bell from deep in the house. "There. I've done it. Whoever comes to the door will invite me in—and then who knows what will be asked of me next."

Mrs. Shields didn't give Kate time to wonder. She opened the door, breathless, to hurry Kate inside. "Come in, come in, Dr. Bushnell. Miss Willard has been expecting you. I'll just get Anna from the dining room."

Embarrassed, Kate stepped back. "Oh, I wouldn't want to interrupt their meal."

"No, no, you're not interrupting them." Mrs. Shields pulled Kate in and shut the door behind them. "Wherever Miss Willard travels, she sets up an office for herself and the secretaries who travel with her. I just felt the dining room would be the most comfortable place, especially with the fireplace at this time of year. Please make yourself at home while I call Anna." She steered Kate to a seat in front of the bay window and rushed away.

Kate noticed the exquisite Tiffany lamp and framed family pictures on the marble table. *Such costly things. I suppose it's good that Miss Willard has generous friends to help her.* She was just slipping her coat from her shoulders as Anna whisked up to help.

"I'm so glad you found us. Miss Willard said you would be early. You impressed her as one of her finest students. She's just finishing some dictation that has to go out on the train this evening. Can I get you a cup of coffee?"

"No, thank you." Kate shook her head. "It will feel good to sit a while in this lovely room."

"It shouldn't be long then." Anna hurried back through the open double doors into the room beyond.

Kate peered after her. She heard the *clack clack clack* of a typewriter in the distance. She could see Miss Willard sitting in a tapestry-covered rocker just beyond the doorway and listened closely.

"Please read back what I've dictated to Miss Henry so far, Louise."

A clear and distinct voice, presumably the Louise whom Kate could not see, began reading: "Dear friend, the fashion in women's dress that requires the constriction of the waist and compression of the trunk not only deforms the body in a manner contrary to good taste but also results in serious injury to important vital organs—"

Miss Willard interrupted, "Move down to where I say, 'you will lend your aid.'"

Silence.

Louise began again. "By making the figures upon your fashion plates conform more to the conditions requisite for the maintenance of health, you will lend your aid to the improvement of female health."

"Let me think a moment about that last sentence."

Kate covered her mouth to suppress a laugh. She remembered when her schoolmate Deborah Smith described Miss Willard as someone having more ideas than a dog had hair. There was nothing she wouldn't tackle.

Through the open door, Kate watched Anna approach Miss Willard.

"How many more letters in that pile, Anna?"

"Just two more that have to go to Chicago on the train tonight. Alma can type them, and you can sign them before we leave for the depot. Dr. Bushnell is here."

Miss Willard pulled off her pince-nez and rubbed the bridge of her nose. "Oh good. I'm glad she came early. You and the others can pack up all our papers." She stood, arched her back, gave it a rub, then turned quickly toward Kate.

Kate rose to meet her.

"Dr. Bushnell! Forgive me for keeping you waiting." She led Kate to a red velvet settee in the far corner of the room. "Come, let's have a little talk." She eyed Kate more closely and smiled. "You have grown into such an accomplished young woman, which is exactly what I expected."

Kate smiled admiringly at her old teacher as they took a few moments to catch up. She felt a bit awed as her former mentor told her about how the WCTU had grown since Miss Willard left the Women's College for the Temperance Union. One rumor was that she left the school over a broken engagement.

"I guess they felt I allowed the girls too much freedom," Miss Willard said, "but look where God has taken me, Dr. Bushnell."

"Oh, Miss Willard, just call me Kate. After all, I was your student. I still feel as though I am."

"Of course, Kate." Miss Willard smiled and inched forward a bit. "You were always a good student too. But as we are each pressed for time, I will come right to the point. You heard my pleas last night regarding the need for someone to superintend the Social Purity Department."

Kate nodded slowly.

"It is another one of those dreams of mine that I get badgered to death about. I speak out enough on other matters of concern for women, and now I am adding sex to my already egregious platforms."

"I was glad you said what you did last night. People need to know. My friends and colleagues are shocked when I tell them I visit prostitutes on my days off. There's so much they don't know that goes on around us."

"Or they do not want to know." Miss Willard looked intently at Kate, then shook her head. "No, I do not suppose how others react, their shock, upsets you any more than it does me. Even some of my board members disapprove of my adding another project—and this one, heaven forbid, deals with shameful women on the streets. But I am not worried a hair. I fancy the explanation is that, unless I am an awfully deceived woman, I am desirous of doing God's will. So the clamor is like the humming of skeeters outside the curtain. It rather lulls me into quiet."

Kate smiled at the picturesque language. "I remember those Evanston skeeters well."

Miss Willard smiled, but there was a seriousness, an urgency in her tone. "Kate, I have had a dream for some time now. I believe there must be an answer for the poor women living lives of shame, often through no fault of their own. Too many people do not think twice about them or care or offer to help. There are hundreds of those awful dens in the red-light district in Chicago, not far from our new headquarters on LaSalle Street. But I think about them, and I care and want to help—only I cannot do justice to heading up what I have envisioned the Social Purity Department can do." She shook her head. "I have just been asked to be ex officio head of the National Department of Education as well."

Kate's heart beat rapidly. Miss Willard put her hand on Kate's arm. "With your experience in missions and evangelism, your training in medical work, your compassion for these women—no, don't shake your head—I have heard how you have been rescuing women here in Denver."

"I've only—"

"No. You are doing good things. We need you. There is so much work to be done."

"But, Miss Willard—"

"Anna and I prayed about this after the meeting last night," she persisted. "I believe you are the right person to become the national evangelist for the Social Purity Department."

Kate stared silently at her former teacher for a moment. Finally she broke the quiet. "I wouldn't even know where to begin in Chicago."

"We have volunteers who can help. Right now, we just have a small room where we bring the women in for the day. I am praying that in time, our White Ribbon women—that is what I call our members—will be able to buy a building that could house these women until they are able to safely fend for themselves."

Miss Willard looked out the window as if seeing a vision. "We could call it the Anchorage, a safe harbor where ruined women find Jesus, the anchor of their soul and the protector of their purity." She paused. "But some of my board members are against it. Even Mrs. Carse, the president of the Chicago union. It wouldn't be an easy assignment."

But Kate's mind was far away. *How Wan and I have wished for such a place here, a place for Bertha and Elsie ... all the others on Halliday Street we haven't been able to help yet.*

Miss Willard pressed Kate's hand tightly. "Would you consider giving up your medical practice here to join me in Chicago in this great endeavor?"

Kate hung her head for a moment before looking up into Miss Willard's eyes. "Dear Miss Willard. I can't answer you without praying about this first. I admit I've felt confused since I came back from China. I didn't go into medicine just to have a job. I wanted to serve God. That's why I went to China even before I completed my residency ... but that was a mistake. I don't want to make that mistake again."

"A mistake?"

"I—I think I was too young for the responsibilities put on my shoulders." Kate struggled to voice what she hadn't articulated fully for herself. "I believe coming home to take care of Ella until she died was God's plan, and working with the women whose lives have been ruined—"

"By drink!"

"Yes, by drink, but also by men who misuse them, who despise them and then demand what they have no right to demand." Kate looked intently at her teacher. "I know I'm helping these women, and that's the best time of my week."

"Yes?"

"I'm just not sure what God wants me to do now." She paused. "I'll think about your invitation and listen to see if this is God's will for me."

"Of course you must listen to God's direction. I understand you cannot give me an answer today. But I do have to make something clear. If you feel the calling, if you do this mighty thing, there are no funds to pay for your support. The work must indeed be God's calling. The WCTU only started giving me a small stipend when I became world president two years ago, but it does not go far, and we are working to fund so many things. This will not be an easy task."

"No, I don't imagine it could be," Kate said. "But wherever God calls me, I know He will take care of me. First, I need a sense of where that is to be."

Anna waved through the doorway at Miss Willard, who rose to take Kate's arm as they walked to the door.

"I will be praying with you," she told Kate. "When you have made your decision, just write me in Chicago." She slipped a card into Kate's hand. "We have new headquarters. It is all written out here."

Kate's thoughts whirled along with the carriage on the way back to the Gilchrists. She thought of Elsie finally accepting a Bible but being unacceptable to Denver society. *Lord, why Chicago? Why not have me work on a shelter here?*

But Miss Willard's passionate pleas rang in her ears: *I have had a dream ... Join me in this mighty endeavor.* Kate shook her head as if to clear it, then stared out the window. She must take the request seriously. Her former teacher, a woman of God, asked her to do this after praying about it.

Kate remembered the turmoil in her heart about making the decision to go to China. She thought God was speaking through Mrs. Gracey's invitation, even though Dr. Jewell questioned the wisdom of it. David too. Did he know from the start that her going to China would be the end of their relationship? Kate closed her eyes as if to shut out all that had happened, but the faces of the women flashed through her mind—the women secluded in the cribs, the girls with bound feet in China. *Show me what to do, God. Make clear what it is I'm supposed to do.* She pulled the Bible she always carried from her bag and opened it. The pages fell to a passage she returned to again and again. Isaiah sixty-one. The first verse caught her breath as the carriage pulled to a halt.

"The Spirit of the Lord ... hath sent me to bind up the brokenhearted, to proclaim liberty to the captives, and the opening of the prison to them that are bound."

Kate waved at the Gilchrists and Bertha through the coach window as the train pulled out of Denver. The catch in her throat surprised her. She was used to getting on trains and boats and saying good-bye. And yet ...

She craned her neck once more as the train gained speed. Colorado, in its spring promise with snow-capped mountain peaks reigning over wildflowers emerging in the plains, would soon be gone, and the city lights of Chicago would draw her forward.

Kate pulled a well-worn packet from her bag and unfolded the letter on top.

> I shared your news with my staff this morning, and we spent time together praising God that He has called you to join us ... I have included some material written by Josephine Butler, the great crusader in England who has been fighting the battle against vice for more than twenty years.

Kate had already pored over the reports about Josephine Butler, but began to read them again, one in particular:

> Mrs. Booth of the Salvation Army sent Rebecca Jarrett to the Butler's House of Rest. Rebecca Jarrett had gone from being a prostitute to becoming a brothel keeper. She had been a heavy drinker and was altogether in a wretched state.

Kate thought of this Rebecca and how like Bertha she was, although at least Bertha hadn't been a drinker.

> When Rebecca Jarrett became ill, Mrs. Booth cared for her and converted her. At the Butler's House of Rest, she sufficiently recovered. When she was able to leave the House, she was also ready and able to help in the work of reclaiming others.

The words thrilled Kate: *She was also ready and able to help in the work of reclaiming others.* She let them ring in her mind as she stared out the window. That was her goal; she was thinking like Miss

Willard now, like this Josephine Butler. Kate wanted to bring women in trouble to the place of healing where they could help others. Even some of Kate's friends in the WCTU didn't think this was possible. They thought such women were born with an innate weakness to sin. *We all sin: each of us needs saving.* She studied the report, this time a quote by Mrs. Butler.

> I was determined not to lose so valuable a helper. So we helped Rebecca and her husband buy a little house, which they called Hope Cottage, not far from our home. There we established Rebecca, who goes out to the most difficult and dangerous reaches of London to bring girls back to a reasonable way of life.

Again Kate shut her eyes and thought of Miss Willard's Anchorage and Rebecca Jarrett's Hope Cottage. And as the train wended east, Kate thought of the rolling waves of Lake Michigan ahead and the lighthouse her father helped build.

His words came back to her: "If I don't ever take on another job, I'll feel I've made a difference with my life. God willing, there will never again be another shipwrecked body." Kate echoed his dream and whispered, "God, let me be a lighthouse of refuge for the broken women on the streets of Chicago. Help me bring them to Your safe harbor."

Kate picked up Miss Willard's letter again.

> Anna has arranged for you to stay with Mrs. Elizabeth Wheeler Andrew, who is one of the editors of the *Union Signal*. I believe you knew her while at the Women's College in Evanston. Her husband died in an accident about a year ago. He was pastor of a local Presbyterian church, and she still lives in the manse. She anticipates your coming.

Kate leaned deeper into her seat, head back. Bess ... what a surprise that they'd meet again after so many years. *Thank you, Lord, for providing me with an old friend in this strange place.* She thought of how she and Bess had led Sunday afternoon prayer meetings at Dean

Sanford's house. Even then they wanted so much to help women find lives of purpose and usefulness. Though Bess was a pastor's wife and quite a bit older than Kate, they had become good friends. Now Bess was a widow, and Kate had never married. She had come almost full circle around the globe to work alongside her friend again. Kate turned her gaze out the window and remarked to herself, "Bess, I hope you're ready for what we are getting into this time."

15
A New Beginning

*T*he iron horse gave up its last puffs of steam as it slid into Chicago's Union Station. Kate buttoned up her long gray coat. She reveled in the steady feel of the coach under her feet after the shaking and creaking of the last four days.

Down the aisle, the conductor called for baggage tickets, and Kate dug hers from her bag. She had clearly marked Bess' address on the top and sides of her trunk. She wanted no confusion about where all her things needed to be since Chicago already seemed a bit overwhelming.

Swirls of people spilled into the cavernous station as the porter helped Kate to the platform. How would she ever find Bess? She stepped into seeming chaos, with porters barreling through the crowd behind baggage carts piled high with trunks and suitcases. Vendors called their wares above the tumult, selling apples and round baked buns.

Kate's mouth watered, especially for the apples. She'd gone to the dining car only twice on the long journey, trying to save her money and stretch the bread and cheese she'd packed in Denver and the cinnamon cookies Mrs. Gilchrist made the night before she left. She allowed herself just one luxury on this journey: the coffee the porter brought through the car each morning. *God, only You know if I will be able to afford coffee now and make my savings last until I can find funding or income. But I won't worry about that now.*

She scanned the platform, searching for her short red-haired friend in the midst of the milling crowd of travelers and porters moving luggage. Anna Gordon had sent her a recent photograph of her new landlady: "Mrs. Elizabeth Wheeler Andrew." In the picture, Bess wore a dark velvet jacket with a frilly white lace collar. Her hair was crimped into small waves along the sides of her face. A spray of flowers on one shoulder indicated she was photographed at some festive event. But the sad, dark eyes and slight downturn of her finely chiseled mouth seemed to belie the occasion.

Kate looked for those eyes in the crowd, then began working her way toward the station. They'd eventually meet up if she stayed on the platform rather than going inside where people from many trains mixed together. The bitter spring winds made her work her way faster toward the station, when above the loud chatter she heard a familiar voice.

"Kate! Kate! I'm so relieved I've found you in this crowd."

Kate turned to see the smile and twinkling eyes of her friend. She wore a muskrat collar topping a black coat and a matching bonnet. A wisp of a red curl attempted to emerge. She had always appeared lovely and well-dressed as far back as Kate remembered.

Kate bent to hug her, relieved to find a familiar face. "It's so good to see you after all these years."

Bess reached for Kate's bag. "Come, you must be freezing out here. I've hired a carriage to take us home. You've been all the way to China and back while I only made it back and forth to Wisconsin these last ten years," she said as she climbed up into the carriage after Kate.

Kate smiled. "It looks like now we'll have enough to do together right here in Chicago." She studied the streets out the window as they wound through the downtown. "How much the city has grown since I've been away." But the gray grime of the buildings, leaden skies, and grubby snow piles made Kate already miss Denver's sun, blue skies, and mountains.

Bess tugged at her sleeve. "Kate, look out this side. You'll see our new building, completed just a few years ago—it's called a *skyscraper*."

Kate craned her neck out the window and kept craning. "I've never seen such a tall building. How many stories are there?"

"Twelve! Can you imagine? It's said the Home Insurance Building is the tallest in the world, and some even taller ones are in the works here in Chicago."

Suddenly Bess pointed to the right. "About a mile down that street is the red-light district. The area is actually named Hell's Half Acre, several square blocks of brothels, saloons, and cribs."

"Cribs, even here."

"Yes, that's the area the Social Purity Department focuses on." As an afterthought, Bess added, "Would you like to come with me in the morning to find a girl who has just been let out of jail? I'm one of the editors of the *Union Signal*, so I don't go down very often, but I told one of our volunteers that I'd go and take you with me." She studied Kate's face. "That is if you aren't too tired."

"Of course. Yes, I'd love to go. That's why I've come all this way." Kate paused at the slight lack of enthusiasm in her friend's voice. *She must be going down there just for me—that's the unselfish Bess I know.* Surely Bess wasn't one of the women who was against buying a house to start Miss Willard's Anchorage?

They left the downtown business district and drove through crowded blocks of brick cottages. Here and there, Kate saw a blackened wooden house wedged between them. The houses were crammed close together. How could any of the structures have survived the great fire in seventy-one?

Bess interrupted her thoughts. "It will take you about half an hour to get to the WCTU headquarters. You'll walk a few blocks to catch the tram that will take you right downtown, within a block of LaSalle."

"I'm eager to meet everyone," Kate responded. "Will Miss Willard be there tomorrow?"

"I think she's due back from New York next week." Bess pointed out more landmarks then nodded ahead: "Here we are." She called to the driver, "Just pull in front of that red brick house next to the church."

Kate studied the small two-story house set back from the road. A fence divided it and a garden area from the muddy road. A long porch stretched across the front of the house, making it look like a smile under the eyes of two long upper windows, each highlighted by yellow-painted brick arches. Lilac bushes, not yet in bloom, lined the sides, and the leftover vines of last summer's wisteria tangled up the porch's wood columns. What a homey place.

It was already beginning to get dark, so Bess struck a match to light the oil lamp standing on a table inside the front door. She led Kate back to the kitchen. "This isn't exactly the way to treat a guest, but you'll find it warmer in the kitchen from the coal stove I stoked before I left."

"Ohhh," Kate said, breathing in something delicious coming from a kettle on the stovetop. Almost like home. "This is so nice, Bess. I am so grateful to be here with a friend. Can you imagine, Miss Willard remembered that we knew each other back in Evanston when your husband was pastoring a church there?"

"Miss Willard remembers everything!" Bess said, laughing. "Before I start dinner, you'll have to meet Jack. He's rather shy around women so it may take a while."

Kate looked around the room. Bess had a man living in her house after the death of her husband?

"There you are, Jack. Come meet my friend."

A large black cat with four white feet stretched and padded toward them from a corner of the kitchen. He looked into Kate's eyes, hesitated a moment, then proudly twitched his whiskers and slunk past her to rub against Bess' skirt.

"Well!" Kate laughed as she reached down to pet Jack's head. "I seem to have that effect on men lately."

"Listening to the stories the women on the streets tell, there are some difficult ones in this world." Bess paused as her eyes locked on a photograph on a side table.

Kate followed her gaze. The picture was of a smiling Bess with a tall man looking adoringly at her.

"But there are precious ones too." Bess turned her back to Kate and lifted the lid on the kettle. "Here," she said haltingly, "I'll dish up this stew, and we can eat right here in the kitchen."

Kate decided not to ply Bess with questions about her husband. Not yet. "Do you know what Miss Willard expects me to do here? I know I'm to head the Social Purity Department, but she didn't give many details."

"No." Bess wiped her eyes and laughed. "Miss Willard doesn't usually give details. She throws out the big picture as bait, and whoever bites gets the fish. I know she's wept over the women down on Custom House Place. She's eager for someone here to help them more than she can since she's pulled across the country so much. I suspect you'll figure out how once you've been down there a few times."

Kate nodded thoughtfully. She supposed the women in trouble here wouldn't be much different than the women on Halliday Street. "She also mentioned something about speaking to WCTU chapters?"

"Oh, yes. She sees this position as more than helping the women here in Chicago. She wants the White Ribboners all across the country to feel the same sorrow she feels for the women of shame in their towns. I suspect that's going to be a more difficult task. We seem to draw protesters at our meetings. The newspapers don't like teetotalers. If you do much speaking, you'll know what I mean."

Light from an oil lamp cast odd shadows across the picture that Bess had eyed earlier. She turned to it again, clearly out of habit.

"You miss him, don't you?" Kate asked gingerly.

"Yes." Bess grew silent a moment. "That's the last photograph of us together before he was killed by a runaway horse."

Kate wanted to ask for more details but chose to listen.

The light from the lamp flickered as Bess began to clear the table and take their emptied dishes to the sink. "He was on his way home from visiting a parishioner—" She suddenly stopped, and Kate sat quietly for a moment while her friend drew a deep breath and swallowed hard. Bess dropped her head and wiped her cheeks with her hand.

Kate studied the picture of the happy couple. You didn't have to be in the Wild West to get injured by a runaway horse. "I'm so sorry, Bess."

Bess turned back from the sink as though physically pushing her grief behind her. She smiled.

She wasn't angry or bitter. But she wasn't the shy woman Kate knew back in Evanston. She was strong. She had found some new confidence and faith and an independent spirit through this. *She's discovered how to be alone. We're both on our own. Maybe God has called us to something far beyond ourselves, a common purpose.*

"Come." Bess looped her arm through Kate's and guided her out of the kitchen to a stairway. "I'll show you your room upstairs. It will be cold up there, but I've put a feather quilt and some other blankets on the bed."

"Don't worry about me. I have a warm nightgown in my case, and when my trunk comes tomorrow, I'll have more warm clothes. You know, Denver got pretty cold in the winter too."

Bess grabbed another oil lamp to lead the way up the stairs to the bedroom on the left. Kate already felt at home in this house. The room made her feel even more so, with its braided rug and four-poster bed piled with an inviting comforter. A small writing desk under the window would be just the place for her to catch up on letters she owed. There was even a shelf for her books. She smiled to herself. Maybe she'd have time to study again.

Bess lit the tallow candles on the shelves flanking the tall mirror on the dresser and turned to leave. "I'll leave this oil lamp with you, and the candles will give you more light when you are in your room."

Kate was grateful to call it an evening and hoped her trunk would arrive early enough the next morning to unpack a little before she and Bess left for the area called Hell's Half Acre. The name stopped her: Hell's Half Acre. If it was anything like Halliday Street, the name was very fitting. She crawled into bed, her feet touching a soft towel wrapped around a hot brick.

An overwhelming sense of God's care blanketed her.

Thank You, dear Father, for going before me on this long journey. Thank You for the courage to follow Your leading, but I confess, I still have questions. I feel so uncertain about the next step, but I'm thankful You brought me here to this peaceful cottage. Thank You for Bess, who shares the same purpose I have.

Kate burrowed further under the comforter as she heard Bess coming back up the stairs to her own room. *And thank You for a hot brick to warm my cold feet.*

Although at first Kate could scarcely hear Bess move quietly around the kitchen, there was no way to dampen the loud swishing sound of coal being poured from a bucket into the stove.

Kate hadn't slept so soundly in months. She must have been feeling that she was where she was supposed to be. What a miracle that God would put her in Bess Andrew's home. When they worked with those proper young women at the Evanston Women's College, they never dreamed they'd be working together ten years later with prostitutes on the south side of Chicago.

She sat up and stretched. The room was chilly, and she quickly pulled on her clothes and boots. As she reached the kitchen, she heard Bess' soft reprimand, "Just a minute, Jack. You'll get your breakfast, but we have a doctor in the house now, so you'll have to learn to be more patient."

She turned as Kate entered the kitchen. "I hope I didn't wake you. I was just filling the water tank in the stove. I've got a roaring fire going, so it should be hot soon."

"You're going to spoil me, Bess."

"I'm the one that's spoiled. The elders have kept up this house so well. They added the modern amenities over the years since Dan and I came to Northside Presbyterian Church almost eight years ago. I never had a bathtub or inside flush toilet before."

"We didn't have those luxuries in China either. But I was spoiled living at the Gilchrists' this last year."

Morning sun poured through the kitchen window, reflecting off the photograph Bess had in her hand. She wiped the picture with the towel in her hands, but it was as if she were caressing Dan's face.

Embarrassed, Bess set it down. "Just dusting." Then, "No. The truth is I miss him. We were so happy. He never stopped loving me, even when I lost both our babies, even when there was never another one." She fell silent. Kate waited. "I often wondered, if Dan had not been killed by that runaway horse, whether there might have been another opportunity to have a baby. But at almost forty-one?"

Kate followed Bess as she carried a tray loaded with a coffeepot and cups and returned them to a cupboard in the sitting room.

"Dan and I entertained a lot of parishioners in here. He often sat in that blue chair there in front of the fireplace, praying with grieving parents or with an abused wife." She turned to Kate. "Do you know how much abuse happens right in the church? Women have come into this room with blackened eyes and bloody noses." Her voice broke. "Dan wept with them, promised he'd pray for them. He struggled. He wanted to do more than send them back home to their husbands with the promise that he'd pray for them."

Kate nodded. "I know what you're talking about. I saw the same kind of treatment in China. I bandaged up many a woman there and in Denver—women who had been brutalized by a drunken husband

151

and thrown out of the house, women who would weep in shame that they had to sell their bodies to buy food for their children."

"Somehow, Kate, it's easier for me to sympathize with those Christian wives who are battered than with the women on the streets selling their bodies to strangers." Bess paused. "Perhaps with your experience, you'll help me understand and empathize with this girl we're going to look for today."

Kate nodded slowly, soberly. "It's not easy. Sometimes I don't know which is worse, their immorality and shame, or the filth—the bodily grime and odor." Kate stopped as memories of Maggie flashed through her mind. "Do you know anything more about this young girl we're to pick up this morning?"

"Just that she's fourteen years old, her name is Huldah Baudisch, and she's being dropped off near an address in Hell's Half Acre."

Dropped off by whom? Kate followed Bess back to the kitchen, where she had already mixed pancake batter and coffee percolated on the stove. Efficiently, Bess poured the batter with one hand and the coffee with her other. Kate reached for a cup to help.

"Just sit down, Kate. You'll have plenty to do once you've settled in. I'm almost sorry we have to go out so soon after your long journey."

"I'm ready." Kate smiled.

Bess frowned. "Just be prepared to see some ugly things. We're going to the worst part of Chicago's red-light district. We never know just where the police will drop off the girls from jail."

Kate practically winced. So the police were part of the problem here too.

"The address in the paper is right down there on Custom House Place. I've only been there a few times. It's a narrow lane, lined with brothels and saloons."

"Do you have any idea how a fourteen-year-old girl could end up there?"

"No." Bess looked Kate in the eye. "But Mary Hasting's brothel is on the same street, and I'm praying this girl didn't escape from there. Mary's pimps roam the streets and don't stop looking for any girl or woman who escapes them. I don't think even meeting a police wagon would stop them from snatching back someone they claimed was theirs. And Kate, they don't like interference either."

Kate sensed the fear in Bess' voice: fear and disdain. She remembered her own uncertainty when she first went on the streets. *I can tell we'll be good for each other.* Bess knew how to get around in Chicago—and the WCTU headquarters—and Kate knew a little of how to work with prostitutes to see God change their lives.

Loud pounding on the front door gave Kate a start.

"I believe," Bess said, "your trunk has arrived."

The trunk was the least of Kate's worries now. She was already wondering how to navigate Mary Hasting's pimps and Hell's Half Acre.

16
Huldah

"You look prepared to face that cold lake wind today," Bess said approvingly. "We'll have to walk several blocks to catch the State Street cable car. Once we get off at Harrison, we have a walk of four or five blocks more to Custom House Place."

Kate nodded. "The lane with the brothels and saloons."

"Yes, only I hope we'll get there before the pimps do."

"So you're not always sure you'll actually encounter the women who are released?"

"No, but at least we have a specific address this time, 249 Customs House Place, which puts her right in the middle of Hell's Half Acre."

"How often do you go?"

"Only when there's no one else to go. And never alone," Bess confided. "Miss Willard has warned us not to go without a companion."

Kate nodded. "Good advice." She thought about her own narrow escape from Blonger in Denver.

"It doesn't look so bad in the daytime." Bess sounded almost apologetic, trying to reassure Kate.

"Really?"

"For several blocks, almost every building on either side of Customs House Place appears to be a saloon, but most are just an excuse for a brothel—though liquor abounds. The saloons and brothels go hand-in-hand really. That's why Miss Willard wants to expand the Social Purity Department, even if her wealthy board members are against it." She cast a pointed look. "Strongly against it."

"I am sorry to hear there is such a struggle between the women at the national headquarters." Kate pointed to the black bag on her arm. "But I'm ready to help. Where there are brothels and saloons, there's usually someone who needs help."

Bess led the way out the door, to the corner, and onto a cable car.

"Hold your nose," Bess instructed. "We're crossing the Chicago River. Some people call this the Stinking River because of the sewage and pollution from all the industry upstream. It's terrible today."

Kate didn't need to be told about the bad odor. She'd already noticed the stench and had pulled her scarf over her nose.

"We hope it will get better. I hear they are planning to reverse the river so the sewage flows into a sanitation canal instead of into Lake Michigan. I can't believe that will ever really happen." Bess covered her nose again.

The car inched slowly down State Street. "If Hell's Half Acre is so notorious," Kate asked, "are the police aware of what's going on? Or ..." She suspected she already knew the answer.

Bess cleared her throat and looked at the passengers around them. She shook her head at Kate and spoke softly. "The police are often actually part of the problem. They protect the brothel owners, warning them of raids and expecting favors in return. How else could Mary Hastings openly carry on a three-story brothel on Customs House Place? She's the worst madam of all. We've been told she travels the Midwest looking for girls as young as thirteen, promising them nonexistent jobs in her 'restaurant.'"

Thirteen? Despite her experience, Kate hadn't heard of this kind of debauchery.

"One girl escaped with the help of the police several years ago." Bess leaned toward Kate's ear. "She was so traumatized that she couldn't even speak. It was weeks before her protectors pieced together what happened."

"The poor child."

Bess lowered her voice to a barely audible whisper. "The girl described being brought to 'the mansion,' locked up on the top floor, stripped, and repeatedly raped by the madam's professional rapists. The girl said the madam told her she did that to"—Bess spoke between clenched teeth—"to break in the girls."

Kate put her hand over her mouth as if she'd tasted something foul. She wanted to speed the car faster, to find Huldah before such a horrible deed happened to her. She tried to ignore the lump of fear that came to her throat.

Bess pulled the cord to alert the driver to stop at the next street.

"Hang on to your bag," Bess said. She pulled a piece of paper from her pocket to check the address once again. "Two thirty-nine should be about four blocks ahead on the other side of the street. Let's check, though, to be sure. Here."

Kate followed Beth into Schultz's Bakery on the corner. The smell of baked bread was a welcome break from the Stinking River they had crossed to get here.

"Hello!" Bess called back toward the kitchen. A short man with a genial smile and bushy mustache came from the kitchen at the back of the shop. He wiped flour-covered hands on his apron. "Ah, madam," he said with a heavy German accent. "How can I help you? I've just taken some delicious *kaffee-kuchen* from the oven."

"Thank you, Mr. Schultz," Bess responded, "but we're just looking for an address—239 Customs House Place."

"Ach, you shouldn't go to Kelly's Saloon. That's a bad place for a good young woman like you."

"We're looking for a young girl." Bess flushed red in embarrassment.

"We're to meet this girl when the police drop her off there," Kate intervened. "We saw her name in the newspaper yesterday. This girl, Huldah Baudisch, is only fourteen. We want to help her before—"

"Huldah!" Mr. Schultz interrupted. "Her family lives on Polk Street. She's a nice little girl. Her mother sometimes sends her to see if I have any leftover bread. You know—bread that I have not sold by the end of the day. She sometimes sweeps out the shop or helps my wife wash baking pans to pay for whatever I give her. I feel sorry for her."

"Why is that?" Kate asked.

"Her papa is a mean man—especially when he drinks. He drinks in the saloon down the street. Huldah always seems hungry; all the children in that family go hungry, never enough to eat."

Bess frowned. "Why would she give her address as Customs House Place? I've heard of that saloon—it's just a front for a brothel."

"*Ach, das ist schade.*" Mr. Schultz shook his head. "I don't know. She came here about a month ago looking for work. She said her father told her she couldn't go back to school. He chased her out of the house and told her that she had to get a job." Mr. Schultz turned

157

to call back to the kitchen, "Lisle, *als Huldah das letzte Mal hier war, erzählte sie uns nicht, dass ihre Mutter gerade ein Baby bekommen hatte?*"

"*Ya,*" a woman's voice called back.

"I asked my wife if Huldah's mama had another baby. My wife doesn't speak English, so she just works in the back," Mr. Schulz said with a nod toward the kitchen. "Ya, Huldah asked if she could work because her mama just had another baby and they needed more money. I told her we didn't need anybody. But I gave her some fresh bread before she left that afternoon."

"That explains how she ended up on Custom House Place," Bess muttered. She turned to Kate. "Like I explained, the place is an alley between Clark and Dearborn, lined with saloons and brothels." She turned back to Mr. Schultz. "What is the shortest way to get there?"

He explained the directions as he wrapped some warm bread in paper for them.

Kate tucked the bread into her bag and hurried after Bess, already out the door. On Customs House Place, Kate looked warily at the men lounging against the buildings.

Bess picked up her pace even more briskly but spoke steadily and quietly as she walked. "You can tell by the curtains on the windows and the women's names on the doorplates that many of these are cribs."

Yes. Kate was familiar with the shades still drawn till late in the day.

Bess hesitated as they passed an alley, then stepped back. Someone huddled behind a trash can, head down, arms clasping knees.

Sobs. Kate and Bess looked at each other and edged toward the figure.

Kate dropped to the ground. "Are you all right? Can we help you?"

A girl raised her blotchy face, eyes red and puffy. As she struggled to stand, her thin coat flopped open to reveal a sheer, sparkling red dress with a low bodice.

She couldn't be more than thirteen or fourteen years old. Kate felt Bess drop to the ground beside her. They looked at one another, and Kate knew they were thinking the same thing.

"Huldah?"

The girl looked up, fear in her eyes. She must have thought they were from the brothel to take her back.

Bess asked, "What happened to you, Huldah?"

"How do you know my name?" the girl whispered, inching back. She began to cry again.

"It's okay," Bess soothed. "I'm Mrs. Andrew and this is Dr. Bushnell—we're here to help you, to get you away from here." She reached to pat Huldah's shoulder. The girl seemed to shiver with fear as much as the cold. "If we walk over to State Street," Bess said to Kate over one shoulder, "we can hire a carriage to take us to the WCTU Reading Room."

Huldah pulled away.

"It's a safe place," Bess assured.

Kate bent down to look Huldah in the eyes. She kept her voice soft and brushed a strand of hair from the girl's face. "We need to get you away from here. The people who did this to you will be looking for you. We want to help you get away from them. Do you understand?"

Huldah nodded.

Bess ran ahead to hail a carriage as a police van drove slowly by. Huldah whimpered and hid her face against Kate's shoulder.

"It's all right," Kate smoothed the girl's knotted hair. "We won't let them pick you up again." But just then the van stopped a little ahead of them. Kate blanched. Where was Bess? *Are they going to pick me up?* A policeman rushed out.

Kate hugged Huldah more tightly against her as the policeman stepped toward them. Then he turned and banged on the door of the next building with his billy club. "Get up, Flossie," he growled. "Let me in."

Kate jerked into action, propelling Huldah ahead and past the police van to catch up to Bess, who waved from the steps of a carriage she'd stopped. Bess reached for Huldah's hand.

"Up, my girl."

Kate scanned the street one more time before climbing in after them. Bess was right. The police shared in the favors. They probably helped round up any runaways too. Just like Denver. What would it take to stop this? The state government? Weren't there laws against such things?

Huldah sank back into the carriage seat between Bess and Kate. Bess reached for a blanket from the bench and drew it around the girl's shoulders.

This shivering was from more than cold, Kate knew. It was shock. She reached down to move the hot bricks the driver had placed on the carriage floor closer to Huldah's feet.

"Where are you taking me?" Huldah finally sputtered. "What is the ... Reading Room?"

Kate put her arm around the shivering girl. "Someplace where you can be safe." She paused and turned Huldah's face to hers. "Do you want to go back home?"

Huldah jerked back. "No! No, I can't go there. Please, no."

"All right." Kate squeezed Huldah's shoulder. "All right. We'll go where it's warm and quiet. You'll be safe until we can find the right place for you to stay." Kate and Bess exchanged knowing glances. Kate didn't know Chicago like Bess did, but she knew how such scenarios had played out in Denver. This child needed their help, but no girl would be welcomed in such an indecent red dress, no matter how traumatized she was.

17
Huldah's Story

"We're almost there." Kate patted Huldah's knee reassuringly. The girl shivered under her touch.

"You can have a warm bath and some food, and we'll find you some clean clothes," Bess said.

Huldah hung her head and stared at the floorboards of the carriage.

Bess tried to get her to talk. "Should we send a message to someone—brothers or sisters—that you are all right?"

Huldah shook her head.

"How long were you in jail?"

"You know I was in jail?" Huldah searched Bess' face.

Bess nodded. "We knew you were getting out of jail. That's why we came—we came looking to rescue you."

"Yes," Kate said. "Yes, that is what we are trying to do, to rescue girls caught down here."

Huldah seemed to measure Kate's words. "Six days," she said. "I think six days."

Kate pressed gently, "Why did the judge send you to jail?"

"He said I was street-walking."

"Were you?"

"No." The tears began again. "No." Huldah was sobbing. "I just want to go home to Mama, but Papa won't let me come back home without money."

Kate pulled the blanket closer around Huldah as the girl burrowed into her shoulder.

"I've heard these stories before," Kate whispered to Bess. "She probably stopped at Kelly's Saloon, looking for a job like she did at the Schultz's."

At the sound of "Kelly's" Huldah lifted her head, nodded, then wiped the back of her hand under her sniffling nose. "He wouldn't give me money. He said I owed for rent and ..." She bent her head again. "And for this awful dress."

Bess called to the driver. "Turn here, please. We're just around the corner." She dug in her purse for coins to pay the driver.

Bess hopped down. "We'll just stop here first for a bath and to eat, and then we'll go to the Reading Room." She led the way through the house to the warm kitchen.

"The water in the tank is hot," Bess announced as she poured a bucket of coal into the stove. "You can show Huldah where the washroom is."

Huldah's eyes opened wide as Kate poured hot water into the gleaming white tub.

"You can put your clothes on the washstand," Kate said, "and here's some soap and a towel." She smoothed Huldah's hair again for reassurance, adding, "I think it would be good if you washed your hair too."

Back in the kitchen, Kate met Bess' questioning eyes with a half-smile. "She's obviously never seen a bathroom with a tub and inside toilet before. So what about clothes? Surely everything I have would be way too long."

"Back at the Reading Room we have used clothes, but she'll need something to put on before then. She can't wear that red dress again. I don't think even Jack would approve!" Bess chuckled. "I know what you're thinking. She's even shorter than I am. But maybe she could wear a skirt and a blouse of mine just till we get to the Reading Room—and I'll find a pair of bloomers she can have. I'll run up and get them."

Kate tapped on the bathroom door. "Huldah, Mrs. Andrew is going to lend you some clothes."

Kate heard a splash and then, "I don't have to put on that red dress?"

"No," Kate said. "You don't ever have to wear that red dress again." She heard another splash. Then she turned back to the kitchen and opened her bag to pull out the fresh bread from Schultz's Bakery. She sliced the fragrant loaf into thick pieces as Bess returned to season the chicken soup simmering on the stove.

"What should we do with her?" Bess asked softly. "By the time we give her some food ..."

"And we get her story ..." Kate added.

"It will be too late to go to the Reading Room today. She can't stay there overnight. Everyone has to leave by six. We'll have to figure out a place for her to go."

"It doesn't sound as though she can go home without money or a job," Kate said as she reached for bowls, cups, and saucers from the sideboard. She set them down, then leaned forward, resting her hands on the table. "What do you think she's doing in there so long?"

Bess grinned. "Probably trying to make some sense and semblance of the outlandish outfit I've offered."

"That bad, huh?"

Bess' eyes twinkled mischievously as if to say *wait and see.*

"Do you think," Kate broached, "it would be all right for Huldah to stay here tonight, perhaps in the living room? You said the Reading Room frowns on taking girls home unless it's for a job, but we can't put her out on the street." Kate looked at Bess for approval but halfway didn't expect it. She didn't know if Bess would approve of bringing the wayward home as Josephine Butler was doing in England. Maybe this was expecting too much.

Bess nodded. "I have extra blankets and a pillow. Huldah can sleep on the sofa."

Just then, Huldah stepped into the kitchen, the disdained red dress wadded under one arm, the other arm hitching the bunched-up top of Bess' skirt to her side. She had tried to belt the skirt into place, but it wasn't working.

Kate fought back a chuckle. Huldah's dark brown hair, the color of walnuts, hung in wet strings to her shoulders. Her sweet heart-shaped face had been scrubbed so clean that her cheeks glowed red. For a moment, Kate thought how Huldah could be an innocent waif playing dress-up in her mother's clothes. Then she looked into the girl's eyes. They should have been sparkling with life and laughter. Instead, they were dull and lifeless, as though a flame inside had been extinguished.

"Well, young lady," Bess broke the silence, "you certainly look a lot better. Did you enjoy your bath?"

"Yes, ma'am."

"Come, sit here at the table." Bess gestured to her place. "I'll take that dress. You don't want it anymore, do you?"

"Oh no, ma'am!"

"So I'll just throw it into the stove, and we'll enjoy its heat." Bess tamped the dress deep into the burning coals with the shovel. The fire licked greedily at it as she announced, "Now let's eat, and then we can talk about how to get you home."

Huldah froze.

"Don't worry." Kate eyed Bess. "Let's thank God for what we have right now—this food and warm house and time together."

Huldah folded her hands like a little child as Kate began to pray.

"Lord, we thank Thee for bringing Huldah here safely, and for protecting her from further abuse today, and for this food for our bodies. In Jesus' name, amen."

Kate passed the plate of bread to Huldah, who took a slice and immediately started tearing off pieces and stuffing them into her mouth.

Bess caught Kate's eye across the table. "There's a lot more soup," she said, "when you've finished with that, Huldah."

"Bess, you are such a wonderful cook," Kate said, and then explained to Huldah, "I just arrived from Denver yesterday by train."

Huldah shook her head, her eyes glued to her bowl.

"Do you know where Denver is?"

Huldah shook her head again. She ate in silence.

"Let's see if Jack will come out and see us," Bess said.

Huldah looked up, alarmed. "Jack?"

"Here, Jack," Bess called.

Jack grudgingly appeared, and Huldah went back to staring into her bowl, now empty.

Bess reached for Huldah's bowl. "Let's get you some more." She stepped to the stove, filled the bowl with more thick soup, and returned it to Huldah, who said only "thank you" and ate again in silence.

When Bess started to clear the table, Huldah jumped up. "I can wash the dishes for you."

"That would be a great help."

They carried their bowls and tableware to the sink. Bess poured steaming water from the kettle into a basin, and Huldah went about the task as though she'd done it before.

"Did you help your mother at home like this?" Kate asked as she picked up a dishtowel to dry the dishes.

"Yes, ma'am." Huldah kept her head down.

"Are you the oldest child in your family?"

"Yes." She was quiet again, then added, "I have four brothers and … and one baby sister." A tear slipped down her cheek. "But I don't even know her name. She was born the day my father chased me out of the house to look for work."

"I'm so sorry." Bess put a hand on Huldah's shoulder, then busied herself putting away the dishes and lighting the kerosene lamp. The kitchen had begun to grow dark as a heavy cloud cover rolled in. An idea flashed in Kate's mind. She would record as much of this as she could for Miss Willard. Kate excused herself to go upstairs for a notebook and pen. When she returned, Bess and Huldah were seated at the table again.

"This is the warmest room in the house, so we'll just stay here if that's all right with you," Bess said.

Kate nodded and sat down. "Has Mrs. Andrew explained our plan for the night?"

Huldah nodded.

"We want to have time tomorrow to get you some suitable clothes at the Reading Room and then help you find work."

Huldah just nodded her head as if in assent.

"You can help us first by telling how you got to Kelly's Saloon and what happened there." Kate reached over and took one of Huldah's hands in hers. She spoke in her softest tones. "I know this will be difficult, but the more we know of what's happening to women and girls like you, the more we can help."

Huldah stared blankly at the table.

"Huldah," Kate tried again, "do you understand that you can help other girls from being treated as you were? You can keep girls like your sister and mother from being hurt too. But we have to know how these things happen. Will you help us?"

Huldah looked Kate in the eyes and nodded. The flame in the

165

kerosene lamp burned tall—like a tiny lighthouse. *Lord, help us light her way.* The light flickered. For the first time since they'd met, Huldah's brown eyes flickered with something too. *Safety? Hope?* Kate wondered. Or was it determination?

"'Get out of here! Go earn your keep!' Father yelled. The day he threw me out, he hollered, 'I can't feed another mouth.'" Huldah slowly began pouring out her painful story. "He looked at my mother the way he does when he strikes her, and ..." Huldah sobbed, "and at my new baby sister in her arms." Huldah paused a moment and took a deep breath. "He shouted at her, 'All you can do is bring me another kid to feed.'"

Huldah put her face in her hands for a moment. She raised her head and said softly, "Then he pointed at me and screamed, 'You can just forget about school. You go get a job.' He couldn't even remember how old I was." The girl grew silent again.

Bess handed Huldah her handkerchief. "Just take your time."

Huldah continued, the hurt in her voice obvious. "He asked me, 'How old are you anyway? Fifteen? Fourteen? I've lost count with so many of you around. Get out. Earn some money to help your ma feed all these kids.'" Her father's bitterness rang in her tone.

Through tears, Huldah told how she'd stood at the door, terrorized that her father would hit her if she moved. "I asked him to just let me get my coat. Then I told Mama not to worry, that I'd find some work and be back soon."

"Oh, Huldah," Bess cried, putting her hand on the girl's arm.

But Huldah hadn't found work. She walked for blocks, visiting every bakery, restaurant, and clothing factory until she came to Custom House Place.

"The men on the street there called me nasty names. They tried to pull me down to where they were lying against the building. I was afraid. I tore myself away and ran into the first door."

Kate stopped writing for a moment. "And right into Mike Kelly's saloon. You thought you were safe, didn't you?"

Huldah nodded. Kate could hardly hear her as she went on. "Kelly offered me work as a waitress. But when I saw the red dresses the other waitresses wore, I knew I was in the wrong place. It didn't feel right, but I told myself if I worked hard serving the food and beer, I could keep away from trouble. I'd try for just that night. I moved fast and was able to steer clear of the men who tried to reach under my skirt and pinch me."

Huldah grew distant for a moment, as though reliving the memory. "The saloon stayed open until midnight, and the men got louder. They began to call me 'sweetie' and 'honey.'" The girl shivered. "When the last customer left, I changed back into my clothes and waited for Kelly to pay me. Instead, he took me to the stairs at the back of the room."

"It's so late," he told me. "I can't let you walk home at this hour."

"I was really afraid then. I told him, 'My mother will worry. I'll just take a cab with the money I've earned.'"

"Kelly told me, 'I don't pay my waitresses until the end of the week, depending on how many tips they have earned.'"

Huldah described how he opened the door and forced her up the stairs. "'You'll be comfortable here,' he told me, but his voice scared me. 'You may even be surprised at how much you'll like it. We give our waitresses all the comforts they desire.'"

"He shoved me into a tiny bedroom and lit the lamp on the table. He locked the door behind him when he left."

Kate stopped Huldah when she started to tell how men in the saloon would pick out the girl of choice and nod to Kelly to visit her in her room. Kate knew what went on in those rooms. It was a wonder Huldah could escape.

"Kelly never paid me. He said I owed him money for my room and food. He showed us a book where he wrote down what each of us owed him."

"He kept a ledger of accounts for each girl?" Kate was incredulous.

Huldah hesitated. "I don't know what a ... a ledger is, but he said if we worked harder and served more customers, he would pay us more to pay off what we owed him."

"Last week, I decided to try to run home. I'd rather get a beating from my father than stay there. In the afternoon, I hid my coat in an empty garbage can at the back door when Kelly's pimps weren't around." Huldah hung her head. "When he was busy with customers at the bar, I slipped out the back door and tried to hide the dress under the coat, but then that policeman saw me." Huldah blinked back a tear.

The bedside candle had been snuffed out for nearly an hour, but Kate kept tossing and turning beneath the feather quilts. She was bone weary after the long emotional day and still tired from her journey from Denver. But Huldah's story kept replaying in her mind. *Get out of here. Go earn your keep.* How could any father yell at his daughter so? Kate wondered why an honest policeman—one who wouldn't return a girl to Kelly's Saloon in exchange for a "favor"—hadn't recognized an innocent, helpless, frightened child?

"Oh, God." She began to weep. "Why do You allow this evil? Why don't these men realize that You value a girl as much as You value them?"

Kate rolled over and pulled the quilt up around her neck. That was one of the problems, she thought. Those men thought that they were worthless too, working meaningless jobs for twelve hours a day, drinking their wages up before they even got home to frightened wives and hungry children. They all needed God.

She raised her hands to pray aloud. "Perhaps no one has ever told them that they are valuable, Lord, that You love them too? So why *should* they think that such a sweet little virgin is more than a body to be used for their own pleasure? Is there any way to convince them? Is there something else I could do?"

"Mama!"

The shriek from downstairs made Kate start, but before she could get out of bed, she heard Bess running down the stairs to comfort Huldah in her nightmare.

18
The Anchorage Opens

"I didn't think we would find a job for Huldah so quickly." Kate took off her bonnet and unbuttoned her coat. "Did you know Mrs. James' husband had started to manufacture light bulbs in his shop?"

Bess shook her head. "No. She's only been volunteering at the Reading Room a few months. But she treats the women kindly, always asking them about their families and whether they need anything. Did you notice how quickly she spoke up when she heard Huldah couldn't go home until she had a job?"

"That did my heart good."

The two women had come directly from taking Huldah to her home to the LaSalle Street headquarters, where Kate would attend her first Chicago WCTU meeting. She rubbed her neck. She hadn't expected her first few days in Chicago to be this full of drama. She was bone weary but was making a difference.

"Wasn't it the most exciting thing you've ever seen when Huldah's mother opened the door and found her there—safe, dressed in a warm coat? She thought Huldah was dead, and then to have her show up on her doorstep! I don't think I'll ever forget her mother's face."

"I just hope it lasts."

Something in Bess' tone surprised Kate. Was this her same friend who was teasing Huldah in the parsonage last night? Before she could ask, they entered the noisy room energized with the hum of women's voices.

Kate whispered, "Are there always this many here?"

"The Central Chicago union is one of the largest, probably because Miss Willard has her offices here." Bess pulled on Kate's sleeve. "There's Mrs. Carse, the president of the union here in Chicago. Come, I'll introduce you before everything starts."

Kate followed Bess, who was full of information this afternoon. "She's building a massive office complex which will house the WCTU publishing house. She calls it the Temperance Temple. She's chairman of the WCTU board and in charge of everything that goes on around here, so it's wise to meet her. She will want to be the one to introduce you to everyone else."

Mrs. Carse looked like someone in charge. She wore an elegantly tailored suit in a color that could only be described as royal purple. She stood out in the crowd as the only woman without a hat—besides Kate. A head taller than those who crowded around, she had piercing, intelligent eyes that continued to survey the room even as she greeted women eager to shake hands with the president.

"She is wealthy, a widow who can hold her own as a businesswoman in a man's world," Bess whispered.

Kate looked at Bess and gave a wan smile. "That means she can be outspoken and aggressive." She stopped. "She looks so busy before the meeting, Bess. Why don't we wait until later?" Kate couldn't explain it but felt unusually intimidated by this strong woman.

"Oh, Kate, she knows me well. She often asks me to write articles about her projects and board activities for the *Union Signal*. Mrs. Carse owns the publishing company that prints our weekly paper. She appreciates good publicity anytime. Maybe I've made her sound worse than she is."

Bess wormed her way through the group of women milling about. "Mrs. Carse, I would like to introduce Dr. Katharine Bushnell, just arrived from Denver to lead the new Social Purity Department."

Mrs. Carse reached out a gloved hand in welcome, but Kate sensed something unfriendly in her gaze, almost resentful. *She reminds me of Eloise Haskins. It's that look that she disapproves of me—but I have no idea why.*

"Good evening, Dr. Bushnell. Welcome to Chicago." Though they stood almost eye-to-eye, Kate couldn't help but feel Mrs. Carse looked down on her.

A bell rang, calling for the women to take their seats and for the meeting to begin.

"Excuse me," Mrs. Carse apologized, withdrew her hand, and turned quickly to walk up onto the platform.

Kate and Bess took their seats. Kate felt increasingly annoyed by the business as usual—the unimportant announcements, the introduction of special guests. She was impatient to get to the purpose of the meeting, but she had to admit that Mrs. Carse handled everything with exquisite professionalism, keeping everyone on time and to the point. Nevertheless, Kate was still uncomfortable.

Bess sensed her unease. "What is it, Kate?" she asked when they were in the carriage making their way home.

"I have the feeling Mrs. Carse doesn't like me, or ... maybe it's what I'm coming here to do? Have you heard her talk about the Social Purity Department?"

Bess smoothed her coat across her lap. "Well, I've heard some talk in the office that she and a few others feel this new department is just one more distraction from our primary focus—to abolish liquor and stop drunkenness. 'It's just another of Miss Willard's countless projects.'" She mimicked the faceless "others." "There was actually some talk that she and Mrs. Phelps, the vice president, were going to veto Miss Willard's latest plan—but you know Miss Willard. She manages to get her way."

"And this Mrs. Phelps? Who is she?"

"Lucille Phelps' husband is the president of Phelps and Fisher Bank. He is Mrs. Carse's banker and also handles the WCTU funds."

Kate threw her head back against the leather bench. "Oh. I'm beginning to see why Miss Willard invited me to head up the Social Purity Department and start this Anchorage. Is she hoping that I can convince these wealthy women—who probably have ways of controlling the funds—that helping the women down in Hell's Half Acre is worth their money?"

"Well, it's not just those two women, Kate. You haven't seen all the other projects Miss Willard starts. Whether they're good or not, they take money and energy from our prime cause."

"But Bess, working with the women down in Hell's Half Acre is part of our prime cause. We just saw how Huldah's drunken father actually drove her out of the house and into the arms of the brothel. Doesn't it make sense that the two go together, the problems of the saloons and prostitution?"

Bess looked out the window, then back at Kate. "What if Huldah is an exception? What if ... what if she goes back to the brothels?"

"You can't believe that, Bess!"

"I don't know, Kate. Some of the WCTU members feel most of these women we are trying to rescue have brought their troubles upon themselves. They don't *have* to go to work in the saloons. I confess, I wouldn't keep a girl like that in my home, not like Mrs. Butler has done in England."

"But you did just last night. What about Huldah?"

"Huldah ... well, Huldah's just a child."

"If that's the way so many women and even Mrs. Carse feel, it will be difficult to see Miss Willard's dream of the Anchorage come about." It was Kate's turn to look out the window. "I can't do this job alone." She turned back to her friend. "Bess, I'll need the help of your influence at the *Union Signal* to get out the message of what we're trying to do here. We can change things, but we have to change minds first."

Bess fell silent and studied her hands in her lap.

Kate followed suit. *Lord, we may be headed the same direction, but we are seeing completely different ways of getting there. Your Word must be my guide.* She closed her eyes and a favorite passage from Jeremiah thirty-one came to mind. She whispered it almost silently. "For they shall all know me, from the least of them unto the greatest of them, saith the Lord: for I will forgive their iniquity, and I will remember their sin no more." *God, You care for these broken women as much as You care for me. I've had all the advantages ... don't they deserve to know You too?*

"I'll take you down to headquarters so you can find your way around and meet everyone working there," Bess said cheerfully as she set their breakfast dishes in the sink and turned back to Kate at the kitchen table. "Unfortunately, Miss Willard won't be back yet, but we can find a place for you to work. Since her office is just down the hall from mine, you might camp in there until—"

A knock drew Bess' attention to the door.

"I'll get it." Kate was surprised that the envelope from the messenger was addressed to her—and even more surprised to find who sent it.

"I was asked to wait for your reply, ma'am," the messenger said.

What could be so urgent? Kate began reading.

> Dear Dr. Bushnell,
> I will be at the WCTU headquarters this afternoon. If you are able, I would appreciate meeting with you at 2 p.m.
> Sincerely,
> Matilda Carse

Kate scribbled a note and handed it back to the messenger. She returned to the kitchen, forehead drawn in puzzlement.

"Is everything okay?"

"That message was from Mrs. Carse—she asked to meet with me this afternoon. What do you think that's about?" Kate paced to the window and back.

"Maybe she just wants to get to know you better."

"No." Kate looked at Bess. "No, it's more than that. I imagine she wants to size me up or set some things straight."

"What?"

"I sensed it last night. As I said, I think she resents my coming."

Bess thought on this a moment. "Well, perhaps she's upset because Miss Willard didn't take her advice."

"Surely she isn't that small."

Bess laughed. "Of course, it could be that she wants some free medical advice."

Kate smiled. "Maybe. But Mrs. Carse doesn't strike me as the kind of woman who wants advice from anyone."

The LaSalle Street headquarters surged with energy.

"I'll just be a couple hours in the editorial meeting," Bess said, "but you're in good hands with our volunteers."

"Here," Kate's young guide offered, "I'll show you Miss Willard's office—it's just at the end of the hall."

Though there was much to look at—framed photographs and pictures covering almost every bit of wall space—a grandfather clock in the corner of the office arrested Kate's glance. It was almost two o'clock. Kate turned to her guide. "I have an appointment with Mrs. Carse in a few minutes. Do you know where I might find her?"

"Yes, she asked me to let her know when you arrived. She plans to join you here in Miss Willard's office. I'll go tell her that you are here."

Of course Mrs. Carse would monitor Kate's comings and goings at the headquarters. Kate walked slowly around the office to study the photographs. Oliver Wendell Holmes ... *I remember he was Miss Willard's favorite poet.* And President Grover Cleveland, a teetotaler. *Didn't she become friends with his wife?* There was Dwight L. Moody, the evangelist. *I'd forgotten Miss Willard preached in his campaigns for a time.* How Miss Willard liked to surround herself with reminders of the poets and presidents and preachers she had met. And there was a photo of her assistant, Anna Gordon.

Another photograph, of a woman smiling slightly with a large cameo brooch at her neck and her hair in ringlets, caught Kate's attention. "Harriet Beecher Stowe," she read from a signature scrawled across the bottom. "I remember reading *Uncle Tom's Cabin.*" Kate mused. "And Miss Willard has her signed photograph! I wonder how they met?"

At Miss Willard's desk, Kate smiled. It was piled high with papers, with more stacks alongside it on the floor. So familiar. Miss Willard always had so much going on—how did she keep up with everything?

"Dr. Bushnell."

Kate turned toward the imperious voice calling from the door.

"I am glad you were able to come." Mrs. Carse moved directly and assuredly to shake Kate's hand, then seated herself in Miss Willard's chair at the desk. "Please, sit down."

Kate moved papers off a guest chair in the corner and sat to face Mrs. Carse, surprised—and yet not—at the authority she assumed.

Mrs. Carse came right to the point. "Miss Willard is delighted that she found someone to help her with the Social Purity Department." She eyed the paper stacks with a lifted brow. "She is overloaded. I don't know why she thinks she has to take on all these pet projects." She looked Kate in the eye. "She has asked me to help you get another one started. Perhaps she has told you about her idea for a house for these street women to stay?"

Pet project? Was that all she thought of Miss Willard's dream? Kate nodded. "Yes," she said cautiously. "She's envisioned a safe pla—"

Mrs. Carse pressed on. "So you know she wants a place where women can be taken until they find work or go home, not anything like what Josephine Butler is doing in England. Thank goodness." She paused. "You know of Josephine Butler? How she actually takes these women into her home and somehow believes women of this nature will not fall right back into sin?"

"Yes. And they can change; they do. I've seen it. I can tell you about—"

Mrs. Carse interrupted again. "I have agreed to pay the rent for one year—more or less as a test. Against my better judgment, I am afraid. Frankly, I don't think these women will change, even if they are pampered. But as chairman of her board, I have agreed to help to see if her experiment will work," she said dismissively. "Find something appropriate down in the red-light district. I will not pay for the expenses to operate the home. I believe that the WCTU women should take some responsibility. Do you have any questions?"

Kate drew a breath and sat up straight, pushing her hair back from her forehead. "I'll be more than happy to find a house. I believe Mrs. Andrew knows the area well and should be able to help me." She paused. *God, give me courage.* "You've heard that Mrs. Butler started a House of Rest in England. It's been quite successful and a sort of model for what we'd like to do here."

Mrs. Carse looked out the window.

Kate drew another breath. *Please, God, help me say this right.* "Since I'll be visiting women in the red-light district and speaking to the WCTU unions about helping us fund the Anchorage and starting Reading Rooms of their own—"

"Yes, go on." Mrs. Carse was impatient.

"We'll need someone in charge at the refuge itself, someone who can take care of meals, help the women with ... Someone who understands the problems they face."

"And?"

"And I believe I have just the right person."

"The right person?"

"Yes. Her name is Bertha Lyons. She was one of the women we rescued in Denver—"

Mrs. Carse put up a hand as though to stop Kate, but Kate continued, determined to speak her mind.

"Bertha is remarkable. She turned her life around. She is faithful and devoted to helping other women turn their lives around too. She brings a wealth of understanding and could be such a help to us." Kate paused, her heart pounding in her chest. *Should I do this? Dare I ask her, Lord?* She looked back at Mrs. Carse, deciding that this woman would not intimidate her. "Would you be willing to pay for Bertha's train ticket from Denver so that she can come and manage things in the house?"

Mrs. Carse remained silent a moment, looking past Kate at some of the paper stacks on the floor. When she looked up again, Kate detected almost a sense of longing there.

Maybe she wanted to believe and hadn't seen the transformation with her own eyes?

But Mrs. Carse shook her head and stood up. "I have always believed these women have a lower nature and easily fall victim to the demands of men," she said as she made her way to the door.

She paused at the door, her head hanging to one side as though listening. To her conscience? "I haven't changed my mind that this is a risky experiment, Dr. Bushnell, but if this Lyons woman is all you say she is, perhaps she can reach her kind better than our WCTU ladies." She turned back to Kate. "I will pay for her train fare, and I will give you one year—one year—to prove that I am right."

She turned and walked briskly down the hall.

"A year," Kate said to herself. "I've bought us a year." She smiled at her one small victory. She'd been in Chicago less than a week, and already Huldah was on a new path and the Anchorage—wherever it would be—had rent for one year. Kate looked at Miss Willard's piled desk. "Well, my teacher and friend, let's see what a difference we can make with Bertha and Bess in the year ahead."

Bess was busy cooking dinner when Kate burst into the house. "You won't believe what happened!"

"Did she chew you out for adding another pet project to Miss Willard's full plate?" Bess grinned. "You know she doesn't like all the 'gimmicks,' as she calls them."

"I could tell that, but she broke down and offered to pay the rent for one year—one year only. It's a kind of test case to prove Miss Willard wrong." Kate smiled as she remembered the rest of the story. "I talked her into paying for Bertha's train fare to bring her from Denver so she can help with the Anchorage."

"Oh, you really stuck your neck out! When will she come?"

"As soon I can get the tickets to her. I know we don't have a place for the Anchorage yet, but I'll start looking right away."

Bess continued stirring the pot on the stove. "And where will this prosti—this woman—stay until the Anchorage is ready?"

Kate was surprised at the sting in her friend's voice. She'd almost taken it for granted that Bess would welcome Bertha. She tried not to reveal her disappointment. Instead, she pressed on, "I can ask the women who come to the Reading Room. Maybe Mrs. James can help. She was quick to step forward when Huldah needed a job."

"But inviting one of these women to live with her? I don't know, Kate ..."

Kate could see Bess was not about to offer an invitation.

A few days proved Bess right. No one offered to take in Bertha for the interim.

Kate overheard the volunteers whispering among themselves.

"My husband wouldn't allow it."

"How can she even suggest we have such a woman around our children?"

Three days before Bertha was to arrive, Kate realized that she had to go back to ask Bess for help. "Can we have a talk in the parlor?" That was where Dan talked with his parishioners, with women who were abused. It's where he prayed with them. *Lord, help Bess to listen with new ears.*

"Bess, I think you know what I'm going to ask. I've spoken to everyone I know at headquarters and the Reading Room about Bertha. They are wonderful people, but somehow they cannot believe that God can change a prostitute's heart, and they don't want to be around someone with that past."

"Well, their husbands wouldn't understand." Bess fidgeted with the knitting wool and needles she'd grabbed from the basket by her chair.

"They won't even ask them."

"They have reputations to think about, Kate. What about their children?"

"Yes, what about their children? Wouldn't such grace and kindness help their children see what it means to show the love our Lord has shown us?" Kate realized she was raising her voice and worked to speak more deliberately. "You've heard Bertha's story. You know she's worked in the Gilchrists' home ever since Ella died and how they love her."

"You don't have to tell me again, Kate. I know she was forced onto the street by her husband. I know her baby died. But I can't accept that she sold her body. How could she do that? I don't care how poor I would be—I could never do that!"

Kate stood and fought to compose herself before responding. "Bess, she hated it, every minute of it. She tried to find work everywhere. No one would hire her. She had no place to go. Frank wouldn't let her back home unless she had money for him."

Bess clicked her knitting needles and pursed her lips, staring into her work, refusing to look up at Kate.

"I've known her for almost two years. I've seen her go with the WCTU women every week to tell others about Jesus. Her past is no part of her life now, except in the understanding it gives her. She is strong in faith and will be a great help to us. If we don't believe we can live with the rescued, how can we work with them?" She gathered up her courage. "Bess, could you allow Bertha to stay in my room with me just until the Anchorage opens? She won't be a bother. She'll even be a help around the house."

Bess sat in Dan's blue chair, her head bowed, her knitting lying still in her lap. She raised her head. "Kate, you and I have been friends for many years. But we don't know each other well. You don't know how I feel. I joined the WCTU to stop the sale of liquor, which is ruining our families. I didn't sign up for this."

She paused and shook her head. "No, I didn't agree with Miss Willard when she started adding the Social Purity Department, working with street women, even the Reading Room. I don't like to tell you this, but some of our WCTU women are against Miss Willard's plan to start the Anchorage, and you may face more resistance from them than from Mrs. Carse." She closed her eyes and was silent.

Their impasse seemed interminable. Kate sat back in her chair, resigned. So that was it then. *I've said all I can say.*

Bess put her knitting in the basket at her feet and stood up. "I'll have to pray about this. I'll let you know in the morning, Kate. I know how much the Anchorage means to you and Miss Willard. I don't want to stand in your way. I just have to be sure that I can do this without ruining my reputation in my church and with my neighbors."

Kate nodded. She wanted to smile, but Bess thinking on the matter wasn't a yes. Not yet anyway. *Thank You, Lord. This is at least a small step forward. I can see You working on Bess' heart.*

A stream of passengers poured off the train. Kate scanned the faces eagerly, watching for Bertha. *There! Doesn't she look smart!*

The woman who stepped through the crowd hardly seemed the same frightened woman Kate met at the Denver hospital. She walked with a new confidence and assurance—almost elegance, Kate thought—in the black traveling suit and matching bonnet. Bless Mrs. Gilchrist. It must have been hard for her to give up Ella's clothes and now say good-bye to Bertha.

"Bertha! Over here!" Kate grabbed Bertha's arm and steered her toward a carriage. "I'm so glad you're here."

"It's a lot bigger than Denver, isn't it?" Bertha eyed the streets with wonder as their carriage moved up State Street.

"Yes, but many of the problems are the same." Kate paused. "First, tell me, are Wan and the others still visiting Halliday Street? What about Elsie? Is she coming to the Reading Room? Have you heard anything about Maggie?"

"The work to help others continues. Elsie is doing fine." Bertha's face pinched as she burst out with the news. "Maggie's dead!"

"Oh no! What happened?"

"One of the girls we visited a few weeks ago told us that Jake held a knife to her throat when she couldn't pay her rent. He threatened her that she'd end up in the river just like Maggie.'"

"Oh, Bertha, how terrible!" Kate stopped in shock. "If only we'd had a safe house in Denver for girls like her." She hung her head for a moment. *God, give joy and peace even in the face of this news.* She wanted Bertha to enjoy her first visit to Chicago. She composed herself in spite of hearing news she didn't want to hear. "We've rented a house right down in the red-light district for just such a purpose."

"This is where I'll be working?"

"Yes. Mrs. Carse, the local president, has paid the rent for a year on this house, and some of the WCTU women are giving us funds to furnish it. You'll be the caretaker. There's a little extra for your salary, not much, but I'll visit other chapters around Chicago for help."

Bertha flushed. "Dr. Bushnell, you will never know what this means to me. A new life in a new place—this is a chance for me to start over, to try to become a decent woman."

Kate linked an arm into Bertha's beside her, trying to restore her own good spirits after the terrible news. "Bertha, you *are* a decent woman. You embody hope." She sat back. "Imagine that, Bertha Lyons, you will be a beacon of hope at this place we're calling the Anchorage."

Bertha beamed. "The Anchorage." She looked out at the city streets again.

How I need that hope too, Kate thought. *We have only a year and a lot of skeptics, not the least of whom is Mrs. Carse.* Kate was determined that Bertha not know how difficult it had been to get her here.

"The Anchorage is where I'll be living, then?"

"When it's ready. You should be able to get settled there in a few weeks. Until then, you'll be staying with me at Mrs. Andrew's home. We put a cot in my bedroom, so it's a bit crowded, but it's comfortable."

Kate didn't tell Bertha that her coming had widened the rift with Bess.

19
To the Road

"*H*ello, Jack." Kate picked up the big black cat and nuzzled her nose into his shiny fur. "Did you miss me?" Jack wriggled out of her arms and ran back into the kitchen. "Bess! I'm home. Something smells good in here. Fresh bread?"

"Welcome home." Bess came from the kitchen with papers rather than dough in her hands. "Bertha came by this morning and offered to bake." She frowned, looking at the papers in her hands. "She brought receipts and bills from the Anchorage. I'm glad you're back. Did you have good meetings? I hope women responded to your challenge to help us at the Anchorage."

"I'm not sure I brought back enough money to cover all those bills. But it's always good to be with the women. It's even better to be back in my own bed." Kate rubbed her back, stiff from her old injury, and took the receipts from Bess. "It was worthwhile," she said, thumbing through the receipts. "WCTU women in other cities admire what we're doing. They're encouraged hearing stories of what's happening at the Anchorage." She looked up at Bess. "Especially about Bertha. How's she doing?"

"Oh, Kate, you know she's everything you told me she would be."

Kate smiled. "I think you changed your mind about her the first time she offered to bake bread for us."

"Well, that was a surprise! But I think I really changed my mind the first time she had dinner with us and asked if she could bless this house and our food. Her spirit of humility when she asked forgiveness—she asks for forgiveness for her past every time she prays—wooed my heart." Bess sat back at the table. "I just wish some of the WCTU women who come to the Reading Room would see that. I don't want to start with problems the minute you get home, but Mrs. Phelps is stirring up trouble again. She even convinced Mrs. Walker to stop coming to the Reading Room. Told her she was wasting her time. And she's spoken to Mrs. Carse about ending her support."

"Well, you of all people can understand that, Bess. She and Mrs. Carse have both been against the Social Purity Department from the beginning. Mrs. Carse is just waiting to prove us wrong." Kate put the receipts back onto the table, trying not to let her discouragement surface. "Their money makes them very powerful. What's going to happen when the rent money runs out?"

"The rent money has already run out!"

"What do you mean, Bess? We have two months left!"

"We had to use up the rest of our rent account to pay bills," Bess admitted. Before Kate could say anything she went on. "More urgent than that, I just got the bill from the plumber. Remember we added a second toilet? He charged us almost double what he'd told me. Then we had to call in Mr. McHenry from the dry goods store to build a room off the back porch for it."

"Oh, Bess." Kate flopped into the kitchen chair. "You should have told me. How do you think we're going to pay the rent? The landlord is just waiting to put us out. You know that he doesn't approve of having all those 'street women' staying there."

"I was hoping that Mrs. Carse would give us next year's rent sooner. But I'm worried about what will happen when the store stops selling us groceries because we are behind in our payments." Bess flipped open the ledger on the table. "When you have a minute, come and look at our expenses this month."

"I'm so sorry, Bess. Maybe I should have talked about our financial needs more openly. But we shouldn't have used the rent money to pay bills."

"We couldn't let the women go hungry. Bertha hasn't even taken her little stipend for several months now."

Kate ran her finger down the column of figures, shaking her head. She remembered how surprised she'd been when Bess had offered to keep the Anchorage books. She'd wondered if Bess wanted to prove her wrong too.

"Our balance has been in the red for the past three months," Kate observed as she paged back through recent months' accounts.

"Bertha has done her best. She seems to do miracles with so little," Bess responded. "She convinced some of the local shops to give her the food they can't sell, and one grocer told her if she could carry it, she could have a twenty-five-pound bag of rice for free. Still, that doesn't pay all the bills."

Kate picked up the additional invoices on the table, noting several past due. *Mrs. Carse would have a heyday with these.* She set down the invoices and receipts and began to fish in her purse. "I haven't enough from my meetings this week to cover them all. It will help pay that big bill to the butcher and a few others, but it won't pay the rent."

"There might not be any need to pay rent next year. I hear some of the women at headquarters complain about what the Anchorage is costing. I'm afraid of what's going to happen at the next board meeting if they get enough supporters to vote it down."

Kate slumped into her chair and mused, "I wonder if I should go to the bank and get a loan so we can cover all these bills and the rent account? That would give us time to figure out what to do."

"But Kate, Mrs. Phelps' husband owns the bank!"

"I know. I've met him at one of the meetings, and I could tell he doesn't approve of me either." *Lord, is the Anchorage going to close down? Did we make a mistake? But we've seen women's hearts and lives changed when we brought them in from the cribs. We need wisdom, Lord.*

"Kate, Bertha and I talked this morning about trying another idea. What if we held an open house and invited all the women from the Chicago union to see for themselves what is going on?"

Kate smiled. "That's a novel idea. We could invite women from the unions outside Chicago too." She stared at the receipts and invoices on the table. "Meeting Bertha and the other women will say more to them than I ever could about the power of grace—and why we need more help."

Bess put a hand on Kate's. "It's taken me a while, but I really believe they are to be friended, not feared." She closed the ledger and began to tidy the table as Kate turned to take her bags upstairs. She called back to Bess, "We might get Miss Willard herself to bring Mrs. Carse and perhaps even Mrs. Phelps."

Kate shared their idea with Miss Willard the next time she was at headquarters. "Do you think we should invite the board—or at least Mrs. Carse and Mrs. Phelps?"

Miss Willard didn't respond with the enthusiasm Kate expected. "Perhaps you should think about this a little more."

"Is there something wrong, Miss Willard?" The last time they'd talked about the Anchorage she'd bubbled with enthusiasm.

"Not wrong. I'm just wondering if the time is right. Some of my women are upset about the costs. They still do not approve of our being involved with street women—'women of shame' they call them."

"I am well aware of that, Miss Willard. But Bertha is living proof that such a woman can change."

Miss Willard leaned back, dwarfed in her huge desk chair, and folded her hands across her lap. "Yes, I know. That is wonderful." But the smile faded from her face as she handed Kate a letter. "I didn't know if I should show you this, but I think it is best to be transparent."

Kate saw the envelope was addressed to Mrs. Lucille Phelps—and was postmarked Shanghai, China! She looked up at Miss Willard in bewilderment. "Is this about me?"

Miss Willard nodded. "Evidently this Eloise Haskins went to school here in Chicago with Mrs. Phelps."

Kate skimmed the letter. Her heart sank as she read.

> Lucille, what are American young people coming to? Mrs. Gracey has always sent well-trained and reliable teachers to my school. But recently she sent us a young woman from Chicago. We were thankful to finally have a doctor on the mission, but it didn't take long for Dr. Bushnell to upset everyone.

Kate looked up in surprise. "Have you read this?"

Miss Willard nodded.

"She's accusing me of speaking against government-approved customs—customs like foot binding. She feared her school would be closed. She says I upset the village elders because I tried to stop the mothers from binding their daughters' feet. It's true I still think foot binding is brutal—but I never tried to stop them. I just told them how much better off their daughters would be walking on unbound feet."

Kate went back to reading the rest of the letter.

"Oh, I see why Mrs. Phelps gave this to you. Eloise says they heard that I was working with the WCTU in Chicago and wanted her to know what a troublemaker I turned out to be—even claiming I questioned the truth of the Bible." She looked back at Miss Willard. "You don't believe this, do you?"

"Of course not, Kate. But you must know that some of the board members are adamant that this project must go. I am afraid Mrs. Carse and Mrs. Phelps are the ringleaders."

Miss Willard leaned forward with her elbows on her desk and pointed at Kate. "You remember when I told you that some of the women attacked my ideas like skeeters humming against the curtain? Well, these skeeters are a bit big, but you are a big girl. Don't let them distract you from what God has called you to do." She paused and leaned back again. "Go ahead with your open house, and I will see to it that those two women come with me!"

Kate stood on the front porch of the Anchorage, careful not to brush against the railing, still sticky in spots from Bertha's efforts to clean and freshen the old house with new paint.

"Mrs. Grimes. Mrs. Thatcher." She shook their gloved hands. "Welcome. Please go on in—refreshments are being served inside. Here's a copy of our new publication about the WCTU Reading Rooms around the country."

Kate smiled and put booklets into the hands of three more women lined up to come inside the Anchorage. *I don't think the neighborhood has ever seen anything like this.* She looked down the street, lined with carriages guarded by nervous drivers. Disheveled men stood outside the doors of the saloons across the street, smoke from their cigarettes wafting into the air.

She stepped inside behind another group of welcomed guests to be sure all was going well. Everything looked wonderful: clean and tidy. The Anchorage was like a rose blooming in a neglected lot. Good thing Bertha was as attentive to the women as to their home. Just before the first guests arrived, she'd prevented what could have been an embarrassment when the new woman—what was her name?—Gertrude saw all the activity and preparations and stumbled in.

"What's goin' on? Ya havin' a party?" Gertrude's voice was rough, matching her dirty face and thatched gray eyebrows. She had been drinking and was unsteady on her feet. Old and worn, her brown skirt dragged in the dirt—hem torn along the back—and buttons were missing from her blouse.

Bertha gently explained they were having an open house.

"Open house? Wa's that? This here house is open!"

In spite of the rush of the moment, Bertha had put her arm around Gertrude's shoulders and guided her inside. "Would you like to sit here in the living room? I'll get someone to bring you a cup of tea and some bread with jam." She helped the heavy woman into a chair and made her welcome in a way that seemed to change Gertrude's demeanor from brash to demure.

Kate looked for Bertha through the crowd already beginning to fill the sitting room. She had such an amazing, natural way of exuding grace. She was a hard worker too. For days, Bertha had organized the women living in the house to polish and clean alongside WCTU volunteers.

Gertrude's very presence changed that. She reeked of cigarette smoke and body odor that Kate could smell clear across the room. Bertha and the other women living in the house smiled at her, saying nothing as they passed by with armloads of clothes and trays of dishes from the kitchen. They were used to women like Gertrude. Some of them had been in her shoes not long ago.

The other guests were not so conciliatory. Kate noticed many avoided Gertrude and shot her disdainful looks from across the room. Claudia and Freda, two of the Anchorage residents, interceded, offering tea and cookies around the room. *If only our guests could have seen those two when they first arrived. They were just as smelly as Gertrude, and today they are clean and refined in their new clothes.* And their hearts! Kate longed for people to see how learning of Christ's love was turning Claudia and Freda into new people. Gertrude would not leave the same as she had come today ... but would the guests?

Kate turned back to the porch to greet more newcomers, just as Miss Willard walked up the steps with Mrs. Carse and Mrs. Phelps beside her. Before Kate could welcome them, men lounging against a doorway across the street called out, "Come on over here. We've got more to drink than they have."

Miss Willard ignored the disturbance. "What a good idea to invite us. I see quite a few of our White Ribboners are here."

Mrs. Carse remained silent, though her disdain was clear in her expression, while Mrs. Phelps called back, "There will be no drinks here."

"I'm glad you came." Kate smiled, ignoring the interruption, and led them inside with an anxious eye for their unwelcome visitor sitting across the room.

Bess hurried forward, calling over her shoulder, "Freda, come and meet our special guests."

Mrs. Carse nodded to acknowledge Bess, who explained that Freda and Claudia were new residents and Bertha was teaching them to bake.

Miss Willard reached out to clasp each girl's hand. "I am so proud of you both."

Kate clapped her hands and began the formal introductions of their guests. "We are honored to welcome our distinguished guests this afternoon. Mrs. Matilda Carse, the president of the Chicago union and chairman of the WCTU board." She smiled and nodded to Mrs. Carse as the women clapped. "And Mrs. Lucille Phelps, the vice-president." Mrs. Phelps nodded and took her seat without a smile. "And of course we are deeply honored to have the World President of the WCTU, Miss Frances Willard join us. She—"

Crash! The women started at the sound of the front door flying open.

A man with bushy whiskers stomped into the room, demanding in a gruff voice. "Where is she? Where's that thieving wife?" He lurched forward, almost losing his balance, then stopped to point across the room at Gertrude. "There, sitting like a queen are ya? Where's my whiskey? Or did you drink it all up yourself?"

He staggered forward again, and one of the guests screamed. Others froze as if captured in a photograph. All conversation stopped as Bertha walked steadily from the kitchen.

"You must be Will. Will, I'm Bertha, and Gertrude was just having a little rest before she came home, weren't you Gertrude?" Bertha helped the frightened woman to her feet. "Come, I'll wrap up some fresh bread and cookies for you to take home to your children."

She steered Gertrude and her shocked husband through the kitchen and toward the back door. "Remember, Gertrude, come back next week, and I'll show you how to bake these." Bertha tucked a sack of cookies into the bewildered man's hands. "You be nice to her, Will." Then she gently closed the door behind them.

Mrs. Carse let herself down onto one of the empty chairs as murmurs resumed around the room. "Frances Willard, who was that?"

"The woman who left?"

"No, the woman who ushered them out."

Kate was proud. "That, Mrs. Carse, is Bertha—Bertha Lyons, our caretaker here at the Anchorage."

"That is the woman you brought from Denver?" Mrs. Carse took a long look around her as if seeing things for the first time.

Kate flashed a smile at Miss Willard, then helped Mrs. Carse up by taking her elbow. "Let me show you around. Down the hall are the bedrooms. We can squeeze three or four women in each room ..." Miss Willard and Mrs. Phelps trailed behind.

"Look," one of the WCTU women remarked, pointing to a bunk bed in the second bedroom. "I slept on one of those on the train to New York."

Kate commented over her shoulder. "We're trying to make room for as many women as possible, and this helps. There are so many who are homeless and destitute in this neighborhood alone.

"This used to be the formal dining room, and now it has become a room for everything. Some of our volunteers teach sewing here, and there's always someone who will read the Bible and pray. So many of the women have come from terrible situations, and they're hungry for the comfort and grace found in God's Word."

"And so they're fed here spiritually, in what was a dining room," one woman murmured.

They see. Kate smiled and nodded. *They really see.*

The temperature had dropped by the time the last guest left the Anchorage. Kate and Bess waved their own good-byes to Bertha, who stood at the railing as they stepped into their carriage for home.

"Hasn't it been a wonderful day, Bess? Oh, my feet and back hurt, but weren't you proud of the girls?"

"And Bertha." Bess paused. "Yes," she said, smiling at Kate, "sometimes seeing is believing. Dr. Katharine Bushnell, you will make believers of us all yet."

Kate looked back at the Anchorage as the carriage started down the street. She could see Bertha in the front window, lighting a candle. "No." Kate nodded for Bess to look back. "God does that." She sat back and said, more to herself than to Bess, "I wish I'd remembered to tell Mrs. Carse how Bertha lights a candle every night, to make sure any woman in trouble on the street can come in to a safe place."

"I think Mrs. Carse sees now how essential Bertha is." Bess laughed. "The best part of the day for me was the way she got Gertrude and her drunken husband out of the house."

Kate smiled. Her mind was spinning like the carriage wheels. "Do you think so, Bess? I wonder what Mrs. Carse really thought. She didn't say anything about the rent, and our final payment is due in a few weeks. But she sure looked into every corner, even the pantry where Bertha sleeps." Kate stared out the window. "No money means no house, no place for the ladies—they'll be back in homes where they are beaten or forced to sell themselves on the street again—no place for Bertha; our whole effort will be discredited." She indulged a sigh and flicked a mosquito from her face. "Do you think Mrs. Phelps will convince her that the Anchorage is wasting WCTU funds?"

"Who knows?" Bess closed her eyes, obviously weary from the day. "But when it comes to Mrs. Carse, you're sure to find out."

Three weeks later, Kate stepped into the parsonage after a long day visiting with women along Hell's Half Acre. An envelope lay on the floor.

"Bess?" Kate called into the back, but there was only silence. *She must still be working at headquarters.* Kate picked up the envelope and eyed the return address: Chicago Construction. Mrs. Carse's company. As she tore open the envelope, a check slipped out and fell to her feet. She stooped to pick it up as she read the letter:

> Dear Dr. Bushnell,
> Thank you for your kind invitation to the open house at the Anchorage. You have proved it can be done. This should more than cover next year's rent.
> Affectionately, Matilda Carse

A new energy filled Kate as she looked at the check in wonder. It was even more than last year! It would pay some of their other bills. Bess would be so surprised. Kate would put the letter by Bess' plate—she would think it was another bill.

Kate started to move her books off the table to the stairs, then stopped at the Hebrew Old Testament she'd left open. She sometimes wondered why she bothered with her studies when there was so much else to do.

The front door creaked open and Bess called, "Kate, are you home?"

"Yes, and I'm just getting ready to fix us supper."

Bess bustled into the kitchen, untied her bonnet, and hung it on a hook next to the stairs. "You know what it's like when Miss Willard is in town. She calls another meeting before the last one's over. I declare, she can keep three secretaries busy."

"I know. Sometimes she brings three of them along when she travels."

Kate piled her books at the bottom of the stairs. "I stayed home this morning before going to Hell's Half Acre. I had a few hours to study, but it's never enough." She couldn't hold back her news. "Speaking of enough—how much money would be enough?"

Bess looked startled. "Kate, you've got something up your sleeve!"

She nodded to the letter at Bess' plate. "Take a look."

Bess noted the return address and looked up. "Do I need to brace myself for this one?" She hurriedly pulled open the envelope, started reading, and then a smile broke across her face. "If I didn't see this for myself, I don't know if I'd believe it."

"You can believe!" Kate pulled out the check from her apron pocket.

Bess looked at the check. "I don't know what surprises me more, rent for another year, or that Mrs. Carse signed her letter 'affectionately.'"

"At least Bertha won't have to worry about a roof over her head for the next year."

"Even though the check is larger than last year's, it doesn't solve the problem of Bertha's salary, small though it is, or the costs for groceries or coal."

Kate sat at the table. "I know." She pulled her chair closer. "Bess, I've been thinking. What if I went on a lecture tour to visit unions farther north and across the country? I've pretty well covered the unions in towns around Chicago. Miss Willard thinks that I could expand the Social Purity Department. We've talked about it for several months. She thinks women would be supportive once they hear how lives can change." Kate closed her eyes a minute. "More than that, I want them to see how God cares for women, even the destitute women on the streets of their own towns. Sadly, women can't vote—yet—but they could persuade their husbands to vote for laws that would ban the cribs and pimps."

Bess leaned forward to look Kate in the eyes. "I think they would. Every time you lecture, we get letters at the *Union Signal* about how powerful your message is."

Bess thought for a moment. "You are the right one to take the vision and the message on the road." She scooted her chair back from the table, ceremoniously handing Mrs. Carse's check back to Kate. "Now, Dr. Bushnell, winner of hearts and minds, we have much to celebrate, so how about if I help you fix that dinner? Let me just run upstairs and get my slippers."

As Kate began peeling potatoes, she pondered where she should go first. She'd hesitated telling Bess about Miss Willard's suggestion, but she'd been planning it for some time. She could go east—she knew from the *Union Signal* that there were strong WCTU chapters in Philadelphia. But maybe it would be best to start in the nearby states, Ohio and Indiana. She glanced over at her books sitting on the stairs. Of course she'd take her books. There would be many long boring hours on the train that would give her lots of time to study.

For a fleeting moment, she wondered if this was a good idea. She'd be living out of a suitcase and sleeping in a different bed every night. She reached a hand behind her back to rub the ache that never seemed to leave anymore. *My back hurts just thinking about it ... and will the women really listen?* If only they could meet Bertha and Elsie for themselves, and now Gertrude.

"Gertrude," she said aloud. "You almost ruined our open house, and today you are baking bread for your neighbors. You're cleaning up your body and soul, and your husband is noticing the difference."

She looked at the check Bess had handed back to her. *Even Mrs. Carse has noticed.* She tucked the check back in her apron pocket and poured the peeled potatoes into a pot of steaming water on the stove, but her mind was already on the road ahead.

20

A Newspaper Story

"Imagine your daughter unintentionally caught in a brothel. Her young body, which you have protected and fed, is in the rough hands of men who care nothing about her innocence."

A hushed silence fell over the audience. It was as though not a soul was breathing. Kate repeated in a soft voice, "Her young body is in the rough hands of men who care nothing about her innocence."

From the back, a man rose and shouted, "Shame on you for filling the ears of our wives and sisters with such language." Everyone turned to see the man pull his wife from her seat and head for the door.

For a moment Kate bowed her head, then continued. "I'm sorry this gentleman was offended," she said softly, and then lifted her voice to the rear of the church. "But truth must be heard, even if it hurts.

"I've seen women weeping in shame because they had no other way to feed their children than to sell their bodies," she told the women who shook their heads in denial. "I wish you could see the faces of the women who come to the Anchorage. For many, it's been years since they've received a gentle touch in love, a nourishing meal, and healing words from the Bible."

As she told how women suffered from the brutality of drunken husbands, she watched her listeners lean in. She wanted them to see the relationship between groggery—drunkenness—and the trade in women.

Then Kate went on to tell Bertha's story. "And every night, she lights a candle in the dark so desperate women on the street know they are welcome and will be loved." Kate saw women wiping their eyes.

After the meeting, she faced lines of women wanting to thank her, and some asked, "How can we start such a place for the women on the street in Hillsboro?"

As the train pulled out of the station, Kate waved back at the women on the platform. Then she untied her bonnet and placed it on the seat beside her, relieved that for the next three hours she could study without being forced to make conversation.

She felt drained after thirty days and almost as many meetings, even though the meetings were going well. She had found the right balance between calling for abstinence pledges and encouraging women to organize Reading Rooms. The hardest part was finding those willing to visit women in the red-light districts. How could she get people to go to the rescue of the lost?

She pulled a notebook from her travel bag and looked again at her careful records of every meeting—especially the gifts for her travel and the separate record with special gifts for the Anchorage. Last night when she'd counted, she had barely covered the costs of her travel. There was not much left to send to the Anchorage.

She leaned back and looked out the window. As the scene outside flew past in a blur, she lectured herself sternly. *Don't complain, Katharine. God has been so faithful. You've been able to pay for every train ticket and all the carriage fares, and the women have generously offered their homes and invited you to meals. You've been able to send Bess money for the Anchorage most of the time.* Still, her whole body and soul ached for a little rest. She hardly noticed the beauty of the thick forests outside the window. And tonight was another meeting.

Kate pulled herself together and exchanged her notebook for her Greek New Testament. She enjoyed doing her morning study in Greek, a language she loved. She had to read much more slowly to be able to catch every nuance, translating as she read. This morning she began in First Timothy chapter two, "Supplications, prayers, intercessions, thanksgivings be made—" *Thanksgivings*, plural! *Lord, I mustn't forget the thanksgivings. For Bertha's faithfulness and Mrs. Carse's generosity ... for Miss Willard's vision, for Huldah, who's grown into such a fine young woman and is helping Bertha. Yes, God, there are so many thanksgivings.*

A few lines down, she came to a verse that she'd had difficulty understanding in the past. She translated the words one at a time, word by word, just in the order they were written, "A woman ... in quietness ... let learn ... in all ... subjection."

Quietness. Something clicked in her mind. She checked her lexicon lying on the seat beside her—*inward tranquility, giving calm attention.* She jotted a note in the margin of her New Testament to remind herself of that the next time she came across the word.

When women are listening to me teach about purity, they should be listening quietly and respectfully too, she thought, remembering two women in the back row the previous night who rudely carried on a conversation while she was speaking.

Kate felt the train slow, then lurch to a stop. The coach began to fill with new passengers. She gathered her bonnet and lexicon from the seat beside her just as a tall gentleman placed his top hat in the bin above her head. "Is this seat taken?" he asked, not waiting for an answer to sit beside her.

Kate shook her head and looked intently into her book. After the last two days of meetings and visiting in homes, she felt talked out and wished for silence, even if she hadn't been studying. Fortunately, after a polite, "Good morning," the man next to her opened a newspaper to read.

She returned to the verse in First Timothy chapter two in her English New Testament. She compared it with the Greek Testament lying on her lap. Ever since her questionable findings in China, she often compared the two. She began to read, *Let the women learn in silence.* Strange, she thought. The grammatical ending of the word for "learn" in Greek was an imperative! Kate sat straight up, her brow wrinkled. It shouldn't read *let* the women learn, but women *should* or *must* learn.

Until she worked at the hospital, Kate hadn't realized how few women went to school beyond the first few grades. So many couldn't read much at all. What would her life have been like if she couldn't read? She would rather be poor than illiterate—but that was a double poverty women suffered more often than men. Most of the women in Kiukiang had never learned to read.

A voice broke into her reverie. "I can't help noticing you're reading a Greek Testament."

Kate started and looked up at the gentleman beside her who spoke as he folded up his newspaper. "Oh, I'm sorry. I haven't introduced myself. I'm Reverend Horatio Cummings."

Kate smiled, mildly irritated. Just when she was getting to a crucial understanding of that verse. "I'm Dr. Bushnell."

He raised his bushy white eyebrows as though doubting her. "Are you practicing in Hillsboro?"

"No, I worked at the General Hospital in Denver until recently. I'm not practicing medicine at the moment." *Why did I tell him that?*

"I see you are trying to read Greek. Why Greek, when you can read much more quickly in English?"

Kate turned to answer him and noticed he was dressed in a black suit and vest with a heavy watch fob across his ample stomach. A minister perhaps heading to a funeral? She looked into his faded blue eyes and noticed he was smiling condescendingly.

"I learn new things when I compare the two, Reverend Cummings. Don't you find it helpful in your preparations?"

A blush spread across his face. Kate inferred that he probably didn't use any Greek, but she ignored his embarrassment.

"I just discovered something I've never noticed before," she said. "The word for *learn* in this verse in First Timothy is an imperative. That actually means that women *must* learn. Isn't that a good reason for me to be studying Greek?" She could almost feel her eyes twinkle mischievously.

"Young woman, you have to be careful not to jump to your own conclusions. That verse also instructs women to be in subjection to their husbands, and if they have questions, they should wait and ask them at home."

Kate repressed a grin. He had the Timothy verse, which didn't mention husbands, mixed up with one in First Corinthians eleven, but she wasn't going to antagonize him further. Instead, she closed her Bible. "How far are you going?"

Before he could answer, the conductor strode through the carriage calling "Chillicothe" as the train began to slow. In a few minutes, the Reverend Cummings wished her a good day, put on his top hat, and joined the people moving down the aisle to the exit.

Kate's mind lingered on the insights she'd just shared. Men like

Reverend Cummings needed to think about truths like this. And women too. What a difference it would make. She glanced down at her notebook, filled with similar insights. She chuckled at the thought of teaching even more controversial truths. Right now she had enough on her plate.

As the train started again, Kate saw with relief that the carriage was almost empty. Before she returned to her studies, she noticed that Rev. Cummings had left his newspaper behind, folded up to the back page. A headline at the bottom of the page caught her eye: "Camp Manager Denies Murdered Girl Held Involuntarily."

A few weeks ago, Bess had written that there was some talk at the *Union Signal* office of white slavery in the lumber camps of northern Wisconsin. Kate had heard nothing about it since. Intrigued, she put her book aside to read the article.

> September 30, 1887
> Ashland, Wisconsin—The coroner's office stated yesterday afternoon that Fannie Clark, working at the Ashland Lumber Camp, was burned to death by W. H. Griffin, a lumberman from Waukesha, Wisconsin. Witnesses report that Griffin poured oil over the girl and set her alight because she refused his advances. The lumber camp manager denies rumors that women are held involuntarily at the camp. Griffin's lawyer declares the death was an accident. No date has been set for the trial.

A wave of anger surged through Kate's body. She put down the paper and looked out the window. The Social Purity Department should investigate, but invitations to speak had her traveling for at least another month. Could the White Ribboners in Waukesha do something? Surely they were already stirred up and making themselves heard. She would write Miss Willard to get the unions in Wisconsin involved. She'd see to it. Something had to be done!

Back home in Chicago, Kate sat at the kitchen table, thumbing through the mail that had accumulated for her during her three months away. She hadn't told Bess about her letter to Miss Willard yet. She pushed the envelopes around and searched for Miss Willard's reply.

Ah—there was one from Lucy. "Listen to this." Kate turned to Bess, who stood at the stove fixing their supper. "It's from my sister Lucy."

> Several people here in Evanston tell me about your speeches across the country. You remember our neighbor, Mrs. Barnes? She has a sister in Hillsboro who attended your meeting! She wrote Mrs. Barnes that she didn't think it's proper for a Christian woman to be talking about such private matters, especially in public. What do you talk about, Kate?

Bess stopped fussing over the pans. "Did you really get that kind of criticism?"

Kate considered this a moment. "Most of the time, the women listen, almost in amazement," she explained. "They just can't believe women live in such shame because they're forced to ... but a few of the women in crowds I've spoken to—women like Mrs. Barnes' sister—have come up to me after I've finished speaking and scolded me. One man was so angry, he shouted right in my face, 'You should be ashamed of yourself!'"

Bess winced.

Kate nodded. "Once or twice, women actually got up and left in the middle of my talk."

Bess continued stirring a delicious-smelling stew that bubbled on the stove. "You remember, Kate, how I felt when you first asked if Bertha could come to stay with us? I felt uncomfortable around women like that. But I have to say that working with Bertha at the Anchorage has helped me understand that a woman who's lived a filthy life can be restored and whole, even after she's allowed her body to be used as merchandise. Bertha was so brutally beaten by her husband and chased away—but you know her story."

"Yes, and look at her now." Kate sorted through the rest of her mail. She stopped at a newspaper article and pulled it closer to the lamp. "Did you read this article, Bess? It's another report about white slavery in the lumber camps in Wisconsin."

"I saved it for you. We've been getting more and more of those reports at the *Union Signal* office."

Kate fell silent, engrossed in the report until she had to set down the paper. "You know, Bess, I wrote a letter to Miss Willard about what's going on in the lumber camps. I asked her to rouse the unions in Wisconsin to take a stand against this. The union leaders could talk with the mayors of the towns or get the pastors to organize a protest. I really expected I'd find a letter from her waiting for me when I got home."

Kate stood up, frustrated, and paced the kitchen. Something was at work in her own heart. She looked at her unpacked suitcase sitting at the foot of the stairs. Would she be repacking it soon? She had a feeling Miss Willard would write, *Dr. Bushnell, this looks like something designed just for you.*

A week later Bess burst into the house. "Kate! I've got something you have to see."

Kate ran down the stairs from her room. "It must be exciting. Is your picture on the front page of the *Union Signal*?"

Bess laughed. She hung her coat and hat on the hook next to the door and pulled out a newspaper from under her arm. "This just came to headquarters today."

She spread a copy of the *Milwaukee Journal* on the kitchen table and opened it to the inside page "Look! A full page article by James Fielding, the special inspector Governor Rusk appointed." She pointed to the headline: "Where Satan Rules."

"He's reporting on his trip to visit the brothels in the Wisconsin lumber camps. He says here ..." She bent over the page and ran her finger down the first column. "Yes, here it is: 'The women in the brothels come in a spirit of adventure and in the hope of making money, having grown tired of leading a similar life in the city.'"

"Pshaw! Where did he get that?" Kate pulled the paper around so she could see it more clearly. "Here's his explanation of why they can't leave. 'The women trap themselves in situations by inescapable debt to their landlords.'"

Kate continued reading silently, her sense of dismay rising as she read. "Listen Bess—well you've probably read this—but just listen to this man. 'No women were held by physical force. Indeed, den keepers had no need to resort to kidnapping; the houses of ill fame enjoyed a steady flow of women.'" She sat back and smoothed the hair off her forehead. "Either he is an outright liar or is being paid by someone to say these things. I've heard from some of the WCTU ladies that the governor will not abide anything that seems to slander the state, even if it's true. I can't help but wonder ..."

Bess nodded. "You're right. But we'll take our chances. We've decided to rerun this article in the *Union Signal*—without my picture of course." She curtsied to Kate. "But we don't have a strong rebuttal except for the newspaper articles that appear elsewhere from time to time, and Fielding repudiates those."

"I think a rebuttal will come. Wait till Miss Willard hears of this."

21

A Campaign in Wisconsin

May 1888

It seemed almost prophetic. Kate was really not surprised when she received Miss Willard's telegram.

WOMEN INDIGNANT STOP

MUST INVESTIGATE WIS RUMOR STOP

FUNDS AVAILABLE FOR YOUR TRAVEL STOP

F WILLARD

As she repacked her bags, Kate turned to Bess, who watched her get ready. "For the first time, my travel expenses are paid by the WCTU. Do you think this is the beginning of a new practice?"

Bess just shook her head.

Now on a train north to Wisconsin, Kate took advantage of the long layover in Madison before going on to Wausau. She hired a carriage to the capitol to find James Fielding. She wanted to know exactly where he got his information and what he was up to. He was so sure all the women working in the lumber camps were there by choice. But from what Kate had read, she was not sure of that at all.

She found Fielding in a small windowless office just feet from the governor's door. When Kate had asked ladies from the WCTU in the area what they knew, she heard rumblings from some that Fielding acted as Governor Rusk's detective, and that he gathered information for him covertly.

She tapped gingerly at the closed door that read *Office of the State Investigator.* The man who answered looked more like an elderly office clerk. Fielding stood several inches shorter than Kate, with rounded shoulders and rheumy eyes behind his thick glasses.

Before he had a chance to turn her away, Kate said, "Good afternoon, Mr. Fielding. I'm Dr. Katharine Bushnell, and I'd like to talk with you about your recent article in the *Milwaukee Journal*—I believe it was titled 'Where Satan Rules.'"

"Of course. Come in, come in. Sorry, it's a bit crowded in here." He whisked a handkerchief out of his pocket and wiped off a chair, then sat behind a desk piled with papers. His desk looked worse than Miss Willard's. "How may I help you?"

"You know that many people are talking about the article? I hear that it's even been reprinted in some eastern newspapers."

"Yes." He smiled, and for a moment his eyes looked bright and intelligent. "Yes, the governor is very pleased."

"Perhaps you could tell me more about your investigations up north. What were the conditions like? Were you able to get into any dens where girls were held?"

"No, no. I didn't have to do that. I spoke with the managers—in fact, just one manager, Mike Leahy in Marinette. He's been working in the forests for many years. So he was an excellent source of information. He provided so much background I really saw no need for further investigation. He said it was totally unnecessary for the state to interfere in the matter, and he convinced me that was true."

Something about his speech and demeanor seemed a little too slick. Kate could see that he could be convincing, but why did she feel he was about to try to sell her snake oil?

"So Mike Leahy vouched for the fact, as you said in your article, that there is no abduction, enticement, or involuntary detention of women or girls? Did you feel confident he was telling the truth?" Kate studied Fielding closely as he answered.

"Absolutely. Of course, some of the girls have their wages withheld until they pay their fines or because of misbehavior. But once they pay their bills, they are perfectly free to leave."

"Yes, that's what you wrote," Kate mused. "But what about other dens outside Wausau—the lumber camps in Hurley and Ashland. Did you visit them?"

"No, Dr. Bushnell. I was confident in Mike Leahy's answers. I didn't have to go way up into the forests. But why are you so interested?"

"I'm a doctor, Mr. Fielding. I'm interested in finding out more about what's going on in those lumber camps myself." She'd better not tell him too much, especially that she represented the WCTU. He'd find a way to warn the den keepers that she was coming. "What do you think I would find in those other dens, the ones you didn't visit?"

Fielding rose and pulled the door shut. "Well, I presume you would find dens where women are detained—probably for payment of fines—maybe a few women who don't want to be there." He stood in front of her, shaking his head. "The stories you may have read about a girl beaten to death or forced to work in a dance hall are just nonsense. That Bonneville woman, Blanche something or other, was found living a fast life. She told Mike she always had lots of fun and was making a bundle."

He studied Kate's face for a few moments as though suddenly suspicious of her intentions. His voice became stern. "Surely you wouldn't think of going up there yourself? It could be very dangerous for an attractive woman like you—and I don't think Governor Rusk would be pleased to know you are doing this. Not at all pleased."

The words expressed concern, but the tone was more of ... a warning? She glanced at the clock on the wall and stood up. "I do appreciate your help, Mr. Fielding. I'll send you a copy of my report. But I have a train to catch." A train to Wausau and then to Ashland— the very place that young girl was burned to death.

Abby Harris made Kate feel welcome from the moment the train pulled into the station in Wausau, Wisconsin. As she talked, she ushered Kate to a one-horse buggy—just big enough for two people—and had her luggage piled behind them.

"You just come along, Dr. Bushnell. I've got dinner on the stove. The boys are waiting to have a real doctor stay in our house," she chattered cheerfully. "I hope they won't wear you out too much."

The round-faced chubby little woman carried on, describing the highlights of Wausau: the school, the Methodist church, even the budding greens of the spring foliage that she pointed out along the way. Kate relaxed as the buggy rolled through town.

It struck Kate that she wouldn't have to answer questions or listen to someone taking her to task for speaking so boldly about women of shame. *I confess, it feels good.*

Still, she was braced for perhaps an even more challenging task ahead. She was not sure if it was the evil of what was happening here in the north wood, or the criticism of women back home.

At the Harris home, Kate freshened up from her journey and went down to meet the rest of the family.

"You can rest here in the living room until Ben comes home from the store," Abby said. Her two little boys clung to her skirts as she introduced them to Kate. "Nathan, Mark, shake hands with Dr. Bushnell."

The boys shyly reached out their hands, then hid back behind their mother.

"Nathan is seven, and Mark is five." Abby pulled Mark forward. "He just had a cast removed from his arm. Show Dr. Bushnell, honey."

Kate sat on a settee by the window and gently took the little arm in her hands. Abby slipped away from her sons and left the room. The boys reminded Kate so much of Sarah's boys when they were little. It had been so long ago when she'd talked with them like this. "How did you hurt your arm?"

Mark hung his head. "I fell out of the tree."

"Oh. I know boys like to climb trees. I took care of a little boy named Timothy who came to the hospital with a broken arm. But he did something very foolish."

"What did he do?" Nathan asked as he gingerly slid next to her on the settee.

"He and his friends climbed a tall wobbly ladder to the garage roof." She made motions as though climbing a shaky ladder. "Then his three friends climbed back down ..." She mimed climbing down a ladder. "Took the ladder away ..." Her hands snatched away an invisible ladder. "And left Timothy up there!" She shook her head with sadness.

Mark moved closer. "We climb high on our rope ladder. Do you want to see it?"

Kate pulled him onto her lap.

"Shhh," Nathan commanded his brother. "Why did they leave him there, Dr. Bushnell?"

"I think they were just teasing him. But he didn't like that."

Mark shook his head. "I wouldn't like that either."

Abby returned to the living room to announce, "Daddy's home. We'll have dinner in a few minutes."

"How did he get down?" Mark asked as Kate moved him gently off her lap.

"Well, that's when he did something very foolish. He jumped and broke his arm. Can you believe he would do something like that? It wasn't very smart, now was it?" The boys' mouths hung open as they shook their heads. "That's why he had to come to the hospital, and I put a big white cast on it."

"We got a rope ladder so Mark won't fall down again," Nathan explained eagerly.

"Can you come and see it, Dr. Bushnell? Can you?" Mark pulled at her hand.

Abby reappeared to call them for dinner.

"I'll come to see it tomorrow," Kate promised.

For just a moment, she wondered if this would have been her life if she had married, then she smoothed her skirt as if to brush away the thought. No, she followed another calling now. She thought of the women and girls who were free from the evil of the brothels. Where would Bertha be if she and Hou Wan hadn't come along? And all those girls in the Anchorage? No. She was content, but not finished. The girls in the lumber camps didn't have the comforts of husband and children. They were bound by evil men. She didn't know what would happen up here, but she knew God had called her to be their advocate.

Late into the evening, after the dishes had been washed, the boys were sent to bed, promising to show Kate the rope ladder in the morning. Ben and Abby reported what they knew about life in the lumber camps and the collusion between town leaders and the police.

Collusion? Kate had suspected as much. "That's completely different from the report the state investigator, James Fielding, wrote in the *Milwaukee Journal*. I saw him when I was in Madison on my way here. He may have been a detective in his younger years, but now it seems he does a little writing and mostly cleans the offices of the State Board of Claims and Reforms. The sign on his door says *Office of the State Investigator*. I can't say he does much real investigating, though. I challenged him on the truth of his article. He admitted that he went to only one lumber camp in Marionette, and as far as he had seen and heard, the women in the camps were there of their own free will."

"He's a liar!" Ben interrupted. "I can introduce you to girls who have escaped, fearing for their lives."

"He admitted that some of the women couldn't leave because of unpaid debts to the camp. He told me no camp manager has to force girls to stay against their will. There are always others willing to take their place any time."

"That's why it's so good that you've come," Abby exclaimed. "These things need to be exposed. We know of police who get special favors for picking up girls on the street and accusing them of prostitution. There's a doctor down in Schofield, about five miles from Wausau, who is known to illegally examine women who are brought in by the police. He declares they are not virgins and hence must be prostitutes. It's not safe for a young woman there to even be out on the street alone at night." Abby stood and clenched her fists. She crossed the room and stared out the window to quell her anger. "And it's not just in Schofield—it's in every lumber camp up here."

Kate jotted down the salient points of what she'd heard. After the questionable reporting and lack of truth evident in Fielding's story, she was determined to validate everything.

"Hasn't anyone from here tried to get into the dens to see for themselves what's going on?" Kate stopped writing. She looked out a north window, toward the lumber camps. "Maybe I should try to get to the dens myself, to discover the real story."

"It would be very risky," Abby warned. "I wouldn't put it past someone like Jack Long up at Big Bear to report you to the police and even take you to Doc Frasier. You're a stranger in the area—and an attractive young woman. You wouldn't be safe."

Kate shivered. How could a man like that work in this beautiful place and do such ugly things?

"I don't know ..." Ben stared at his feet stretched out before him. "If you thought you could do it, I'm sure the union women and their husbands would help to keep track of where you were at all times." He looked back at his wife and then at Kate, shaking his head. "No. Abby is right. You must never go into the dens alone, and not even near without letting us know where and when you're going."

Kate sat back in her chair, not resigned, but thinking.

Ben and Abby also appeared deep in thought. Then Ben broke the silence. "I do have an idea," he said, hesitating. "This may be the last chance before the season ends. You might be able to get into Big Bear, several miles beyond Schofield, with a lesser degree of danger, since I usually take a wagonload of supplies from my store to the camp once a month. People are used to seeing my wagon in that area. I leave in a couple of days for my last trip of the spring. The camps have already started logging on the Chippewa. Many of the men will leave for their homes and farms in another month or so. But I could try to get you into the Big Bear Camp without Jack knowing you're there."

Abby seemed excited about the possibility. "You could go as a peddler, Kate. I've gone with Ben on occasion to sell items to women in the camps and farms along the way. You would certainly get better information talking directly with the women than we can give you." She looked to her husband. "Do you think that would work, Ben?"

Kate wasn't sure if she should be amused at the Harris' excitement and flair for disguise, or skeptical of the very idea. What was she thinking, anyway? These people knew this part of the world, the trails, the camp layout. Yet no one else had been willing to confront the problem. Maybe this was what she was sent here to do.

"Getting into the shanty where the girls are kept is another story," Ben said. "A few months ago, I made the mistake of stretching my legs and taking a walk around the camp while waiting for Jack to get back. I'd heard rumors of girls being held there against their will. I noticed an unusual building outside the camp and moseyed over out of curiosity."

"You never told me that." Abby studied her husband's face.

Ben turned to her. "I didn't see anything really. There's a high stockade fence around the shanty. At the time, I thought it might be a place for their animals." He shook his head and looked back at Kate. "There was an animal in there all right, a huge black dog who tore at his chain, lunging at the locked gate. I didn't try to enter."

Kate sat forward in her chair though she felt as if she were reeling. If she got lost or encountered the dog ... Or if she was caught, would it be a beating, imprisonment, something worse? Killed? This wasn't at all what she had envisioned when she told Miss Willard she'd come up here. She knew visiting with the girls and women in the camps would be the best way to get to the truth, but this was no small thing.

Kate drew a deep breath. "Do you really think it could be done?"

"May I?" Ben gestured to borrow her notebook and pencil. "Let me show you what we'd face." He drew a rough sketch of the layout of the camp. "All the buildings lie between the main road and the Chippewa River. The girls' shanty sits south of the cookhouse and men's quarters." He tapped his pencil on the road and then the shanty site. "This is where you'll want to go, and it will be the nearest building as we approach the camp. I could let you out at the turnoff into the camp, and you would need to head straight toward the Chippewa River. You'll come to a clearing here." He pointed to a spot outside the high stockade fence he'd drawn. "The shanty is surrounded by that high fence, but it is the only building you'll see, and it is nearest the road. All the other buildings are closer to the river, so if you're careful, and we time it right, the men shouldn't be able to see you walk right in."

Kate studied the diagram. "How do I get past the dog you mentioned?"

"The gate probably will be locked, and the dog is always chained during the day, as far as I know." He paused a moment, studying the diagram and apparently searching his memory. "When Long caught me wandering around that one time, he told me they kept their calves in the shanty to protect them from 'those drunken thieves that live up here.' I suspected differently but didn't question him."

"Yes, but the dog," Abby pressed.

Ben sat back in his chair and stretched his long legs in front of him. "I think," he said slowly, "if you're able to get over the fence in back near the outhouse, you could get into the shanty or talk to the girls through a window." He sat forward and drew his legs back under his chair. "Yes, that way the dog couldn't get to you."

"But, Ben, she couldn't climb over that fence." Abby frowned at the drawing of the camp layout.

"Maybe I could use a rope," Kate burst in. She looked at Abby, then Ben. "You know, like that knotted rope the boys told me they use to climb the tree in the yard!" *Am I really serious about this insane idea?*

Ben rubbed his chin. "That might work. We could put a hook on one end to throw up over the top of the stockade."

Abby laughed in astonishment. "But this is outlandish." She studied Kate's face. "Do you think you could do something like that?"

Kate felt a remarkable calm. "I do," she answered, surprising herself. "I'm pretty strong. Let me try tomorrow." She smiled. "The boys are eager to show me their rope."

"Good," Ben said, getting up from his chair. "We'll have a busy few days ahead of us. What do you think about taking Kate over to the Davis' tomorrow morning, Abby? I'll take the boys to the store with me. She needs to hear Agnes' story. That will remove any last smattering of doubt that Fielding's reports are a pack of lies."

Before climbing into bed, Kate made notes in her journal of the people she needed to see while in Wausau. There was the Davis family and the girl named Agnes whom Ben mentioned. She would try to talk with the police chief too—to find out if he knew anything about what was going on at Big Bear Camp. Sometimes the police were helpful, or this would help her gauge if the chief was in cahoots with Jack Long.

She put down her pen and turned out the light. But she couldn't sleep. The enormity of the foolhardy plan was sinking in—it had never occurred to her that the police could apprehend her and declare her a prostitute. What if the camp manager whisked her away to another den before Ben discovered what happened? What if one of the lumbermen forced himself upon her? She shivered as a sudden wave of fear poured over her. What had she gotten herself into? Was she really going to climb over a stockade to get to the girls? How did Ben know the dog was tied up all day? Or that it couldn't reach to the back of the shanty? *Lord, is this what You want me to do? It's crazy.*

She sat up in bed. Moonlight streamed across the quilt and pulled her gaze out the window. The branches of a tall pine brushed against the house, and Kate tried to imagine what it would be like to be trapped in a shanty, deep in the woods, shackled to what she recognized was pure horror. *God, I will do whatever it takes to meet these girls and tell their story. Whatever it takes.*

She felt an assurance pour over her, and a verse from her morning's reading in Isaiah came back to her: *Seek judgment, relieve the oppressed, judge the fatherless, plead for the widow.* "That's why I'm here," she whispered. "I'm seeking justice and fighting for the rights of the oppressed." She turned and plumped up the pillow, saying out loud, "And I will trust You to protect me. But Lord, You're certainly going to have your work cut out for You."

The next morning, Mark and Nathan were waiting for Kate to come out of her room.

"Can you come and climb our rope now?" Mark asked as he took her hand and pulled her toward the back door.

Nathan led the way and showed her the rope hanging from a limb of the huge oak in the backyard. "Just put your feet on the knot before you reach for the next one, Doctor," he explained eagerly. "Do you want me to show you how to do it?"

It looked easy for him. Kate tried not to let him see how insecure she felt. The boys peered down at her as she hiked her skirt up between her legs and tucked it into her belt like she used to do when washing her mother's floor. Her cheeks warmed with embarrassment. "Here I come," she called with false bravado. "Oops!" Her foot slipped and she had to let herself down with her hands.

"Come on, Dr. Bushnell," Mark called down. "You can do it."

"Are you certain you wouldn't rather talk with the pastor of the Presbyterian church and the chief of police?" Abby asked as she stepped out of the kitchen to watch.

"I'll talk with them when I get back." Kate was resolute. "I have to see for myself how these girls live. But first, I have to tackle this oak tree."

On her third try, Kate reached the top, to the cheers of the boys and a sharp whistle of approval from Ben, who'd come out to harness the horse for Abby.

The women rode across town in the open buggy. Abby handled the reins expertly through the crowded streets, at the same time giving Kate a running commentary about the town. She rounded the corner at the Methodist church and deftly turned the horse into the yard. A small clapboard manse stood at the back of the fence line where Abby tethered the horse to a hitching post.

Ruth Davis opened the door and came out to meet them, smiling a warm welcome. She exuded both strength and compassion. Kate instantly felt this woman to be a kindred spirit. Abby had told her that Mrs. Davis was "getting up in years," but only her crown of heavy silver hair revealed any hint of age. Ruth stood erect as she reached out to clasp Kate's hand in a strong grip.

"You've no idea how eagerly we've been waiting for you, Dr. Bushnell," she said as she led them into the sitting room. "Scott should be home shortly. He's just gone to the post office down the road. Can I get you some coffee?"

Abby shook her head. "We can't stay very long. Ben took the boys to the store with him, and I'm sure he'll be glad to see us back. I brought Kate to hear Agnes' story."

Ruth nodded, "Of course." She turned to Kate. "And you should hear it from Agnes herself. She'll be home soon. She works early in the morning at the bakery, and she's usually home about now. While we wait, would you like to hear some of her background?"

Kate liked Ruth even more. She knew how to get to the point. Kate nodded and reached into her bag for her notebook. "Please. That would be very helpful." She looked up. "I hope you don't mind if I make a few notes. I'm trying to verify everything I hear. It's not going to be easy to convince the governor to take action unless I can dispute Fielding's reports with authenticity. And I've come to believe that change is not going to happen without legislation. I'd started to realize that, working back in Chicago, but now it's clear.

The state government must pass a bill if this corruption is going to stop. I'm determined to try though I'm not entirely sure how. I do know, however, that hearing about Agnes' experience will be an important start."

"I'm so glad someone is finally taking this to the authorities," Ruth remarked. "Agnes' story will shock them." She paused. "Her family came here from Germany eleven or twelve years ago. Her mother died of tuberculosis when Agnes was ten. She took on a woman's responsibilities, caring for her father and two older brothers who work in an iron mine."

Abby interrupted, "She learned to bake even before her mother died. Haupt's Bakery here in Wausau is famous for Agnes' strudel."

Ruth nodded. "Yes, she became quite a baker and competent little housekeeper, even as a girl. But when her father brought home his new wife, there wasn't room for two German cooks in the kitchen. Agnes heard of a job in Ashland about twenty miles from her home, and her dad agreed to let her go. In fact, he even brought her to town to make sure of the job."

Ruth looked down, saddened. "Within just a few months, the job was gone. The bakery had to lay off workers, and Agnes was left without work almost overnight. One of the clients who'd come into the bakery now and then told her about a job in the kitchen at the Moore Lumber Camp a few miles from Ashland. He offered to take her out in his wagon that very Saturday. Desperate, she accepted the invitation. She didn't even have time to tell her father."

Ruth stopped at the creak of the back door opening. A tall, rugged man, gray hair falling over his steel-rimmed glasses, burst into the room. He smiled apologetically at Ruth, who extended an arm toward Kate.

"Scott! Come and meet Dr. Bushnell."

"Please, just call me Kate."

The Rev. Davis greeted her in a booming voice. "It's so good to meet you." He reached down and took Kate's hand in both of his. "We've needed someone with your experience to clean up the mess in the camps."

He greeted Abby, then folded his tall frame into the chair across from Kate. "We've tried everything, even writing to newspapers, but we've failed to get the attention of the authorities."

Ruth nodded at her husband. "I was just giving Kate a little background." She turned back to Kate. "So that's how Agnes ended up at the Moore Lumber Camp."

Kate thought of the map she'd studied of the region. "But how did you help her? Ashland must be almost two hundred miles from here."

"Ruth and I go up every winter to hold evangelistic meetings in the camps," Scott explained. "Often women attend the meetings. Some men bring their wives to work in the kitchen. We've been suspicious of what the younger girls are doing there, but were never able to talk with them."

Ruth shook her head. "The girls are whisked out of the meeting before we can get to the back of the room where they usually sit."

Kate couldn't help but admire these two elderly people. It must be a difficult journey up north in the winter. "How were you able to talk with Agnes?"

"We heard her coughing and coughing in the back of the room," Scott replied. "Ruth is a nurse and usually brings a bag of medications with her. She knew she wouldn't be able to see this girl once she returned to her shanty. So she left me preaching and went to her in the back."

"When I saw this thin little girl, I knew she was seriously ill," Ruth explained. "There was just a look about her, as though she was going through a horror."

Kate nodded with understanding. *Just like I knew Seen Fah was seriously ill.*

Ruth turned to the sound of the kitchen door opening again, then quickly finished for Kate. "I convinced Thorpe, the manager, that Agnes might have tuberculosis, and he was more than happy to have her taken away from his men."

Ruth stepped to the doorway to invite Agnes into the sitting room. "Come meet our guests, Agnes. You know Mrs. Harris, and this is Dr. Bushnell. I've told you about her."

Agnes stood shyly in the doorway.

This was the girl who had tuberculosis? Kate was pleasantly

surprised by Agnes' shining golden braids, wrapped around her head, and her rosy cheeks brightened from just coming out of the warm bakery. She seemed to glow with health ... and something more. Kate had seen this same sense of peace before—in Bertha.

Kate stood to draw Agnes next to her on the settee. "I hear you make the best strudel in Wausau. Perhaps my friends will bring me to the bakery to buy some while I'm visiting."

Agnes smiled shyly.

"Miss Ruth tells me you speak English well. Where did you go to school?"

Agnes looked bewildered, as though she didn't understand the question.

Ruth stepped in. "There was no school near the iron mine, and when her mother died, Agnes became the woman of the house. But she's learning quickly." Ruth turned to Agnes. "Dr. Bushnell is here to find out how she can help the other girls at Big Bear. Will you help her?"

Agnes hung her head.

"I know it must be hard to talk about what happened in Ashland," Kate spoke slowly. "But we must stop this terrible thing. I just need to ask you a few questions."

Agnes looked shyly at Ruth, then turned back to Kate. "I can answer."

"How old are you?"

"Sixteen."

"How old were you when you started to work at the Moore Lumber Camp?"

"Fourteen."

She had been as young as Huldah—just a child! Kate paused, considering how to phrase the next question. She decided the best thing was just to ask outright. "What kind of work did you do?"

Agnes hesitated and looked pleadingly to Rose. "*Ich* ... I work in the kitchen, and ..."

"It's okay. You can answer plainly, my dear." Rose smiled kindly. "Dr. Bushnell has helped many girls like you. She understands."

Scott stood and excused himself. *He knows it's even more difficult for her to talk in front of a man.*

Agnes began speaking in halting English, so softly that Kate bent her head closer to hear her. "We live ... ten girls live in house. *Zwei frauen*—two—Tess and Blanche—they tell us to put rouge on our cheeks, make hair pretty. *Schnell, schnell*. Men come after dinner." She stopped herself and wiped the tears that began streaming down her face. Kate noticed her hand trembled.

Then, seeming to realize the importance of her testimony, Agnes composed herself and continued. "We wear thin dress—neck comes to so." She put her hand to the middle of her breast. "Tess say, 'Smile.' Blanche say, 'Look happy.'" She paused to swallow back tears. "The men come every night—"

"Agnes," Kate interrupted. It was cruel to make the child go through those horrors again. "Were there other girls your age?"

Agnes wiped her eyes with the palms of her hand. "Ya. Luella and Claire—sisters. Luella was fourteen and her little sister—" She stopped to control herself. "Her little sister, Claire, twelve and so pretty, but not good in the mind."

Kate felt sick. A twelve-year-old, with mental problems.

Ruth asked Agnes softly, "Tell Dr. Bushnell about Fannie."

Agnes shook her head.

Ruth put her arms around Agnes' shoulders. "It's all right. Go get some lunch in the kitchen, and I'll tell her for you."

Agnes forced a smile for Kate and rushed from the room.

"You may have read about the murder at the camp last year?" Ruth asked.

"Yes, that was the first article I read about white slavery."

"Well, Fannie Clark burned to death when one of the men, Griffin, threw a lamp full of oil at her in a rage because she was afraid of his advances. She'd already tried to run away once, but the police brought her back. Fannie and Agnes were best of friends and were plotting to escape together." Ruth shook her head and added grimly, "Griffin has never been charged."

Kate bristled and started to get up. "I think I've heard enough."

As she thanked Ruth and said her good-byes, Kate realized the investigation was going to take much longer than she had expected. But no matter how long it took, she was not stopping until she visited those dens and saw for herself who was responsible for these horrors.

22
Inside the Den

Kate sat deep in thought as Ben drove the horses through the narrow road in the pristine forest. She'd watched him load the wagon high with supplies: bags of grain for the horses, rice, sugar, flour, barrels of kerosene, boxes of soap, matches, bottles of cooking oil, and tins of spices. He'd added items for the women living on the farms along the way: sewing thread, scissors, several bolts of colorful cloth, and scarves and brooches that men might buy for their wives.

"Don't look so serious."

Kate looked up at Ben, suddenly aware of her anxiety. How would she convince anyone in the camp she was there on business with Ben? She'd never been a saleswoman before. She'd feel embarrassed trying to talk anyone into buying something.

Ben seemed to read her thoughts. "You'll pass just fine as my assistant. Of course, don't let them look into your bag. You'd have a hard time explaining that climbing rope."

"I might have a harder time explaining why I'm your assistant instead of Abby. I'm almost glad Mark came down with a fever last night. At least you can honestly say I've come all the way from Chicago to take her place since Abby needed to stay home with him."

"Well, I won't try to explain the Chicago part," Ben chortled.

Kate drew her basket closer as if to protect it. "How much longer before we get to the camp?"

"About an hour. The horses are pulling a heavy load, so I don't like to drive them too hard. We're getting close. You can see how thick the forest is here, but you should easily find the camp if you head toward the Chippewa River on your right. Listen for the river—it's rushing after the spring thaw."

Kate reviewed the map Ben went over with her last night.

"All the buildings lie between the main road and the Chippewa River," he reminded her. "Remember, the girls' shanty sits south of the cookhouse and men's quarters—the shanty will be the first building you'll see as you approach camp."

"Are you sure I'll see the shanty before I get too close to the river?" Kate kept studying Ben's sketch, which she'd pulled out of her pocket. Could she really get to the women and girls without the men seeing her?

"I'll let you down at the turnoff to the camp. Ben squinted to see farther down the road ahead. "If you head straight toward the river"— he pointed a long arm to the right, straight across her face—"you'll come to a clearing. You'll see the shanty surrounded by a stockade."

It had all sounded so simple, so workable the night before, but now that she was here ... She shut her eyes and prayed. *God, I must trust You to accomplish what concerns me.*

The wagon lurched along. Kate stiffened when she saw a lone rider coming down the road toward them. Ben bent close to her. "Kate, quick, wrap your scarf around your face. You have a toothache, so you can't talk. This may be Fielding coming toward us. I heard in town yesterday that he was out at Bear Camp."

"Fielding! If he recognizes me, it will be over. News of the investigation will get into the papers. I'll never get into any of the dens or meet any of the girls." Kate tightened her scarf around her face and pulled her bonnet forward over her forehead. "And what is he doing here anyway?" she whispered. "He told me he only went to the one camp before he wrote the article. Why is he up here now?"

"Hopefully, he'll just ride by."

But instead, the little man on the oversized steed held his hand up to stop the wagon. He rode to Ben's side and doffed his cap. "How do you do, my friend? I'm a stranger here, and I'm afraid I'm lost."

Ben pulled on the reins to quiet his restless horses and reached out his hand. "I'm Ben Harris, shopkeeper down in Wausau."

"James Fielding, secretary to Governor Rusk."

He couldn't even tell the truth when there was no need to lie! Kate rocked back and forth as though in pain. *And here I am pretending to have a toothache.*

"Toothaches are a bear," Ben said with a nod toward Kate. "We have to deliver this load and get her back to Wausau. How can I help you?"

"I'm on my way to Schofield, but I'm afraid I took the wrong turn." The two men discussed where Fielding should have turned off. Then Fielding bent over, looking into the wagon. "So sorry about your painful tooth, Mrs. Harris. I hope you'll get some help in town."

Kate nodded her head but didn't turn to look at him. Was he suspicious?

She heard Fielding rear his horse around and head back the way he'd come.

"I think you're safe now, Kate. He's left us in his dust."

Kate kept the scarf wrapped around her face. He'd looked her right in the eyes at his office. What if he had second thoughts now and came back?

But they reached the turnoff without incident. Ben helped Kate down. "I should be gone about two hours. Jack makes sure to check off everything I unload, and I'll keep him talking as long as I can. Come back to the turnoff, but stay out of sight until you hear me. God be with you, Kate."

Kate walked quickly toward the camp, then stopped to review the picture of the layout in her mind again. She slipped through the underbrush along the road and then into the thick forest. The soft rustle of leaves in the trees and the call of the birds above broke the silence of the woods and might have been peaceful under other circumstances. But every step forward crackled the dry brush, and each seemed to echo through the trees.

Then, a rustle. Definitely not the wind this time.

What was that? Kate ducked behind a tree to listen again. A soft step, barely audible except to her highly strung ears. She quickly scanned the area. The bushes ahead of her moved. She froze as the branches moved again. Even her breathing stilled.

A deer darted out. It paused for a split second, then disappeared into the forest.

For a moment, she leaned against the tree and exhaled. *You asked me to be here, Lord. I will trust and not be afraid ... I will not be afraid ... I will not be afraid.*

With renewed courage, she started out again, slowly heading toward the faint sound of rushing water. Just as Ben had told her— the Chippewa River was ahead on the other side of the camp. She stepped slowly and softly, trying to keep hidden behind large trees or thick bushes. Oh—she should've taken off her bright bonnet. It could be easily spotted through trees. She slipped her bonnet into her basket and tied on a dark kerchief. Suddenly, she heard a soft thud and pulled herself back. A squirrel scampered off with an acorn in its mouth. *Take a deep breath, Kate. You can't jump at every small animal.*

A few minutes more of moving stealthily forward, she saw the clearing Ben had noted on his map. Smoke! The cookhouse. *Keep well to the right,* she reminded herself. As she inched forward, ever watchful for someone wandering around the camp, the den suddenly appeared, huddled at the edge of the forest. It was just as she had imagined. The split-pole stockade surrounding the shanty seemed even taller than described as she drew closer. She prayed for just enough time to make it unnoticed over the wall and talk with the girls. Ben had told her that the lumberjacks would be occupied by moving freshly hewn logs down the river at this hour, and no doubt the cook and Jack Long were helping Ben unload his welcome supplies.

As she neared the stockade at the back of the building, she dug into her bag for the piece of raw meat Abby had wrapped in a napkin.

"Too good for a dog," Abby had murmured. "This bone would make enough soup for the whole family for several days." But it should keep the dog happy long enough for Kate to get over the stockade and into the shanty itself. That was what mattered now.

She peeked through the cracks in the wall but couldn't see anything on the other side. Ben had assured her the dog was chained near the front gate during the day. Her heart pounded as she inched around the front of the stockade. No barking, no girls talking. Could the women have been moved?

She reached the gate and found an unlocked padlock hanging on the clasp. Gingerly, she pulled the heavy gate open a crack. The dog's chain lay on the ground, unattached to anything. All was quiet. She shook the gate, sure the dog would come roaring around the shanty towards her. Nothing. She slipped through the gate and quickly pulled it shut behind her.

Ahead, the door to the shanty stood ajar. Strange. She pushed the door open wider, calling softly, "Is anyone here? Hello?"

Silence.

Kate stepped in and quietly shut the door behind her. It was difficult to see anything in the gloom. She stood motionless as her eyes adjusted, then focused on three rough-hewn wooden chairs and a table. A bucket of water stood beside the stove, where a kettle spewed steam. Someone had to be around. Along the back, drapes shielded three doorways. The open drapes to one of the rooms revealed a single cot and rag rug on the floor.

Kate stepped into one of the tiny rooms, practically filled by the metal bed frame. A flimsy lace robe hung on a hook inside the doorway. She drew a sharp breath as she noticed the chain dangling from the bars at the head of the bed.

Kate fled back to the main room and slumped onto one of the chairs, pulling the scarf from her head. *I've seen this all before in Chicago.* She surveyed the room again: one tiny window, a heavy lock hanging on the door. But she would not forget the chain—obviously used to keep a girl in her bed. If only she could speak with them.

"Here you are, girls. Home sweet home."

A man's gruff voice startled Kate. *He must be just outside the gate. Don't panic—hide.* But where? She grabbed her bag and rushed back to the far room, pulling the curtain tight.

"You did a pretty good job in the kitchen. I might bring you back another day to work for me. What would you think of that? 'Specially you, feisty Fran."

Kate heard a girl's whimper.

"Aw. I forgot you hurt your arm." His voice was heavy with sarcasm. "Good you kept your mouth shut when I told Fielding you tripped over our tomcat running through the kitchen."

"Leave her alone!" A coarse-sounding woman shouted at the man. "You probably broke her arm with your roughhousing last night. She can hardly move it. She did her best to sort the hulls from that cheap rice you bought."

"Whoa, Bella. This fight's not yours." The man sounded menacing. "I wouldn't have to hurt her if she didn't fight me." His voice softened. "You girls did just what you were told. Fielding was impressed with our cooks in the kitchen. You did all right. Maybe I'll give you a special treat. How would you like me to come and give you a treat tonight, Frannie?"

"Leave me alone." The voice was softer.

If only Kate could see their faces, especially that man. Could that be Greiber, the cook? Ben warned her that he was cruel.

"You girls have a good time in the yard. Don't get any ideas just because Rufus isn't here. Jack will bring him back from the men's bunkhouse as soon as he finishes his business with Harris." He laughed. "Jack didn't want to give Fielding any ideas about us having dangerous dogs in the camp."

Kate heard the man stomp away from the shanty, then the gate slam and the padlock click.

"Good riddance," one girl muttered under her breath. "How I hate that man."

"I hate them all," another cried. "Bella, I didn't come here to live—" Her voice broke and she stammered, "to live like—like this."

"Don't start that again, Cora." Bella turned gruff herself. "You don't have anything to cry about. You weren't the one chained to a bed like Fran."

Cora changed the subject. "At least we can sit out here in the sun as long as Rufus is gone. Fran, I'll bring out a chair—you'll be more comfortable than on the ground."

Kate heard the door of the shanty creak open. She pulled the drape back just enough to peek through as a girl with disheveled blonde hair tied in a blue bandanna walked past with a chair. *Now or never.* Kate gulped, then spoke softly. "Cora. You are Cora, aren't you?"

The girl dropped the chair she was carrying. A look of fear flashed in her eyes as Kate stepped past the drape.

"Don't be afraid." Kate smiled. "I've come to—"

In terror, Cora darted across the room and out the door.

23
Caught in the Den

Now she'd done it! What if Cora told the other two that she had seen Kate? What if Jack came with the dog just then? Kate looked around the room once more, but there was no escape.

She stepped to the window, her back against the wall. She could hear soft murmurs outside but couldn't make out what was being said. She could see Cora point animatedly toward the shanty.

Did she want them to come in and see the stranger for themselves? They must have been wondering how Kate got in. She was wondering how to get *out*. How long had it been since Ben dropped her off? Kate turned to scan the room for a clock but whirled back at the burst of the opening door.

A buxom black-haired woman marched in, followed by two young girls. All eyes focused on Kate.

"What are you doing here?" the buxom woman boomed. "How did you ever get in here? New girls don't show up here like this."

"I—"

Cora interrupted. "If you want to get out of here, you'd better go now. Jack is going to bring back the dog as soon as he's done unloading Harris' supplies." Her voice dropped its bravado. "He won't let you go."

"Don't worry about me," Kate looked the dark-haired woman in the eye then turned to the girls. "I'm here to help, but I won't be staying long. I'm going back with Mr. Harris."

The older woman stepped belligerently between Kate and the girls. "I don't know who you are or what you want, but you're trouble for us. We'll get blamed for whatever happens."

Kate turned. "You are Bella?" Was she angry or just suspicious? "I'm not here to make trouble. I'm here to help. I'm a doctor."

Bella smirked. "We've had enough of *doctors*, lady."

Kate studied Bella's face. "No," she said finally. "Not that kind. I came in with Mr. Harris. I'm here to help you find a way out of this place. Let me start by examining Fran's hurt arm." She pulled her medical kit out of her bag, set it on the table, and stepped past Bella to lift Fran's chin and check her bruised face. Those dull eyes should have been sparkling with joy instead of flat with despair. She spoke softly to Fran as she helped her into one of the chairs and gingerly lifted her arm. "Let's take a closer look at what's going on here." Carefully, Kate unwrapped the filthy rags wrapped around the thin arm. "What's your full name?"

Bella, who stood watching Kate warily, answered, "Just Fran. Greiber beat her."

"He bullies her," Cora added.

"I can see that," Kate murmured as she gently felt Fran's arm. "I'm Dr. Bushnell."

Fran grimaced.

Kate stopped a moment. "I'm sorry. I'll move it as gently as I can, but I need to work fast." She eyed Bella and then the door before focusing again on the arm. "I think you've got a fracture, young lady." She lifted Fran's chin again. What kind of a beast would do this to a young girl? Her bruises would heal, but would her heart ever be free? "I'm going to put some ointment on these cuts to keep them from getting infected. I think you'll be more comfortable with your arm in a sling, too." She looked around the room for something to use.

Bella followed her gaze, then stepped into a back room, returning with a thin towel. "Will this work?"

Kate nodded. "Thank you." She wrapped it around Fran's arm and tied the ends together, thinking how many times she had done this for other girls: binding and unbinding wounds. She handed Fran a small tin of salve. "Hide it under your bed, and use it till you're healed."

"Thank you," Fran whispered.

Cora stood near but kept looking at the door. "Won't Jack notice that someone has been here?"

"Tell him that Bella found the towel for the sling—that it hurts less wrapped this way."

"You've got to get out of here," Cora insisted. "If they find you, they'll keep you."

Kate spoke softly. "Mr. Harris assured me he has a pretty full load, and there will be mistakes in the inventory that he and Jack will argue about. I think we have at least an hour." She hoped they did. How would she know when Long was coming back? The thought of being caught in the den sent a shiver down her spine. She looked to the girls. "Help me. I need to know some things so I can make a plan to get you out of here." She looked to Bella. "To get you all out of here and somewhere safe, but not today."

"Can't you take us with you?" Cora implored.

Bella stopped her. "Don't be stupid, Cora. You know Rufus would be after us in no time."

A glimmer of hope flashed in Fran's eyes. "We could get on Harris' wagon ..."

"No," Kate spoke gently. She hated to diffuse that hope. "That won't work just yet. I need to gather more evidence about all the camps first. I so wish I could take you now, but we've got to shut them down for good to keep you and others like you safe." She looked at Fran and Cora. "You've got to be strong. Can you do that?"

Cora slumped to the floor beside Fran's chair. Kate knew she had to work faster. She turned to the two girls. "How old are you?"

Fran looked to Cora. "I'm fourteen. So is Cora."

"And you, Bella?"

Bella looked hard at Kate for a long, silent moment.

Kate could see her uncertainty, and wondered if Bella would help or hurt this rescue. But she was as trapped as the other two were.

Bella seemed to be measuring things. She turned from Kate and looked out the window, then back again before answering. "Twenty-four."

Kate felt relief. *She wants out.* "Bella, how did you get here? How did you all come to be prostitutes?"

"Oh no!" Cora covered her face with her hands. Kate realized the word was too terrible, too harsh for her to hear.

Fran became animated for the first time. "That's what everyone calls us. The police forced me to come. I lived on a farm with my family but came to Schofield to work. One night, I was running back to the boarding house from a dance." She paused and supported her broken arm with the good one. "I should have stayed there."

"What happened?" Kate searched her face.

"A policeman picked me up, said I was a prostitute. He took me to Dr. Frasier." She began to cry. "He examined me." She shook her head at the memory. "Then the policeman brought me here to Bear Camp. He told Jack that the doctor said I was a prostitute, that this was a good place for me."

"And you, Bella? How did you get here?"

Bella answered defiantly, "I was a prostitute in town—I was my own boss, kept my own money, but here ..." She spread her hands to take in the room. "Here, we're locked up like animals." She looked at Kate. "I heard it paid well here. I was wrong. These two—" she waved at Fran and Cora. "These two don't belong here. Look at Fran. Greiber beats her because she tries to fight him off."

"Have there been other girls here?"

All three started to talk at once. Kate stopped them. "Bella, you tell me."

"Lila." Bella stood at the window as she talked. Was she watching for Jack Long? "She was tricked into coming here too. She came before these two. Lila was determined to get away and planned for weeks how to do it." She turned to Kate. "I confess I helped her. I would have gone with her if I could."

Fran and Cora stared at Bella intently. It was clear they never knew. Bella looked at them apologetically. "Lila waited one night until Jack was in my room. I was very nice to him, even rubbing his back until he fell asleep—just like Delilah in the Bible story." She looked at Kate. "I heard that story once in church." She gave a scornful laugh.

"The keys were in his pants, which he'd left hanging on a chair. Lila fished for the keys to unlock the gate. She'd secretly saved a rare piece of meat from dinner and threw it as far she could. Rufus raced to retrieve it. She unlocked the den door and opened the gate. Jack hadn't bothered to lock up when he visited, and he never heard a thing. She disappeared into the forest. We never heard if Lila got back to her home in Wausau, but Jack would have dragged her back here if he could."

Cora pressed Bella. "Didn't Jack ever question if you knew what Lila was going to do?"

"Lila was clever. Once she unlocked the door, she threw the keys back into the shanty so it would look like they'd fallen from Jack's pocket. He had no idea how handy that rag rug turned out to be—muffling the sound. He growled at me a lot about her escape, but I really think he believes he forgot to lock the den that night." She shook her head. "He'd never admit it though."

Kate studied the girls' faces. Escape sounded so good that even the possibility seemed almost something they could taste.

"Now we're watched more closely than ever," Cora said.

Fran looked to Kate. "Couldn't you do something to help me get away?"

Sadly Kate shook her head and turned to Bella. "Not yet. If we were caught, it would be the end of my plan to rescue you and many more women. But I promise I won't forget you." She smoothed Fran's tear-stained cheek. "I have a few more questions. Do they ever test you for disease?"

Bella nodded. "Once in a while, when one of the lumbermen comes down with symptoms, they haul us all in to Doc Frasier to see which one of us gave it to him," she said bitterly.

"Have any of you been infected?"

Bella shook her head. "Not so far. Jack would throw us out. Which wouldn't be all that bad."

Kate cleared her throat. "No, be thankful. I wish I could tell you how to avoid infection, but for now, just keep yourselves as clean as possible. If Jack does throw you out, try to find a good doctor."

"Like Frasier?" Bella asked.

Kate ignored Bella's sarcasm. "What would happen if you got pregnant?" She hated to ask that question, but there was no skirting it.

"You see that chart on the wall?" Cora pointed to a roughly drawn monthly calendar, with checks on some of the squares.

"That's to make sure we don't." Bella practically spat the words, she was so angry. "Jack doesn't want any pregnant girls here, so we have to mark down our monthlies."

"At least that's five days a month we are left alone," Fran said. She whispered to Kate, "But if we do get pregnant, Jack has ways to make sure we aren't anymore."

Kate fell silent. To hear a girl talk about such things instead of school and games was unsettling, no matter how many times she'd heard and seen them. "Do you have one of those calendars I could take with me?"

"Sure." Bella turned from the window, pulled the calendar from the wall, and handed it to Kate. "This one is full, so I have to put up a new one." She forced a smile. "One of my honors for being the oldest."

As she folded the evidence and put it into her bag, Kate could hear horses' hooves in the distance. That must be Harris leaving. She needed to get back to the gate and then the road.

Bella was back at the window again. "Oh, oh. Jack is coming."

Kate pulled her things into her basket, her heart pounding in her throat. "What should I do?" she found herself asking helplessly.

"You can hide in my room," Cora cried out. "No, that won't help."

She was right. The curtain in the doorway wouldn't hide anyone for long.

"It's okay," Belle called softly. "He's walking away. I think he forgot to bring Rufus back."

Fran whimpered. "Jack will bring Rufus soon. He just took him away to fool Harris. What are you going to do, Doctor?"

Kate pulled out the knotted rope ladder from her bag. She hoped she looked more confident than she felt. *Lord, help me to get out unseen, not only for my sake but also for these girls.* They'd suffer if she were caught. No one would come back to free them.

"Cora, come around to the fence behind the outhouse with me. I'll use this rope as a ladder. You can hold it steady for me."

Cora looked frightened but followed Kate to the door.

"Bella, talk to Jack when he gets here. Complain about something, anything—just keep him occupied!"

"I can keep him busy with complaints all right. But Rufus will know there's something going on."

"You're right," Kate said. "Here." Her hand was shaking as she reached into her bag and pulled out a bone with meat still attached. "Go outside and throw this to the other side of the shanty. That's all the scent Rufus will want for a while."

A distant whistle sounded.

"Hurry!"

Bella pushed Cora and Kate out the door. "Jack lets Rufus run wild in the forest before chaining him up here. Sometimes Rufus doesn't come right away, so you may have a minute or two."

Another shrill whistle pierced the air, this time closer to the shanty. Kate knew she had to hurry. She put her arm around Cora's shoulders as they ran around the shack to the outhouse.

How can I leave her behind? The longing in her eyes, the hatred of the things she has to do here. She could probably climb that rope ladder faster than I can. It almost broke Kate's resolve to leave her behind, but she knew she could still free Cora and rescue hundreds of other girls too with more time and evidence.

"Stand back a moment," Kate whispered.

She hefted up the rope with Ben's hook attached, praying it would hook at the top of the stockade. It missed and fell to the ground with a thud. Quickly, she picked up the hook, aiming carefully for the top before hurling it again. It stuck to the edge of the fence. Kate gave Cora a quick hug and whispered, "Hold on until I get to the top."

She grasped the rope and pulled herself up. The rope burned her hands. She felt a sharp pain in her back. *Please don't fail me now.* Hand over hand, she pulled her way up and within moments was at the top of the fence. She undid the belt holding her bag and tossed it over, into the bushes below. Turning to haul up the knotted rope ladder, she looked into Cora's eyes, watery and red with tears. *How can I leave her to endure another moment at the hands of these men?* "Here," she whispered. She clung to the top of the rough-split logs and tossed the hook to Cora. "Hide it in the outhouse until you're sure it's safe to escape. Run for town and ask for me or Abby Harris. If I'm gone, Mrs. Harris will know how to help you."

A dog barked in the distance.

Kate perched on the stockade fence and clawed her way down. She grabbed at the scraggy surface of the logs and tried finding tree knots for footholds. Midway, she fished with one foot for some bump or ridge of log to step on as she edged down. She slipped and fell into a bush. Another spasm in her back seized her. She held still, partly in fear of the ache continuing deeper and longer. *Oh, Lord, don't let me fall apart now. Help me.*

The dog's bark sounded closer.

She pulled herself free of the bush. With her bag in one hand, she hoisted up her skirt with the other and ran blindly into the forest. Even in her own fear, she could not forget Cora's pitiful face.

Kate kept running. Her heart raced in her chest. Her lungs burned. After a while, she realized every tree looked the same and there was little light to help. She looked up through the canopy of branches and leaves. The sunlight that had filtered through earlier was gone. The sky must have clouded over ... or was she going in the wrong direction? Kate turned around. Which way was north? No paths, no footprints to follow. She glanced back the way she had come.

Where's the cabin? I could be running in circles.

Wild barking sounded from behind. Was Rufus running loose? He could find her in a minute! She tore through the trees ahead. Anywhere to get farther from the barking dog—and Jack. Kate panted hard. Limbs and thorns in the underbrush snatched at her skirt. She lifted it to keep from tripping.

The trees thinned. *I think I see him!* She had a glimpse now of the road and a wagon on it. She could still hear Rufus barking in the distance. *Oh thank you*—there was Ben's wagon at the edge of the road. She hadn't noticed until now that her hands were bleeding and skirt torn—but it didn't matter, she was almost safe.

24
Revealing the Truth

*I*gnoring her scratches and lacerations, Kate took a train the next morning to Hurley, about an hour away. After hearing about influential mayor Mike Mahoney, she had sent a message to Mrs. Farwell, a Hurley union member, requesting a meeting with Mr. Mahoney. Kate had heard such exaggerated rumors of fierce dogs milling around the dens and women living behind barricades that she was determined to follow up every lead. She would record truth, not rumors. Hopefully, the mayor would give her the facts she needed.

"I'm glad you came to see Mr. Mahoney," Mrs. Farwell said as she led Kate from the train to the carriage. "He's a fine man—a deacon in our church."

"When I heard that from some of the union women, I decided to come to see if he would help in exposing the slavery of girls in the lumber camps," Kate replied.

"After your visit, you must come back to our house for coffee. Some of our women would like to meet you."

The carriage stopped at Mahoney's Dry Goods Store on Hurley's Main Street.

"With your learning, Dr. Bushnell, you'll be pleased to know that Mr. Mahoney has a small library in the back room of his shop," Mrs. Farwell told her eagerly. "Not many towns up here can boast a library."

Mahoney, a short, stocky man with a thick black mustache, which seemed intended to compensate for his nearly bald head, was engrossed in conversation with two men who stood across the counter from him. But with one glance at Mrs. Farwell and Kate, Mahoney wiped the flour from his hands and reached out his arms in welcome as he walked over to greet them.

"Ah ha, you are the doctor visiting us all the way from Chicago?" He didn't wait for an answer. "Welcome to Hurley." He reached for Kate's hand and surprised her with his strong grasp. "What can I do for you?" he asked pompously, then glanced back at his friends as though confirming this was the visitor he was expecting.

For some reason, Kate immediately felt wary. Perhaps his tone. *Why is he so patronizing with me? I don't even know him. Lord, set a guard around me today.*

"Glad to meet you, Mr. Mahoney." Kate withdrew her gloved hand from his, which had gripped hers a little too long. She winced. "Is there some place private we could talk?"

Mahoney raised an eyebrow. "Of course, Dr. Bushnell. I wanted to show you our town library in any case. I'm sure you'll be surprised by how educational we are up here in the wild woods."

He'd be surprised to learn how "educational" I am! She tried not to let the man's poor grammar lessen her respect for him.

Mahoney nodded to Mrs. Farwell. "Won't you join us?" But Mrs. Farwell shook her head and waved to leave.

Mahoney led Kate to a rear room, away from the customers at the front. When he turned back to her, his expression had changed. It held a stern, knowing look that said he knew why she was there. And that he didn't like her.

Kate followed him uncertainly. The "library" was a room with two shelves of old books along one wall. A table and chairs that seemed to serve as Mahoney's office filled most of the room. He gestured for Kate to have a seat. "Now, Doctor, how can I help you?"

"I've heard that you have a great deal of influence in these parts." Mahoney leaned back, visibly flattered. "So you may have heard that I've been looking into rumors of white slavery here in the north woods. The governor's inspector, James Fielding, wrote an article in the *Milwaukee Journal* denying such a trade exists, but I've come to believe that women are being held against their will in the camps. You must hear a bit of everything that goes on from all the people who pass through your store. What do you think?"

Mahoney cleared his throat. "It's true a certain kind of ..." He paused. "Let's call them cheap women ... they don't know any better and don't care where or how they live. They come up here for money. There will always be that kind of woman. Why bother about them?"

Kate bristled to her very core. *Cheap? Don't care?* "Perhaps you don't understand. There are many held against their will."

"Ah. You've been talking to the rumor mongers—probably from that united Christian women something group. I don't think *you* understand, Dr. Bushnell. In every town there are girls—women— who go home with quite a bit of money from what goes on in the camps. Men are lonely up here without family, so they visit the dens and bring business to Hurley." He laughed loudly. "Everyone's happy, see?"

Kate stood. "You can't believe that. You can't accept that this is anything less than evil."

Mahoney's gaze turned icy. "That depends on one's definition."

"I see." Kate turned to leave the room. Her gaze caught a picture on the wall of Mahoney on a hunt with ... Why was the other face familiar? Wasn't that Jack Long from Big Bear Camp? She'd seen his face in the Wausau newspaper. Proof! Mahoney *did* accept evil. He brokered in it! She reached to open the door.

Mahoney called after her. "Things work the way they are—the system is like a sewer that drains the muck collected in the big cities. Why do you think so many of the fine wives in this town shut their eyes to what's going on?"

Kate tried to put on a happy face at Mrs. Farwell's tea. But she was discouraged and glad to be returning to Wausau that afternoon.

A few days later, women from all over the region streamed into the Wausau Methodist Church where Kate sat in the front row of the main hall, waiting to speak. She played with the gloves she wore to hide the lacerations still healing on her hands. There would be enough drama in what she had to tell the women of the Wisconsin unions about her work in Chicago. They didn't need the melodrama of her escape.

She had begged Abby not to tell about her trip to the shanty at the camp. "If word gets back to Jack Long through one of his friends in town, those girls already enduring the unthinkable will be in even more danger. That's why I couldn't ..." Her voice broke. "That's why I couldn't risk even trying to bring them with me."

Now she was concerned about the outsiders Abby had invited. She knew that resistance to her investigation grew among certain groups in town—even some union women. She listened to the chatter as women took their seats. Two women filed into the row behind her. She couldn't help overhearing them.

"Mrs. Harris has invited me to these WCTU meetings for years. I've not been interested in fighting the battle for temperance, but I wanted to hear for myself what this doctor has to say on the matter. Mrs. Harris speaks so highly of her."

Kate shifted in her seat. The woman sounded skeptical.

"I've heard the union members in Chicago give jobs to the women of shame—jobs *in their homes.*"

"I could never do that. My sister is in the Chicago union. She says that the board is not at all happy with this new Social Purity Department. I understand that the Wausau union wants to do something akin to Chicago."

"No! That would pollute our community. Surely this Dr. Bushnell will advise us against such a thing."

"I don't know. I'm not so sure she is the sort of doctor we need. My brother-in-law is a doctor—Dr. Frasier—and is doing a good job examining the women who come to work in the camps. He knows how to contain their kind there, and I say that's just what we need. I don't want that sort of women near my sons."

Everything in Kate wanted to whirl around and shout *stop*! She drew a deep breath. They had no idea what they were saying. What if Cora were their daughter and not some stranger? Wouldn't they do everything in their power to rescue her? Would a daughter caught in the unpardonable sin—against her will or not—become an untouchable, someone forever banished from family and community?

"Dr. Bushnell, we're about ready to start," Abby said. "I want to introduce you to our president, Mrs. Branson. Won't you join us on the platform?"

Kate quickly glanced behind her as she stood to follow the women to the platform.

"I'm sorry, I can't shake your hand." She smiled apologetically at Mrs. Branson though she was angry inside. "I hurt mine while out in the woods a few days ago." *Oh, if you ladies behind me only knew what I was doing.*

Kate followed her host to the platform and waited to be introduced, but she could not shake off the conversation she had overheard. She scanned the faces of the women, wondering how many others felt this same indifference. Most of these were good church women. Would they be willing to help Cora or Fran if the girls made an escape to town, or would they turn in pleading, fearful girls to the police who would drag them back to Dr. Frasier?

Mrs. Branson's voice jarred Kate from her thoughts: "And now we'll hear Dr. Bushnell tell us of her work with the Social Purity Department in Chicago."

Kate rose to her feet and knew tonight she wouldn't need notes. She began by telling Bertha Lyons' story as if for the first time, with passion and righteous anger—how alcohol caused Bertha's husband to brutalize her so that she ended on the streets to sell herself, how the same Bertha was now rescuing others from the same hell. "We work among those in the dance halls and brothels. Yes, right on the same street where ..." Kate paused a moment. *Dare I use the word in this audience of proper Christian women?* "We've established a home for reform right on the same streets where prostitutes turn on their red lights for business—"

"Shame!" A woman's strident voice called out, "A woman of shame is just half a woman—"

"Sit down!" Voices across the hall began to clamor. "Quiet. Let the doctor talk!"

The angry voice continued, "A woman of shame is just half a woman—no matter how much she *claims* to be innocent!" The woman sat down.

Kate had heard this kind of reaction before. As the audience began to settle down, she repeated, "We've established a home to reform women right on the same streets where prostitutes turn on their red light for business—red lights that welcome men to their little rooms, *cribs* they call them—for fifty cents worth of sin."

A surge of gasps and whispers rippled through the audience. She focused her gaze directly on the two women who'd sat behind her and who stared back intently. "And Bertha, who knew the life on those streets personally, now keeps a candle in the window of the Anchorage, a candle that burns not with a red light, but with a pure flame to invite anyone from the streets to come inside, welcomed in the name of Jesus. A place where they can accept Christ's invitation and 'go and sin no more.'"

For one moment, in the complete silence, Kate wondered if she'd failed to rouse compassion and justice. Then roaring applause and cheers filled the room as the women in the audience rose to their feet—all but two. The conversationalists in the second row eventually stood as well, to turn and march from the church hall.

A long line of women formed in front of Kate to thank her.

"We want to start a Reading Room here in Wausau."

"You've opened my eyes to the truth right here. Thank you."

"I would love to meet Bertha. I was so moved by her story."

Suddenly Abby broke into the line, leading a tall woman with golden hair framing soft pink cheeks and deep azure eyes. Kate had heard there were many Norwegians and Swedes here in the North, but this was the first one she'd met. "Kate, this is Senator Grossman's wife, Susannah. She plays an active role in our union."

"I'm delighted to meet you, Mrs. Grossman. We need laws passed restricting these den keepers. I'm glad to know that someone closely connected with the legislature is interested in justice for these women."

"I'll try to convince Michael with what I've heard tonight, but—"

A woman behind Mrs. Grossman pushed forward to grab Kate's hand. "That was so good, so good."

Kate looked back at Mrs. Grossman, disappearing down the aisle. What had the woman started to say? She took a quick glance at the line, relieved to see only two women left.

The last woman was large of build and bone, her gray hair combed flat against her head then caught in a huge bun where her black straw hat sat precariously. Her jowls were heavy like a man's, and Kate noticed her scruffy shoes were half-again as large as Kate's. As she reached out her hand, Kate realized this was the woman who had interrupted her lecture.

"I wanted to wait until the end so I could speak more clearly to you, Dr. Bushnell. I'm Dorothea Maddington. You don't know me, but I've read all your reports in the *Union Signal*."

"That's very kind of you Mrs.—"

"*Miss* Maddington. On occasion, I write for the *Chicago Tribune* and have also read James Fielding's very fine report of his visit to the lumber camps. I was glad to catch your lecture while visiting up here. I think you are naïve, Dr. Bushnell. You may have learned about the Chinese culture—"

"How did you—"

"I told you, I read the *Union Signal*. Not that I agree with all that temperance talk. And I certainly think you are wasting your time trying to *save* these misguided girls. I spoke with Mr. Fielding when he was here last week. He's taken the right approach—one that Governor Rusk and his legislature appreciate."

The woman straightened her back and looked at Kate with chilling intensity. "The governor doesn't like such lies being spread about our good state, neither does Fielding. Especially from a single woman who has no business even speaking of such trash in public. An honorable woman would not dream of doing that. Which makes me wonder, just what kind of a woman must *you* be?" Her eyes grew icy. "I'm not naïve. I understand you have no salary. So let me be direct. How exactly *do* you support yourself? You don't practice medicine. But you do spend an awful lot of time in those cribs ..."

She paused while Kate stood aghast, then continued. "Well, let's just say I'm surprised that Fielding hasn't written an article about *you*, Dr. Bushnell. Of course, maybe he still will, if there's a reason to. So don't give him one." The woman turned to leave. "Just a friendly warning!"

25
Fearful Threats

The rustle of the elm trees in the breeze stopped Kate from her typing. She looked out the window at Bess' mums lining the front walk below. Their beauty was like medicine to her heart. Since returning to Chicago from her investigations north, she couldn't seem to get enough of the peace in Bess' home and garden or time alone in study.

The four months in northern Wisconsin had taken their toll. She tried to erase the conversations with those who told their stories, like Agnes in Ashland or Fran in Big Bear Camp. She dreamed of holding a shaking young girl who had risked escape and was willing to tell her story.

The typewriter sat silent now, Kate's hands immobile on the keys. She remembered entering dens like the notorious one in Ashland, all alone. She'd tried to interview Griffith, who'd thrown burning oil at Agnes' friend, but no one seemed to know where he was. That was strange. *I think he suspected I knew the truth.* Pictures of injustice and cruelty crowded her mind, scenes that followed her thoughts like a black cloud overhead.

She looked back at the typewriter. She had to finish the report of all she'd seen. Again she pecked at the keys: *The system is in the hands of shrewd businessmen who own dens of prostitution in several towns. They have become adept ...* She stopped. Adept? Maybe *expert* was more precise. She wanted to be absolutely clear. Yes: *expert at...* She tapped her lips in thought.

> They have become expert at accusing young innocent girls of already having engaged in unchaste behavior so that the procurers are protected by a loophole in the law

that applies to prostitutes. This enables den keepers to be able to show in self-defense, if trouble results, that records cast doubts upon the women's characters even before they began working in the dens.

She stopped again, thinking how Jack Long could use Bella's police report to argue she was a prostitute before she came to Bear Camp. That would prove that she was qualified and willing to work for him.

She sat back and tried to rub the weariness from the back of her neck. It had been difficult to plunge right into writing these reports after she returned from Wisconsin. But she didn't want the girls trapped in the camps to be kept there an hour longer than she could help. She planned to appeal to the WCTU National Convention in New York in October—perhaps even get something on the ballot? She had sent a short report simply summarizing her findings to the Wisconsin governor and to the misled editor of the *Milwaukee Journal*. There was no time to waste and too many people to rouse. They needed to know the truth of what went on in the camps.

Kate also sent short articles to other newspapers throughout the state of Wisconsin and received poisonous responses. But she didn't let that stop her. She'd talked with physicians, businessmen, lawyers, pastors, even church women, and had been shocked at their apathy. Too many people who seemed so decent outwardly were tacitly approving of the den system.

"Well, I can't document all of them," she said to herself. "The insidiousness is everywhere. But Mahoney is a prime example—well respected in the community, even the church, but wicked to the core."

She continued writing.

> Mahoney not only found it acceptable for girls to be imprisoned in the camps to experience unspeakable crimes. He also owned them in two of the dens outside of town.

She put her elbow on the desk and rested her forehead in one hand—the weight of what she'd seen was palpable. How had he and other men come to consider women as property rather than human beings created in the image of God? How could Mike Mahoney think that he was right and just in buying ten girls for forty dollars apiece when Pres Wade's den had been closed down in Washburn?

Kate sat up straight, arched her back, and continued typing.

> A woman who had escaped told me Mahoney charged the forty to each of their accounts—they had to work off that much more before receiving payment for their "services." With that system, a girl can never earn enough to pay off her debts. If they complained, he pulled out the ledger to show them how much they owed him, and he also added a percentage for poor behavior.

The rumble of a large wagon drew Kate's attention outside the window. Four horses strained to pull a load of lumber down the street. That timber probably came on the same train that took her from Wausau to Marinette, Merrill, Ashland, Washburn, and Hurley—and some towns more than once.

Kate reflected on her trip north to Ashland to verify the death of Fannie Clark. The coroner concurred that Fannie died as the result of burning oil intentionally thrown at her. The finding read *burnt to death by W. H. Griffin*. And the perpetrator was never charged! But that must change. Kate was preparing legal documents proving there was a white slave trade in practice. And that it was actually an encompassing business!

She came to the end of a page and inserted a new sheet and three carbons into the typewriter.

> Having amassed a fortune, the men who own these places readily influence a certain class of newspapers to whitewash them. Their money commands votes for the candidates of their choice; they gain the friendship of influential businessmen through financial favors.

She sat back and her jaw dropped. Suddenly Fielding's involvement made sense. It wasn't only the businessmen up north that benefited from the dens, it was the politicians in Madison too. Whose lackey was Fielding? Governor Rusk's, or was there someone else?

"Kate, lunch is ready, if you're at a good place to stop." It was a relief to hear Bess call up the stairs.

Kate pushed away from her desk. *I think she's as eager as I am to see this report sent to the governor.* She stepped to the mirror to smooth her hair back into the bun at her neck. The other day, she thought she had seen one or two gray strands. She never expected she'd be doing this at thirty-three.

As she'd done every day since returning home, Kate reached into her pocket and retrieved the crumpled piece of paper Bella had given her from the shanty wall. The recorded calendar of the girls' monthlies—Bella's bold checks across five squares and Cora's tiny marks in five corners, overlapping Fran's by three days. Vacation days, they'd said. Kate tucked the calendar back in her pocket. *Lord, help me find the way to keep such a memory alive. I must never forget.*

"How's it going, Kate?" Bess called up again.

Kate hurried downstairs. A copy of the *Milwaukee Journal* lay on the table next to her place. Her heart sank. "Has Fielding written another article about me—that I'm a liar?"

"No, no, Kate. But there is a short article on the back page by a Miss Dorothea Maddington. Do you know who she is?"

Kate's heart flipped. She turned the paper over to the back page. "Yes, she came to one of my meetings—in Hurley, I believe." She read for a few minutes, then threw the paper down. "Just what I expected. She defends Fielding's article and claims I'm manufacturing reports of white slavery to gain attention. She's even questioning my purity!" Kate shook her head. She had braced herself for this, but still it hurt. And it concerned her. "Maddington hasn't even seen my reports, but she and Fielding are determined to destroy my credibility."

"Are you really worried about their threats?"

"I'm concerned that they could mar the reputation of the WCTU and keep people from hearing the truth. As for me, I have to trust that God will take care of me. I think I've pretty well disproved all Fielding's claims in the *Milwaukee Journal* that girls are never abducted or detained by den keepers."

"Someone's putting pressure on him," Bess remarked dryly. "I've already reserved space in the next *Union Signal* for your report. The women on the editorial team are all eager to read it. I've told them some of your experiences, and they are awestruck. I think maybe some of the naysayers are coming around."

"The report may be a bit long." Kate shook her head. "I'm going to have to cut out a lot if I want to read it at the National Convention in New York."

"Imagine." Bess marveled. "You'll be on the stage of the Metropolitan Opera House in one of the most treasured time slots— the final Sunday afternoon. God is giving you favor, Kate."

"Yes." Kate frowned. "I think some of the women come to hear me speak because they want to hear lurid details, the gossip of sensational newspaper reports." She shook her head. "But this isn't gossip, and I'm going to make sure they know the truth—thoroughly documented with reliable sources."

Kate grew quiet. She didn't want to spellbind with stories as much as rouse hearers to action. "They'll know I've never relied on newspaper articles and have double-checked every story directly with various people and sources." She looked at Bess. "And, yes, if I have to, I'll tell how I've visited the dens myself."

Kate touched Bella's crumpled chart in her pocket. The proof was in her hands.

Kate climbed the stairs to her lodgings in a private home. She'd come to New York for the WCTU Convention, which would be held at the famed Metropolitan Opera House. She found a cheerful-looking young woman unpacking a suitcase.

"Hello," Kate called out. "We must be roommates. I'm Katharine Bushnell."

The young woman looked up from her unpacking with a bright smile. "Oh good, you've arrived, Dr. Bushnell. I'm Ruby Franklin. She reached out her hand with a warm smile on a heart-shaped face framed by unpinned waist-long brown hair. She had an impish upturned nose, sprinkled with freckles. But Kate saw sadness in the hazel eyes as though the shine had been dulled.

When Ruby changed for the meeting, huge discolored bruises on her arms explained the reason. Kate had seen those marks before. They brought back visions of Maggie and Bertha. That's what had taken the glow out of Ruby's eyes.

Ruby saw the look on Kate's face. "It shows?" she asked softly. "Joseph is a good man. He works in his father's lumber store. But he's drinking more and more." She pulled her dress over the bruises. "That's why I joined the WCTU. I hoped I'd learn how to help him."

"Has it helped?"

"No. Not yet." She gave a weak smile. Then the hazel eyes seemed to darken. "He became angry that I went to union meetings. He ordered me to stop."

"Did you?"

"I didn't know what to do. At first I did because he has the authority. Isn't that what the Bible says?" She looked searchingly into Kate's eyes.

"I've read that," Kate responded dryly. She remembered conversations with Bess. It was the same situation faced by the women whom Dan tried to help.

"I couldn't stay away, Kate. I needed the comfort and fellowship of the White Ribboners. They understood—better than the women at church. Sometimes I think my minister thought it was my fault when Joseph hit me." She looked down. "Joseph doesn't know I'm here. He thinks I'm visiting my mother."

Ruby shook herself and brightened. "But we need to finish dressing for dinner and the opening meeting tonight."

Before the meeting began, Kate stood alone for a moment at the back of the hall, elegant with its domed ceiling and five layers of encircling balconies.

She watched the frenetic activity. Four thousand attendees, she'd been told. Above the hum of conversation, she heard squeals of delight as delegates with lavish hats welcomed one another and greeted friends with a kiss on the cheek. Kate shook her head. How different to be among these women with a common purpose and convivial spirit than in the shanties filled with fear and longing.

Suddenly a man's voice broke into her reverie.

"Excuse me, may I speak with you a moment?"

Kate whirled around. An unexplained tremor of fear raced down her back as she faced a giant of a man with a shock of black hair and short beard outlining his chin. He loomed over her by at least a foot, which in itself made Kate uneasy, since she was usually the tallest woman in the room.

"Do I know you, sir?"

"I'm Senator Jonathan Grossman. My wife plays in the brass quartet."

"Oh, I didn't know she played. I met her after one of my meetings in Hurley several months ago."

Grossman looked startled at her comment, but he asked again, "Could we step into the foyer for just a moment so I can speak with you?" He put his hand under her elbow so that she found herself moving up the aisle with him until they found a relatively quiet corner in the foyer.

"I understand that you are going to speak to the women on Sunday afternoon about your experiences in the lumber camps in Wisconsin."

Kate nodded.

"Can I give you a word of advice? Governor Rusk is very disappointed in your report."

"I don't think he—"

"Oh yes, he's received it and read it. He finds that it slanders the state of Wisconsin and our public servants. The earlier reports in newspapers around the state disturbed him, and he sent his own person to research and report on what he found."

Kate shook with anger. "His own person—Fielding—did not visit the dens nor write the truth."

Grossman gave her a dark look and jabbed his finger at her. "But his report is the official position Governor Rusk and the senate are taking. He has asked me to warn you not to spread rumors that will stir up our emotional sisters. You may not be aware that the Rev. Davis has already been accused of libel for defending your findings. He's awaiting trial."

Kate stepped back and covered her mouth. Ruth Davis' husband! *Arrested because of me?*

Grossman spoke sternly, a warning note in each word. "It would behoove you to keep that in mind. The governor is thinking about asking James Fielding to write another article in the *Journal*. What it contains depends entirely on you." With that, he turned and walked back into the hall.

Shocked, Kate stood in the foyer, oblivious to the crowds and the music coming from the hall. She could only think of Scott Davis. She never thought that her enthusiasm for revealing the truth could hurt others who tried to help her. She sank to the nearest bench and wiped her forehead with her handkerchief. *He threatened me!* She took several deep breaths, then stood and raised her chin just a little. *But you haven't frightened—or stopped—me, Senator Grossman.*

Kate straightened her shoulders and walked purposefully back into the hall. The sight lifted her spirits. Flags flew over each union delegation's area. White Ribbon banners in silk, satin, and velvet hung over the platform. Huge vases stood on each side, bearing grain, fruit, and flowers, all surrounding a moss-covered well. The whole auditorium was decked with red-white-and-blue slogans. From the other side of the heavy curtain, the White Ribbon quartet could be heard warming up their cornets.

Kate felt herself warming to the occasion as well. A sudden exhilaration poured over her, not so much from the noise and color, but from the sense of how she was part of a great force for good. The women in the hall were driven by the same passion she was. But could she persuade them to open their hearts and homes to girls like Cora, Fran, and Bella? Like Huldah?

She didn't have time to think on that. A young volunteer pressed a thick conference program into her hand, then paused upon reading the button on Kate's jacket with her name. "Dr. Bushnell! Your article was on the front page of the *Kenosha Courier*. I can't wait to hear the rest of your report Sunday."

Kate thanked her and moved slowly through the crowd toward her seat in the staff section. *This is what God intends—to let my passion for justice spill over to a young woman like that. She's no older than I was when God called me to China.* A sudden homesickness for her father washed over Kate. She thought of her plea to go to med school and how he supported her in each new endeavor. *Make a difference. Leave a legacy.* His words never failed to rouse her. She wondered what advice he would give her now.

"There you are!"

Kate turned to see the welcoming smile of Abby Harris. "I told Ben you'd be here. Are you going to speak?"

"Oh, I'm so glad to see you here." Kate hugged Abby. "I feared you might not be able to come from so far away."

"There are three of us here from Wausau. Come join us."

"Oh." Kate was moved. "I would, but Bess has saved a seat for me in the staff area. I hope I can introduce you to her."

"I figured as much, but we will cheer you on from the Wausau delegation. You have much to say, Kate Bushnell, and we know it."

Kate smiled. "What I really want is to hear some good news. Have you heard anything about the girls, the three at Big Bear Camp?"

Abby's face fell. "I meant to write you. Cora did try to escape, using the rope Ben made into a ladder, the one you left for her. She managed to get as far as Schofield, but something happened. We don't know if she couldn't find someone to help her get to us or she lost her way. In any case, one of the town constables picked her up on the street, and she was sent back to the camp. The constable's mother comes to our union, and she heard him telling their neighbor about it. If only she had found Cora instead."

Everything inside Kate grew heavy. Following Grossman's threats, she felt even more helpless. Even though she had the truth, powerful men would not believe her. Should she have brought Cora out with her? At least then no one could have doubted the reality of the evil playing out in the forest.

Abby's arm slipped around Kate's waist. "I'm so sorry. I know the dangers you faced going into that den. I know you risked everything so they could be free. But it's not over. When Governor Rusk gets your report, he will find Jack Long guilty. The girls will be freed."

"Maybe not." Kate's stomach churned. She felt truly shaken. "He has my report, and we haven't received any response." Swallowing the lump in her throat, she hugged Abby and turned to find her seat.

She realized that thousands of girls, degraded by liquor and lust, could never be part of a joyous gathering like this. Would they even be welcomed here?

Suddenly everyone around and in front of her started cheering and rising from their seats. Miss Willard had stepped up to the platform to give her annual address, and there was so much applause and shouting, Kate could hardly hear the brass quartet playing the crusade hymn. White handkerchiefs filled the air like thousands of fluttering birds, and union banners were raised high toward the ceiling.

In spite of her inner pain, Kate found herself clapping and cheering for her mentor, who looked so tiny on the stage, looking severe, dressed all in black.

Miss Willard waved to the adoring crowd. Kate waved back, but her mind replayed the senator's words while her inner eyes saw Cora's pleading face outside a shanty sequestered in the Wisconsin forests that hid its awful secrets.

As the women finally sat down to listen, Miss Willard began her annual message without a note in her hand. She reminded the delegates that after fourteen years, more than a half million women followed the WCTU cause. Her powerful voice reached the highest balcony, and people stood again in joyous jubilation, white handkerchiefs thrown into the air. The sight looked like sea spray.

By Sunday afternoon, stories of Kate's adventures in the northern woods of Wisconsin had circulated. Kate fielded many questions as delegates recognized her. But she was still surprised to see the hall nearly full when she stood to give her report.

"Beloved co-laborers," she began. She glanced at the pocket watch lying conspicuously on the podium. "I present this with humble gratitude to God for His protection and guidance during this four-month ordeal." Kate raised a thick packet for the audience to see. "There is more than enough proof in this report to recant all the falsities printed in the *Milwaukee Journal* and other newspapers across the country. We have indisputable evidence that white slavery exists in northern Wisconsin!"

The women clapped and cheered. Kate watched patiently as they settled down so she could continue. "Our time is limited this afternoon, so I will briefly share a few highlights." She placed her report on the podium and stepped forward to one side to speak directly to her audience.

"My story is really about a fourteen-year-old girl, a girl who could be your daughter. I found her locked up in a shanty, guarded by a big black dog. She wanted to escape with me, but I had to leave her behind. I still see her pleading face."

Kate glanced around at the women as she told her story. Many were wiping their eyes. Would they have taken Cora in if Kate had brought her to them? Her voice grew stronger. "I met with 576 degraded girls and women, most of them young girls. I have records of fifty-nine dens. I visited many of them several times. Sometimes, I confess, I was afraid—afraid I would be caught and examined and forced to work in a den, afraid I would be branded for life like Hester Prynne in the *Scarlet Letter.*"

Kate paused, noting the shocked expressions on many faces. "But my medical bag and credentials often helped, as did the protective husbands of White Ribboners." Cheers broke out from the back of the crowd.

"The root of the problem lies in the hearts of corrupt businessmen who amass fortunes at the cost of innocent girls' purity." Her voice rose in anger as she told of a town health officer who proudly showed her a copy of the Contagious Diseases Act that had recently been passed through his influence. "That act is patterned after the English act that Josephine Butler fought for more than fifteen years to repeal.

"Listen, sisters. Listen to what that law does. It requires all degraded women to be examined regularly. The term degraded simply means the poor. It includes any woman or girl picked up—often without any cause—by the corrupt, yes, even corrupt constables, and taken to a doctor for examination. As a doctor, I could describe the specifics of such an examination, but it would not be proper in this gathering. The girls are then provided with a physician's certificate of 'purity from infectious disease,' often signed by the town mayor." Kate paused to let the words sink in. *Lord, let them hear.* "This allows a man to commit lewd acts with her because she is virtually a licensed prostitute. She becomes a piece of valuable property for the owner of a den or brothel."

She glanced at the watch on the podium and picked up her notes. "In closing, let me read a story dictated to me in Hurley, way up on the Minnesota border, by a Christian woman whose veracity was vouched for by a dear friend of mine." Kate read: "It was the week before Christmas. I was coming along Second Avenue from town when I heard something that sounded like the clinking of a chain. I thought it must be horses running away with part of the harness. I kept hearing the noise but could not see anything." Kate looked up and met the eyes of woman after woman in the audience. She didn't have to read the account; she knew it by heart. "Then I saw a woman coming toward me from the direction of Le Claire's den two blocks off. I will never forget the awful look on her face in the glow of the gas streetlight. She had a cape flowing loosely around her and spread out with the wind. Her dress was held up on one side by a chain attached to an iron ball she held in her hands and fastened to an iron cuff on her ankle. With every step, the chain rattled against the cuff."

Kate swallowed again. "She was running as hard as she could across the track just in front of an oncoming train. Two men followed in a cutter. They were gaining on her, but she dashed past the train and they had to wait for it to pass. The woman got a little ahead and ran up the embankment on the other side, then down across the Lake Shore railroad and up on the other bank of the ditch."

Kate paused, turned back to her notes, and read each word deliberately. She wanted to nail the words into each listener's heart. "When the train passed, the men drove on and overtook her. They thrust her into the sleigh and took her back to Le Claire's den.

"Dear sisters. I'm sure your hearts are broken for that young woman and you're saying 'I wish I could do something.' You can. Open your eyes to what's going on in your town or city. Find ways to reach out *with love* to women and girls caught in prostitution—many out of desperation. Remember Jesus forgave the woman caught in adultery and encouraged her to go out in purity from that day forward. Should we do less?"

Kate stepped off the platform, but her words hung over the hall where nearly four-thousand women sat hushed, except for the occasional sniffles breaking the silence.

26
Overcome by Fear

1889

$\mathcal{T}$he carriage waited in front of the house to take Kate to the train station. It rent her heart to say good-bye. She'd been home in Illinois for Christmas with her family. Now she was going on to Pittsburgh. But Father just didn't look like himself. He didn't have an appetite even for Mother's special dishes made just for him.

Kate hesitated at the carriage before climbing in, then ran back to give her father one more hug.

"I'm proud of you, girl," he whispered in her ear. "Even though Mother acts shocked when you tell her the things you've seen and are talking about, in her heart she's proud too."

"Keep praying," Kate said. She ran down the stairs to the carriage. "I should be back in the spring. I want to go to the lighthouse with you again."

But only a few days after she arrived in Pittsburgh, she received the telegram:

FATHER DIED PEACEFULLY STOP

FUNERAL SATURDAY AT TWO STOP

COME HOME

SARAH

Mrs. Brady, her hostess, had delivered the telegram and sat quietly beside Kate, respecting her grief.

"I can't go home for the funeral." Kate sobbed. "I have meetings scheduled all weekend."

"They'd understand if you canceled your lectures."

"The women have invited people from other towns," Kate

251

responded. "And besides, I don't think I would make it home by Saturday."

The gloomy winter skies mirrored her spirits though she tried to hide them from her eager audiences. Even though she was committed to speak at meetings all weekend, she checked the train schedules to Chicago, just in case. But as she'd expected, she could not have reached home in time for the funeral.

Her heart was broken. *I couldn't even say good-bye. I don't understand why I have to be torn like this, why I can't go home?* As she lay in bed, unable to sleep, she drew upon her only source of peace. *Lord, I sense You calling me to keep my commitments. Bertha and the women she's caring for depend on the income I bring in from my lectures. Please, please help Mother to understand.* And the tears she wept into her pillow washed away her pain for a little time.

After the busy weekend, Kate had a free evening. She desperately needed the time away from meetings to heal and grieve, even if work still required her attention. She pulled out a folder filled with mail and willed herself to catch up on correspondence. *I'm so behind. How does Miss Willard do it?* Kate smiled a little. *Of course! She has a typewriter and a secretary.*

At the sound of a soft knock, she put down her pen and went to the door.

Mrs. Brady carried a tray in her hands. "I brought you some coffee, Dr. Bushnell. It's such a cold night. Are you warm enough?"

"Oh yes. I admit I'm more exhausted than anything." Kate sipped the coffee. "Your home is so comfortable. Thank you for this welcoming fire, for everything."

Mrs. Brady smiled. "We're so grateful for you, for all your work. I'll let you rest, and perhaps we can chat at breakfast before Mrs. Foster arrives to take you to your next meeting."

Kate sat back at the writing table. The reports beckoned, but she felt such an urge to write a letter to her sister. She pulled out a fresh piece of paper.

Dear Sarah,
I hope you received my telegram in time to share it at the funeral. My heart is spent. You know how close Father

and I were—and to think I couldn't even get home for the funeral.

She explained why she hadn't been able to come. *They knew I'd have been there if I could*, she reminded herself as she wrote.

This has been a doubly difficult trip. The reports of my work in northern Wisconsin have preceded me everywhere. I seem to be a sensation—and it's distressing. You won't believe the exaggerations and untruths newspapers have published. The *New York Herald* wrote that "packs of bulldogs surrounded the dens," and one paper said I'd been captured and barely escaped. Even the *Union Signal* had its facts wrong. I wish—

Another knock sounded, this one more insistent. Kate got up to pull the door open to find Mrs. Brady's husband with an envelope in his hand.

"I apologize for interrupting, Dr. Bushnell, but a telegram just arrived for you. I hope it's nothing serious."

Kate reached for the buff-colored envelope, remembering the last telegram she'd received. "It's probably a change in my schedule again." She thanked him, shut the door, and pulled the message from the envelope.

DR KATHARINE BUSHNELL

REQUEST YOUR PRESENCE AT SPECIAL SESSION OF WISCONSIN STATE LEGISLATURE STOP MARCH 15 1889 STOP BRING PROOF OF ACCUSATIONS REGARDING NORTHERN LUMBER CAMPS

S. J. CLARK

CLERK OF WISCONSIN SENATE

Kate sank back in her chair. Finally. Her reports were being taken seriously. Or at least she hoped so. The subtle threats from Governor Rusk and Senator Grossman accusing her of slandering the State of Wisconsin had made her fear her findings would languish—and that the governor would call for action against her. They had tried the Rev. Davis for libel, but he was finally acquitted.

She stood and looked out the window. The storm had passed, and the gas lamp down the street illuminated the snow glistening against the ink-blue sky. It looked so pristine, like the untouched forest. But by morning, the horses and wagons would come down the street. What looked so pure now would be churned into mud. She thought of all the ruined girls and women in the camps, all the months of work investigating their horror, then documenting it, and now this summons before the lawmakers. Suddenly her hands began to shake as she put them over her face. She felt more fearful of all the work falling on deaf ears than she had of getting caught in the camps. What if the powerful men in Madison thought she truly was churning her findings into slander? How could she make them see the truth? What if they accused her of libel, too? What if this turned into a trap to discredit her further?

Kate stood at the window a few more minutes. Huge flakes of snow began falling on the city again. She thought of the mud and the mire hidden beneath the purity. An old hymn she'd sung in the tent meeting that changed her life so many years ago came to her mind. *Oh, precious is the flow that makes me white as snow, no other fount I know, nothing but the blood of Jesus.*

She bowed her head. *Father, I need You to handle this one for me. I don't know what I'm getting into, or what I need to say. But You do. Please go ahead of me.* Gradually, she felt peace and confidence fall on her like the snow outside, and she turned back to finish her letter. *Better for Sarah to hear about this from me.*

Kate's pen flew across the page as she told about the telegram.

> This means rescheduling my meetings in New York. But I'm glad for it. Now those men will hear the truth. Please pray for me.
> Give my love to Mother.
> Your loving sister, Kate

Kate twisted her fingers nervously around the handle of her bag and gazed out the window of the carriage. She was thankful that Mrs. Bascom, the president of the Madison WCTU, and her husband had picked her up at the station. She hadn't realized how much their support would mean.

Mrs. Bascom patted her hand. "It's going to be all right, Kate."

She wasn't so sure. As the carriage drew closer to the Wisconsin capitol, her heart constricted. A little more tightly, her hands clutched her bag where the fearsome telegram lay, the words indelibly imprinted in her mind: *Bring proof of accusations.*

Kate smiled weakly at Mrs. Bascom and eyed the capitol building they approached. The whole thing felt like a trial. What if the doubters brought Fielding before the senate to present his slanderous accusations against her chastity? Would they take his word over hers? If word about her like that got out, no one would believe her research. Those women she had talked to would still be trapped, or worse. The WCTU would be damaged. Kate would be discredited. She'd seen firsthand how powerful these people were. They'd stop at nothing to—

She shook her head to clear her mind. *Enough! Are you believing in yourself or in God? Whose work is this, after all?* She closed her eyes a moment.

Mrs. Bascom patted her hand. "Once they hear your report, they will take action against those—"

"Oh, I hope so, Mrs. Bascom," Kate interrupted. She paused, then asked the question on her heart. "You don't think there's danger that they will accuse me of libel? Governor Rusk wrote me an angry letter, saying that I'm slandering the state."

"Of course these men don't like to hear the truth. They have too much at stake. But once they *see* the proof you've unearthed, they must face it."

Richard Bascom leaned across his wife to face Kate. "I just want to warn you. There's been a lot of talk around town about your testimony today. The chairman of the senate is an irascible fellow, and I don't trust him."

His wife tugged at her husband's arm as though to quiet him.

"No, Edna." He was kind to his wife but resolute. "Kate should be forewarned." He turned back to Kate. "Men from the breweries in Milwaukee have threatened to come today. They were furious at the Temperance Union's stance even before you appeared on the scene. The newspapers spread stories of how the women go to pray in the saloons."

"Do you think they'll come into the senate?" Kate felt her anxiety growing again.

"I doubt the police will allow that."

"Police?" Kate had expected an appearance before the legislature to be stately. *But police?*

Richard Bascom eyed his wife. "I'm afraid there's more. There are others—"

Mrs. Bascom became insistent. "Hush, Richard. You're frightening the poor girl. She needs calm to be collected. She needs peace." She turned to Kate. "Take confidence in the truth."

"I need to know what to expect." Kate eyed the capitol building, now in full view. The large dome supported by tall pillars was imposing, but its north and south wings seemed outstretched like welcoming arms. Her heart settled again as a realization dawned. She turned back to Mrs. Bascom. "I'm embarrassed that I've been so nervous. There are hundreds of women praying for me today. I've had peace up till now. But I'm not alone."

Mrs. Bascom placed a hand over Kate's. "God will be with you."

"That I know and have preached."

The driver turned the carriage onto North Hamilton Street and the capitol's entrance.

"Richard and I will go into the rotunda with you." Mrs. Bascom pointed to the doors. "We'll take you to the office of the state clerk on the second floor, and we'll go up to the visitors' gallery. We've arrived in plenty of time for your two o'clock appointment."

Kate nodded. She looked at the beautifully carved columns that surrounded the oval portico. But the beauty was shattered by hundreds of men, some holding placards: *Get out of Wisconsin. Keep your nose out of our state.*

"Those men! Do they really see me as an enemy? Where are the women?"

The men milled about and lined the path up the capitol steps. As Mr. Bascom had warned her, police lined the steps too, chatting amiably with the men in the crowd.

When Kate stepped out of the carriage, someone shouted, "There she is!"

Others joined in a mean chorus: "Liar!" "Go back where you came from!" Words far worse floated through the air.

Kate began to climb the steps, the Bascoms just behind her, as men in the crowd began to boo and wave the placards high in the air. They closed in. One pulled her sleeve.

"Stand back!" police officers called. "Get back."

But the men surged forward. A burly, bearded man bumped into Kate so that she almost lost her footing. Stunned, she raised a hand to her throat as she hurried along. *Is this all about me? Or are they angry at the Temperance Union?*

A young policeman, wielding a billy club, jumped to her side. "Take my arm, ma'am," the officer said quietly. "I'll see that you get into the rotunda. These roustabouts won't be able to follow you in there."

The angry men didn't follow, but their curses sounded louder and they raised defiant fists.

Kate wanted to cover her ears with her hands to shut out the ugly words the men yelled. Instead, something arose in her. She squared her shoulders and looked straight into the angry men's eyes. She thought how Miss Willard would give such a look and stare down unruly students. The men seemed to back away as she moved up the steps through the crowd.

As she reached the top, Kate turned to see the Bascoms, surrounded by several police officers, close behind her. She felt relief as they slipped inside, then heard one last angry outburst.

"You whore."

Kate felt her face blanch at the cruel accusation.

The door closed behind them, shutting out the commotion. Kate determined to put these men out of her mind as she and the Bascoms hurried toward the stairs leading to the senate hall on the second floor, their boots clicking loudly on the marble tiles.

At the door to the office of the chief clerk, Mrs. Bascom kissed Kate on the cheek and whispered, "You'll do fine. Just give them the awful truth so they will have to take action for justice or slink away in shame."

Clark, a wizened little man in a black suit shiny from wear, opened the door to his office and offered Kate a seat. A red mark encircled his neck from his highly starched collar.

"You can wait here until you're called in, Dr. Bushnell. Governor Rusk is giving a speech." Without waiting for a response, he turned and left her alone.

She should have realized that Governor Rusk would be there to listen to her report. But she wouldn't let him keep her from making a bold presentation. She answered to God, not him.

The clock above the clerk's desk ticked loudly, the only sound in the room. Kate tried not to look at it, conscious of how the hands seemed to barely move and time seemed to be standing still. She started to take her report from her bag, then thrust it back, staring at the desk, empty except for a silent telephone. Clark would come back for her any moment. She mustn't let him think she was nervous.

She sighed and looked at the clock again. Only five minutes had passed since the last time she'd looked, but it was already two-thirty. Why were they taking so long?

Suddenly the door opened and the clerk beckoned her to follow him into the senate hall. Kate rose and for a moment paused at the door into the hall. On any other occasion, the beauty would have mesmerized her: curved walls stippled in pale lilac, a high ceiling with delicate pink cornices, at least a dozen gas chandeliers hung over the circular rows of polished oak desks. And below, flowered carpet stretched underneath the pale-green domed ceiling. But at this moment, Kate could only focus on the men in dark suits and starched collars searching through seas of papers that spilled over almost every desk. She studied the faces turned toward one another in serious conversation and thought how intense they were. Then she closed her eyes and pictured other faces: young, wounded, helpless faces—Cora, Bella, Huldah.

She drew in a breath, stood tall, and stepped into the hall.

Every chair swiveled around to face the podium, the sea of serious faces turned angry. Some men raised their fists as though threatening her very presence.

Kate felt as though she inhaled the anger. The senators looked as though they'd already passed judgment. She could not see a single friendly face; even the Bascoms were above and behind her in the visitors' gallery. There was no applause or acknowledgment of her presence, just an ominous muttering.

She noted that the governor's chair on the podium was empty. She didn't recognize any of the senators as her eyes swept her audience. Oh yes, there he was: Senator Grossman! He sat at the rear, leaning sideways in his chair, his arm flung over the back, and his grim face sending a threatening message.

God, help me to ignore him. Kate exhaled and stepped forward, admitting her fear to God. Where were the women? She'd sent telegrams to the unions in the region. Didn't they receive them? Did no one believe her? *Lord, let truth be heard.*

The clerk pointed to the huge wooden podium, arched like a half moon. The president and vice president of the senate sat on either side of the speaker's lectern; the governor's chair was empty, but no one offered Kate a seat.

She tried to control her shaking hands as she pulled her report from her bag and placed it on the lectern. Her right ankle began to quiver. *I've done this hundreds of times in the last year. This audience may be different, but the message is still true. God, You are here.* She took a deep breath and began to speak. "Honorable Governor Rusk, president of the senate—" She nodded to the right. Was she even looking in the correct direction? "And honorable senators of the state of—"

The sound of a door opening forcefully caused her to turn to her left and stare.

The clerk stared too, rooted to his seat, unable to stop the entrance of women pouring into the senate chambers from the ladies' lobby.

They did come! Kate watched the women quietly march around the back of the hall, heads held high. They circled the room, and several moved onto the podium itself.

Kate recognized the wives of several senators and ministers, one from as far away as Milwaukee. She looked into the eyes of friends.

She spotted Senator Henry's wife, pulling her two young daughters along, and Miss Cook, the ninety-year-old schoolteacher everyone in the union admired. She had probably taught many of the senators seated there. And Mrs. Grossman—she came in spite of her husband's threats? There was Dr. Nichols' wife, Sheila. Thank God for Dr. Nichols. Kate remembered his words that all prostitution must be eliminated rather than be accepted as a necessary evil. He was a rare man indeed.

One of the senators started to stand to offer Miss Cook a seat, but the man behind him put his hand on his shoulder, forcing him to sit back down, and grumbled something indiscernible into his fellow senator's ear. Kate didn't need to know the words to know he was complaining about her.

It was clear they didn't want to face the truth. What had happened to these fine gentlemen? She couldn't wait another moment.

Kate lifted her head and faced the mixed audience. She quieted her heart and sent up a final prayer. Her ankle stopped quivering and hands stopped shaking. *This is where I belong today. You've brought me here as Your messenger, to speak Your words. Lord, open their ears.*

"Ladies and senators ..." Kate began again, this time in a voice so strong and confident that she knew even the visitors in the gallery behind her could not miss a word. "Her name is Cora. Her family has a small farm up north in your beautiful state, but with many children to feed, her parents agreed to send her to Schofield to find a job. The plan was for her to work and earn money to help her family. But it didn't turn out that way."

Kate paused. Every eye was focused on her. The muttering had ceased. "Instead, Cora was stopped on the street as she walked to visit a friend. She was taken to the police station, accused of indecent intentions, and sent to a doctor to be examined. In other words, she was forced to endure surgical rape." Murmurs of disbelief came from the women listening, but most of the men sat stoically though several shook their heads in disgust. Michael Grossman admired the green ceiling, feigning disinterest.

Kate took a deep breath and spoke even more forcefully. "Cora was sent to Bear Camp and locked in a den for the pleasure of the lumbermen." She paused and bent over the lectern, looking directly into the eyes of a senator in the front row. "Cora is fourteen years old."

Senators shifted uncomfortably in their seats, but they remained silent.

"There is a persistent determination to maintain these dens as a necessity for the men working in the lumber camps. The evil is compounded by compelling any girls who look even slightly suspicious to live in them. Gentlemen, if your daughter walked down the streets of those northern towns, she might end up like Cora." She looked directly at Senator Grossman in the back, who'd lifted his head to look at her for the first time.

Kate forged ahead, reporting case after case of women and girls trapped in the camps, stories from places like Hurley, Ashland, and Wausau. "I found that the real obstacle that keeps these girls from returning to a virtuous life is a total lack of sympathy for their terrible fate, lack of sympathy on the part of men, women, and even officers of the law." She raised her voice. "Nobody cares about them." She paused to look into the faces of the senators around the room and whispered again, "Nobody."

She sent a grateful glance to the women standing around the room, even to Senator Henry's girls and their mother who'd been listening intently. Then she locked eyes with one senator after another. "I plead with you to remember the very words of Christ who came to heal the brokenhearted, to preach deliverance to the captives, to set at liberty those who are bruised. Cora, and others held like her, are in your hands."

In silence, she put her notes back in her bag. *Have I failed? Has even one word registered?* She teetered on despair and then lifted her head at the sound of one lone person clapping. In the front row, a senator had risen to his feet and stood alone, applauding loudly.

Then one by one, around the room, others joined him, until all but a few stiff-necked hardliners stood clapping heartily.

Kate nodded gratefully and slowly followed Mr. Clark back to his office and out to the rotunda. The women had filed from the senate chambers through the ladies' lounge and were already gathered to welcome her.

Susannah Grossman greeted her first. "You have stunned them

all." She leaned over and whispered, "And I'll make sure my husband gets the message. I know exactly how to handle *him*." She winked.

Others gathered around. Their victorious mood was infectious, but Kate warned, "We haven't won yet. They still have to pass a law."

"They will," one of the women said.

"How can we be so sure?" Kate wondered aloud.

Edna and Richard Bascom each put an arm around Kate's shoulders. "Senator Fitch—that first senator to stand?" Edna whispered in Kate's ear. "His daughter's name is Cora."

As the women continued talking in excited clusters, Kate gradually moved away down the hall, passing the governor's office and approaching Fielding's windowless cubbyhole. She planned to put her report on his desk so he would see her proof for himself.

Unfortunately, a group of senators in animated conversation crowded the hall. She didn't want to pass them and draw their attention. If only there were another way to get to Fielding's office. As she neared the group, she caught one of the men saying, "She claims there are fourteen-year-old girls being held up there!"

"What proof does she have?"

Kate recognized Fielding's voice even before he turned to see her standing nearby. His face was flushed and rigid with anger. Had he been drinking?

"You think you have them convinced?" he asked her sarcastically.

Kate forced a smile on her face. "Why, good day, Mr. Fielding. I'm glad to find you here. I brought you a copy of the report I gave to the senate." She heard a few snickers from the bystanders.

"Just because you've written up a pretty story doesn't mean it's true. I was up there, you remember, Dr. Bushnell." His cheeks puffed out as his voice rose. "I saw the conditions with my own eyes, and they were nothing like the slander you're spreading about our state."

By now, the men standing in the hall had stopped talking and were listening intently. Not only the senators but also Governor Rusk himself had come out of his office to see what was going on. Kate had never met him, but he looked like his picture with that bushy silver beard and thick white eyebrows pulled together into a frown. She knew he'd been in the senate hall giving a message. Why hadn't he stayed for her report? He had previously refused to take the matter up and dismissed her findings, but he might have changed his mind after hearing her speak.

"But you haven't read my report, Mr. Fielding," Kate persisted. "I contacted more than 550 women and girls personally, and many of them were held against—"

"You're a liar, Dr. Bushnell!" Fielding shouted. He clenched his fists in frustration. "It's easy to count people. Count as many as you want, way up there in the woods." He paused and moved closer; for a moment Kate thought he would strike her. "I know your kind. You live down there in Chicago. Why don't you look for dirt in your own backyard?"

Kate drew herself to her full height and looked down at the short blustery man. "You have no right to call me a liar. You're just afraid to read the truth—the truth you refused to print in the *Journal*."

"The truth, ma'am? You're not only a liar. I had a long talk with Mike Leahy, who has a business in Marquette. He told me how you carried on up there with all your *questions*. But people saw you traveling alone with that shopkeeper Harris. You can't deny that." He turned to face his stunned audience.

"Yes, she traveled alone with a married man. Leahy saw them together. He told me she's just as unchaste as those women she talks about—but more of a hypocrite—at least they admit who they are. You'd better believe I'll have plenty to say in the paper about all this."

One of the senators called out, "That's enough, Fielding."

Nervously, others began moving away, shaking their heads. The governor had slipped back into his office.

Kate stood stunned, clutching her report. She felt tears beginning to form. *I won't, I won't let them see me cry.* Even as her tears dried, a surge of anger rose through her body, and she had to bite her tongue not to shout back at Fielding, who disappeared down the hall.

But one senator stayed and came to stand next to her. Kate recognized him—Senator Fitch, the first senator to stand and clap for her. "I'm so embarrassed, so sorry that you had to listen to that."

Still in shock from the altercation, Kate thanked him. She looked directly into his face. "Did you hear him call me a liar and accuse me of being unchaste—in front of all these senators, even the governor?"

"Yes, ma'am, I'm afraid I did."

"Do you think I'm a liar and a whore? Do the senators believe that?" Kate asked anxiously, controlling the fury she felt.

"No! No, of course not, Dr. Bushnell. Your report has stunned us all, even the skeptics. We're ashamed that something like that has gone on in our state."

"But these men heard Fielding, the governor's *detective*. He has many friends in this building. What if he writes another report about me in the *Milwaukee Journal*?" Kate hung her head as she and the senator walked slowly back towards the rotunda. "Is there any way to stop him?"

"How long will you be in Madison, Dr. Bushnell?" Senator Fitch asked.

"I have to leave on the afternoon train tomorrow to get back to my lectures in the East."

"I'll bring my lawyer, Joshua Olin, to see you at the Bascoms' this evening. I think the only way to make sure Fielding doesn't do more damage is to sue him for defamation."

"Do you think this could affect the legislature's decision about accepting my report as evidence? We desperately need a law to imprison those men. Right now men like Leahy and Jack Long just pay a fine if they are caught with illegal girls. But that small fine is like paying for a license. It's just the cost of doing business. I wouldn't want a lawsuit to jeopardize this legislation from happening."

They were almost to the rotunda where the women were still milling around discussing the new revelations they'd heard. Senator Fitch stopped and spoke confidentially to Kate. "If I can read the legislators right, I think the overwhelming majority were not only shocked by your report but are also determined to do something about it." He turned to a woman coming toward them. "Here's my wife. She probably wants to go home. But one more thing, why don't you jot down your thoughts about what this law should look like, and I'll take it to the legislature."

27
Go Home

Fall 1889, Chicago

It felt so good to be back in Chicago after all the months on the road, Kate thought as the carriage stopped in front of the little house on Cedar Street. She was eager to see Bess, but when she unlocked the front door, only Jack came to meet her. He rubbed his back against her legs, begging to be picked up.

"Are you all alone, old boy?" She nuzzled her face into his soft neck. "Has Bess gone out?" She walked into the kitchen and saw a note on the table.

> Kate,
> I am so sorry I won't be here to greet you after your long travels away. I'll be back on Monday. Mother isn't feeling well, and I could tell she really needed me to visit her. Jack will take care of you until I get back.
> Bess

Kate looked Jack in the eye then set him down. "It doesn't do much good to talk things over with you." She shot him a sideways glance. "But maybe I will anyway." She carried her valise upstairs, disappointed. "There are so many things I need to discuss with Bess. She sees the big issue I'm trying to work out. She listens without interrupting. I need that." Kate saw Jack following her. He stopped when she did and cocked his head to one side. "Then she responds with a few words of wisdom that make me wonder why I didn't think of that. She might know why Miss Willard has called me in. Does it make sense that Miss Willard would summon me, Jack?" Jack just pawed his whiskers.

Miss Willard's note simply read: *When you get back, please come to see me as soon as you are able. I will be in the office after the fifth of October.*

Kate wondered whether people had been complaining about her lectures. They wanted details of what happened in the dens. *Lord, I'm so weary of sharing the ugly details. I just want to tell people how they can help.*

On a brisk sunny fall morning two days later, Kate headed downtown, still feeling anxious about Miss Willard's request. She'd been asked to make major decisions by powerful women before! *What does Miss Willard want this time?*

But when she got off the streetcar on State Street, her spirits lifted. She craned her neck at the latest skyscraper. A few steps later, she couldn't help but glance up again. The buildings seemed to stretch taller into the sky every time she returned to the city. Her father had built the tallest lighthouse in his day. Had he ever come into the city to see the construction here? He had been too weak to come for most of this year. How she missed him.

She drew closer to the familiar WCTU headquarters and felt a tingle down her spine again about why Miss Willard had asked her to come. She didn't usually call Kate in for a special meeting unless there was another skeeter buzzing. Kate smiled. *As usual, Miss Willard, you get your way.*

Kate walked toward Miss Willard's office and thought about what she would say if a complaint arose about her lectures. She neared the door and straightened her shoulders. *Lord, please don't let her ask me to go on another long speaking tour. I want to stay here and work with Bertha and the women in the Anchorage again. Perhaps I can help them change their minds about feeling they are worthless.* She could see Miss Willard at her desk through the open door. She tapped lightly and Miss Willard jumped to her feet.

"Kate!" Energetic as usual, Miss Willard rushed from behind her desk to scoop papers off a chair and pull it near her. "Sit down, and let me look at you."

In an uncharacteristic gesture, she squeezed Kate to her before sitting in a chair next to her. "You have had a long and arduous trip, haven't you? I was shocked to learn of your father's passing when you were out in Pennsylvania. I am sorry you couldn't even get back for his funeral. How is your dear mother doing? We were all praying for you."

Kate smiled wanly. "Thank you. I visited my family for a few days since I've been back. The house seemed so empty, even though it was full of people." She cleared her throat for composure. "It's good to be back in Chicago. I haven't had time to go over to see Bertha. Is everything going all right at the Anchorage?"

"I hear good things. Your Bertha has certainly made a turnaround in her life."

"She's one of my best stories to dispel the myth that 'once a fallen woman, always fallen.'" To her embarrassment, a tear trickled down Kate's cheek. She had determined not to reveal her pain—she knew how Miss Willard felt about emotional weakness. But she couldn't help it.

Miss Willard was silent as Kate composed herself, and then spoke quietly. "You are making a difference around the country, Kate. Even those tough Wisconsin senators were impressed enough to draft a law regarding age of consent and sending den keepers to prison. Any word on that?"

"Nothing yet. Senator Fitch asked me for suggestions as to what should be included. I'm sure I asked for a lot more than we'll get."

"Isn't that always the way of compromise? What is the minimum you will be satisfied with?"

"That the den keepers be put in prison whenever they're caught putting girls to work at too young an age or keeping girls against their will."

"The legislation will happen, Kate. Keep holding on to your faith." She tapped Kate's knee with her finger, enforcing her words. "Everywhere I go, I hear encouraging reports that you speak with conviction and passion. Because of your work, many of our chapters have added a Social Purity Department to their agendas."

Kate nodded and wiped the tears that would not stop. "I'm sorry," she murmured. She choked back more tears. "I guess I'm just tired ... and missing Father."

"I know you are. You have worked so hard. Perhaps it is time that you go home for a few months."

That's what Dr. Hart said when I sat in his office in Kiukiang. Am I just a failure?

"You have spent so little time with your family since you joined us three years ago." Miss Willard spoke quietly as if her own thoughts were far away. "I think your mother needs you now." She lifted Kate's chin. "Spend a few days with Bertha and your colleagues at the Anchorage, and then go home."

Kate sat up and wondered whether this sympathetic woman was the Miss Willard she knew?

"You are no doubt wondering why I asked you to see me."

"Have there been complaints about my lectures?" Kate asked tentatively.

"Those of us with a passion from God know there will always be complaints." She sat back and smiled at Kate. "It has nothing to do with your lectures. Our first two round-the-world missionaries have been so well received wherever they have gone that we have decided to add two more. We want to reach more countries and organize women to pray and promote the message of the WCTU. You know we have already established unions in Britain, Australia, and New Zealand."

Kate listened warily. What did this have to do with her?

"We have asked Elizabeth Andrew to become our third round-the-world missionary next year."

Kate felt as though she'd been pinched.

Miss Willard noticed Kate's shock. "Yes, your friend Bess." She paused, then looked even more intently at Kate. "And we would like you to be our fourth."

Me? A missionary? I tried that once. What did she mean by a "round-the-world" missionary?

"Bess has not yet agreed but indicated she is seriously praying about it. As you know, the denomination has asked her to vacate the manse before the end of the year for the new minister, so the timing is perfect for everyone."

"Perfect," Kate mumbled, nodding her head. Bess had written she'd have to find somewhere else to stay when she got back. She wished she'd been able to talk to Bess before coming into the office. Just the thought of another move on top of Father's death and the months of travel shook her. What did Miss Willard expect of her? She'd had one bout being a missionary.

"I've not seen Bess since I returned," Kate responded slowly, looking at her lap, searching for the right words, the right questions. "She'd written me about the house." She paused then looked at Miss Willard. "I'm not sure what you mean by a 'round-the-world' missionary." She hesitated, then added, "I've already had one experience as a missionary. It was a mistake."

Miss Willard was not swayed. "Give it careful thought and much prayer, Kate. Our plan is for you to spend some time in England, and then South Africa, and perhaps Australia. The women there are ready to take a stand against alcohol. You and Bess could challenge them about temperance, as well as about establishing Social Purity Departments. Your being overseas for a while would also allow time for the sensationalism of your experiences in the lumber camps to die down."

Miss Willard pulled her chair closer to Kate's and spoke gently. "But you must know. I ask this with the understanding that the WCTU has no funds for such a project. I wish we could help, but unfortunately, we are barely able to fund the work in this country. I am afraid you can't expect any financial help from us, not even for stamps."

Kate almost laughed. "Miss Willard, money has never been the allure of the work. You know I came from a big family and we never had much money. If God wants me to accept this offer, He'll provide as He has all these months I've traveled across the country." Kate shook her head. "If I were to become a missionary again, I'd have to be sure this is really what God wants me to do." *I made a quick decision once—not this time.*

Miss Willard didn't answer. Instead, she stood and rummaged through a pile of papers on her desk. "Ah, here it is. This is the latest report about Josephine Butler's work in England. Take this home and read it. It might help you decide." She handed Kate an article from *The Times* of London.

Kate began to utter, "Perhaps—" then thought better. "I'll think on this," she said as she clutched the paper and her bag and said her good-byes.

She left the building, grateful to be out in the fresh air to clear her thoughts. But the wind had risen, and as Kate reached up to tie her bonnet more tightly, a gust tore the article from her hand.

She chased it down the sidewalk, only to see the paper land in the lap of a disheveled-looking tramp slouched against a building. She stopped in front of him to retrieve her paper and saw the drunken glaze of his eyes.

He looked vacantly at the paper he half-held in dirty hands, as though trying to read.

Kate was tentative. "May I please have that paper? It's very important."

The man tried to stand but fell back on his knees. "Dish yours, lady?" He reached out with one hand while trying to balance himself against the building with the other.

Gingerly, Kate leaned forward to take the paper from his hand and whispered a relieved, "Thank you."

He slipped back against the wall. "Shorry. A shentleman should shtand up fur a beautiful lady."

Kate slipped *The Times* article into her bag and walked away, but something in her heart broke a little. Poor man. He was in bondage too. Who would help him? Were the WCTU women just blaming men for letting liquor ruin their lives? *Shouldn't we be helping them too?*

On a rare sunny January day in Evanston, Kate rushed home after a quick visit with Dr. Jewell, who'd just returned from his studies in Egypt. It was hard for Kate to break away. "But I promised my sister Mary I would be home by two to take her and young Billie down to the lighthouse," she said. "They're here from Minneapolis, and I want Billie to see his grandfather's legacy." As she hurried home, she mused how the lighthouse had become a symbol of challenge for her. Her father had left his legacy to keep people from losing their lives. *It's strange how often I think of it—such a perfect reminder that God has called me to leave a legacy too—for women who have already lost theirs. How do I do that?*

"Are you almost ready?" Kate called up the stairs as she entered the house.

"Coming," Mary called down. "Billie is looking for his gloves."

Kate smiled, knowing how scatterbrained her ten-year-old nephew could be. But he was bright. That child could figure out mathematical problems better than Kate could. He was going to be famous someday.

Unfortunately, neither Billie nor anyone else could solve the problem of what Kate should do next with her life. Miss Willard still waited for an answer, and so did Bess. *Bess!* Kate needed to write her soon with a decision about whether to join her as a round-the-world missionary. She would leave in just a few months. Kate looked out the door. *Why, God, is it so hard to know Your will when I pray every day for direction?*

"At last, we're ready." Mary came running down the stairs with Billie in hand. Her trim figure belied that she'd married a man named Stout, a family joke she took good-naturedly.

"Are you sure you're dressed warmly enough to walk to the lake?" Kate asked her nephew. "You'll have to tie that scarf over your nose and mouth when we get outside, Billie. The wind off the lakeshore can be powerful."

"Aw, Aunt Kate, it's not that cold."

"You'll find out, young man." Kate tapped him lovingly on the head. "Let's go. This is the best time of day to see the sun reflecting off the lighthouse."

Gusty winds blew off Lake Michigan, but it was an unusually sunny day for Illinois in winter. Billie skipped ahead. Kate relished the walk with Mary, who wasted no time. "Why do you think it's so hard to make up your mind about Miss Willard's request?" she pressed. "Is it the money? John and I could help you."

Kate was reminded of how well her sisters knew her even if they didn't always understand her choices. "No." She smiled. "It's not the money, though you know I've never had much. God has taken care of me ever since I gave up my medical practice, and I know He will do the same whatever I choose next."

"So?"

"I'm not sure. Women get the *Union Signal* wherever the World WCTU operates, so even those overseas have read about my experiences in Wisconsin. Is that really what I'm meant to do if I go overseas? Tell all the same stories all over again? I've got to do more than just tickle the ears of my listeners with sordid stories."

They watched Billie pick up stones along the shore and toss them into Lake Michigan's churning waves. Kate turned to Mary. "I often wonder if the women would listen if I brought one of these degraded women to the meeting with me. Josephine Butler has brought prostitutes into her home and cared for them until they died. I don't—"

"Billie!" Mary shouted. "Come back here!"

Kate followed Mary's gaze to see Billie start up the stairs to the base of the lighthouse. She thought back to the walks here with her father when the lighthouse was under construction. He always warned her about the spray washing over the stairs and leaving sheets of ice. "Billie!" Kate echoed her sister's calls. "Don't go up there!"

But Billie was already on his way. Perhaps he couldn't hear her over the noise of the waves. *Or*, Kate thought, *he doesn't want to.*

She began to run for her nephew, but her foot, clumsy in the heavy boot, turned on a stone. She tried to right herself. *Ice! Oh!* She slipped on an icy patch. Thrashing the air with her arms to keep balance, Kate screamed. She was falling and there was nothing to stop her. She landed against a boulder lining the path. *Crunch!* She heard a crack in her ankle. She felt the snap.

"Aunt Kate, Aunt Kate!" Billie shouted as he scrambled down the bluff. "What happened?"

Mary tried to help Kate to her feet, but Kate grabbed her arm.

"No, don't move my legs. Please, flag down a carriage to take me to the hospital. I am pretty sure I've broken my ankle." *And now I know I have my answer for Miss Willard. It doesn't look like I will be going anywhere for some time.*

28
A Miracle

"*Just* a moment!" Kate called out from the living room where she lay on the couch. The knocking continued. She shook the confusion from her head and tried to compose herself. The nightmares of things seen in the lumber camps kept haunting her.

Cora's pleading eyes.

The chain on the iron bed frame.

The despair and gloom of the shanty.

She couldn't shake the nightmares. They came more frequently now that she had been incapacitated by the broken ankle.

Kate wrangled the crocheted afghan to one side and scooted to the edge of the couch. She leaned down to pull her crutches from the floor and fumbled to raise herself up off the couch as the knock continued, more impatiently.

"Coming," she called again, trying to orient herself to the room. Mother and Sarah were out at the school for a recital. There was no one else to get the door. Kate hobbled in pain on the crutches. She inched her way across the floor, but just as she reached for the doorknob, the crutch slipped from her hand and she helplessly watched it slide to the floor.

Balancing on her good leg, she bent to retrieve the lost crutch, accidentally brushing the toes of her broken foot against the floor. Electric pain shot through her body. She braced herself against the doorjamb and leaned her head on the door, praying for the pain to subside. There had to be more wrong than just a broken bone. It had been almost six months. The specialist said he'd never seen a break take so long to heal. Neither had Kate, and she'd set plenty of bones. Maybe he was right that there was a pinched tendon. Frustrated and aching, she steadied herself again on the crutches and opened the door.

"Bess! Oh, Bess." Finding her dearest friend on the veranda buoyed Kate more than she would have expected.

"Kate, I'm so glad to see you at last." Bess hugged Kate, careful not to upset her balance. "I've come to pick up the rest of my things, and then I'm back to Chicago." She paused. "Did I write you that I'm living at the Anchorage while getting ready to leave for England?" She laughed. "I have so much on my mind, I think I must be losing it."

"Oh, Bess, yes. You did, and I want to hear all about it. Mother and Sarah will be back soon. Until then, we can talk without interruption." She grinned. "Well, you talk and I'll interrupt!"

Bess followed Kate slowly into the parlor. "The Anchorage is going strong, Kate. You would be proud."

Kate sank into a chair. "We've seen God work in the lives of many girls and women."

Bess nodded. "Since way back when Ella Gilchrist accepted Christ in that Sunday afternoon prayer meeting."

"And Bertha's life turned around as she knelt at Ella's bedside," Kate added.

"And without Ella, you wouldn't have come home. You never would have been asked to be the fourth round-the-world missionary for the WCTU."

Kate avoided the implication. *She still thinks I'm going to join her.* The throb in her ankle drew her hand to put pressure on it for relief. *Isn't it obvious God has other plans for me?*

"I want to hear all about what you've been doing all these months, Kate."

"Well, I've been writing back and forth with Senator Fitch and his lawyer in Wisconsin. We sued Fielding for defamation for calling me a liar and unchaste in front of a group of senators. Mr. Fitch felt that was the only way to keep him from defaming me in the *Journal*."

"I haven't seen anything by Fielding lately."

"No, he hasn't written an article about me, but after three continuations of the hearing, the judge exonerated Fielding."

"Sounds like he was paid off."

Kate nodded. "But everything isn't lost. At least one thing has happened to make me feel that my work hasn't been in vain. The best news came just yesterday. I was trying to find a way to contact you before you left."

"News from Madison?" Bess asked eagerly.

"Yes—I received a telegram. Look, it's right over there with my papers."

Bess jumped up and retrieved the yellow envelope lying on the table. "Can I read it?"

Kate nodded, a broad smile on her face, which just minutes before had been tight with pain.

Bess smoothed the telegram on her lap and read aloud.

WISCONSIN LEGISLATURE PASSED KATE BUSHNELL BILL
STOP IMPRISONMENT FOR DEN KEEPERS STOP LETTER
FOLLOWING
EDNA BASCOM

"You've won!" Bess jumped up and threw her arms around Kate. "You won't have to worry about Senator Grossman's threats anymore. I would like to see Fielding's face now!"

"I wasn't worried about them. But just think, Bess: Jack Long, Mike Mahoney, and Jack Leahy will go to prison for their evil doings, and Cora, Fran, and Bella—and so many others—will go free. Of course, it will take some time. Justice moves slowly, you know."

"But can't you see, Kate, how God has confirmed your call to this work?"

"I haven't stopped praising God since the telegram arrived yesterday. But there's more to do than getting a law passed. I've seen so many women suffer injustice. Their bodies and lives are broken— and worst of all, they've been told they are worthless." She leaned forward to reach down and press her ankle again. "I can help heal their bodies, Bess, but I believe that God wants me to help heal their souls—to free them from their own disobedience, from injustice, from others."

"You can do that as you spread God's message around the world. That's why Miss Willard asked you."

"She wants us to speak to Christian women in churches and unions. Important work, no doubt. But I believe God wants me to directly help those who are shamed and blinded to their full humanity—women who don't understand that they have potential in Christ." She looked down into her lap. "That's the call He's pressed upon me in these weeks of immobility. I don't believe that He intends women to live in bondage—whether it be with three-inch feet or three men a night."

They sat pondering the implications of Kate's words. Finally, Kate turned to Bess. "And what about your plans?"

"I'm planning to start out on this grand venture in July. I just bought my ticket a few days ago." Bess' eyes dropped to Kate's ankle. "I saved Dan's insurance money. I found I have enough to pay my fare to Europe: eighty-two dollars, second-class."

Kate winced. "Eighty-two dollars? That seems expensive, Bess. How will you live once you're there?"

Bess leaned forward, beaming. "I've been corresponding with Lady Henry Somerset, the president of the British WCTU. She assures me that I'll be able to stay in members' homes, and she'll arrange meetings for us to speak on behalf of the World WCTU." Bess paused, looked down at Kate's bandaged leg again. "Are you able, Kate? Is your leg healing so you can join me soon?"

Kate shook her head. "You know I've been ambivalent about this decision." She rubbed her ankle. "But it seems God is not. He's made it clear that I won't be able to go. My leg has not healed, and not even the specialists understand why."

Bess leaned closer. "I've noticed you wincing whenever you move. That isn't like you, Kate, not like you at all."

Kate leaned back in the chair. Bess might as well know. "I try not to say much, but I am in constant pain. Any movement of the leg, the least weight on my foot, sends shooting pains up my body. I've consulted the best doctors here in Evanston, and you know they have the best at the medical school." She shook her head. "They have no answers." She looked up at Bess, her eyes brimming with tears. "I can't go to England, not even if I wanted to."

Bess reached toward Kate and grabbed her hands. "You can't give up, Kate. I can't do this alone. You're the speaker and teacher. I can organize, plan, and write letters, but without your teaching and your inspiring talks, Miss Willard's vision won't come to life. She expects us to start local unions wherever we travel. She wants us to collect one million signatures of men and women who promise to abstain from alcohol. She wants you to teach the Bible about—"

"About purity. I know. And she wants us to meet Josephine Butler. That's a pretty big agenda for two women!" *What am I saying? Even with God's help, I can't do that on this crutch. I can't get to the door without being spent.*

Kate looked into her friend's eyes. "In spite of all the hardships and difficulties I've faced, I have never doubted God's power. Never." She looked down at her hands, opened in her lap as if to accept a gift. "And yes, I believe God can heal me if He chooses."

"Well then." Bess kneeled beside Kate and gently placed her hands on the damaged ankle. "Let's put the force of the two of us to work. God told us that where two or three are gathered, He is in their midst." Gently, she rubbed the injured leg. "I will pray for you, Kate. I believe that God has called us both to be round-the-world missionaries. What better way to give His full affirmation than by healing your leg today, right now?"

Kate reached down and put her hand on Bess' shoulder and squeezed it, urging her to begin.

"Father, dear caring Father. Thou art able to heal all our diseases. I believe—yes we both believe—that Thou hast called Kate. Thou hast gifted her. Now we ask in the name of Jesus to heal these broken bones. Release Kate from the pain. Give her the strength she needs to continue serving Thee." Bess paused. "Give us the faith we lack. We believe, but help our unbelief—"

The door burst open, drawing Kate and Bess from prayer. Sarah's daughter Peggy and her brother John rushed into the room, followed by Sarah and Kate's mother. Bess stood and greeted her friends warmly.

Sarah smiled broadly, happy to see Bess and Kate together. "We're so glad you came to see us before leaving for England. I can see in Kate's face that you've brought happiness already. Let me run to put the kettle on the stove, and I'm sure we can find some of Mother's famous sweet rolls. You made some this morning, didn't you, Mother?" But Mrs. Bushnell had already disappeared into the kitchen.

Bess was eager to help. She turned to Kate. "Do you feel up to joining us?"

Kate reached for her crutches. "Go ahead. I'll be there in a minute."

But as Bess and Sarah headed to the kitchen, Kate stopped herself. *No! I don't need these! Where is my faith? We just prayed that God would heal my ankle. I can do this. I will do this.*

Kate stood on her good leg and turned toward the kitchen, but the moment she put her other foot on the floor, it crumpled under her in agony. She grabbed the back of a chair to keep herself from falling. Had she really expected a miracle?

"Kate," she heard Sarah call. "Do you want to come in here for coffee, or should we bring it out there?"

Kate swallowed the pain and called out, "I think it will be more comfortable here."

Mrs. Bushnell brought out a basket of aromatic rolls. As Sarah poured tea for each of them, Bess sat down and looked quizzically at her friend.

Kate shook her head. She could see that Bess understood. *The pain is still there. My faith feels fragile. It's not your fault.*

The women exchanged pleasantries. Conversation paused as Bess commiserated with Kate's mother. "I understand. There was a knot in my stomach for months after Dan died. I'm doing better, but ..." She looked down, then said softly, "It's never the same." After a bit, Bess made motions to leave and said her good-byes. She bent over Kate and whispered in her ear, "Good-bye, dear friend. I haven't given up."

After Bess left, Kate excused herself. "I've had a big day. I think I'll make my way up to bed early tonight." This was no small task. She found the only way to get upstairs was to sit on each stair and lift her body up to the next one. It was a slow, agonizing effort, and she dreaded another long night of pain. This was how the girls in China must have felt while the broken bones in their bound-up feet healed. But Kate felt broken all over, not just her ankle. She was bound here at home. She couldn't even help Mother in the kitchen. The night hours would pass so slowly—and when she did sleep, she was caught in the dens in the lumber camp.

Morning sun streamed across the bed. Kate opened her eyes, then sat up rubbing them. What time was it anyway? She'd slept hard and found waking hard. She looked at her alarm. Nine o'clock? She couldn't remember when she'd slept so late.

Gingerly she swung her legs over the bed, noticing a cup of tea on the nightstand. Her mother had checked on her. She stood and reached to see if the tea was still warm.

Suddenly she looked down at the floor. "What?" she said aloud. "I'm standing! On both feet—and no pain. I've slept through a night without pain." She took a step and then another, slowly walking to the window and back to the bed. *Is this a dream?* She rubbed her eyes again. For months, her legs had felt weak, like rubber. "I'm walking. Walking!"

She walked round and round the room, then danced over to the window, looking at the morning sun. "O God, Your mercies are new every morning." She sat back on the bed to massage her healed leg. She couldn't help crying out, "It's really healed! I can massage the muscles, once so sore, now without pain. You have made it very clear, Lord, that You're not done with me. There is still a job to do."

Suddenly Kate remembered: Bess would be leaving for Chicago on the afternoon train! She looked again at the clock. "I have to get word to her that I'll be coming to England once I raise the money to get there. You've got me on my feet again. Let's see where You'll take me now."

She stepped to the stairs. "Mother," she called, running down the stairs. "I've got news!"

29
A Vision and a Dream

August 1890

"Whew." Kate wiped the perspiration from her forehead as she walked home from the post office. She swung the bag of mail she'd picked up back and forth, excited about what she would find. Would she be able to finalize her meetings into December?

Sarah was shelling peas on the porch. "There's not a breeze off the lake. Stay out here a bit. It's worse in the house." She eyed the mailbag. "Anything interesting today?"

"I haven't read anything yet," Kate responded as she poured the letters onto the porch. "It looks as though quite a few of these are from chapters in Ohio. I wrote the national vice president, Mrs. Phinney, who lives in Cleveland, that I could spend most of November lecturing in Ohio before going on to Philadelphia in December."

Sarah looked up. "That's quite a schedule."

Kate nodded as she read through one of the letters. She needed the proceeds from as many engagements as possible to work her way east to New York in order to sail for London by January.

"Do you really think you'll receive enough offerings in these meetings to cover your rail fares and food along the way and still have enough for the steamer to London?" Sarah grabbed another handful of peas.

"That's not my worry—I'm more concerned about letters like this!" Kate handed her sister the reply from Mrs. Phinney. "Read the last paragraph." Kate sat on the stairs with her head in her hands. *Is there no end to this?*

Sarah read aloud. "All our chapters want to invite you, Dr. Bushnell. I've had a hard time selecting only the ones you have time for." She looked at Kate. "Good for her. You'll be worn out before you ever get to New York if you don't have people like Mrs. Phinney to control your schedule."

"No." Kate shook her head. "That's not it. Go on. Read the rest of the paragraph."

"The others are very disappointed. They want to hear your firsthand reports about your findings in those wretched dens in Wisconsin. I've told them—"

Kate pulled the letter from Sarah's hands. She didn't want to hear any more.

Sarah went back to shelling peas. "You know, Kate, perhaps you're letting yourself get angry and frustrated because you don't understand these union women. They want to hear truth. They aren't getting it in the newspapers. Their pastors don't ever talk about these things. No one's ever told them about the awful things happening."

Sarah pulled Kate's hand from her face and turned her chin to look her in the eye. "But when they hear you—you who have shaken hands with prostitutes, heaven forbid—and talked with fourteen-year-old girls caught in white slavery! When they hear the truth from you, they start paying attention to what's happening in their towns. They urge their husbands to look into these matters. Laws will begin to change."

Kate reached into the basin and picked up a handful of plump peas. "If I were a pea, I'd know exactly why God created me—to be boiled in water, doused in hot butter, and eaten for dinner." She forced a smile. "But my life isn't as simple as that. I know what I'd like to do. I'd like to rescue girls like Cora and Huldah." She snapped the top off of a full pod of peas. "I'd like to introduce them to Jesus and watch Him make something beautiful out of their lives." She shook her head. "Evidently that's not what the women expect of me. I would like to teach them what God says about purity so they can pass it on to their children—and they just want to hear about the impure." She gathered the letters and stuffed them into her bag. "But you're right, Sarah, if those sordid stories are what they want, that's what they'll hear—and perhaps their eyes will open to what's happening right around them."

Upset at her own reaction, Kate headed up the stairs to her room under the eaves. She tossed the mailbag onto the bed and threw herself beside it. She knew she wasn't being fair. Sarah understood. Many of the women wept over the conditions of the camps and asked how they could help.

Kate curled up on the bed. She remembered Bess' recent letter from London where she was setting up an itinerary among the British WCTU unions: *They can't believe you will actually be here. They've read so much about you.* Was this going to happen in London too? *Surely, God, You have something more for me to do than tell shocking stories.*

She eyed her Bible at the corner of the bed where she'd left it open from her morning reading. Scripture had been her source of direction in the past. As she pulled the Bible toward her, pages leafed open to the story of Joseph and his brothers in Genesis. A verse caught her eye: "And Joseph dreamed a dream, and he told it his brethren: and they hated him yet the more."

She rebalanced the book in her hands and flipped through more pages, this time to the New Testament, looking for something, but what? She stopped in the Gospel of Matthew, where the wise men traveled to worship baby Jesus. Again a verse caught her eye, "And when they were departed, behold, the angel of the Lord appeareth to Joseph in a dream, saying, Arise, and take the young child and his mother, and flee into Egypt."

Kate smiled. *You do have a sense of humor, God. You're not trying to send me to Egypt, are You?* She laughed at the thought. At least no one in Egypt would know about the Wisconsin episode. Kate shut her eyes. *Really, Lord. Where are You? I need answers if You mean for me to keep telling the stories.* She picked up her Greek New Testament, where she had been reading the story of Peter falling into a trance: an *ekstasis* or vision. God used the dream to direct Peter to preach in the house of a Gentile.

"Dreams, dreams, dreams," Kate murmured. She shut her Bible and stretched out on the bed. She'd turned to three great men: Joseph. Jesus' father. Peter. Dreams directed their destinies. *Can't You direct my destiny, God? I'm sorry I'm so self-centered.*

Even though she was weary of seeking more direction, she felt confident about joining Bess in England and about the ministry as a round-the-world missionary. How could she doubt after the miraculous healing of her ankle? But was her ministry to be exactly the same old storytelling? She felt that she had so much more to share.

An errant fly buzzing at the window broke the silence in the room, and, exhausted, Kate felt herself lulled to sleep by the hum and the heat.

Black skies rumbled with thunder. Lightning danced all around. Kate stood at the prow of a ship at sea. Cresting waves shot into the sky, then fell back into the turbulent waters. *Where am I going?* Over the howling winds, she heard someone calling her name—

"Kate! Kate!"

She started at the loud pounding on the door and jumped—but from bed, not a boat. Kate rubbed the sleep and confusion from her eyes.

"Aunt Kate."

Johnny.

"Mom wants to know if you want some lemonade."

A dream. It was a dream. Kate tried to focus on the door. "No … No … Not just now, thank you." She rubbed her face and took a deep breath. "Tell your mom I'll be down in a bit."

She couldn't have been asleep more than a few minutes, yet she felt as though she'd already crossed an ocean—the ocean to England to ask for Josephine Butler's help. Mrs. Butler knew the shame Kate had seen. She too had faced the revulsion of society wanting to hear the dirty details but unwilling to have anything to do with girls and women in need: women who were defiled, trapped in a dark underworld.

Kate's heart pounded. Suddenly everything became clear. She would begin her call as a round-the-world missionary by asking Josephine Butler to help her do more than excite crowds with sensational stories—to instead find ways to arouse passion and a united voice against the evil taken so lightly. *I must write her.* Kate rose from the bed and paced the room. *I'll let her know I've got meetings almost every day at least through November but don't have any money yet—that I'm not exactly sure when I'll get to London.*

Kate sat at her desk piled with letters and pulled a piece of paper from the drawer. Remembering her dream, she whispered to herself, "Mrs. Butler will understand. I'll write her that I'll arrive in—I'll arrive in God's time."

Epilogue

November 14, 1890
Berea, Ohio

Dear Bess,

Thank you for your good letter. I was so glad to read that things are going so well for you in London. I can sense your excitement. But I know you too well. Reading between the lines, I can see you're ready for some help. You'll never admit it though! You wouldn't want to put pressure on me. I can't wait to join you, but I've been facing some difficulties on my lecture tour to the East Coast.

When I picked up mail that had been forwarded to Brunswick, I found a letter from Abby Davis. Wonderful news about the girls in Big Bear camp in Wisconsin! Ben and Abby rushed out to the camp as soon as they learned that the senate had passed a law making it illegal to entice and "use" young girls. But they found the shanty empty. Of course, Jack Long had disappeared—to avoid prison for trapping young girls like Cora and Fran. They finally found someone who knew something about the girls. Evidently Bella has gone back to her old "job," but Cora and Fran are home with their parents. What joy!

I left Brunswick not feeling well and had to detrain at Wooster, Ohio, because I came down with influenza. The carriage driver took me to a boarding house—cheaper than a hotel. I saw myself in the cracked mirror across the room. You wouldn't have recognized me. I looked like a street woman. (Please don't laugh at the irony of that.) Even hot water to wash up costs money.

Finally, in the middle of the third night, I woke up drenched in sweat; my fever had broken. A doctor came every day—he charged me $3 for three visits. More than I ever earned to treat an influenza case! You can only imagine the discouragement I felt about being so run down. You know I usually take such things in stride. By the time I paid Mrs. Schultz, who ran the boarding house, and bought the ticket to Berea, I didn't even look to see if there was anything left in the blue crocheted bag Mother gave me to keep my travel money. I determined to trust. Why is that always so hard to do, dear friend?

I tried to reschedule the meetings I missed. They were all very sorry, but no one was able to rebook any of them.

There was nothing left to do but send a telegram to Ruby Franklin—you remember I met her in New York at the convention—that I would be arriving early. It took the last fifty cents from my bag. Now I am here in Berea, getting ready for another meeting tomorrow. Ruby says women are coming from many towns in the area. Perhaps this will start the turnaround we need.

Good news! I received a letter from Josephine Butler inviting us to tea. I look forward to spending time with her. Maybe there's something we can do for her?

I believe God wants me to join you, so hopefully the next letter will have better news. Until then, continue strong in His work, and I'll do the same here.

Affectionately,
Kate

December 14, 1890
New York

Dear Ruby,

Your peaceful home was such a comfort to me. Thank you for caring for me and feeding me such good meals—and for your godly counsel. Praise God for the generous gifts the women gave to send me on my way. Did you know that I didn't have a cent for my fare to New York when I arrived in Berea?

Now I'm in Mary Burt's luxurious home. But more beautiful than her abode is her spirit of giving and serving people in need. Remember when she provided lunches for all the delegates at the convention in New York?

When I arrived, she insisted I rest up. Her servant drew a bath, and I soaked in a bathtub so large I could almost lie flat in the water! Hot water came from the faucet! I felt pampered.

Mrs. Burt invited me to stay here as long as necessary, but I'm praying to be on board the HMS *Boundless* on January third. I have to purchase my ticket in five days. I don't have the funds yet, Ruby, but I'm hanging on to God.

The New York White Ribboners are coming for a meeting tomorrow evening. I saw the lounge set up with more than fifty chairs. I'm clinging to the verse in Matthew: "Every one that hath forsaken houses, or brethren, or sisters, or father or mother ... or lands for my name's sake, shall receive an hundredfold." I still need the hundredfold to get to London.

Perhaps I will be able to see you when I'm back in America—whenever that is. But I send my love to you, and I'll write again soon. Hopefully from London.

Kate

December 16, 1890
New York

Dear Mrs. Butler,

Thank you for your kind invitation to tea after Mrs. Andrew and I have settled in London. I have read about your courageous effort to defeat the degrading Contagious Diseases Act. I would count it a privilege to help your work in some way.

I hope to purchase my ticket for the January third departure of HMS *Boundless*. I should arrive in Southampton by the eleventh of January, Lord willing. I'll contact you soon thereafter.

Prayerfully,
Katharine Bushnell, MD

HMS Boundless

Captain Jonathan Whitehall
January 3, 1891

Dear Sarah,

Just a quick note. The ship will be leaving port shortly, and I want to get this into stateside mail. I received your letter just before I left the Burts for the dock. I can't believe Peggy is getting ready for preparatory school next year. Give her a hug from her Aunt Kate. Saying good-bye to you all proves the hardest part of leaving. Promise me you'll write often.

Getting to New York was nip and tuck. Ruby organized a meeting with the women from many towns around Berea, and their offering paid for my ticket as far as New York, but no farther.

God gave me such confidence that He would provide the "hundredfold" I needed, but frankly, I had only two dollars and change in the blue crocheted bag when I arrived here. You can imagine my confusion. Wasn't God calling me? If so, why wasn't He providing? Faith is an ongoing lesson for me. I wish I had a portion of your unshakable faith, sweet sister. How many times have you turned my eyes back to trusting God?

But listen to what happened! (I can hear you say, *I told you so.*)

The meeting in Mrs. Burt's home was one of the best I've ever had. Well-educated women listened intently and asked questions. They gave generously, but it wasn't even enough to go steerage! And that was my last scheduled meeting.

I came back to my room and knelt beside the bed in despair—I'd been so fully convinced God would provide. Mrs. Burt knocked at my door with a bag of mail her husband had just brought from his office. Letters from across the country with small gifts, some offerings— some just coins wrapped in hand-embroidered handkerchiefs. Then I found a letter from Mrs. Carse with a generous gift. You know that there is more value in it coming from *her* than the money itself.

Bertha is now in good hands. Another one from the Gilchrists with a photograph of Ella. I still miss her.

I'd been so busy reading letters I hadn't noticed Mrs. Burt putting the coins and bills in piles on the bed. She touched my arm, pointed to the money, and asked me, "Are you ready?" I wasn't sure what she meant. "Are you ready to have tea with Bess and Josephine Butler?" I looked down at the piles in amazement—each one came to five dollars. It was enough. I'm traveling second-class, not steerage. So please put Mother's mind at ease about my travels. God provided.

Oh, the ship's horn! Must close and mail this. All my love to Mother and your children—and to you and Will of course.

With much anticipation,
Kate

Author's Notes

Katharine Bushnell

*H*ere's the real story: the actual people and what went on behind the scenes in Katharine Bushnell's life.

In 1860, the *Lady Elgin* collided with a barge and sank in Lake Michigan's turbulent waters around the Evanston Grosse Point promontory. More than three hundred people lost their lives in the icy waters. In the midst of the Civil War, there was no money to build a lighthouse to avert danger. But by 1870, bids were out to find a contractor. William Bushnell won the bid and moved his wife and nine children from Peru, Illinois, to Evanston. Katharine Bushnell, sandwiched between the three youngest boys, was just sixteen. She must have joined her siblings to check on the progress of the lighthouse that would become Evanston's number one tourist attraction. Though no longer operating today, the lighthouse is visited by over two million people every year—and in 2010, I was one of them.

A year or so after the Bushnell family moved to Evanston, the Reverend Maggie Van Cott, a flamboyant Methodist evangelist, held meetings in town. There's no evidence that Kate attended the tent crusade, but we know she made a personal commitment to Jesus as her savior.

While studying at the Evanston College for Women, where Frances Willard was president for a short time and which later became part of Northwestern University, Kate changed her studies from literature to medicine. She went on to attend the Women's Medical College of Chicago, which would eventually be integrated into Northwestern Medical School. Only thirty years earlier, in 1849, Elizabeth Blackwell became the first woman to graduate from medical school with an MD. Women were slowly entering the medical field, but it was not considered proper for a lady in the nineteenth century. Kate also studied neurology for two years with her neighbor and family friend, Dr. James Jewell, a leading neurologist and co-founder of the American Neurological Society. Unfortunately, David Russell lives only in my imagination.

Mrs. J. T. Gracey, the first president of the Women's Missionary Society of the Methodist Episcopal Church (1870), has never been named in any of the literature about Kate. Nonetheless, she was most likely the sophisticated woman who asked Kate to go as a missionary doctor to the Kiukiang Mission in China.

The Reverend Doctor Virgil Hart founded Kiukiang Mission in 1866. Hart was a highly respected mission statesman and had moved on to establish other mission stations when Kate arrived in 1879. Even though he wasn't there to give her personal guidance, I suspect that they actually met. I found pictures of the original two-story mission house facing the Yangtze River. A covered veranda ran along the length of the house in an attempt to keep it cooler.

The climate at Kiukiang was draining—with severe heat and humidity. Kate suffered frequent bouts of malaria. Overworked at the clinic, she had no medical help until Ella arrived. Kate was also determined to learn Mandarin to get closer to the people. Chinese customs, like foot binding, seemed strange and cruel. She was shocked when a father brought his daughter to the mission for help. His wife had "trimmed" her feet to fit into the conventional three-inch embroidered shoes. The incident with the man attacked and left for dead did cause the people to believe that Kate could raise the dead.

Two years after Kate arrived, Ella Gilchrist, a fellow student at the medical college, joined her in Kiukiang. Ella soon became ill, and she and Kate spent several weeks in the Lushan Mountains, staying in a cabin retreat for missionaries who were often plagued with malaria. Kate described her sense of freedom during this stay in her short autobiography, *A Brief Sketch of Her Life Work*: "I was inclined to be athletic and was like a young colt let loose, in the beautiful mountainous surrounding." At some point while in the mountains, Kate fell and injured her back, which would give her lifelong problems.

Perhaps the key turning point in Kate's life occurred while in China. She was a gifted linguist and eventually learned five languages in addition to English—Latin, Greek, Hebrew, Chinese, and German. She loved to compare the Chinese and Greek Bibles, which helped her to learn Mandarin. During that stay in the mountains, she discovered an inaccurate translation of Philippians 4:3 about Paul's female helpers. In the Chinese Bible, the name of one of the women is rendered *Euodias* while it is spelled *Euodia* in Greek. The added *s* changes the female name to a male name. This raised Kate's concern about inaccurate and possibly biased translations by male translators and began her lifelong study of the Bible's teaching about women.

In 1882, Kate accompanied Ella, seriously ill with tuberculosis, to her parents' home in Denver. Kate helped the Gilchrists care for Ella but was also able to develop a small practice through a local hospital. Because she used her Mandarin to work with the Chinese chapter of the Women's Christian Temperance Union, I created Hou Wan to work with her in helping women who sold their bodies on the streets. Kate began on Hamilton Street, the red-light district of Denver at the time, and rescued Bertha Lyons, who accepted Christ at Ella's bedside. We don't know Bertha's past, but we do know that she went on to work at the Anchorage.

Lou Blonger (1849-1923) ruled as crime kingpin of Denver's gambling activities and ran extensive "con" tricks among tourists during the years Kate worked in the red-light district. Though there is no record of his controlling hand over the illegal sex trade, we know he had strong ties to politicians and law enforcement, including the mayor.

Frances Willard, Kate's former teacher in Evanston and later president of the WCTU, invited Kate to come to Chicago to help start the Union's Social Purity Department. In 1886, Kate began working with the WCTU and with Elizabeth Wheeler Andrew—Bess. She and Bess, a pastor's widow, had served together years earlier in a prayer group in Evanston.

There's very little information about Bess until she and Kate began to work together in Chicago. Nothing was ever said about them living in the same house—but it works, doesn't it? In reading the lengthy handwritten reports about later investigations in India, it is obvious that the handwriting belongs to two people: Bess' is neat, clear, and easily readable; Kate's is more flamboyant and less easy to read. The two women traveled and served together around the world for almost twenty-six years.

Fifteen years after the great fire, Chicago was a growing boomtown, with the world's first skyscraper. The Home Insurance Building (1885) rose ten stories, with two added in 1890. Chicago eventually turned the polluted Chicago River and its sewerage away from Lake Michigan and into a planned drainage canal. This wouldn't happen until 1900—hence Bess' comment about "the stinking river."

Frances Willard, the woman with more ideas than a dog has hair, gave one to Kate. With the help of Bess and Bertha, the Anchorage (1887-1974) opened to provide a shelter for prostitutes and homeless women. Since Mrs. Carse was president of the Chicago union, she and Kate just had to meet somehow. I found a picture of this imperious woman and gave Kate an adversary.

In *A Brief Sketch*, Kate describes her experiences at Customs House Place, but the women and girls she meets there and in Denver, including Huldah and Maggie, are figments of my imagination based on her writings.

Somewhere Kate read the newspaper article about W. H. Griffin killing a young girl entrapped in a brothel in a Wisconsin lumber camp. Governor Jeremiah Rusk didn't like the rumors going around about the state and assigned one of his assistants, James Fielding, to investigate. Fielding wrote a false report for the *Milwaukee Journal*. At Willard's request, Kate spent four months exposing the truth of forced prostitution in the camps, taking risks to visit girls in the dens. Cora, Bella, and Fran are my creations, but their plight was real. Kate had the cooperation of the local WCTU women and their husbands wherever she went. Ben and Abby represent them. The Reverend Scott Davis was indeed arrested and tried for libel but was acquitted.

It became clear to Kate that "the business" was assisted by crooked police, immoral doctors, and dishonest politicians. Girls never gained the freedom they were promised, for they could never pay off the bills held against them by the den keepers, who accumulated vast sums of money. Some women in the towns convinced themselves that these girls in the dens would never change, so they turned a blind eye to the police and doctors who kept them in the camps and out of town.

News spread around the country once Kate finished her report and sent it out to several newspapers. Though she did not speak at the 1891 WCTU convention held at the New York Metropolitan Opera House, I couldn't resist that setting for her report. Many of the quotes given in that speech and the one to the Wisconsin senators in Madison are taken from her speeches printed in the *Union Signal*. The appearance of the women encircling the senate and standing on the platform behind her must have been one of the highlights of Kate's experiences that year.

Willard had deep respect for Kate, but it is believed that she offered the unpaid position of fourth round-the-world missionary in part as an attempt to stop the sensationalism Kate had caused. Money was not an issue to Kate, but she did not have peace about going to England, fearing it would be a repeat performance of what she'd been doing. Kate suffered a foot injury and was incapacitated for more than four months, seemingly confirming her doubts. Bess, who was to go ahead to England as the third round-the-world missionary, prayed for healing. Although we have no details, there seemed to be a miraculous cure. Kate agreed to join Bess but would have to raise funds for her fare.

As she scheduled her lectures, Kate found that women again wanted the sordid stories about her experiences with the girls in the dens. Her frustration continued even as Bess was arranging meetings in England; Kate feared she would be expected to retell the same accounts there.

While at home in Evanston preparing for her journey, Kate opened her Bible for assurance about her plans. She haphazardly turned to three passages, all speaking about dreams. Kate wondered if God would guide her that way. Lying on her bed in the warm summer afternoon, she fell asleep and had a vivid dream in which she heard Josephine Butler calling her name.

Josephine Butler (1828-1906) is considered one of the greatest Christian advocates for women in the Victorian era. She rescued women of the street and cared for them in her own home, which shocked genteel society. She traveled widely in Europe, speaking for justice for women. In England, she and the Ladies National Association worked for fifteen years to end the Contagious Diseases Act. The act was purported to prevent the spread of venereal disease, but it was actually meant to protect men visiting brothels. Under the act, the police could pick up any suspicious woman on the street. She could be forced to undergo a vaginal exam and be declared a prostitute, whether or not she was. Butler and her team waged a campaign against the act until it was finally repealed in 1886.

When Kate heard the call from Butler in her dream, she felt assured that Butler would help her do more than tell lurid stories. She sat down immediately and wrote that she would be coming to England.

However, Kate had to raise her own funds: not only to get to New York but also to purchase a ticket to cross the ocean. She felt confident that gifts and offerings would cover her expenses. But halfway to New York, she fell ill and had to cancel meetings and lie up in a hotel. In *A Brief Sketch*, she wrote, "The struggle to *believe* and accept the terms for my future was sharp, but soon settled. I went forward, earning barely enough money to reach New York City and with nothing for my voyage to England. But I found on arrival money from several unexpected sources in letters awaiting me. God sends no one out to labour without wages. Although I have made no charge for my services (with a few reasonable exceptions) since that experience, God has never failed me."

Daughters of Deliverance ends with Kate on her way to her next adventure. She will indeed meet and work with Josephine Butler, who asks her and Bess to go to India to investigate rumors that the CDA has not been repealed in the British military barracks there.

Why I Wrote a Biographical Fiction

*M*ore than ten years ago, my friend Mimi Haddad and I were rooming together at a women's conference when she told me of a woman she'd been reading about. "You've got to write a book about Katharine Bushnell. She's made great contributions advocating for justice and equality for women, backed by years of study of the Bible. And few people know about her!"

At the time I just laughed off Mimi's suggestion. I figured I'd written all the books I had in me and was busy encouraging women around the world to use the gifts God had given them.

But the challenge had been planted in my mind. I hadn't acquiesced yet, but I wanted to know more about this woman. And as I read about her, I was surprised that her name had fallen by the wayside. We know of other women like Hannah Whitall Smith, Frances Willard, Catherine Booth, and sisters Angelina and Sarah Grimke—but little about Katharine Bushnell.

In 2006, the idea of writing about Bushnell had taken root, and I began to research her life. I started at the Frances Willard library in Evanston, Illinois, and in November of that year I flew to London to the Women's Library of the London Metropolitan University. What great support the staff gave me as I delved into the archives! I found short biographies, articles, reports, and a lengthy journal about the investigations she and Elizabeth Andrew conducted in India.

Books by Dana Hardwick and Kristen Kobes Du Mez (see Acknowledgements) provided rich documentation and personal insights into Bushnell's life. Bushnell herself wrote several short books about her experiences, including *A Brief Sketch of Her Life Work* and *The Queen's Daughters in India*, which she wrote with Bess Andrew about their investigations in India. I downloaded a short book by Bushnell from godswordtowomen.org: *The Reverend Doctor and His Doctor Daughter*, a fictional dialogue between a doctor and her father that summarizes Bushnell's teaching about the love of God and His perfect justice in all His dealings with women. Her groundbreaking work, *God's Word to Women*, first published in 1916, is considered a classic and is still in print today.

But nowhere did I find intimate letters to or from Bushnell, nor a private journal, and very little that expressed her inner feelings. Bushnell died seventy years ago, and I was unable to find anyone who had met her. And without Bushnell's thoughts, quotations, and insight into personal relationships, a biography could be a very dry read.

Somewhere along my research journey, I talked with a literary agent about this lack of personal sources either from or about Bushnell, and he suggested I write a fictional biography. Voila! I could do that! I had all the facts of her life to form the framework of the story—and fiction gave me the freedom to expand on that framework with how I think events might have happened. That was the fun part, though I often agonized over how Kate (she was that to me by now) handled people, disappointments, and physical weakness. I do know one thing—she was a woman devoted to the Bible and prayer, and so you see lots of references to that in this story.

In the midst of my research on Kate, my husband was diagnosed with cancer. I dedicated myself to his care and set aside my writing. After he died in October 2008, I didn't realize that the mourning journey would be so draining of energy and creativity. But a few years ago, I was able to pick Kate's story back up with vim.

Bushnell had a full life; to do it justice will take a second book, which is on its way. I hope you like the flesh-and-blood Kate that I constructed on the bones of the truth I discovered about her.

Coming Soon
From Heritage Beacon!

The Queen's Daughters

by
Lorry Lutz

Kate arrives in London to find that her friend Bess seems to have everything organized. She wonders if she's needed at all, or will she just be telling stories from the lumber camps in Wisconsin again? But when she and Bess have tea with Josephine Butler, the famed British activist, Kate is confident that God has brought her to England. But to do what?

At their first public meeting Kate meets Lady Henry Somerset, the wealthiest woman in England and several members of parliament who've helped Mrs. Butler change laws to protect girls on the streets. The women travel to Pontefract with the MPs to campaign for removal of a corrupt judge. In a room above a stable, the only place available, Mrs. Butler challenges the village women to convince their husbands to vote. Suddenly smoke pours through the floor, and they barely escape a fire set by agitators. Kate begins to see what Mrs. Butler has gone through to protect girls forced into prostitution. She is impressed with the men's concern and work for the poor. But what does Mrs. Butler want of her? Only on their journey back to London does Mrs. Butler ask the question which will change Kate's life.